HEART OF FIRE

Suzann,
Enjoy the magic!
Kristen Painter

PUBLISHED BY:
Kristen Painter

Heart Of Fire
Copyright © 2010 by Kristen Painter
Print ISBN: 1453617221
Digital ISBN: 978-1-4524-6131-1
Kindle ASIN: B003L2008G

Cover by Jax Cassidy

ೞﮩೞ

HEART OF FIRE

Kristen Painter

ೞﮩೞ

Dedication

To my parents for their unyielding support.
All my love.

Chapter One

A shout ripped Ertemis from sleep. He bolted to his feet, yanked his sword from its sheath at his hip, and in a blur of flashing metal, prepared to deal death to the intruder.

There was no one in the room.

He relaxed and sheathed his sword, groaning as the remnants of last night throbbed anew in his skull. Cheap human ale. He rubbed his eyes, still stinging from the smoky tavern air.

An aching head, gritty eyes and naught to show in his hunt for his birthfather. How the edge of his Feyre hungered for the bastard's blood. He scrubbed his eyes again. Other than the Traveler's tales, he had little to go on and time was running out. Surely, the Legion knew he'd deserted. If only his bond price weren't so high.

Midday sun spilled through the old wood shutter slats, slashing the dusty air into light and dark slices. He leaned his Legion-issued sword against the bed and picked his leather breastplate off the floor. Another shout rang through the air. He clutched his head. Vile, stinking, babbling humans. At least the residual effects of the ale dampened his heightened senses. More shouting broke out.

What in Saladan's name was going on? He dropped the breastplate onto the bed. The ruckus erupting outside needed squelching if there was any chance of further sleep. The more he slept, the faster his elven blood would work the healing magic that enabled him to pickle his brain night after night and kept his black skin scar free despite his many battles.

He drew on his trousers, grabbed his sword belt, and unwedged the room's only chair from beneath the rusty door latch.

The scarred, faded leather notched easily into the silver buckle at his waist as he trudged down the steps. The belt settled low on his hips, the weight of the sword as comfortable as the press of a woman but far more reliable. His fingers tightened around the hilt as he stepped onto the crowded street.

The brilliant noonday sun drove daggers into his head. He grimaced, shielding his eyes with his hand. People rushed through the streets, their faces drawn into worried masks. Even with his faculties dulled, the tang of panic hung in the air like burning refuse.

The daylight, the noise and the crush of unwashed human flesh reminded of why he'd had the ale in the first place. Blunting his acute senses made time spent among humans a little less wretched. Night's quiet solitude was preferable, and since quitting life as the Legion's fatal messenger, night offered a security day did not. The Legion would soon realize their deadliest weapon had no plans of returning. They would place a hefty bounty on his head, send men to hunt him. No one left the Legion until the Legion decided it was time.

Snarling a curse, Ertemis narrowed his eyes against the glare. He scanned passing faces for someone who might know what was going on. Few returned his gaze, but the flow of humans split, giving him a wide berth.

The frightened expressions as mothers pulled their children closer, the timid glances of men...none of it was new to him. Few sane people were of a mind to engage a dark elf, especially one of Ertemis's size and current disposition. He hadn't earned the nick 'Black Death' for being kind and sweet.

The crowd's collective gaze crawled over his body like a regiment of ants, staring at his telltale black skin and the silver runes tattooed down his spine and up his slanted ears. With less ale and more thought, he would've donned a tunic and trousers. His clothed appearance drew stares enough but the sight of him shirtless stalled traffic.

He wanted to shout at them to stop staring, that he wasn't one of the Travelers' curiosities to be gawked at. Instead, he ground his teeth and held his tongue. An outburst would only make them stare harder.

A bright spot of green bobbed toward him through the sea of humans. He reached into the crowd, snatching the vibrant cloak of a small man coming toward him. The left side of the man's face was a bunched mass of scars that disappeared beneath his tunic collar.

"What's this ruckus about?" Ertemis muttered to his captive. The little man stumbled and put his hands out to catch himself. He looked up, fear registering on his face. He stared at Ertemis in dumbfounded silence, mouth agape, eyes large.

In his peripheral vision, Ertemis saw a crowd developing at a distance around him. The only thing he missed about the Legion was being left alone.

He dragged the little man into the alley between the tavern inn and the mercantile beside it. "Just tell me what this commotion is about and you're free to go."

The man whispered, "Quarantine," then cleared his throat before speaking again. "Quarantine's been called on the whole city. Half of the north quarter and all of the eastside have come down with Speckled Fever, and they ain't lettin' anybody out. The gates are locked up tighter than an Ulvian's pocketbook." He added, "Sir," as if hoping to gain enough favor to be allowed to live.

"Don't call me sir," Ertemis snapped. He released his grip on the man's cloak. Raking a hand through his hair, he swore under his breath. "Codswallop."

His elven half could protect him from human illness, even if he had to suffer through it first. But being quarantined wasn't going to help him find the man who'd ruined his mother's life. Slodsham was a passable place to spend a few days, but that's where it ended. Staring past the man, he exhaled in frustration.

An enterprising light flickered in the man's eyes. "I don't much wanna be here, either. I got goods ta buy and coin ta--anyway, maybe we..." Another upward glance at Ertemis and the man stopped.

"Begging your pardon, master elf...I best be off." He shifted his gaze down to the alley and tried to back away.

Ertemis tightened his fist in the man's cloak. "Speak."

The man's gaze darted to the alley's entrance then back to Ertemis. "I know a way out."

"I don't need your help to ditch this slum." He'd find a way on his own, after his head stopped throbbing.

The man frowned. "But I need yers, master elf."

"Why? What's in it for me?" Ertemis watched the alley's entrance for company. He released his grip on the man's cloak.

"I'm owed a favor from a rather shady fella. I reckon he won't pay up without some persuadin'. The kind you could provide, if ya understand. It's worth fifty silvers when we're out."

Everyone always wanted something, but Ertemis needed the coin. "Seventy-five and not a silver less. What's your name?"

"Haemus Brandborne at yer service, fiber merchant, seller of the finest colored fabrics, yarns, and other textiles ya could ever want."

He grinned, showing a few missing teeth as he extended his hand. "An yers?"

Marbled burn scars matching the one's on the merchant's neck covered the man's hand and extended up his wrist and under the sleeve of his rich tunic. Ertemis crossed his arms over his chest. "Master elf will do."

Haemus's gaze went to the sword at Ertemis's side. The merchant's eyes widened in sudden recognition. "Ain't you the..." His voice trailed off as if he no longer wanted an answer.

Narrowing his gaze, Ertemis finished the man's sentence. "Black Death? And what if I am?"

"The Black Death." Haemus breathed the words out like a curse. "I didn't think ya came out during the day...ya in Slodsham for work or pleasure?" His eyes suddenly went wide and he shook his head. "Don't answer that."

With his scarred palms up, he stepped back. "I just want out of the city." He swallowed. "We got a deal, then, right? And that makes us partners, don't it?"

"We have a deal," Ertemis nodded slowly, the pain in his head not yet subsided, "but we are not partners."

ဆ

On one last walk along the placid shores of Callao Lake, Jessalyne watched some of the resident herd of cervidae, the deer people, gather ahead. Fairleigh Grove had been home to the skin-shifters since long before Jessalyne's father had brought her mother to this secluded vale.

A few of the young cervidae, in human form and dressed in simple linen tunics, played on a cluster of boulders, their mothers and fathers close by. The cervidae reproduced so slowly, each child became a carefully guarded treasure.

Her jaw tightened. How wonderful to grow up with adoring parents. A father to protect you. A mother to teach you.

One of the male cervidae kissed his companion's cheek. Jessalyne looked away. The sight made her ache for something new, something she could never have. Who would love someone like her? Not even the cervidae dare touch her.

But then, they had good reason not to touch. They knew exactly why her father had left.

Her mother had been the cervidae's healer, caring for the deer people until her death. The skin-shifters had become Jessalyne's only family after her father abandonment. They were kind but never affectionate, and the hole left by her mother's passing widened with every season.

Jessalyne inhaled the crisp air, tipping her face toward the sun's buttery heat. A patchwork of fragrant wildflowers bordered the path along the shore. Honeybees and dragonflies buzzed by. In the distance, waterfalls tumbled from the jagged Wyver mountain range shaping the lake's furthermost shores. Rainbows shimmered in the mist. A place this beautiful should bring happiness, and it did, but not in a way that felt like home deep down inside.

She sat beneath a tree, twisting a lock of hair around one finger. She scowled at the snowy strands and pale skin. I look as though I've been left in the sun to bleach.

She didn't belong here, didn't even look like she belonged here. In human form, the cervidae were so beautiful – slender builds with elegant bone structure, large russet eyes, sun-kissed skin, and tawny-gold hair.

A fish jumped and circles rippled across the lake's surface. She closed her eyes and rested her head against the trunk. If she packed this evening, she could leave at firstlight.

"Lady Jessalyne, come quick!"

Jessalyne's eyes snapped open. The alpha buck's daughter, Corah, was running toward her, panic distorting her pretty face.

"Orit fell and hurt his leg on the rocks. Come, please." Corah's hands clenched, as if she wanted to grab Jessalyne and pull her along.

"You should practice what I've been teaching you."

"I can't, not on my brother. We need you." Tears welled in Corah's eyes as she glanced over her shoulder toward the small gathering by the rocks. "Please, it looks bad. Very bad."

Orit was the alpha buck's only son. Jessalyne nodded. "I'm coming."

The cluster of cervidae surrounding Orit parted to let her through. She knelt beside him. The young cervidae's eyes were dark with pain, and he'd reverted to his fawn form, another indication of how badly he was hurt. She gently ran her hand over his warm dappled coat. A long deep gash along his rear flank exposed shattered bone.

"Oh, Orit..." Jessalyne held her pity. The child needed reassurance, not further hurt.

"Should I get mother?" Corah asked.

"Not yet," her father replied. "Your lady mother need not see this in her condition."

Jessalyne glanced up at Lord Tyber. Not once had her father held such concern for her in his eyes. "I can't do this here. Bring him to my cottage, but move him as little as possible."

He nodded and tenderly lifted his fawn-son. Orit bleated in pain at the movement. Tyber winced.

"It's father, Orit. Rest now," he whispered, moving quickly but carefully into the woods toward her home.

Jessalyne sent Corah to gather herbs before hurrying after Lord Tyber. Even with Orit in his arms, he arrived ahead of her. He settled Orit into the small second bedroom, then took up pacing the braided rug in her front room.

Jessalyne paused on her way to the kitchen. "Please, cease that. You'll wear out my rug, and besides, I know what I'm doing."

He stopped, resting one hand on the dagger tucked in his belt. "My apologies. I know you're skilled, but I cannot help my concern for my son."

"I'll do my best to heal him."

His expression was stony. "I expect nothing less."

The words spun in her head but she shook them away. There was too much work to do to worry about what Tyber expected.

Into a kettle she measured valerian, skullcap, and nightflower to dull Orit's pain and make him sleep, then asked Tyber to fill it with water and set it to brew on the stove.

Corah came in as the kettle trickled steam, her arms full of fresh herbs and roots. "How is he?"

"Hurting. Take a mug of that tea to him and see he drinks as much as possible. I'll be in to clean the wound shortly."

After adding the few last ingredients to the cleansing solution, Jessalyne grabbed some clean linen towels and joined Corah and Tyber at Orit's bedside.

Evening approached, muting the light filtering in the windows. The muscles in her neck tightened. She didn't want her fear of the dark to disturb her efforts to care for Orit. Nothing bothered her so much as the loneliness of night, the empty stillness when memories turned into nightscares and unbidden thoughts ruled her dreams.

At the cursory flourish of her hand, every candle and lamp in the cottage sparked to life.

Lord Tyber and Corah glanced at one another, a brief wordless communication, before returning their attention to the now slumbering Orit. Jessalyne ignored the look the pair exchanged. She knew what they were thinking. Their shifting magic was harmless. Her magic was not. She frightened them.

Just one more reason to leave.

Lord Tyber finally broke the silence. "Corah, go home to your lady mother and gently tell her what has happened. Let her know Orit is in Lady Jessalyne's capable hands." Jessalyne knew the cervidae called her lady out of respect for her as their healer, but now she wondered if their fear had prompted the title.

"But I want to stay with Orit." Corah remained seated.

"Now." Tyber's stern tone put Corah on her feet.

She bent to kiss her brother's head. "Yes, Papa. Good eve, Lady Jessalyne."

Jessalyne nodded and went back to her work. Cleaning the bits of bone from the wound and setting Orit's leg left her drained and aching for the beautiful fawn child. Although she had done her best to stitch the deep gash neatly, it would leave a scar. He would forever bear a reminder of the pain he'd suffered.

Hours later, Jessalyne perched on a short, carved stool near the bed sipping a cup of anise tea and watching Orit's rhythmic breathing. Firstlight softly brightened the sky. She glanced through the doorway at Lord Tyber. He'd drifted off in one of the twig chairs by the fireplace. Would he be happy when she told him she was leaving?

Chilled by memories of her own father, she pulled her loosely woven shawl tighter around her shoulders. She pushed hair out of her eyes and pressed her palms against her forehead to blot out the thoughts of the day her mother died.

Those thoughts turned the sweet tea bitter in her mouth. She could count on one hand the times she'd seen her father since the day he'd left. Giving her a share of his merchant's take seemed to fulfill what little paternal obligation he still felt, whether he did it in person or by leaving a sack of coins on her flagstone porch. Didn't he know coin meant nothing here? Where would she spend money in Fairleigh Grove? She sighed.

Orit moaned but didn't wake. She got up and smoothed the coverlet over him. As soon as he was well, she was leaving. Waiting for another worthless sack of coins held little allure.

℃

Glass globes of phosphorescent angelmoss washed the cobbled streets with weak light. By the position of the crescent moon, Ertemis knew it was well past midnight. There was no sign of the merchant in any direction.

Ertemis exhaled in frustration. If he hadn't needed the coin, he never would have agreed to this arrangement. Even with Dragon, his warhorse, he could have gotten out of the city on his own. Somehow.

A rat scurried through the gutter. Ertemis cloaked himself in elven magic and merged into the shadows, disappearing against the grimy wall of the butcher's shop behind him. Once shrouded by the enchantment, only elven eyes could see him. There was safety and a sense of comfort in being hidden this way.

His fey blood had healed his throbbing head, but the hush night brought to the city pleased him. He relaxed against the wall and opened his senses. A full spectrum of sounds filled his angled ears.

The thump of his own heart, the soft snuffling of Dragon hidden in the alley behind him, the whoosh of wind through the streets, water dripping, the distant scutter of nocturnal creatures. The quarantine had made Slodsham unnaturally quiet. Focusing, he shut out those sounds and listened again.

This time footsteps echoed in the distance. Footsteps that had better belong to Haemus. Before long, the merchant arrived at the meeting place.

Ertemis reached out and gripped the merchant's shoulder. The man stiffened, his breath caught. Haemus whirled around, his face gnarled in fear.

Ertemis dropped the enchantment, stepped out of the shadows, and revealed himself. Haemus slumped with relief, then opened his mouth to speak. Ertemis put a finger to his lips and motioned for the man to follow him into the alley.

The dank lane stunk with the butcher's refuse. The fetor evoked memories he longed to forget – battlefields littered with sun-bloated corpses, puddles of blood dotted with flies. He forced the thoughts from his head. Dragon snuffled in recognition of his master, and Ertemis greeted the big grey with a hearty nose rub.

The shadows sculpted Dragon, magnifying his size. Haemus eyed the beast warily. "That's the biggest horse I ever seen. Whaddya pay for him?"

Ertemis focused on the merchant and bolstered his gaze with a dose of elven magic to set his eyes afire. The look had the desired effect, stifling the man's question and sending him back a step.

"You ain't gonna hurt me, are ya, now?" Haemus rubbed at the scars on his throat.

Ertemis ignored the question. "Is your contact in place?"

"Aye. We best go. I don't know how long he'll wait." Haemus coughed nervously.

The man needed be quieter. Ertemis checked the wraps on Dragon's hooves, a precaution against clatter waking any light sleepers or busy bodies. Killing someone would only complicate his night. The wraps were snug. He nodded his readiness.

Dragon's leads in hand, he followed the merchant through a series of back streets and side lanes, until they arrived in Slodsham's Stew. The mosslights here held devil's fire, the same lights used by the Legion for night patrols. The warm-water algae shed a red glow over the bawd houses.

Tonight, the regular bustle and hum of the Stew was silenced. The bawd house balconies stood empty of their usual painted faces. Even the pink skirts didn't work during quarantine. Only healers were allowed on the streets during a quarantine curfew.

Ertemis studied the rusted, rundown postern. Easy to see why it was the least used gate in the entire city. It looked barely wide enough for Dragon.

Lantern light shimmered through the dirt-streaked window of the dilapidated guard shack beside the locked passage. Haemus walked toward the shack and Ertemis hid himself and Dragon with magic. Might as well let Haemus have first go.

The merchant rapped twice, paused, and then rapped once. The door creaked open. A stunted creature with watery eyes and swamp-colored skin emerged.

"Haemusss," the goblin hissed through large, wet lips. "Twuag wasss about to leave."

"Good of ya ta stay since ya owe me," Haemus said.

"Perhapsss a little gold would help Twuag find the key fassster." The goblin offered up his warty palm suggestively.

Haemus sighed. "I thought ya might feel that way. Twuag, meet my banker." He jerked his thumb over his shoulder as he moved out of the way. "Ya want gold, ask him."

Ertemis dropped the enchantment slowly, revealing only his eyes at first. Experience had taught him just how effective the sight of two glowing, disembodied eyes could be.

Twuag shuddered and herked his bulk back into the guard shack, peering around the doorframe. "What givesss?"

Dragon slid his head over Ertemis's shoulder. He dropped the enchantment altogether. Man and beast came into full view, outlined by mossglow, a glimmer of moonlight and the unmistakable sheen of elven magic.

An uneasy smile twitching on his lips, Haemus crossed his arms over his chest. Twuag whimpered, taking obvious notice of the high, tattooed ears. Goblins rarely fared well against the fey, be they half-blood or full.

The squat-legged creature dug the keys out of his pocket and scuffled toward the gate. Frantically trying each key, Twuag peered over his shoulder every few moments, keeping one bulging eye on the dark elf's whereabouts.

Ertemis grinned slightly when he saw the smug look in Dragon's eyes. By Saladan's britches, that horse is full of himself. He stepped a little closer to the fumbling goblin. "Hurry, goblin," he whispered into the creature's knobby ear, "or Speckled Fever will be the least of your worries."

"Twuag isss hurrying," the goblin whined under his breath.

At last the lock popped open. Twuag dropped the keys and disappeared into the city.

Haemus grinned his gap-toothed grin. "I knew ya was goin' ta be handy with that one." Spinning on his heel, he sauntered through the gate.

Ertemis shook his head and began easing Dragon through the narrow space. He walked backward through the corridor, leads in hand, mindful of the limited room for his own passage. "Head down, one shoulder at a time," he urged. "Come now, you can do it."

He worried the beast would be caught at the hips. "Steady now, almost through -"

But it was not to be. Dragon stuck fast and fumed about it, snorting hot breath, nostrils flaring, eyes wild. Knowing the horse's strength and persistent nature, Ertemis goaded Dragon further.

"Pity you haven't the strength to get through, old friend. If you hadn't gorged on that second helping of oats, you might be standing next to me—"

Dragon burst from the gate with enormous force, knocking his master back. Ertemis stifled his laughter as the beast pawed the ground indignantly, snorting and stomping his still-muffled hooves. "All right, hush, you've proved me wrong."

He righted himself and shook the dirt from his cloak. He reached for Dragon's front hoof and stripped the wrapping off, working his way around until all four were freed. After stuffing the wraps in his pack, he adjusted the cinch on his scarred black leather saddle.

Haemus coughed again. "That's quite a piece of horseflesh ya got there."

"Do not refer to my fine equine friend as 'horse flesh', unless you prefer to deal with him directly." Humans were such bothersome creatures.

Dragon tossed his head and snorted.

Eyeing the horse, the merchant swallowed hard. "Does the beast understand what yer...never mind. My apologies. Dint mean any disrespect."

"Fine." Ertemis held his hand out. "My coin."

"About that..." Haemus rubbed his scarred hands together. "I have another proposition for ya."

ᏸ

Jessalyne awoke with a start, the remnants of the same familiar nightscare fading as she remembered her patient. Corah and her very pregnant mother sat at Orit's bedside. Elegant in a robe of pale green linen, Lady Dauphine held Orit's small hoof and whispered soothing words to her sleeping son. She gazed at her child with a tenderness that made Jessalyne's heart ache.

"I'm sorry, I meant to stay awake with him." She'd fallen asleep perched on the stool, head against the wall, the shawl still draped around her shoulders. She rubbed her neck.

Corah nodded. "I'm sure you needed the sleep. Papa left already to attend the morning council."

"Orit should have a mug of willow broth." Jessalyne arched her back, trying to wake up.

"I'll make it." Corah headed to the kitchen.

"He will be fine." Jessalyne tried to comfort Dauphine. "He just needs rest." The words rang false even to her own ears.

Dauphine kept her gaze on her son, her hand trembling slightly as she caressed his head. "He is very warm."

Jessalyne rubbed at the stiffness in her neck again. "It might be best if you gave me a moment to check his wound."

With a soft grunt and a hand under her belly, Dauphine pushed to her feet and joined Corah in the kitchen.

Once alone, Jessalyne pressed the back of her fingers against the little fawn's nose. Fever burned through him. She pulled the coverlet back and flinched. The gash on Orit's flank puffed around the stitches and oozed yellow fluid. A sick-sweet odor filled her nose and knotted her stomach.

No poultice or balm alone could fix this. Thoughts of the cervidae who'd been bitten last season by a water serpent filled Jessalyne's head. Tyber had forbid her to use magic. The elder buck had died. She recovered Orit and went into the kitchen.

"He isn't healing like he should. I need to...to try something else. Something Lord Tyber may not like." Something I may not be able to control.

Dauphine blanched in comprehension, more tears spilling. "I'll speak with him."

"I'll wait for his decision then."

"Nay," Dauphine's voice wavered. "Don't wait. I'll make Tyber understand."

She closed her eyes briefly. "Can you heal him, with your...gifts?"

"I can only try." Jessalyne wished she could promise more.

"Please do your best. He is our only son." She cupped her very pregnant belly. "So far."

Another tear slanted down Dauphine's cheek and Jessalyne started forward to hug her. Dauphine shifted back out of reach.

Jessalyne dropped her hands to her side. "I didn't mean..."

Sadness softened Dauphine's tone. "I know." Hesitantly, she put her arms around Jessalyne.

The rare contact nearly brought Jessalyne to tears. She inhaled. The scent of new earth and sun perfumed the expectant mother. She felt the faint kick of Dauphine's unborn babe. If the woman was willing to touch her, Jessalyne knew how desperate she must be.

Jessalyne pulled out of the embrace, knowing what the contact cost Dauphine.

"I will heal him." Jessalyne prayed her words weren't a lie.

Once Dauphine and Corah were gone, she checked on the sleeping fawn again. "I'll be back soon," she promised.

She headed through the garden and into the woods behind the house. There a grove of tall, fragrant rowan trees encircled a moss-carpeted patch of ground. A solitary stone marked her mother's resting place.

"I wish you were here, Mama. I need you. There's so much I don't know, and now a life rests in my charge. I wish you'd left me books to teach me about this magic. I know it comes from you."

Her sigh disappeared on the wind. "I don't know if I will heal Orit or hurt him, but I have to try." The lingering sensation of Dauphine's arms around her sharpened the pang of missing her mother.

She wrapped her arms around herself but it was a cold comfort. "I hate this useless, misplaced feeling. I hate it!"

Clenching her fists, she struggled to calm herself. "It can't be this power is just for lighting candles and warming bath water.

"If I heal him, maybe the cervidae won't be so afraid of me. Maybe they'll be willing to touch me."

Her voice quieted. "Not that it matters."

She dropped to her knees in the grass. "Dauphine hugged me today, Mama. That's the first time anyone's held me since you died. I can't live like this. I can't. I have to leave, Mama. I need to. I need to go somewhere people aren't afraid of me."

Jessalyne knelt with her arms outstretched. She willed the leaf-filtered sun to melt her doubts and strengthen her spirit for the work ahead.

Orit showed no change when she returned.

There was no reason to delay. She waved her hand and lit the beeswax candles in the wall sconces. After easing the coverlet back, she stood at the footboard and blocked out all but the wounded child. Occasional moans punctuated his ragged breaths.

The room blurred as she focused on Orit's innocent face, on his small body racked with fever and infection, and the angry seeping gash. Heavy magic prickled her skin as power flowed through her.

She closed her eyes and visualized Orit's flank perfect and blemish free. In her mind, she saw him healthy and well in both his human and deer forms.

Holding her hands over him, she wished she could bear his injury herself. She imagined his wound as her own. Heat coursed over her in rippling waves, lifting the hair off her face. Sweat trickled down her spine. A shard of pain stabbed her side. Orit's hurt was hers for one long, hard moment and then dissolved, extinguishing the fire within her as it faded.

The heat drained out of her and she wobbled, her balance gone. She opened her eyes but couldn't focus. She clutching for the footboard, as her knees give way. She dropped to the floor with a sharp crack. She gasped and her eyes watered at the jolt.

On all fours, she tried to catch her breath. She blinked, unable to clear her vision. Then she heard a child's voice.

"Lady Jessalyne?"

She tipped her head up, the action spinning another wave of dizziness through her.

"Lady Jessalyne, are you sick?" A blurry Orit stood before her, in his human form.

Small hands wrapped around her waist trying to help her up. She laughed weakly.

"Orit, Orit..." Her voice trailed off as she pulled the boy against her and hugged him, kissing his little cheeks. He squirmed out of her embrace.

She studied him, searching for a mark. Nothing remained of the wound.

"What's wrong, Lady Jessalyne?"

"Nothing...absolutely nothing." Cool relief filled her as she collapsed to the floor.

Chapter Two

"Our business is concluded, Haemus." Ertemis swung into his saddle.

"But wait, ya haven't heard what I have to say!" Haemus looked as if he might weep. He rubbed his throat again.

Ertemis peered at Haemus, impatient to be paid. Dragon tossed his head, ready to go.

"Yer a man fer hire, ain't ya?"

"Aye."

"Well, I want ta hire ya."

Ertemis wrinkled his brow. "For what? And how much?"

"Guard my way ta Drust and then Callaoja River. Ten pieces of gold." Haemus pulled a small pouch off his belt and tossed it up.

Ertemis counted the coins in the pouch. Seventy-five as promised. Haemus might be human but his money was good. Ten pieces of gold. Perhaps Haemus could be quieter. "Twenty. And conversation is not provided."

"Aye, agreed! Again, we have a deal." Haemus started to reach for a handshake but stopped short, clapping his hands together instead. "Now, ta the stables ta gather my steed."

As Ertemis expected, the stables outside Slodsham were deserted, no guards anywhere. He shook his head with disgust. Only the wealthy and careless left their mounts at the city mews. They might lodge the animal well enough, but here was a prime example of what happened in time of crisis. When the cry of quarantine went up, the guards on duty probably took the best mounts and got as far away as possible. Anyone could walk in and help himself to any horse he wanted. Ertemis wondered if that wasn't exactly what Haemus planned to do.

An unusual quiet greeted them as they went inside, no shuffling of hooves or whinnied greetings. The pitch-black gave way as Ertemis's elven sight took over. There was good reason for the

21

quiet. "Your horse is gone with the rest of them. Nothing left but one scraggly donkey."

"I beg ya pardon, she ain't one bit scraggly!" Haemus dug in his waist pouch for a flint and began sparking it to locate a lantern.

As soon as he got one lit, he found the jenny's stall and led her out, scratching the animal's head. The donkey had a marking around one eye in the shape of a flower. "Petal, my sweet girl, did ya miss me? Here's a carrot for ya." He pulled the promised treat from a pocket inside his cloak and fed it to her, stroking her neck. "I don't see my cart."

Ertemis shrugged. "Probably stolen as well. You'll have to ride that animal."

Haemus grumbled something about the cost of the cart, but soon found a light blanket and some tack and fixed Petal up to ride. Hoisting himself onto the donkey's back, he followed Ertemis out of the stables.

By firstlight, they were well beyond Slodsham. Haemus pattered on non-stop about buying a new cart, the price of silk in Drust and many other things Ertemis wished he could shut out.

He pulled his hood down against the rising sun. They traveled through the low country forests all morning, finally breaking at midday for Haemus's sake. Dragon and Petal grazed near a small shaded stream, while Ertemis and Haemus ate bread and hard cheese from their packs. Ertemis finished first. He contemplated how much longer he would have to abide his noisy human companion while he refilled his waterskin.

Another day's ride and the foothills of Shaldar's Wyver Mountains would spread before them. The port city of Drust lay slightly further east on the Callaoja River. Maybe someone in Drust would have the information he needed to find his father. Time was slipping away. Once the Legion declared a bounty on his head, he'd have to be more cautious than ever. Maybe he should go to Shaldar City first, see if what the Travelers had told him was true. Or maybe he should abandon the idea of punishing his birth father until his bond was paid and he was truly free.

Perhaps in Drust he would ditch Haemus and find passage on a ship. He had heard rumors that the games in Myssia were about to begin as their new queen sought a husband among the fittest men. The thought tempted him. Myssia's queens were fierce warrior women, not soft, pampered nobility. He doubted they would be afraid of him, and they'd have coin enough to buy his freedom. Even so, the thought of himself as king of anything was laughable.

Maybe he would seek work through the black markets. There was always someone willing to pay a hefty fee for some scurrilous deed. No. Black market dealers were not the kind of people a wanted man did business with.

If he could just earn enough to buy his freedom. Freedom. He couldn't imagine what it would feel like. He would find a quiet spot in the mountains somewhere and disappear, away from the stares and whispers. Concentrate on other ways of finding the blackguard who'd fathered him. Plan the weasel's slow death.

Haemus snored loudly. Ertemis shook the man awake. "You can sleep tonight. Time to ride." Ertemis mounted Dragon before Haemus' eyes opened.

"I'm up!" The merchant started. "Ya needn't bruise a person!" He no sooner finished speaking before a coughing fit bent him over. Red-faced, he gasped, "Hold yerself still a minute." Haemus went to the stream and drank his fill. Finished, he hoisted himself onto Petal. He motioned his hand forward, still winded from coughing. "This wretched country air could kill a man."

With a nudge, Ertemis moved Dragon forward. His mind wandered in the possibilities of his future. Haemus found his voice and began another one-sided conversation.

The air cooled as the elevation rose. The tall pines of the low country gave way to the scrubby brush of the foothills, and the broad open sky blushed with the setting sun. The night calmed Ertemis. He reveled in the silence before he realized Haemus had not asked to stop in some time. In fact, he could not recall exactly when the man's chattering had ceased. He heeled Dragon and looked back.

Haemus was slumped unmoving over Petal's neck.

ॐ

Jessalyne dreamed of freshly baked bread, warm from the oven, and a big bowl of something hot and savory to dip it in. She opened her eyes, unsure for a moment of her surroundings.

The coverlet was hers, as was the bed. Stars sparkled before her when she sat up too quickly. She let out a great sigh just as Corah popped her head in the room.

"How are you feeling?"

"Fine. Have I been asleep long?"

"A while. It's almost lastlight. Are you hungry?" She smiled broadly. "Orit was very hungry."

"Orit! How is he?"

"Perfect. Wonderful. Papa announced a day of celebration at the lake tomorrow in your honor."

"How did I get here?"

"Orit came running home and Mama almost fainted when she saw him. He was yelling you were sick and needed help. We all rushed back here. Mama and I put you into bed..."

They had touched her.

"...and Papa rekindled your stove fire. Orit gathered vegetables from your garden and I made stew and bread."

"That's what I smell! I'm starving." Jessalyne swung her legs out of bed.

"Mama and Papa took Orit home, so I'm the only one here. I'll set a bowl out for you."

Still in her everyday tunic, Jessalyne hurried to the table. Her stomach growled as she took the first bite. The vegetable stew tasted even better than it smelled. She ate slice after slice of the hot brown bread drizzled with honey.

Despite weakening her, the use of her magic to heal had left her with a great lingering peace. Warming bath water had never done that.

She moved from the table to her chair near the fire. "Sit with me. Do you ever wonder what your purpose in the realm is?"

Corah cocked her head as she took the other chair. "I'm cervidae. My purpose is to serve the greater good of the herd, to watch Orit, mind my father, help my mother with chores and in time, to be a good wife to Emmitt."

"Beyond that I mean. What are you here to do?"

Corah gave her the same quizzical look. She shook her head. "I am doing what I am meant to do."

Jessalyne started to ask again but then just smiled. Perhaps she should adopt Corah's view of life in the grove. Perhaps she should concentrate on the good feelings from healing Orit, think more about the present and less about the future.

"You're a good friend. You are indeed doing what you are meant to do." She turned the conversation to herbs and quizzed the girl on remedies while trying to convince herself her simple life contained all the purpose it needed. As much as she wanted to leave, she really had nowhere to go, and no idea how to find whatever it was she was looking for.

୫

"Haemus!" Ertemis wheeled Dragon around and rode to Haemus's side. He shouted the man's name again. Still no answer. He grabbed the man's shoulder and tried again to get a response. Haemus was burning up. Ertemis eased him back. The merchant groaned. His head bobbed, chin to chest. Blotches of red and white mottled his skin. Sweat dripped from his forehead, and his hair stuck to his cheeks in damp wisps. "Don't feel sa good," he whispered before collapsing over Petal's neck again.

Playing nursemaid to some human was not part of Ertemis's plan. The fates must be out to get him. Nothing ever went right in his life.

He made a hasty camp near a large clump of Devil's Toothbrush. The warrior in him sought the most protected spot at all times. Soon he had a fire blazing against the night's chill.

He plucked Haemus from Petal's back and got him settled onto a cleared section of ground between the fire and cluster of scrub brush. A weak moan escaped Haemus. Ertemis tried to give him water, glad the merchant had filled his waterskin at the last stop.

The man sputtered and water spilled over his chin. "Where are we?"

"Camped. You cannot ride further."

Haemus coughed. His body shook as he struggled to sit up. "I got the fever, ain't I?"

"Aye."

Leaning toward the fire, Haemus shivered. Ertemis pulled the thin saddle blanket off Petal and draped it over the sick man's shoulders. Humans were such weak creatures. Hardly any of them had magic. How could his mother have lain with one? Was it any wonder the gutless cretin had ignored her once he'd gotten what he wanted?

"I ain't got long then," Haemus muttered through chattering teeth.

Ertemis didn't know what to say. Death was a familiar thread in the cloth of his life, and most often he was the weaver, not the wearer. At least this time, death had not come from his own hands.

"Rest. I'll get food." Ertemis started toward the packs.

"Wait, stay. Please..." Hacking coughs cut Haemus off. He caught his breath and continued. "A word."

Ertemis trudged back and crouched beside him. "What?"

"I know I ain't gonna get over this, and I got something needs doin'." Filmy eyes looked up at Ertemis as the man reached beneath the collar of his tunic. He pulled a brown suede bag from a cord around his neck. No bigger than a fist, it was sweat stained by years of being worn close his body.

"There's a key in here. Give it ta my daughter." His gaze drifted, unfocused. "The box is buried under the garden bench. Tell her I'm sorry. I weren't a good pa and I'm sorry. Tell her I don't bear no ill against her for what she done—"

A fit of coughing came over him, and some time passed before he could finish. "Tell her it ain't her fault she is the way she is. And I don't blame her for it." His voice weakened. "Poor thing, all alone." He coughed again. "Take a sack of coins from my pack fer payment an' give the rest ta her."

He mumbled directions, something about following the Callaoja River to Callao Lake and someplace Ertemis had never heard of. His mumbling ceased as he drifted off to sleep.

Ertemis studied the man's disfigured hands and face, the hardened mass of burn scars. He shook his head. Just like a human to be careless with fire.

He added a few branches to the fire, then rummaged in his pack for cheese and bread. Haemus coughed in his sleep, wheezing.

Ertemis stared into the fire as he ate. Part of him wanted to ignore the man's request, take the money, and continue on to Drust. He cursed under his breath. A dying man's request was not something to be denied. He would deliver the key.

Haemus said his daughter was alone, so she must be unmarried. With the dowry a merchant could provide the girl must be either truly homely or a bitter shrew not to be married off.

Maybe both. Definitely well fed and spoiled. Although obviously not high born, Haemus wore fabrics as rich as those draping the nobles who oft hired the Legion's men to fight their battles. Haemus must have a lavish home, no doubt with servants. The girl had probably never lifted a hand on her own behalf.

Tell her it ain't her fault she is the way she is. Ertemis grimaced as he pictured a plump, overdressed twit wailing about her father's passing while showing her revulsion for the halfling who'd brought her the news. She would look at him with the same distain most women did.

She would anguish over who'd supply her next meal or trinket. Or she'd worry that the lowborn creature before her might desire her favors. He snorted. Not blasted likely.

The absurd idea of this arrogant brat imagining he wanted to lay her bones amused him. He flicked a rind of cheese into the flames. His mixed blood might repulse most decent women, but to the wanton few, his fey half made him a highly desirable bedmate. He hadn't bothered in a long time, but finding companionship when the mood struck presented little problem. He closed his eyes and almost forgot the sick human sharing the circle of firelight as sleep overcame him.

Awake before firstlight, Ertemis knew without opening his eyes that Haemus lay cold. He heard nothing but the sounds of the world rising around him. No coughing, no wheezing breaths, no other heartbeat broke the morning calm but his, Dragon's, and Petal's.

Low-spirited by such needless death, he chose a spot and used the dagger in his boot to dig a slim trench in the hard ground. He wrapped Haemus in the thin saddle blanket and placed the body in the swale. He piled stones over the site over then murmured a prayer in his mother's native tongue.

As Haemus had promised, there was money in his pack. Ertemis found five heavy sacks of coin in the bottom. No wonder Haemus had wanted a little traveling protection. Two sacks of gold and three of silver, almost enough to buy his freedom. He weighed the sacks in his hand. With what he already had, maybe exactly enough. The girl wouldn't know how much money her father was carrying.

He tied Petal's leads to a cinch on Dragon's tack, and set off straight toward Callaoja River. He was unsure how far up river Callao lake was, but the sooner he handed over the key to whatever spoiled brat Haemus had fathered, the sooner he could buy his life back. He smiled, the promise of freedom sweet on his lips.

ഓ

Jessalyne didn't regret the late night spent with Corah in front of the fire, even as firstlight woke her. She stretched and listened to the birdsong outside her window. Last night she'd slept without a single nightscare. Was that a sign her decision to leave was the right one or a sign she should stay? She didn't know.

She also didn't know what the day would bring. Would the cervidae treat her differently now that her magic had worked some good? If they did, her desire to leave might fade. Her head swirled as she dressed in a pale blue silk tunic, so weightless it was like wrapping herself in sky. She added a simple bleached linen overvest.

In front of a reflection glass, she brushed her hair until it shone and left it loose, save two small braids at her temples tied with silk ribbon in a matching shade of blue.

The remainder of Corah's bread went into a linen square. Jessalyne took a basket from a hook in the low kitchen ceiling and knotted the free ends of the linen around the handle.

In the grove beyond her garden she picked fragrant stonefruit until her basket overflowed. Their sweet scent wafted thick in the gentle breeze, and she couldn't resist biting into one as she walked to the lake. A drop of juice rolled down her chin. She wiped it away with the back of her hand. Perhaps the grove was the most perfect place in all of Shaldar.

The entire cervidae herd had gathered at the lake, all of them in human form.

Orit approached first. "I made this for you, Lady Jessalyne." He held out a circle of yellow starflowers.

"Thank you." Jessalyne accepted the garland with a smile. She draped his handiwork around her neck. "I love it."

There were all sorts of games: tag, hide and seek, foot races, jumping toad. The children and adults alike skipped stones across the lake's placid surface.

Blankets spread on the ground held a multitude of goodies. Jars of sticky fruit preserves sat next to seeded breads. There were honey cakes scented with lavender, savory vegetable cakes, piles of stonefruit, purple and gold grapes, seedberries, apples and lily root. Pitchers of alderberry wine and spring ale passed from group to group. Laughter and singing echoed around the sheltered lakeside, accompanied by the lilting sounds of wooden flutes.

By afternoon, the children reverted to fawns and nestled against their mothers, napping in the drowsy warmth of the midday sun.

Jessalyne sat with Corah and Dauphine. Orit dreamed at his mother's side. The woman chatted about nothing and everything. The day slipped peacefully by. More and more, the idea of leaving melted away. She could live this peaceable life after all.

Then Corah and Dauphine went silent, their eyes rounding. They stared over her shoulder. Other heads turned. The entire herd went still.

She turned as well. She furrowed her brow, not believing her eyes.

A donkey with a flower-shaped marking around its right eye plodded toward them along the river. Her father's donkey had a marking like that. Petal. But it was what followed the jenny that had undoubtedly drawn the crowd's attention. A huge warhorse carrying a dark figure.

As Petal came closer, Jessalyne stood for a better look at the figure on the horse. Definitely not her father. Whoever it was, he was slumped over the horse's neck like a dead man.

"Dark elf." Tyber whispered the words uneasily.

"What?" She swung around to look at Tyber. "What does that mean?"

"You remember the council of elves that came for Orit's naming ceremony?" He spoke without taking his eyes off the creature.

She tipped her head toward the dark skinned, ebony-haired man coming ever closer with Petal's guiding. "Yes, but they looked nothing like that." The elves she recalled glimmered with light and magic; elegant, graceful beings closer to her own fair coloring than any other creature she'd seen before.

Jessalyne eyed the dark elf once again.

Tyber continued. "They were high-born elves, light elves, fully imbued with the magic of old Shaldar. This one is a mixed-breed, a mud blood, a halfling. By any name dark elves are dangerous creatures with tempers as black as their skins. They have their own magic, but few survive birth when the midwives do their jobs properly. Neither elf nor human claim them, and for good reason. They are trouble in the flesh." Tyber spat on the ground.

Petal stopped just paces from where the herd stood watching and bent to drink from the river. The warhorse came along side, putting the dark elf in plain sight. Jessalyne stared. The parts of him not covered by cloak or battle leathers revealed broad curves of thick muscle. His smooth, luminous skin was the deep charcoal grey of iris root dye, but with the subtle glistening sheen of oil on water. She wanted to touch him to see if the color would rub off on her fingers. The thought of it made something quicken inside her.

Black as a starless night and partially tied back with a leather thong, his long hair hung over one shoulder, exposing his most telling feature: his ears. Angled skyward, they were undeniably elven and covered with strange silver runes.

Even unconscious, he was intimidating.

Her mouth hung open. She closed it. "I don't think he's well."

Tyber snorted. "Lady Jessalyne, I know your heart on this already. But no good can come of helping this creature. It's best to let nature do what the midwives did not."

She faced the alpha buck. "I am a healer. I cannot dismiss the sick so easily. Beside, I need to know why he has my father's animal." She tossed her hair back and walked toward Petal.

"Lady Jessalyne..."

She kept walking.

Tyber muttered something she couldn't hear.

At Petal's side, she stopped and gazed at the strange horse and rider. She swallowed hard. They seemed much bigger up close. She made eye contact with the slate-colored warhorse. The animal snuffled softly.

"I mean your master no harm," she told the horse. There was a tremor in her voice she didn't recognize.

Sweat dampened the dark elf's hair. She reached out and rested her fingertips on his forearm, unwilling to touch his face. His skin blazed with fever. He moaned, and she jumped, snatching her hand away. Tyber and his men started forward.

"I'm fine. He is not. He burns with fever." She grabbed at the horse's reins expecting protest, but the horse dipped his head lower, giving her a better grip on the leather.

"I'll lead them to the cottage, but I'll need assistance getting him off his mount and inside. I also need Corah's help making enough antidote. Whatever sickness this is, the herd must be protected."

Tyber opened his mouth to argue, but Jessalyne raised a hand to cut him off. "Then don't help. I'll do it on my own. I need to know why the elf has my father's animal."

Setting his jaw, Tyber grudgingly agreed. "Territt, Willem, go with Lady Jessalyne. Help her with this...creature. Confiscate his weapons, then stand watch outside her cottage. Corah may go to help with the antidote."

Jessalyne led the big gray while Corah walked next to her with Petal. The guards stayed on either side of the warhorse. Despite Corah's attempts to disguise her glances, Jessalyne noticed the girl's attention to the dark elf.

"Just take a good look and be done with it, will you? I doubt he'll notice you staring in his current condition."

Corah shook her head, but her gaze danced over the elf. "I've never seen anything...anyone...any elf, whatever he is, like him." She smiled at Jessalyne. "I dare say you have either."

Jessalyne returned the smile. "I haven't. That's a sure thing." Life in the grove had shown her very little.

She directed the guards to carry her newest patient into the room so recently occupied by Orit. The boy hadn't taken up quite so much of the bed.

After asking twice, Jessalyne got Corah into the kitchen to boil water. She then asked the guards to take the animals to the old stable. One task remained, one she'd have to do herself.

The guards had taken his leather breastplate but left his cloak. It lay over the stool where they'd thrown it. She picked the length of fabric up to hang it. The fragrance of horse, leather, and something darker filled her nose. The spicy scent was unlike anything she'd smelled. She shook her head, forced herself to focus. She dashed the cloak over a peg to get it out of her hands.

He lay on his back, legs sprawled out, feet hanging off the sides of the bed. She unlaced the first of his knee-high boots and pulled it off. A slim blade clattered to the floor. The guards' search hadn't been very thorough. Tyber would be angry if he knew. She turned the blade in her hands, recognizing the design. The dagger was a Feyre, elven steel, twin to the blade the elven council had given to Tyber. Perforations honeycombed the blade like metal lace, making it as light as a wasp's nest, but elven magic made it nigh unbreakable. She set the dagger atop the stool to give to the guards.

After his other boot, she untied the laces at the neck of his tunic. The worn grey linen clung to his hot, damp skin, outlining the contours of his chest in soft relief. Her fingers brushed the sooty vee of skin beneath the laces. She inhaled. The feel of skin beneath her fingers was rare. Her belly tightened. She would have to touch more of him to get the shirt off.

Loosening the wrist ties, she took his hands in hers one by one and eased his arms through the sleeves. His broad palms were calloused, his thick fingers rough. What would that hand feel like against her skin? She pressed her palm to his, comparing the size. Her hand looked like a child's.

Unable to lift him, she see-sawed the bunched fabric between him and the bed until she had it at his shoulders. Avoiding contact was impossible. Her fingers grazed his chest and her breath caught in her throat. His skin was so smooth, the muscle beneath so hard and hot – like river stones warmed in the afternoon sun. She laid his tunic over the footboard. The patched fabric was torn in two places and needed washing.

His sweat-glossed skin shone like tarnished silver against the ivory bedclothes. Thick black locks splayed out around his muscled shoulders. What color eyes hid beneath those velvet-fringed lids? Glancing at the blade she'd found on him, she studied him more carefully. No scars that she could see. Nothing marked him but the runes on his curious ears.

He was as different in his coloring from the cervidae as she was. His strong jaw and straight nose gave him the countenance of man used to getting his way. She stared, unable to look away. Like the time she'd stumbled upon a den of sleeping wolves, watching him ignited two senses; fear and longing. He was beautiful in the way of all wild creatures, and if Tyber were right, just as deadly.

His chest rose and fell rhythmically. She wanted to touch him again, to know once more the feel of his skin, any skin, beneath her fingers. Tentatively, she traced one of the silver runes on his ear.

He moaned and she pulled away. She stepped back, thunderstruck by the acute nearness of him and the way his palpable maleness permeated the room. There was something about him darker than his skin.

"What have I done?" she whispered. "Why have I taken this man into my home?" To find out why he had her father's donkey? He might have robbed her father. Or worse.

She backed out of the room, grabbing the Feyre as she went, and shut the door harder than necessary. She pressed her hand against her mouth, and composed herself before going into the kitchen. With so much work to be done, she did not want Corah to think she doubted her decision to help the elf.

She squared her shoulders, and took a deep breath. I'm a healer. He won't harm me. Still, she vowed to see him well and on his way with as much haste as possible.

After depositing the Feyre with the guards outside, Jessalyne strode into the kitchen. "I need you to start an elixir base while I study my mother's books for some hint at what this illness is. Now, what would you use?"

Startled by Jessalyne's burst into the kitchen, Corah almost dropped her mortar and pestle. She stammered for a moment, "Um, let me see, angelica root, dried monk's blossom, hyssop – no hyssop would be for a bath, this is an elixir, so ground parsley seed and..."

"And?"

"Alder flower?" Corah asked hopefully.

"Yes! Well done." Jessalyne pulled one of her mother's books from a shelf and began flipping through it. She looked up at the girl, lost in some daydream. "Will you be making that elixir today?"

"Of course, sorry," Corah nodded, head down.

Jessalyne knew who occupied the girl's thoughts. "Mind the work at hand, not the creature in the bedroom. Besides, you are betrothed." Corah's cheeks colored. She dipped her head lower.

Jessalyne pulled one of her mother's books from a warped shelf. She scoured the text for some indication as to what malady they were fighting. The faded scents wafting from the yellowed pages reminded her of her mother. She smiled. Her mother would have helped anyone in need.

"I think this is it." Her finger stopped at a passage near the bottom of one page. "We need a few more ingredients."

Lastlight settled as they finished the brew. Jessalyne and Corah strained the concoction through a bit of fine linen into a narrow-necked jar. They each took a dose, then plugged the jar with a cork stopper and sealed the cork with wax.

"Be sure everyone gets a dose, fawns and elders first. There's no way of telling who was exposed." Jessalyne smiled at her shape-shifting apprentice. "You're a good student. Thank you for your hard work."

"You're a patient teacher," Corah said.

Jessalyne waved the comment away. "Off you go."

Corah left, her precious cargo cradled in the crook of her arm.

I'm alone in the house with him. Jessalyne shivered. Stop behaving like some foolish chit. There are guards outside the front door. He's too weak with fever to be dangerous. And even if he were, I have my magic. Just give him the elixir and be done with it.

She took a measure of the elixir in a mug and a cool damp cloth with her into the back bedroom. She nodded her head toward a small oil lamp on the bedside table, and it flickered to life, brightening the room with a soft glow. He slept fitfully, the covers tossed aside. Light from the oil lamp danced across his skin.

She set the cloth on the table and hesitated. Giving him the elixir required touching him again. She sat on the edge of the bed, as close as she dared, and studied his face. He didn't look that dangerous. In fact, he looked more feral than dangerous, and wild creatures could be tamed. Sometimes.

Dark elf. She mouthed the words silently, not knowing his name. The shadows in the room caressed him as though they knew him and for a brief moment, she envied the darkness.

She slid her hand behind his head. He moaned softly, but this time she didn't jump. He wouldn't hurt her for helping him, would he? She lifted his head enough to bring the mug to his mouth, trying not to think about the silkiness of his hair between her fingers or the lushness of his lips. She trickled as much of the liquid as she could into him, then eased his head back onto the pillow.

The last few ribbons of blue-black hair slipped through her fingers. She reached for the cloth, eager to occupy her hands with something else besides him. No, not eager. Reluctant, for in truth his skin infected her with the desire to touch, the urge to caress. She shook her head. This was not the proper behavior for a healer.

She mopped the sweat from his brow with the cool linen and left, taking his shirt with her to wash. The cottage was too dark. She slashed her hand through the air. Small flames flickered to life in response, the pair of candles on the mantel, the tableside lamp by her chair. Better. The light calmed her.

His life relied on the healing power of the elixir now. She had no intention of using her gifts to heal him. None. Ever. Tyber had said dark elves had their own magic, and she knew too little about the alchemy of such things to chance clashing with whatever power flowed through him. It simply wasn't a risk worth taking.

Chapter Three

A concert of drum-pounding pixies played in Ertemis's head. What tavern had he spent last night in? The Dirty Dwarf? The Fig and Gristle? Nay, neither of those was right. He opened his eyes a slit.

"What the..." He sat up too quickly, and the pixies pounded harder.

If this was an inn, it was one of the nicest he'd slept in of late. The room was sparse but clean. And wretchedly sunny. It wasn't like him to leave the curtains open. It also smelled better than any place he'd ever stayed. He smelled food – hot griddlecakes and smoked trout by the scent of it.

"That will do nicely." He swung his legs around and the instant his bare feet hit the floor he realized he had been undressed and stripped of both sword and Feyre. Someone had disrobed him down to his trousers. He inhaled, then lifted his hands to his face and sniffed. The scent of a woman lingered on his skin, his hair.

Wanting more information, he stood near the door and listened. Only soft muffled sounds reached his ears. He imagined a plump cook bustling about. Plump cooks always made the best food.

He tried to sense more, sending tendrils of magic into his surroundings, but a wall of mist drifted around him. He blamed his overindulgence, although he still couldn't recall the tavern responsible.

The door opened without a sound. Two chairs sat in front of a fireplace, a basket of knitting next to one. A braided scrap rug covered a stone floor. The room was simple and tidy. This was not a tavern. Where was he?

Wonderful smells wafted through a doorway on the far wall. A woman hummed an unfamiliar tune. He followed his nose into the kitchen and there she stood. With her back to him, she alternated between slicing seedberries and flipping griddlecakes.

He inhaled, her scent filling his nose. She was the one who'd undressed him. Pity he didn't couldn't remember what else she'd done to him.

A sly smile lifted the corners of his mouth, and he moved closer. He'd not had a woman in ages for many reasons, but he complimented himself on the one he'd picked to break his fast. From the back, she looked a fair prize. Tall for a woman, but well shaped – even her loose tunic couldn't hide a slender waist and well-curved hips. If only he could remember last night. Her scent caressed his senses with warm, feminine sweetness.

He came a little closer. Her hair was so uncommonly pale, it could have passed for elven. He tried to get a glance at her ears to be sure she wasn't. A seedberry rolled off the counter. She bent to pick it up, placing her nicely rounded backside inches from his groin. He could not recall a lovelier sight.

His stomach growled loudly.

She whirled around, dropping the utensil in her hand, and inhaled sharply, almost colliding with his naked chest.

"What are you...why are you...you should be in bed!" she sputtered, her pale lavender eyes wide.

A fair prize, indeed.

&

What nerve! The creature dared sneak up on her in her own home, half naked, and that smirk – like a cat full of milkbeetles. Jessalyne breathed deeply to calm down. She willed herself to stop staring into his silver-edged onyx eyes.

"Why are you out of bed?" She asked again, bending to pick up the dropped utensil. Her scullery felt too small and very warm at the moment.

"Good morning to you as well." He backed away and sat at the table.

She ignored his jab at her lack of politeness, relieved by the distance he put between them. "You shouldn't be up."

"Why, pray tell?" His devilish grin widened. "Were you bringing me breakfast in bed? If that's so, I'll gladly go back and wait for you there."

Jessalyne felt blood surge to her cheeks at his words. What was he implying? "If I had known you were such a lout, I would have left you to the mercy of the fever."

At the word fever, his smile dissolved.

"I saved your life. You should be thankful," she said.

He scowled. "You didn't save my life. Illness doesn't affect me."

Hah! It apparently affected his brain. She snorted. "Then why were you boiling with fever? Why did I bother poring over books and crushing herbs and straining mixtures and making an elixir to heal you? An elixir that did indeed cure you!"

"My body uses fever to burn illness out of the human portion of my blood. I would have gotten better with or without your elixir."

She glared at him. "And now I suppose you expect me to feed you."

"That's the best offer I've heard so far." He smiled wickedly. "Although the day is young."

Ignorant lout. She turned her back and begun heaping food onto a platter. She dropped a plate of trout and griddlecakes in front of him and made to go. He planted his foot on the chair across from him and shoved it out.

"Sit. I can't eat all of this alone."

Undoubtedly a lie. Most men could eat their share and then some without breathing hard. She hesitated, unwilling to bend to the whims of this creature. But she was hungry, and it would give her a chance to ask the questions plaguing her. She took another plate from the cupboard. He watched everything she did but said nothing.

The silence and the staring made her uncomfortable. Not to mention sharing breakfast with a bare-chested man. Elf. Whatever kind of beast he was. The sight of him shirtless left her speechless. How did a man's shoulders get so wide? He must think her simple.

In the light of day, his skin shone like raven's feathers. She knew the softness of that midnight-colored skin and longed to touch it again. Just once, to be sure her memory was true. The thought flooded her face with heat. She pushed a seedberry slice across her plate as she tried to refocus and was just about to ask about Petal when he spoke.

"I didn't mean to startle you."

She looked up through her lashes. "I wasn't startled."

"You were." He paused, a griddlecake halfway to his mouth.

"I am fine."

He started as if to refute her again but paused, the faintest twinkling in his eyes. "Do you have a name, or shall I come up with one of my own?"

"I have a name." She popped the seedberry slice into her mouth to stall.

He waited for a moment, then leaned closer. "Are you going to tell me what it is?"

She swallowed. "You haven't told me yours."

"Master elf will do."

"I am not about to call you master, and elf is not a name. It's what you are."

He shook his head slightly. Was that a smile? "Ertemis."

Satisfied, she leaned back. "I am Lady Jessalyne."

"Lady Jessalyne? You're nobility?" He peered out the window and laughed. "Living out in the woods? I doubt that."

The urge to strike him was thick. She pushed away from the table, grabbed her plate and headed out to the slop sink. She needed to get away from him for a moment, to breathe air untainted by all that maleness. And nakedness. His laughter wafted out behind her as she pushed through the side door.

Ertemis. His name rolled too easily around on her tongue. She hadn't expected him to recover so quickly. At least now her conscience was clear. He would be on his way, and that would be the end of it. But she still didn't know what he was doing with her father's donkey.

She left the plate to soak and went back inside, but he wasn't in the kitchen. She peeked into the rest of the house. The back bedroom door swung shut.

Good. She would speak to him when he was dressed. She straightened her kitchen and had almost emptied her head of the sight of his bare chest when he came back in. He wore boots with his trousers this time, but still no tunic.

She balled her hands to keep from touching him. That would not do. "I imagine the sort of woman you're used to finds your lack of dress appealing. I do not." In truth, his bare chest was far more to her liking than she cared to admit.

An irritating smile danced across his lips. "I would be happy to put my tunic on, Lady Jessalyne. Simply show me where you put it when you undressed me."

He stressed the word in a way that gave her wicked thoughts. She chastised herself for not remembering she'd washed and hung the shirt to dry after giving him the elixir. Brushing past him, she hurried out to the clothesline. She snatched the garment off and stormed back into the house.

"There." She threw the tunic at him. "Now dress. Please." Or not. No, he needed to dress.

He held it out in front of him. "Laundered and mended. Do you treat all your guests this way or are you hoping I'll reward your kindness again?"

"Again?"

"Perhaps you'd like another taste of last night?"

"A taste of you feverish and sweating in my childhood bed? I don't think you're well after all." The man was unbearable.

"Did we not..." He raised his brows.

"Whatever you're implying, no, we did not. Do most women fall at your feet so quickly?"

"Actually...," he began with a slight grin.

She cut him off with a glare, trying to damp down the building heat of anger and unwarranted jealousy. Let him rut like the beast he was. What did she care?

His expression softened, and surprisingly, he held his tongue and yanked the tunic over his head. Jessalyne looked away, unwilling to give her overactive imagination further fuel. As soon as he was decent, she would ask him about Petal. Then he could be on his way and out of her life. Her front door creaked. She turned around. He was gone.

ဆ

Ertemis found his way blocked by two cervidae guards, hands on sword hilts. Why he hadn't discerned them earlier? Testing his senses again, he found the fog in his head was gone and he could read the guards. They were wary of him.

His hands came up in a show of peace. "Just looking for my horse. As soon as he's saddled, I'll be about my business."

The guards relaxed their stance. The tall one spoke. "Territt will take you to your mount. Fine beast, I might add."

"He is indeed, thank you." Ertemis knew enough to take peace when it was offered.

He followed the guard through the woods on an overgrown path. Before long, they came upon Dragon and Petal in a rundown willow pen attached to a small, three-sided shed. From the shed's state, it hadn't housed animals in many years.

Dragon whickered a greeting and Petal, not to be left out, brayed softly. Dragon nudged Petal's neck with his nose.

Ertemis raised an eyebrow at Dragon's behavior, but he had other things to worry about. He needed to get his bearings so he could start looking for Haemus' daughter again. He nodded to the guard and promised to be on his way.

His mind wandered to the lovely Lady Jessalyne as he went through the mechanics of preparing Dragon's tack. She was a uniquely beautiful woman and oddly unafraid of him.

He smiled at how flustered she'd become in the kitchen, nose to chest with him. The sight of her fair face flushed with indignation, her chest rising against the thin fabric of her tunic with each deep breath, tightened his insides like no other woman ever had. Maybe the fever had affected him. And she had not denied she was the one who had undressed him. The thought of her hands on his skin caused parts of him to stiffen.

Perhaps after he delivered the key, he would return and let her undress him again. He shook his head. Fool. She only helped you because she thought you were dying. What would she want with an ex-Legionnaire? She was a simple country healer. Probably not frightened of him because she didn't know better. He couldn't imagine she'd think him worthy of more time than she'd already given him. In his scarred, battered heart, he knew she would sooner dally with Saladan himself before she would choose the company of a lowborn halfling.

He wanted to leave more than ever. With renewed purpose, he finished saddling Dragon. Once done, he turned to ask the guard for some bearings, and found himself alone in the wood.

"Saladan's hocks!" Ertemis kicked the ground. He was so addlepated by the curve of Jessalyne's hips and the depth of her heather eyes that he had no weapons, no cloak, and no idea where he was. He hadn't even heard the guard leave.

Temper simmering, he started back to the cottage, berating himself for succumbing to a woman's wiles. What point is there in getting wrapped in the charms of some esya who doesn't want me anyway? I don't need the misery.

He turned a section of path half-circling a huge acacia thicket, and as he came round the blind bend, Jessalyne crashed into him.

She fell flat on her backside, glaring at him with fire-filled eyes. She looked mad as a faerie with fleas. Ertemis stifled a chuckle.

"Oaf!" she snapped.

"Am I to blame because you didn't watch where you were going? Women!" He extended his hand to help her, but she ignored it, and got up on her own.

Jessalyne shook bits of leaves and dirt from her clothes. "I thought you left." She brushed her hair back.

He stared at the curve of her ear and wondered what it might taste like. "Miss me already?"

"No." She shook her head for emphasis.

"I started to leave, but your guards –"

"They are not my guards."

"Well, they belong to someone. They left before I could get my bearings and find out where my weapons are."

"Oh." She sucked in her cheek in a most becoming way.

He glanced down. "Were you rushing up here for a reason or do you normally run barefoot through the woods?" Maybe she wanted to ask him to stay. Or to kiss her.

She hitched up her skirt a bit to look at her feet. They were filthy. Her ankles, however, were lovely. A sunset glow colored her cheeks as she hastily dropped her skirt. "I wanted to ask you about how you came to have Petal."

"You know the jenny's name?"

"Of course. She belongs to my father."

The wind from a dragonsprite's wings could have knocked Ertemis over. He cleared his throat. "Well, that answers one question."

Back at her cottage, Jessalyne's stoic demeanor confounded Ertemis as she listened to the news of her father's passing. She didn't wail and bawl expected. Not until he told her of Haemus' dying admission did any emotion rise to the surface.

"He said he knew he hadn't been a good father, and he was sorry for it."

A single tear spilled down her cheek. She stared at the kitchen table, eyes not really focused. She made no effort to wipe the tear from her face, just let it slide off her chin and onto her hands, folded in her lap.

Ertemis shifted in his chair. Sobbing and squalling he could have dismissed as typical female behavior, but her single quiet tear unsettled him. He wasn't the comforting type, which mattered little, for comforting didn't seem the correct response either. He tried to read her, but the fog was back. Perhaps the house was warded with a protection spell. Who would ward a house in the middle of nowhere? Haemus certainly hadn't. The man had as much magic as mud.

Jessalyne finally brushed the wet trail from her cheek and glanced at Ertemis. "What else did he say?"

He furrowed his brow. "He said it's not your fault you are the way you are. What does that mean?"

She ignored his question and shook her head. "Nothing."

"He gave me a key to give to you. I have it in my packs, on Dragon."

"A key for what?"

"He said it opened a box under the garden bench." Ertemis stood.

Her expression changed to one of intense curiosity. "Did he say what's in it? Is it something from my mother?"

Ertemis saw hope in her eyes. "I don't know. I'll get it."

Jessalyne flicked a wisp of hair out of her eyes and stood. "I'll meet you in the garden."

Chapter Four

Shovel in hand, Jessalyne smiled as she approached the stone bench beneath an arbor of her mother's climbing roses. The pale pink blooms were almost at the peak of their beauty. She came here often to sit and inhale the sweet perfume. After her mother died and her father left, it was comforting to know at least the roses always came back.

She dropped the shovel, and tried to pick up the bench. It wouldn't budge. She shoved it again, trying to turn it over. Nothing.

Behind her, a throat cleared.

She spun around, startled. Ertemis stood behind her, a worn suede pouch in one hand. How did he move so quietly?

"Need some help?"

"No. I can manage." Jessalyne wrapped both arms around the seat and tried to lift again.

He leaned against the nearest tree. "I think the sun's going down."

"Fine!" She wiped a misting of sweat off her brow. "You do it."

"Are you ordering me or asking me?"

"You offered."

"And you refused." He didn't move off the tree, his half-lidded gaze sweeping the length of her before returning to her face.

Obstinate creature. She stood silent for a moment, chewing her bottom lip. Sighing loudly, she stared skyward. "I'm asking."

He peeled off the tree and came toward her. The suede pouch dangled from his fingers. She pointed at it. "I assume that belongs to me?"

"Aye." His fingers brushed her palm as the key tumbled into it. The glancing touch sucked the air out of her. She squeezed her hand around the key, her traitorous heart thumping.

Her reaction seemingly unnoticed, he lifted the bench then grabbed the shovel. Hands that large could easily encircle her waist.

He stomped the spade into the ground where the bench had been and started digging.

Turning the key in her fingers, she watched his thick shoulders bunch with the movement. His sleeves were pushed back, revealing sleek, corded forearms. She cleared her throat, but not her mind. "I can do that."

He stabbed the shovel into the dirt again. It struck something solid.

"Too late." He dug a bit more then tossed the shovel aside and dropped to his knees, reaching into the hole. He cleared the rest of the dirt with his hands, working the box back and forth until it was loose enough to lift.

Pulling up the box wrapped in dirt-caked sackcloth, he set it on the ground at her feet. It was no bigger than a loaf of bread. He clapped the dirt from his hands as he stood.

She dropped down next to the box and pulled off the wrapping cloth. The box was as ordinary as the key, built of unfinished wood, with two hinges on the backside and a locked clasp on the front. She hugged it to her chest and stood.

"Aren't you going to open it?" He shrugged. "Not that it's my business."

"I want to look at it inside." She started toward the cottage.

"I'm not leaving until I get my weapons back." Ertemis crossed his arms over his broad chest, his feet planted wide.

"Oh." She stopped. His trousers clung to his thighs, outlining legs as muscular and distracting as the rest of him. "I forgot about that."

"So I noticed."

Heat blossomed in her belly like spring flowers after a warm rain. "I…I have to ring for Corah."

He raised a brow.

"You can wait inside." Inside, with her. The thought made her shiver, but nothing about her felt cold.

He looked at the position of the sun. "Might as well. It's almost time for you to serve me supper."

"Serve you supper?" She scowled, all thoughts of his muscled shoulders and sleek skin gone. "This is my home. I am not your servant. The more you speak, the more I regret saving your life." The sooner he left, the better.

The lout did nothing to suppress his laughter as he followed her to the cottage. Just outside her front door hung a weather-worn bell on a carved post. She yanked the bell pull twice before hurrying inside. The need to know what the box held consumed her. She set it on the kitchen table and pulled out a chair

Ertemis planted himself opposite her as though he was lord of the manor. She refused to acknowledge him. He irritated her almost as much as he intrigued her.

The key fit the lock, but she had to wrench it to break through the rust. The hinges moaned when she lifted the lid. The unlined box held two items. Beneath an object wrapped in sackcloth lay a folded leaf of yellowed parchment.

Jessalyne picked up the object first. Without unwrapping it, she knew what it was by its shape. She pulled off the fabric and held in her hand an intricately etched dagger with a large oval lunestone set at the cross point of blade and hilt. She slid it from its sheath. The blade bore unfamiliar runes matching those on the hilt. The handle warmed quickly in her grasp. There was a lethal beauty to the piece. She slipped it back into its sheath and set it on the table.

Next, she unfolded the parchment. It was a letter from her mother. She blinked back tears as she sat. How long she had wished for a message, a brief note, anything from her mother? Now she held that anything in her hands.

Dearest Daughter, I have instructed your father to give this to you on your tenth year. How I wish I were still there with you. As I sit in the garden writing this, you play but a few steps from me. I am sure you have become a beautiful young woman. By now, you know you are gifted. I believe you are more gifted than even I imagine. I will explain.

Her father had kept this letter from her, ignoring her mother's request. Her stomach knotted. She should have read this many years ago.

All my life, I ached for a child, but I was not fair of face and found no man willing to wed me. Being a magewoman did not help, either. Many years passed and my time for bearing children grew short. I wept to think I would never have my heart's desire, but I refused to accept fate's hand. I sought aid from the most powerful sorceress I could think of, Mistress Sryka, magewoman to King Maelthorn. She took pity on me and gave me the spells and potions I needed. In return, she told me I must relinquish my child to her as an apprentice when the child came of age. Of course, my darling, that child is you.

Jessalyne reeled. She was the product of a sorceress's spells and potions? She'd never heard of this Sryka but King Maelthorn was Lord King of Shaldar, so if Sryka was his magewoman, she must be very powerful indeed. Jessalyne couldn't believe she might actually become this woman's apprentice. Finally, someone who could explain her gifts to her. She took up the letter again.

You must travel to her, Jessalyne. She is a mighty sorceress but she grows old. I think she means to train you in her stead. According to Sryka, you must remain chaste or your gifts will disappear. It is not such a grand sacrifice, I promise you.

Think of it, Jessalyne. Magewoman to a king! My precious daughter, you will be all that I was not.

The dagger is a gift from Sryka to guide you on your journey. In your hand alone, the lunestone will glow when the blade points toward her.

I am sorry our time together was so short. The spells Sryka gave me to bind your father to me and gain you have taxed my strength, but you were worth it. I love you, Jessalyne. You are my life.

Tears blurred the words as Jessalyne tried to reread the letter. It ended too soon. She still had so many questions. Her belly twisted as she pondered what lay ahead of her. Leaving had suddenly become a reality.

"Well?"

She'd almost forgotten the elf. She scrubbed her eyes. "It's from my mother. She died when I was very young."

At the word mother, a flicker of something passed over Ertemis's face but disappeared before she could name it. It didn't matter. She had a journey to pack for. She would find Sryka and hope the magewoman was still alive and still wanted her after so long. Maybe Sryka could answer the rest of her questions.

A rapping at her front door reminded her she'd rung the bell. She put the letter back in the box, closed the lid and went to answer the rapping. She opened the door. Corah's hand was raised to knock again.

"The elf is gone, then?" Corah was transparently disappointed.

"Nay, I am not gone yet." He walked from behind the door, again coming up so quickly Jessalyne hadn't heard him. "Although I would be if those guards had not taken my weapons."

Corah stared at him with a coy smile. "I didn't know you were still here, Master Elf."

"Obviously." He flashed a blinding grin and rested one brawny arm against the door frame. Why must he stand so close to her? "Why do you call her lady?"

"You don't have to answer him, Corah." Jessalyne frowned.

"We call her lady as a term of respect. She is our healer. And our friend."

Jessalyne made an impatient noise. "Corah, your father's men still have his things. Take word to him that the elf is ready to leave."

"I'll tell him." Corah glanced at Ertemis again. "But he's gone to a settle a territory dispute with the neighboring herd's Alpha Buck and won't be back until morning."

"Firstlight then. Please tell him I desire an audience with him and Lady Dauphine at that time also."

"Very well." Corah curtsied, something Jessalyne knew was entirely for Ertemis's sake. "Good evening, Lady Jessalyne and..." This time, she looked up through a thick fringe of tawny lashes.

"Ertemis." Jessalyne grimaced at the girl's blatant flirting. Sickening.

"Good evening, Master Ertemis." Corah completed her curtsey and gave Ertemis one last smile as she left. Jessalyne rolled her eyes and Ertemis caught her.

"Your friend has impeccable taste in men. Perhaps she wants company for dinner." He was close enough that his spicy scent stroked her skin.

She stepped back. "I'll be sure to mention that to her betrothed. There is bread and cheese in the larder if you're hungry. I have packing to do." She turned toward her bedroom.

"I knew you were smitten with me, but I had no idea you planned on becoming my traveling companion. First you undress me, now this. Who knew that innocent face hid such a saucy wench." He gave her a wink when she spun around.

"How dare you speak to me that way after what I did for you?" Her cheeks burned with indignation. "You flatter yourself with such big thoughts, halfling."

To his credit, he didn't respond to her name calling. "Why are you packing then?"

"Not that it's any of your business, but according to my mother's letter I am to apprentice with King Maelthorn's magewoman so that I may take her place."

Surprise washed the expression from his face. The satisfaction she felt at shutting him up was short lived.

"Magewoman to King Maelthorn? Are you deluded? You have to actually have magic to be a magewoman. You do know that?" He shook his head. "Humans."

"You know nothing about me. Don't assume otherwise." Her hands were tingling. She bit back the remainder of what she wanted to say in an attempt to quell the heat snarling in her veins and ground out an angry, "Good night," before stalking off to her room.

"Shaldar City will eat you alive," he called out.

She slammed the door.

Firstlight broke in streaks of pink and gold. Sleep had only come to Jessalyne for a few hours as packing had kept her up. She went into the kitchen, eager for a cup of tea and a bite of breakfast before she packed some foodstuffs and herbs for travel.

Her scullery lay in shambles. Crumbs and crusts of bread mingled with sticky smears of jam dotted the table. A single half-eaten sweet cake remained as the only proof of the dozen once piled on an earthenware platter in the larder.

She opened the hatch to the cold box. The milk jug sat empty and most of the smoked fish was gone too.

"Dash it!" Jessalyne knew exactly which ill-mannered elf to blame.

She stormed toward the second bedroom and shoved the door wide, ready to blast him for his ungracious behavior. As soon as the door burst open, she knew she should have knocked. The dark elf wore only the skin in which he'd been born.

Sweet mercy. Her jaw unhinged. His hind parts were to the door. A line of silver runes like those on his ears trailed from beneath his long black locks down the length of his spine, stopping above the cleft of his buttocks. Her fingers itched to trace the marks marring his perfect flesh. A sigh slipped from her lips.

He turned. Her eyes, frozen to the spot where his backside had been, now saw a great deal more of him than she had seen of any man. Ever.

A roguish grin bent the corners of his mouth and he scratched, unashamed. "Something I can do for you?"

Her mouth hung slack, but she couldn't close it. Supple curving muscle and the dark, radiant smoothness of his skin stole the breath from her body. Like the silver runes tattooed on his skin, his image inked itself into her mind.

Her hand flew to her eyes. "Ohmy – I did not mean – please, my apologies!" She slammed the door.

She leaned against the wall and shut her eyes, but all she saw was skin. She had never seen a naked man before, elf or otherwise. Were they all so... Was he always that... Her shame at intruding was compounded by her burning desire to see him again. Something between panic and need sluiced through her. She tipped her head back against the wall and sucked air into her lungs. Laughter echoed through the door.

Wretched halfling. Blast him! He wrecked her kitchen, depleted her food supply and now this. Of course, she was the one who'd burst into the room unannounced. But she refused to claim fault. He shouldn't have been naked in her house. She stomped off to repair her kitchen, muttering under her breath about the bothersome creature occupying her spare room, still unable to wash his image from her head.

ဢ

It pleased him that Jessalyne had caught him while morning's rigor still engaged his body. He only hoped he hadn't frightened her. He tried again to read her, feeling with his mind for the wards that held his senses captive. The magic was weaker than before and he quickly found a way through it.

She rushed into his head like new wine, her quickened breaths, the thrum of blood in her veins, her pounding heart. He realized with a start there was no fear in her. She was a mix of curiosity, longing, embarrassment, and indignation.

No lust, no prideful desire. None of that existed in her, just a sense of need he wondered if she understood. She was a true innocent, not some wagtail in one of the taverns he frequented. Neither did she look at him as a conquest to be bragged about over her cups. She'd probably never even been in a tavern.

As flattered as he was with her reaction, guilt racked him. Life in the Legions had brought few true innocents his way. He resolved to treat her more gently and provoke her less.

But the rogue in him found it nigh impossible to look at her and not imagine her beneath him, her moonlight skin glistening with sweat, her heat drawing him deeper, her honeyed scent rising around him, her voice ragged with need as she whispered his name. He shook his head free of the image too late to keep his body from responding. No wonder she thought him a beast.

His thoughts turned to the remainder of her father's money. He would keep one bag of silver for payment and give the rest to her. If she were truly going to Shaldar City to find the king's magewoman, she'd need it. Weighing a bag of gold in his hand, he growled. Freedom would have to wait.

છ

Jessalyne attacked the mess in her scullery, trying to scrub his image out of her head at the same time. What it would feel like to be in his arms? Or any man's arms for that matter? Maybe he would kiss her. Heat swept through her hidden parts. She cleaned with renewed vigor. She could never let him get that close. Tyber said dark elves were known for their temper. Burning Ertemis would be a quick way to see if Tyber were right.

In short order, she restored the room and checked her remaining supplies for something to turn into breakfast. She settled on oatcakes and blackberries fresh from the thicket outside her kitchen door. Batter sizzled as she poured thick puddles onto the oiled stone griddle. She cleaned the berries while the cakes cooked. It didn't take long for Ertemis to appear in the kitchen.

He was dressed, but her mind knew too well what hid beneath. "You cannot possibly be hungry after eating the larder bare last night." She busied herself with flipping oatcakes.

"Aye, but I am." He stayed near the door, giving her space. "May I have some after I feed and water Dragon and Petal?"

That he asked almost felled her. He was being oddly civil. She glanced at him. "Yes. Thank you. I am not used to having a beast to look after."

He exhaled softly. "It has been ages since anyone felt I needed looking after."

Jessalyne scooped the last oatcake off the griddle. "I didn't mean you were a beast." She turned when he didn't reply. He was gone. For a man of such size, he moved with unnatural silence.

Not long after breakfast, Lord Tyber showed up with Ertemis's weapons. As Jessalyne had asked, Lady Dauphine accompanied him as well. Corah tagged behind.

"Good morning." Jessalyne ushered them in. Tyber nodded at Ertemis leaning against the wall near the kitchen. Ertemis nodded in reply. Both men eyeing the other warily.

She took a deep breath before she began. "As you know, I was very curious about how Petal came to lead Ertemis here. As it turns out, my father hired Ertemis to protect him while he traveled. The fever that incapacitated Ertemis was my father's undoing. Before he died, he charged Ertemis with delivering a key to me. That key unlocked a box holding a letter from my lady mother. In the letter, she revealed I am to apprentice with Lord King Maelthorn's magewoman, Sryka. And I plan on leaving today."

Corah looked stricken. Lady Dauphine covered her mouth with her hand and shimmered as if she might shift right then and there. "But we need you. What if Orit falls again?"

"I'll leave my mother's books behind for Corah, and I am certain Orit will be more careful from now on."

Lord Tyber, ever practical, spoke next. "If your mind is made up, I'll send two of my guards with you."

Jessalyne sighed. She did not want to travel escorted like a child. This was her chance to discover life on her own. "Lord Tyber, I appreciate your offer but it's unnecessary. I'm a grown woman. I can find my way."

"You may be a grown woman, but you know little of the world. A woman traveling alone, especially one such as you, is easy prey. All the realm is not Fairleigh Grove. They will ride with you as far as Shaldar City's gates."

Tyber might be right, but she still didn't want cervidae guards accompanying her. If Mistress Sryka turned her away or had already chosen another apprentice, she wanted to return with her dignity intact. She caught Ertemis's gaze and held it while she spoke. "Lord Tyber, I didn't want to tell you because I knew you wouldn't approve but I have already contracted the elf to be my shield."

Ertemis raised a single eyebrow but said nothing.

She kept talking, "He agrees it is the bare minimum he can do to repay my healing him. Besides, I insisted on paying him. The deal has been struck."

Jessalyne looked back at Tyber. "I feel it's best. No need for your men to make a return trip."

Lord Tyber shook his head. "I'll honor your decision." He looked hard at Ertemis. "I would speak with you outside while the women say their farewells."

Ertemis followed Tyber through the door and faced the Alpha Buck on the flagstone path. He was not surprised to see a quadroon of Tyber's men waiting outside. Tyber shut the door. His men tightened their stance by a hair.

Crossing his arms, Ertemis leaned against the bell post. "Is this where you tell me you'll hunt me down and kill me if I touch her?"

Tyber snorted and shook his head. "Touch her and she may kill you herself."

Ertemis narrowed his eyes at the man's words, unsure how Jessalyne would manage that.

Tyber notched his head up. "I wasn't at a border dispute yesterday. I was confirming my suspicions about the dark elf with the Legion-issued sword. The Legionnaire I spoke with recognized your sword, but I only told him I purchased it from a band of Travelers."

"I don't know what you're talking about." He kept his body still, his muscles loose and ready. The Legion hadn't wasted much time.

Tyber ignored him and continued. "If you harm her, I will take great pleasure in collecting the price on your head, halfling. And for your knowledge, the Legion doesn't require you alive. Do I make myself clear?"

Ertemis uncrossed his arms and met Tyber's cold gaze with his own. "Aye."

ୠ

Back inside, Jessalyne said her farewells. Corah promised to look after the cottage and tend the garden. Dauphine thanked her again for healing Orit. Tyber gave Ertemis his weapons. Jessalyne saw something flicker in the eyes of both men as Ertemis buckled his sword belt.

Once the cervidae were gone, she steeled herself for his protest about her quickly hatched scheme. It didn't take long.

"As tempting as you might think it sounds, I have no intention of traipsing through the countryside with you on some foolish quest. I have better things to do." Ertemis slipped his Feyre into his boot.

"I said I would pay you and I meant it."

"I've got all the herbs I need."

She ran to her bedroom and grabbed one of the sacks of coins left by her father over the years. She plopped the heavy pouch into Ertemis's palm.

He opened it. Gold. He looked at it again. "Where did you get this?"

"My father. He soothed his conscience by giving me money."

"How much of this do you have?"

"More than I need."

Shaking his head, Ertemis dug in his bag. "Your father wanted you to have these as well."

Jessalyne took the bags, but shot Ertemis an odd look. "Did you forget you had them?"

"It slipped my mind."

Not blasted likely. She stared at him for a moment. "Then you accept what I've proposed?"

"Aye, for this much coin I would carry you there." Ertemis gave her a half-hearted smile.

"That will not be required." This was going to be a long journey with such company. "Will you fetch Dragon and Petal and bring them to the house? I'll bring my bundles outside to meet you."

"Bundles? Perhaps I should educate you on packing for travel. Let me see these bundles."

Despite her misgivings, Jessalyne led him into her bedroom, dumping the coin pouches onto the bed next to a mound of parcels—rolled and folded, tied and ready to go.

"Hah!" Ertemis surveyed the pile with his hands on his hips. "Surely, you jest. Not half of this will be coming."

"What? Why?" Jessalyne watched Ertemis rifle through her things, appalled with his lack of regard for what she considered necessary. After she stopped him from discarding an item for the third time, he growled at her.

"You cannot take all this! You have coin enough to purchase what you need." He sighed. "Petal may be a donkey, but there is no need to overload her."

"Fine. But this goes with me." Jessalyne patted the box holding her mother's letter and the dagger.

"Just the contents." He shook his head. "Not the box."

Resigned, Jessalyne folded her mother's letter and tucked it into the pouch on her belt. She lifted the sheathed dagger and stuffed it into her bedroll. Ertemis caught her hand, his rough fingers gently snagging her wrist.

"Always keep your blade handy." He unlatched her waist belt and ran it through the loop on the dagger's sheath, then refastened the tooled leather around her hips. Heat flared over her. For a man with such large hands, his fingers were surprisingly nimble.

℘

Ertemis struggled to concentrate as Jessalyne's scent curled around him. The gentle rhythm of her beating heart filled his ears. She smelled of flowers, sunshine and sweetness. Heat radiated off her like a blacksmith's shop.

"Thank you," she said, her voice small and breathy.

He lost himself in the liquid lavender of her eyes. Less than the length of his Feyre separated them. Her lips moved. He realized she had said something else. The urge to kiss her overwhelmed him. He stepped away to give himself recess. He couldn't think. Couldn't breathe. "What?"

For the first time, she smiled at him. "I said that is better than having it hidden away in my bedroll." She patted the dagger.

The smile lit her face from within. Ertemis just nodded. Saladan's britches, she bewitched him. This was going to be a very long trip. Think of the coin, he told himself. Being paid to go somewhere he needed to go anyway was no burden.

"I'll go pack what little you left in the larder." She almost laughed.

"Uh, good, the animals." Ertemis gestured toward the outside, stumbling over his words. "I'll be back." He needed fresh air. His head swam with her perfume. Perhaps she had magic after all. He felt utterly bespelled.

The air cooled his blood as he brought the animals down from the stable. He finished adjusting his saddle. Dragon stomped the ground, eager to be off.

He turned to ready Petal and frowned. There was no saddle for Jessalyne. He doubted she was schooled in riding or had ever ridden at all. Without proper tack, she would suffer more than necessary. He could share his saddle with her but having her so near, her backside pressed against his—he started calculating sums in his head until his blood cooled.

They would stop at the first town and purchase a decent saddle. He would buy it using some of the too-generous sum she'd paid him.

Jessalyne came out of the house, bedroll tucked beneath one arm, rucksack in her hand. Her hair was braided in a plait down her back.

He hooked the clasp of his cloak and tugged his hood down over his eyes. Without asking, he knew she would not be willing to wait until nightfall to travel. "There's no saddle for Petal. Do you know how to ride bareback?" He already knew the answer to that question as well.

"No. Is it hard?"

"It isn't easy even if you're skilled." He sighed. "You may share my saddle with me, if you wish." He regretted the words as soon as they left his mouth.

She stayed close to Petal, stroking the jenny's back. "I'll be fine without a saddle."

Mostly relieved, he nodded. "We'll stop at the first town and purchase one."

As Ertemis mounted, Jessalyne placed both hands on Petal's back and pulled herself up. He turned. She laid belly over the donkey. "What are you doing?"

"I am trying to get on, what does it look like?"

"Not that," Ertemis muttered as he hopped off Dragon. He knit his fingers together to form a step and held his hands below Petal's side. "Step up."

Jessalyne placed her foot into his hands and rested her palm on his shoulder. Her light touch shot warmth down his spine to pool as hunger in his belly. He hoisted her onto Petal's back but she fidgeted, trying to get comfortable.

"In a gown you cannot ride straddle as a man, so bend your knee..." He nudged her slippered foot to bend her leg. "And hook your foot beneath your other leg like so." His hand lingered longer than necessary on the slim arch of her foot.

"How does that feel?" He swallowed, remembering to breathe.

She stroked Petal's mane, her voice soft. "Thank you, I think that will do."

Indeed it would. Touching her was a great distraction. She was job. A package to be delivered. Nothing more. Ertemis jumped astride Dragon once again. "Off to Shaldar City then."

"You don't know that."

"Where else would the king's magewoman be except near the king?" Why did she have to smell so good? Feel so soft?

"Do you know what direction Shaldar City is from here?"

He frowned and stared into the distance. "Once we're out of the wood the way will become clear."

"Yes, I'm sure it will be. Until then…" Jessalyne slid the dagger from its sheath and gripped the handle. She swept the blade through the air. Halfway across the horizon line, the lunestone flared to life.

"There," she said, pointing with the blade.

Chapter Five

Crisp winds scrubbed the wall walk around Sryka. She pulled her robes tighter, loose gray locks tangling in an updraft. The sun shone brightly but the winds carried a faint chill, and old bones held little heat.

She peered into the courtyard below, but the height of the tower and her age prevented her from discerning much detail. Prince Erebus pranced about down there somewhere, no doubt preening for the simpering skirts that clung to him like flies to dung.

If only the child would come. The Prince grew angrier with her, but she had done all she could. Her spells hadn't failed. The glamour she'd cast on the child's mother had worked well, transforming the homely woman to a jade-eyed, scarlet-haired beauty before Sryka's eyes. She'd watched the pathetic woman drink down the potions, heard her chant the words. The fertility spells must have worked. Sryka's magic was as sure as the king's mortality.

In her heart, she believed the child would come. But after so many years, she held little hope the girl would still be acceptable. Prince Erebus would expect a virgin bride, and the spell required untainted flesh. Bride. As if the King had already blessed this one fit to wed his son. If necessary, she would charm the King into blessing the union, just as she would charm Erebus into accepting the girl. Whatever it took, she would do.

Sryka spat over the parapets. She hoped the juicy gob landed squarely on Prince Erebus' vain head. The thought made her smile. He would get his. Once she controlled the child. The kingdom, youth, power...it would all be hers.

Small warmth spread through her, and she thought little of it until it centered itself in her chest. Sryka paused, gripping the stone ledge, wondering, wanting it to be true. She reached into the folds of her robes and pulled the amulet free. The lunestone pulsed warm and lively in the amulet's center. Her hand trembled. The girl child came.

℃

The scenery they traveled through was so different from the grove, but still not as interesting as the elf in her company. She focused on the way his broad shoulders tapered to the slender vee of his waist. How his cloak flowed over his expansive back. Time and again her mind imagined the trail of silver runes and the fine curve of backside that brought them to a halt.

The image built such heat in her, she thought it best to think of something else before she melted. She broke the stillness with a question. "Have you been to Shaldar City?"

"Nay." Ertemis slowed Dragon and dropped back beside her.

"Why not? It's the capital. It must be very beautiful." She wondered how her ideas compared to the reality.

"The king has men enough to fight his battles. No need for a man like me." His jaw went tight.

"But you haven't even visited there?" Jessalyne imagined bustling streets and colorful shops and felt a tingle of excitement at what her future held.

"Nay," he snapped. "I told you that already."

Whatever brooded in the dark elf, Jessalyne didn't pursue it. She had no desire to rouse his temper.

Ertemis changed the subject. "Why did Tyber tell me if I touched you, you would kill me?"

Taken off guard, Jessalyne searched for an answer that was neither a lie nor the truth. Tyber should have kept his mouth shut. "He was only trying to protect you."

"Protect me? From what? You don't look very dangerous."

"Looks can be deceiving."

Ertemis shook his head. "Not usually."

"You don't think so?"

"Do I look dangerous to you?"

She hesitated. "Yes. You do."

"No deception there."

She narrowed her eyes at him. "So what do I look like then?"

ଙ

Ertemis opened his mouth to speak but nothing came out. What she looked like was a kind of dangerous he had kept himself free from, the kind of dangerous that addled a man mind with soft curves and sweet perfume and whispered words. "You look like the woman I work for," he growled. "Let's leave it there."

"Hmmph." Jessalyne stopped talking to him after that.

He glanced over. Petal's rhythmic stride and the warmth of the sun in the cloudless sky made her eyelids heavy. The last thing he needed was for her to drift off and fall.

"There. Do you see it?" Ertemis pointed toward the horizon.

She looked up, yawning. "See what?"

"The town."

She was squinting into the distance. "I don't see anything but trees."

"Ah. I forget my sight surpasses human. Trust me, there's a town ahead. One I think I know. We'll break there."

"You can see that far ahead? What other gifts do dark elves possess?" She nudged Petal into step with Dragon, curiosity shining in her eyes.

Ertemis threw his head back in a laugh. "You aren't timid, are you? Few have been brave enough to question me so directly. You have mettle, esya."

She smiled back. "What does esya mean?"

"Girl."

"I'm a woman," she countered.

"If you say so, esya." He grinned at her insistence.

She sparked with irritation. "You aren't the first elf I've ever met."

"Really? In the grove? That surprises me." He watched her while he rode, his eyes unwilling to leave her face.

"A council of elves came for the naming ceremony of Lord Tyber's son. They gave him a Feyre, like the one you carry."

"I'm impressed you know the name of my blade."

Her cheeks pinked. "Those elves looked very different from you."

"They were light elves, high born. Like my mother." His smile waned and he faced forward again. "Your coloring is very much like hers."

"You must miss her."

"I miss no one." He urged Dragon on, breaking stride with Jessalyne and pulling ahead.

ॐ

The town finally emerged before Jessalyne's eyes. The sign above the main gate proclaimed it Warren on the Wick and she rejoiced, knowing reprieve from Petal's hard back was on its way.

Ertemis drew his hood in a way that hid his face. From his pack, he retrieved leather gloves and donned them as well. Once in the town, he stopped at a tavern called The Thirsty Troll. He tethered Dragon's reins around the hitching post with a few deft loops. "Tie up. Bring your bags. We'll eat, then buy your saddle."

She tried to mimic his movements, almost duplicating his knot, then followed on his heels, trying to keep up and absorb the sights around her at the same time. People bustled about with packages, dogs and children ran through the dusty streets, vendors spieled their wares. Shouting, barking, babies crying, cart wheels creaking – so much clatter and jangle from every direction.

The women's clothing emphasized their curves. Blouses and skirts, cinched about the waist with wide, boned belts that pushed their chests into soft mounds spilling out of their tops. Jessalyne felt shapeless in her tunic and overvest. No one dressed like her.

Near the alehouse's entrance, a painted tart with cleavage to spare brushed by, giving Ertemis a lusty growl. He turned and winked at her.

Jessalyne glared at the woman as she passed. "Do you know her?"

"I know what she's about."

"And what is that?"

"Pleasure. But don't worry, I never mingle business with pleasure." He pushed through the tavern doors.

Jessalyne barged after him, wanting to snap back but didn't know what to say. You look like the woman I work for. She was nothing but business to him.

The stink of sour ale and smoke mixed with unwashed flesh stung her nose. A tumult of languages filled her ears. A sordid mix of creatures packed the dim tavern. They crowded around tables, drinking ale and telling tales. She moved closer to Ertemis. Better the beast she knew than those she didn't.

From the shadowy recesses, a bristled figure emerged. Dressed in a fine loose linen shirt and brushed cotton trousers, he stood a head taller than Ertemis and twice as wide. Flexing fists the size of hams, the creature headed toward them.

Ertemis pushed his hood back. A soft murmur swept the crowd.

"Saladan's strumpet mum," the creature growled. "Who let this muddled blood lowlife into my fine establishment?"

Tiny pointed teeth filled the brute's mouth, but it was his ears that drew her gaze. Little shells of skin, they sported dangling gold hoops. His ears were too small by half. Even faeries had bigger ears than he did.

Ertemis snarled right back. "Fine establishment? This dunghill? How fine could it be if it's run by a troll?"

Jessalyne looked back at the door. If any chance for escape remained before the bludgeoning began, it was most likely now.

The two scowled at one another, gazes locked, fists clenched. Not a single creature in the alehouse moved. Jessalyne expected blows any moment.

They lunged and Jessalyne shut her eyes.

"Ertemis!"

"Valduuk!"

She peeked. They were pounding each other on the back in friendly sort of way. Childish oafs. The rest of the patrons, bored with the lack of bloodshed, went back to their carousing. Ertemis and Valduuk cuffed each other a few more times.

"How does the day find you, my friend?" Valduuk's voice resounded low and gravely.

"Well, and you?" Ertemis stood, hands on hips, his back to Jessalyne. She crept closer.

"I am the most contented troll in all of Warren on the Wick. What's taken you so long? I've not seen you in ages." The troll leaned close, his voice soft, "Have you finally paid your bond?"

"I have no excuse other than too many battles to be won and too much coin to be collected. As for my bond, let's just say I'm working on that."

Arms crossed, Jessalyne cleared her throat.

"Ah...Valduuk, please meet my current employer, Lady Jessalyne of Fairleigh Grove." Ertemis mocked a courtly bow in her direction.

Valduuk extended one enormous hand, catching Jessalyne off guard. She reached her hand out, not sure what else to do. He took her fingers and lightly brushed his thick lips across the back of her hand.

Jessalyne blinked at him, dumbfounded.

"Best manners I have ever seen in a troll." Ertemis shook his head, adding, "At least when there is a fair-faced skirt involved."

Valduuk ignored the elf and offered a crooked arm to Jessalyne. "My Lady, if you would care to join me in my quarters, I'll have my staff prepare whatever eatables you desire." He glanced at Ertemis. "Don't mind the elf, he's always been jealous of my good social graces."

Jessalyne reached up to take his arm, suddenly tickled by the gentleman troll. "Thank you, kind sir." She rested her palm on Valduuk's arm, surprised by the softness of his pelted skin.

"What? No arm for me?" Ertemis followed the odd pair through a private entrance at the rear of the tavern.

Valduuk's quarters were as paradoxical as the troll himself. Instead of duplicating the rough-hewn scheme of the tavern proper, his chambers were luxuriously appointed.

"Since when did you become exiled nobility?" Ertemis asked as he surveyed his friend's dwelling.

Thick Ulvian carpets covered finely waxed wood floors. The furniture, sized to match Valduuk, was exquisitely crafted. Upholstered chairs sported plush fabrics, antique tapestries hung from the walls and yards of diaphanous silks draped the windows.

"Oh my. Your home is lovely. I've never seen such beautiful things." Jessalyne wanted to touch everything.

"Thank you," Valduuk tipped his head toward Ertemis. "How is it that such a fair lass as yourself has ended up in the company of the Black Death?"

"The company of the what?" Jessalyne wasn't sure she heard Valduuk correctly.

"Valduuk." Sinking into one of the overstuffed chairs, Ertemis shot the troll a look. "There will be time for tales when we eat. Our mounts need tending."

Valduuk made short work of ordering food then sent someone to feed and water the animals. He led his guests into the dining room, where they seated themselves around a spacious table in wide, high backed chairs.

After her time on Petal, Jessalyne lounged happily on the well-padded seat. "What was that name you called him?" she asked Valduuk.

"The Black Death?" He glanced at Ertemis, who was shaking his head back and forth. "Nothing, just a little ribbing between old friends."

Ertemis regaled Valduuk with the events leading up to his joining company with Jessalyne, and Valduuk kept their goblets full of honeyed wine. Before long, tavern staff began setting heavy platters of food before them.

Valduuk pulled one of the workers aside and whispered something to him. The man nodded and left.

Jessalyne looked out over the table and beheld foodstuffs the likes of which she had not known existed. Smoked eels stuffed with garlic and leeks, capons wrapped in bacon, fresh and cured sausages, cabbage stewed with onions and tansy, rice soup with spinach and walnuts, blue-veined cheeses, thick brown bread, crocks of fruited butters. The last plate brought in was a footed dish holding small shiny brown cakes decorated with flower petals. It must take a vast quantity of food to satisfy Valduuk.

As they feasted, she exclaimed her love for everything she tried, which caused Ertemis to roll his eyes and Valduuk to smile with extreme pleasure. She ignored Ertemis as best she could. She sipped her wine before speaking. "So, Valduuk, how do you know Ertemis?"

Valduuk wiped his mouth with a square of linen and sat back in his chair. "We met many years ago. We were youngsters then, conscripted to the Legion for different reasons. It wasn't an easy life, but we learned. We grew up quickly."

She could only imagine what that life must have been like.

Valduuk hesitated, eyes trained somewhere in the past. "None of our squad wanted to spar with a troll or a half breed, fearsome creatures that we be. So we sparred with each other." He chuckled. "Truth be told, it was for the best. We outsized and out-muscled the others by a fair measure."

"Well, you certainly did," Ertemis interjected.

"As I am in the presence of a lady, I'll ignore your remarks until such time as I may deal with them properly."

Ertemis snorted and returned to his meal.

Valduuk's attention belonged to Jessalyne's once again and he continued. "We fought together in many campaigns. But as I grew older, I tired of Legion life. I had enough money saved to pay my bond and purchase my freedom. I took what was left and bought this tavern. And here I am." He stretched his arms out toward his surroundings. "I am content with my life. What it lacks in excitement, it makes up for in stability, unlike my brother here who has no stability but plenty of excitement."

"Stability is overrated." Ertemis pushed back from the table. "It's good to see you again, Valduuk. I'm glad the years have been kind to you."

"They have indeed. And I insist you stay the night. The least I can do is give you a soft bed," Valduuk said.

Ertemis lifted his hands. "I'd as soon press on, but I'm only the hired help."

Hired help. Must he constantly remind her of their arrangement? He had said yes, after all. Why make such a point of it?

Valduuk turned to her. "I know you must be anxious to continue your journey but lastlight comes soon. Surely, you'd prefer a feathered pallet to a bedroll on the hard ground?"

"A feather bed sounds wonderful. We don't need to travel at night. Besides, we still have a saddle to purchase."

Ertemis stood and shoved his chair in with more force than she thought necessary. "I'll see to the bags and the beasts."

"No need," Valduuk beamed. "Your bags are already in your rooms and your mounts in my stable. I set my staff about it before dinner. Lady Jessalyne, if you wish, I'll have a hot bath sent up. Ertemis and I can purchase the saddle."

"A bath sounds even better than the feather bed. You're a marvelous host, Valduuk." Jessalyne smiled at the gentleman troll. Too bad Ertemis wasn't more like his friend.

Ertemis sat back down as Valduuk rang for his valet to escort her to her chambers. She bid the men good evening and headed off to the promise of a hot soak.

ဢ

Watching his friend's face as Jessalyne left, Ertemis suspected Valduuk had fallen under her spell as well. "She isn't hard to look at, is she?"

"Aye. A definite step above your regular paramours," Valduuk said.

"She's not my paramour. Far from it. I doubt she knows much of what passes between a man and a woman. Anyway, she's not my taste."

"Then perhaps you should hide the heat in your eyes when you look at her, my friend." Valduuk chuckled. "A blind man could see you want her."

"Pah."

"Then why deny what you're called? She hired you, she must know who you are."

"She doesn't. Not really. I just don't want her frightened of me for no reason. It's been more years than I can count since I've met a woman who doesn't run from me in fear or wish to bed me just to tell the tale."

Valduuk smiled. "She has the look of the high born light fey, don't you think?"

Ertemis nodded. "Her father certainly carried no elven blood and if her mother had, she'd look like me."

Valduuk stood. "Let's go get that saddle. You can explain what in Saladan's name made you desert the Legions."

Ertemis rose to his feet, raising an eyebrow as he slipped his hood over his head.

"Did you think I wouldn't know? This was one of the first places they came looking. For the price on your head, I could have a tavern in every city in Shaldar." Valduuk tossed his voluminous cloak about his shoulders. "Fortunately for you, one is all I can handle."

℘

"Fynna!" Sryka screamed for the girl.

Fynna scrambled into the room, her head already ducked as she anticipated Sryka's predilection toward ear cuffing.

"Worthless pixie, never around when there is work to be done," she muttered.

"J-just washing the mixing pots, mistress." She peered at Sryka, trying to determine the magewoman's mood.

"Get word to Prince Erebus I require an audience with him immediately. I have very important news. And be quick about it! No dallying with the stable boys or you will be sorry." Sryka stared at her.

"You are such a mess, Fynna." She sighed. "Be gone."

Fynna scampered off, taking the stone steps in little hops. She thought of her wings, locked away in Sryka's closet. With them she could have flown down the steps in no time.

She smiled anyway, for any task that took her out of Sryka's immediate range was a task worth doing. Fynna detested the old crone but was debt bound to serve her.

If only Sryka had not saved the life of Queen Menna. No, no, she must not think such things. The pixie queen was not to blame. It was Sryka who had demanded bond service of the next born female child in payment. Such is my luck to be that child.

When she reached the great hall, she looked about for Prince Erebus' valet. Most likely, they were all out in the yard, playing at swords or hand-to-hand in front of a crowd of giggling females. She wandered in the direction of the yard.

She was torn between wishing the King would name one of the Prince's foolish women as the Blessed Bride and hoping that Erebus never took the throne at all. Prince Erebus filled her with as much dread as Sryka did. She could not imagine him as king. If only King Maelthorn was not sick abed. Poor man. He was the only compassionate soul left in the kingdom.

Fynna located the Prince's valet and gave him Sryka's message. She exited the courtyard as quickly as possible but not before some of the Prince's tootsies got a few jeers in. They didn't speak to her. Rather, they spoke about her and always loud enough to be heard.

"Pixies are a rather homely breed, are they not?"

"I hear they eat pixies in some kingdoms."

"What do you think they taste like? Blue-berries?"

At the last comment, the cluster erupted into laughter and Fynna crept away, head down.

୨౨

Jessalyne took one look at the bathing tub being carried into her chambers and erupted into a fit of giggles. Perhaps the volume of wine she had consumed made Valduuk's tub look so enormous. But of course, it was sized to fit him.

His staff, used to filling it for Valduuk, brought the water level up in no time. Finally alone, she disrobed and climbed in. There was something so wonderful about a hot bath after a day's traveling.

She stretched her legs and tried unsuccessfully to reach the end of the tub with her toes. She nudged the soap with her knee, sending it drifting along, a rudderless ship in a vast sea. A tub this size could hold two people. Even if one of them was the size of a dark – she failed to stop herself from completing the thought and a delicious tingle ran up her spine. Valduuk's honeyed wine had befuddled her. She closed her eyes and imagined life in Shaldar City but it was hard to picture something she'd never seen. Her mind kept wandering back to Ertemis.

The water cooled before she was ready to get out. A bathing tub of such magnitude was a rare and luxurious treat. She wiggled her fingers over the water's surface and the temperature rose. She wondered how Ertemis and Valduuk were getting on with the saddle purchase. The elf's room was right across the hall from hers, and she hadn't heard him come back yet.

Ertemis smiled at his own subterfuge. While Valduuk bargained with the craftsman for the best price on the tooled leather saddle, he slipped off to the shop next door. Baubles of every description filled the glass cases. The shopkeeper eyed him warily until Ertemis jangled the coin pouch on his belt.

At last, in a small locked case on the back wall, Ertemis saw something befitting Jessalyne. He pointed to a large, polished amethyst dangling a massive black baroque pearl. Caged in gold, the pendant hung from a cord of lavender silk.

The amethyst's hue matches the hint of lavender in her eyes. The pearl's charcoal nacre danced with an oily sheen of green and purple.

"You have excellent taste, Master elf." Hands trembling slightly, the shopkeeper slipped it from the case and laid it on a velvet cloth. "Tis a most exquisite piece."

Translation—expensive. "Aye, lovely. How much?"

"You have a fine eye. Very hard to come by black pearls from the Thracian Sea these days, with the pirates and what not."

"How much?"

"All set in the finest gold in the kingdom, crafted by His Lordship's own—"

Ertemis smacked the counter, rattling the glass. "Don't make me ask again."

"Aye," the shopkeeper swallowed hard and gave Ertemis the price.

"I only want one."

"That is for one and a very good price for such an exquisite piece."

"Codswallop! Do pirates run this shop? I'll give you half."

"Perhaps you would prefer something less expensive?"

Ertemis growled. The shopkeeper blanched and began to put the pendant back into the case. Nothing else Ertemis saw suited her nearly so well. "Wrap it."

Valduuk was still haggling over the saddle when he returned. He assured his friend the price was satisfactory. Ertemis added matching saddlebags to the purchase. At last, the pair headed back to the Thirsty Troll.

Valduuk handed the goods to one of his staff. "Let's sit and enjoy an evening like we used to. I assure you none of these sad souls has the wherewithal to even think of taking the Legion up on its offer. Between us, we'd make lunch of them and they know it."

Ertemis followed Valduuk to his private table in the back. The troll beckoned a serving wench.

"Aye, Master Valduuk, what might I do for you?" She asked, her gaze fixed on Ertemis.

"My usual. My friend?"

"Ale." The girl was pretty enough but too buxom, even for his taste. A silver coin sparkled in the deep cleft of her cleavage. Apparently, tips were greatly appreciated.

She licked her lips. "Back in a moment."

"I see you haven't lost your touch with the ladies."

"Calling her a lady is taking liberties." Ertemis said. The girl had none of Jessalyne's sweetness or grace.

Valduuk laughed. "She works hard and gives me no lip. The customers love her."

"I can see why. As can everyone else."

Valduuk grinned wickedly. "I am sure Dalayna would willingly keep you company, since Lady Jessalyne lacks what you seek."

"You're the one in need of company, my friend." Ertemis changed the subject. He was glad Valduuk knew nothing of the lavish bauble hidden away in his pocket. "How did you come to own this bastion of sophistication and charm?"

"You're smitten with her." Valduuk laughed.

"I am not." Ertemis scowled at the troll. "I've not had a woman since the siege at Batton Falls and I don't intend to start now."

"All the more reason—"

"Here you go, lads." The barmaid set a mug of ale in front of each of them. She leaned so far forward Ertemis thought the coin in her cleavage might dive into his drink. "Anything else I might do for you?"

He smiled at her, eager to disprove Valduuk. "Nay, but don't wander far."

Dalayna winked at him, thoroughly pleased and sauntered off, an extra swaggle in her hips.

"That can only bring you trouble, brother." Valduuk smirked. "Lady Jessalyne would be so disappointed."

Ertemis raised his glass to Valduuk. "Get stuffed."

After a long draught, Valduuk wiped the foam from his lip with a linen square. "How will you earn the bond money? I have a little I can spare—"

Ertemis stopped him with a hand. "I'm not here begging.

"I wasn't implying—"

"I know." He stared into his ale. "She's paying me. Too much really. I was headed to Shaldar city sooner or later anyway."

Valduuk raised a brow. "Work?"

Ertemis shook his head. "Right after I deserted, I came across a band of Travelers. They'd heard stories of me, my mother. According to them, my father lived there."

"Travelers will tell you anything for the right coin."

"I didn't pay them."

"Fear then."

Ertemis shrugged. "It's the only thread I've found. Best I unravel it."

"It's been a long time."

"I'll find him."

"And then?"

Ertemis drained his mug. "Kill him."

Valduuk shook his head, then emptied his mug as well, bringing Dalayna back to the table with refills and ending the conversation about Ertemis's father. Dalayna's gaze never strayed from Ertemis. For the rest of the night, he and Valduuk reminisced about old times.

When the final customer made his way to the door, the hour was late. Valduuk swallowed the last sip of his ale. "We shall break bread before you leave in the morning. I look forward to more of Lady Jessalyne's company."

"In the morning then." Ertemis clapped his friend on the back and headed up to his room.

∞

Jessalyne fell asleep after her long soak but an ache in her legs and backside woke her when she shifted. So much for being unaffected by bareback riding. She eased herself to the side of the bed and bent to pick her rucksack off the floor. She searched through the bag for a tin of white willow salve.

She found it just as she heard a door close across the hall and realized Ertemis was just now turning in. He and Valduuk must have been up reminiscing. It was nice to know he had a friend like Valduuk. Surprising actually. Now that the elf was in his room, she

69

could ask him to knock on her door when he rose in the morning. The thought reminded her of another morning when she'd barged in on him. Remember to knock. She grinned. Maybe he'd try to kiss her goodnight.

Maybe she'd let him.

She hobbled to the door, wincing at her aching lower half. This will not do. If he sees me limping he'll think me weak. Steady yourself, it's just a little ache.

Jessalyne inhaled deeply and closed her eyes. Ignore the pain. Just for a few moments.

She opened the door slowly, not wanting to wake any of the other guests. One of the serving girls from the tavern stood before Ertemis's door. Jessalyne remembered her because of her excessive bosom. As if the girl's assets were not enough, she was additionally blessed with thick chestnut waves and large hazel eyes.

Jessalyne closed her door to a sliver and despite the slow twist of her insides, kept watching. Without so much as a knock, the girl turned the knob and slipped inside.

Stung, Jessalyne shut the door and stumbled back to bed. Betrayal was a feeling she had no right to. She was only business to him. Still, she wasn't paying him to…to…do whatever he was doing across the hall. She snatched the salve from off the bed and rubbed it into her sore muscles. The pain brought clarity.

What he does is his business. I'm behaving foolishly. Obviously, he prefers a much different sort of woman. A sort of woman I will never be.

"I never mingle business with pleasure." Ertemis's earlier words echoed in her head. Fine. Business she would be. She tucked the pot of salve back into her bag, wrapped herself in the coverlet and mercifully, fell asleep.

∞

How would he present the necklace to her at the end of their trip? He stuffed one arm beneath his pillow and stared at the ceiling. She wore no jewelry but perhaps that was because she had none, not because she disliked it. Would she kiss him in thanks? That would be worth the price alone.

He rubbed the bridge of his nose. What was she doing to him? He was the most dangerous creature in the kingdom and he was buying pretty baubles for a woman who didn't even like him. Just the thought of her face lighting up with that smile—the door creaked softly and light leaked in.

Someone had entered his room.

What little ale he'd had did nothing to dull his senses. He picked up a rapid heartbeat and the mingled smells of ale, stale smoke and oversweet perfume. A woman. But not Jessalyne, unfortunately. He inhaled again. The scent was familiar. Dalayna. Lust came off her in waves.

He was in no mood for games. If Valduuk had sent her, he would deal with his friend in the morning. To his fey eyes the darkened room was lit like lastlight, dusky but not too dark to see. He watched her for a moment before slipping silently out of bed. She stood by the door, trying to get her bearings.

He pulled his trousers on, and drew back the curtains to give her some light. Moonlight spilled into the room. "Did Valduuk send you?

She jumped, then giggled. "Nay, I came on my own. I thought you might like some company." She walked toward him, hips swaying. "I know I would."

Ertemis groaned. He should have known better. "I don't need company. I need sleep."

"Mmmm..." she purred, staring at his bare chest. "Very nice." She reached out and drew her nails down his rippled stomach muscles. "Just think how well you'll sleep afterwards. I promise you won't be disappointed. I've heard enough stories to know I won't be."

She put her hand out to touch him again. Ertemis stepped back. She followed and Ertemis grabbed her wrist. "You need to go. Now."

"I know you want me, I saw the way you looked at me downstairs," she pouted. "Do you deny it?"

"It was the ale, nothing more," he said.

"I don't believe you." Dalayna slipped her free hand into the waist of his partially buttoned trousers before Ertemis could stop her. She wrapped her fingers around him, gasping in delight. "Those stories don't lie, do they?"

Ertemis snatched her hand away and in one swift motion, captured both her wrists. "Don't ever touch me again."

"You're hurting me," she whimpered.

"I'm just giving you a story to tell." He sneered. "Isn't that what you want?"

Humiliation welled in her eyes. "Muddled blood fool." She wrenched her hands away and cupped her breasts. "You would turn these down for that shapeless mare you're traveling with? How much coin has that whey-faced princess given you? Or perhaps you dream she's a high born elfess when you're inside her?"

How dare she speak of Jessalyne that way? Ertemis grabbed the girl and hauled her to the door. She kicked and mewed as he opened it. He put his lips to her ear. "What makes you think I'd want what everyone else has already had? How pathetic. I'd sooner have my hand than lay you." He pushed her out. "Stay gone or Valduuk will hear about this."

She snarled and took off toward the stairs. Ertemis looked across the hall at Jessalyne's door. Why hadn't she snuck into his room instead? Thoughts of her sweet and willing in his bed almost made him moan. He thought of the pouch on his belt that now held her gift and he smiled. He eased the door shut so as not to wake her, and went back to bed where dreams of moonlight skin and lavender eyes lulled him to sleep.

ℂ

Jessalyne tipped her head forward and brushed her hair slowly, dragging the bristles from the nape of her neck down. The salve she'd reapplied to her sore legs and backside upon waking had barely taken the edge off the ache in her backside and legs.

The knock at the door must be Ertemis making sure she was up. Still brushing her hair, she called out so he'd know she was awake. She couldn't bear to look at him knowing how he'd spent his night.

The door opened and a feminine voice bid her good morning. "The master has sent tea for you, miss."

Jessalyne smiled at Valduuk's continued hospitality. "He's too kind." She tossed her hair back and stared straight at the girl she'd seen slip into Ertemis's room last night. Her stomach pitched and heat tingled at her fingertips.

"Honey in your tea, miss?" the girl asked.

"Yes, please." Jessalyne composed herself. No reason to be upset with the girl. Ertemis was the whorehound. What chance did any woman have against those silver-edged eyes or that promising smile? "What's your name?"

"Dalayna." She handed Jessalyne a mug of fragrant tea. "Did you sleep well, miss?"

"Yes, thank you." Jessalyne carried the teas over to the small vanity. She sat in front of the oval reflection glass and began plaiting her hair.

"Good, then." The girl giggled. "I'm glad to know the ruckus across the hall last night didn't keep you up."

A hot, thick wave of nausea rolled through Jessalyne. She met the girl's eyes in the mirror. "What do you mean?"

"Your traveling companion, miss. I served him last night in the tavern." She giggled again. "I guess I served him above the tavern as well."

The tingle in Jessalyne's hands increased and her fingers lost their way. She started the braid over. "How nice for you," she mumbled. She couldn't imagine any of the cervidae women talking so boldly about private affairs.

"How could I resist? He's devilishly handsome. Anyway, I had to see for myself if the old rhyme was true." Dalayna occupied herself with making up the bed. She did a poor job of it.

"What rhyme?" Jessalyne stopped trying to braid her hair altogether. She crushed her palm against the bristles of the brush, watching the girl in the mirror.

"You know the one, elves of light give smiles all night but the darker skin brings a bigger grin," she chanted. "Sure enough, he was a fine toss. Best I've ever had, and quite impressive in his all-together. That dark skin..." She sighed with longing.

Jessalyne's blood rose. Pricks of heat danced along her spine. She didn't know if the girl toyed with her apurpose or spoke brashly as a rule but she would not be made the fool.

She forced a smile and faced the wench. "He is most pleasing in his natural state, isn't he?"

Dalayna's smug expression dissolved.

Jessalyne continued with what she hoped passed for condescension. "Poor thing, he would dally with an old mother when the drink is in him." She clucked her tongue. "Pity such fine flesh is so thinly spread."

Dalayna's face bleached. Her brown eyes gleamed with fury. Perhaps she wasn't as simple-minded as she appeared. .

"Will that be all?" The trollop's voice frosted the air between them.

Jessalyne turned back around to braid her hair. "I can think of nothing else you're needed for."

Chapter Six

Sryka swallowed a simple potion to dull the ache in her bones before she left to speak with the prince.

"Fynna, while I am gone, I want these floors scrubbed spotless. I have begun to think you nigh worthless. This is your chance to prove me wrong." Sryka tapped her staff on the floor for emphasis. She cared very little if the floors were clean, keeping the pixie occupied was the true task.

"Yes, mistress." Fynna nodded.

Sryka slogged down the curved stairway, pausing to rest twice. There were too many blasted steps between her and Erebus. Her aged body needed the spell of renewal soon. Patience. The child was on her way.

At last, she stood at the door of the conservatory. The prince was a man of rare and dubious tastes. He boasted of his collection of exotic plants and made a show of feeding the carnivorous ones in front of guests.

Sryka pushed through the foggy glass doors. The warm dampness sucked at her, as if it knew how much she loathed the place. Too much green, growing energy. Too much color. An earthy stench befouled the already unbreathable air.

Poisonous bloodfruit hung from vines threading up the walls like green veins. Thorns covered the branches of one tree. Another oozed corrosive sap. She found him in the thick of the conservatory, stroking the furred leaves of some hideous weed.

"Sryka." He spit her name out like a piece of spoiled meat. "What pressing matter brings you out of your wretched tower?"

"Prince Erebus, so good to see you," she lied.

He dangled a mouse by its tail. The creature squirmed and squealed, its tiny feet scratching the air. He dropped it into the plant's fleshy maw. A sucking sound filled the air. Erebus nodded. "Get on with it."

Sryka sneered. If she didn't need the renewal so badly, she'd let him twist in the wind like that rodent. She reached into her robe and extracted the lunestone amulet, facing the glowing gem toward the prince with great satisfaction. "The child comes."

⅋

Jessalyne threw on her overvest and slippers and raced down the stairs to Valduuk's quarters.

He opened after the second knock. "Good morning, my lady! Come in. I didn't expect you so early but let me call cook. She can have breakfast for you in a moment."

She shook her head. "I'm not here for breakfast, not yet. I need some help."

"Anything, of course. What can I do for you?"

She looked at her clothes. "This," she plucked at her simple tunic, "will not do. I need something more...something like what the townswomen wear."

"Ahh," he nodded. "I understand."

Valduuk scribbled directions on a scrap of parchment. "Tell the proprietress I sent you."

"Thank you." She smiled. "I won't be long."

Jessalyne found Valduuk's map easy to follow and in minutes she stood before the clothier he'd directed her to.

A bell jangled as she walked in. The shop overflowed with ready-made women's clothes. An older woman with elaborate braids in her grey hair greeted her. "Good morning, miss. May I help you?"

"Master Valduuk sent me. I need something better to wear." She looked around. "I don't know where to start."

The woman smiled, blue eyes twinkling. "I'm Mistress Chara. Let's see what suits you, shall we?"

Chara dressed Jessalyne in a pale green blouse scooped low at the neckline and matching long full skirt. "This color does wonderful things for your eyes but the most important part is the bodice."

She showed Jessalyne one of the boned tapestry belts she'd seen many the townswomen wearing.

"Is this the nicest one you have?"

"I have another t'would go with this outfit, but it's a few more silvers than this one. Very beautifully worked leather. I'll fetch it."

Tooled flowers and vines covered the deep green leather. Thin slices of animal bones stitched inside kept it rigid. Chara laced the bodice around Jessalyne's waist. The tighter she pulled, the higher Jessalyne's chest rose, creating deep cleavage between the pale crests of her bosom.

"How does a person breathe in this?" she gasped.

"Takes some getting used to, doesn't it?" Chara laughed.

A few minor adjustments and Chara led Jessalyne to the long polished glass.

"You look lovely."

Jessalyne stared into the glass. A stranger stared back. She didn't quite have Dalayna's curves but the bodice worked wonders. No longer did she see an odd, out of place girl. Instead, she gazed at woman of the realm, a woman fit for Shaldar City. At least fit on the outside.

"Yes," she whispered, "this will do." Let that blasted halfling look at her now and call her girl.

The woman went into the back room, returning with a tray of hair combs. With deft fingers, she coiled and twisted Jessalyne's braids, slipping in a comb here and there. Chara's touch relaxed her like a hot bath. She opened her eyes and smiled. "I never imagined my hair could look like that."

"I was a lady's maid for many years." Chara showed her how to attach her dagger and coin pouch to the leather loops hidden around the bottom of the bodice. She slipped a matching pair of green leather slippers onto Jessalyne's feet.

"May I wear this now? I couldn't bear to put my old clothes back on."

"Of course. I'll bundle your other clothes." Chara rolled the tunic and overvest and wrapped them in paper and twine.

"Thank you so much. I feel transformed. I'll be sure to tell Valduuk what a great help you've been." Jessalyne held out a handful of coins, unsure of how much it had all cost. Mistress Chara counted out the right amount and bid her farewell.

On her walk back to the tavern, Jessalyne's stomach grumbled. Hopefully, she hadn't missed breakfast. She couldn't wait to see the look on Ertemis's face. She hoped the outfit made him want her so badly he begged to kiss her. Telling him no would be a great pleasure.

She knocked on Valduuk's door again and he answered promptly, as though he were waiting. He smiled and nodded approvingly when he saw her. "We are just sitting down to the table. The food will be out soon. Come, I think my halfling friend should like to see this." He winked at her, putting her wrapped bundle on a nearby chair.

Valduuk walked ahead of her into the dining room, blocking Ertemis's sight line. "Your tardy mistress has finally graced us with her presence." He stepped to the side, allowing Ertemis full view of her as she entered the room.

Ertemis looked up from a steaming mug of tea. Jessalyne took great satisfaction in the drop of his jaw. She lifted her chin slightly. "Good morning."

He stared at her, wordless. She held his gaze, daring him with her eyes not to respond. The soft swish of her skirts pleased her as she moved around the table to her place. Valduuk pulled her chair out and she fluffed her skirts out over the seat. "Thank you, sir."

Valduuk sat across from her and rang a small bell. The cook came in with the first of the trays. "Ready for your vittles, sir?"

"Aye, cook. Thank you." Valduuk ignored the still speechless elf. "I must compliment you, Lady Jessalyne. You look more beautiful than yesterday. That color is lovely on you."

"You're very kind." She couldn't help but smile. Compliments were not something she was used to.

Ertemis remained silent. Valduuk moved in his seat and she heard a soft thunk. She suspected Ertemis had just been kicked and when he shot Valduuk an angry glare, she felt sure of it.

"Aye. Lovely," Ertemis mumbled.

Cook set the platters down and the trio tucked into heaps of fried eggs and sausages, buttered mushrooms and biscuits topped with seedberry preserves and thick whipped cream.

"You spoil us, Valduuk." Jessalyne licked a dollop of cream off her fingers.

Ertemis missed his biscuit and bit his finger.

"I trust you both slept well," Jessalyne said.

Valduuk helped himself to another sausage. "Very well, thank you. I had cook pack food for your trip. Bread, cheese, apples, that sort of thing."

Ertemis spoke around a mouthful of food. "Good of you." He finished chewing and added, "My bed was sufficient."

Jessalyne lowered her eyes and bit back a retort. I'm sure your bed was sufficient. Sufficiently full of tavern wench. She sipped her tea. I am just business.

So what if her new outfit brought little response from him. By the distracted look in his eyes, he was probably still lost in

Dalayna's ample charms. So she couldn't fill a gown like that little chit. Valduuk thought she looked beautiful. Even if that blasted halfling didn't.

"Did you purchase the saddle?" She directed the question to Ertemis in her most businesslike manner.

"Aye. And saddlebags." His eyes swept her newly exposed bosom before picking at the crumbs on his plate. Probably comparing her to that tavern hussy. She doubted that tart could afford an outfit like this. Unless Ertemis had paid her for last night's pleasure. With her gold. New rage crackled over her skin.

"We should be about it, then." She snapped. "If you would please excuse me, I'll gather my things and we can resume our trip."

Valduuk stood as Jessalyne got up. He gave Ertemis a look, but he didn't budge. Who cared if he stood or not? He was just the hired help.

∩

When Jessalyne left, Valduuk's smile disappeared. "What's wrong with you? Would it have killed you to give her a compliment? To rise when she left?"

"Certain circumstances made it wiser to stay seated." Ertemis cursed his body's response to her new look. Not a chance in Hael he would show her his straining trousers. She thought little enough of him as it was. "Where did she get those clothes?" That body?

"She came to see me before breakfast. It seems her old clothes became unacceptable overnight. I think she wants to catch your eye."

"Not likely. She's off to serve the king's magewoman." He drew a breath. "Codswallop! Who knew such curves existed beneath those rustic threads." He leaned back in his chair. "The woman confounds me."

"Woman, eh?" Valduuk laughed. "Yesterday, she was a child and by your own words, not to your taste."

Ertemis stood, throwing his linen on the table. "I don't have time for this. I have animals to saddle and miles to travel in daylight." He spoke the last word through gritted teeth before storming out of the room. Valduuk's laughter echoed in his ears.

What if Valduuk was right? The thought of traveling beside her all day, seeing so much of her in those new clothes, rattled him. He threw himself into saddling the animals. Finished, he brought them round the front of the tavern and hitched them before going

78

inside to fetch Jessalyne. Dalayna was nowhere in sight, which suited him fine.

Jessalyne sat with Valduuk at his table, sipping a glass of cold tea, her rucksack at her feet. Dwarfed by Valduuk's size and dressed in those clothes, she looked like a beautiful doll. He wanted her to the point of pain. Her lavender eyes met his and he looked away, unwilling to let her see the torment she caused him.

He extended his hand to Valduuk. "My friend, your hospitality was much appreciated."

Valduuk rose and clasped Ertemis's hand between his massive palms. "May fewer years pass between us before we meet again."

Jessalyne embraced Valduuk. "I hope to see you again some day, too. You're the nicest man," she glanced at Ertemis, "I've met in a long time.

Valduuk kissed her hand as he had when they first met. "It's been my pleasure, Lady Jessalyne. Let me walk you out."

Arm in arm, the two headed for the door, leaving Ertemis behind. "You left your bag," he called out.

Without looking back, Jessalyne called out over her shoulder, "Haven't I paid you enough?"

Ertemis stared at her, mouth open. "What?"

Valduuk howled with laughter. "Just bring the lady's bag, will you?"

Muttering, Ertemis snatched the bag and strode after them. Now he was her servant? Where had that come from?

Dragon and Petal stood at the hitching rail, Petal's nose tucked beneath Dragon's neck.

"Seems Dragon has found himself a ladylove," Valduuk said. Ertemis rolled his eyes.

Jessalyne examined her new saddle. "This is lovely. Much better than bareback."

Ertemis plopped the rucksack at her feet. "Put your things into one of the saddlebags."

She glared at him but did it. He placed the foodstuffs supplied by cook into the opposite side. He mounted up and Jessalyne followed suit, placing her foot in the stirrup as he had placed his. Her full skirts allowed her to sit straddle, which was the only redeeming quality he could see in her new clothes.

They rode in silence. Once beyond the town limits, Jessalyne checked the dagger. She pointed and they took up the trail, each lost in their own thoughts.

What a fool he'd been for buying that necklace. She didn't want him for anything but protection. What had gotten into her? New clothes, new attitude, she barely spoke to him except to give him an order...an order! It made no sense and he didn't like any of it. Well, in truth, the clothes were not that wretched.

He mused on the way she'd looked walking into the dining room that morning. With her hair up, the sweep of her neck had beckoned him, a sweet to be savored, an expanse of skin so fair it deserved small tender kisses that trailed lower across her bosom. His body responded to his thoughts and he groaned. Once again, this was neither the time nor the place.

"Something wrong?" Jessalyne's eyes were straight ahead.

"Nay." He watched her out of the corner of his eye.

"You groaned." She dragged the words out like they were painful to speak.

"Just thinking."

"I'm sure you have plenty to think about."

"What is that supposed to mean?" Why were women so difficult to understand?

"Nothing."

He shook his head. "Do you like the saddle?"

"It's fine."

"Valduuk picked it out." He was relieved to talk of something else.

"Then I love it. How much did it cost me?"

"Nothing."

That got her attention. She finally looked at him. "Please don't tell me Valduuk paid for it. He did more than enough."

"He didn't pay for it."

She furrowed her brows.

"I did."

She turned away again. "I will reimburse you."

"You will not. You've already overpaid me."

She tucked her chin so he couldn't see her face, but he heard the smile in her voice. "Thank you."

"Your smile becomes you."

The smile disappeared. "Was that a compliment?"

Was there no making her happy today? "A thousand pardons. I didn't mean to overstep my bounds as your hireling, my lady."

"I didn't mean...oh, you're impossible. You could learn a great deal from Valduuk. He's a gentleman."

Ertemis snorted. "He's a troll!"

"You're more troll than he is."

He glanced at her. Her jaw set in a way he had not seen before. "I've done nothing to make you think that."

"Hah! You're a crude, ill-mannered, skirt-chasing whorehound!" She sputtered.

He reached out and snagged Petal's reins out of her hands, bringing both animals to a standstill.

She stared into the distance, her fists clenched. An angry flush spread over her chest. Saladan's britches, she tempted him when her blood was up. "Explain yourself."

She locked eyes with him. "I'm aware of your appetites. In truth, it's none of my business, but I find your dalliances repulsive." She turned her face away.

"Appetites? Dalliances?" He shook his head. "I know less now than when you started."

"Don't play innocent. I saw her!"

He threw his hands up. "Her who? The more you speak the less I understand."

"Dalayna."

"The tavern girl?"

She rolled her eyes.

"And?" Had Valduuk said something about the flirtation between them in the tavern?

"I saw her go into your room last night. Don't deny it."

So that was it. "She was in my room but –"

Jessalyne threw her hands up. "Don't give me details unless you want me to retch my breakfast all over you. You're a cad. I'm ashamed to keep company with you. The sooner we part ways the better."

"You don't know what you're talking about." Half-stunned she might care, he opened his senses to read her. Jealousy rolled off her like steam.

"Indeed I do." She glared at him. "That trollop was in my room this very morning, boasting of what a fine toss you were. She made sure to inform me you were, 'quite impressive in the all-together'." She crossed her arms beneath her chest, pushing it up and out even further.

"Enough!" He leaned over and grasped her shoulders, very aware of how close his hands were to other parts of her. "Listen and do not interrupt me." He looked her straight in the eyes and tried not to smile as her jealously continued to flood his senses. "I slept alone last night."

"I saw her—"

"I am not done speaking."

"She told me—"

"Not another word until I'm done." He was tempted to silence her mouth with his.

She huffed but kept silent.

"She did come into my room, but I promptly escorted her out. She was furious I refused her. I'm sure her visit to you this morning was just an attempt to get back at me." The angry light in her eyes faded. He smiled. "Your jealousy flatters me. I can't say I've felt that from a woman before."

"I'm not jealous. I don't even like you." Jessalyne tried to pull away but he wasn't ready to let her go.

He read her again. She was a bad liar. The jealousy tapered off, but hurt rose to take its place. "I didn't compliment you at breakfast because the sight of you made me lose my tongue." Among other things. He couldn't believe he was telling her this.

"But Dalayna is so, so –"

"Dalayna is a plump little tart who mistakenly thinks men should bow at her feet." He released her and sat back.

"Truly?"

"Aye."

"Why should I believe you?"

"Have I lied to you yet?"

She shook her head. "Not that I know of."

A small pain shot through him at her lack of trust. He gripped his sword hilt. "I swear on my blade, it's the truth."

Happiness flowed off her, filling him with warmth. "I'm sorry for being cross with you." She took Petal's reins back from him. "But I'm not jealous."

"You are jealous. Sensing strong emotion is one of my gifts, so don't bother denying it." Against his better judgment, he reached into the pouch at his belt. He wanted to feel her intoxicating happiness again.

"Here," he said, holding the amethyst and pearl pendant. The bauble sparkled in the sun. "Just to show I harbor no ill will against your name calling."

Jessalyne stared at the necklace, her mouth slightly open. "Where did you get that?"

"I see receiving gifts is not your strong suit."

"I've never seen the like before." Her eyes shone with the same lavender as the gem.

"My arm grows numb."

She cupped the necklace in her palm, and he let it drop. She held it gently, caressing the amethyst and rolling the pearl between her fingertips.

"Does it please you?"

"Oh yes, it's lovely," she breathed. "I'm sorry, I just forgot myself for a moment. I don't own any jewels."

"You do now. Put it on."

She undid the catch and slipped it around her neck. "I can't fasten it."

Ertemis guided Dragon closer until he touched Petal's sides. He took the pendant from Jessalyne and she turned the bare curve of her neck to him. He looped the pendant over her head. His fingers grazed her silky skin. She was so warm. He stroked a fingertip down her neck and fought the desire to kiss the flesh beneath his fingers.

"There. Turn toward me." He nodded. "Beautiful."

"Thank you."

"The necklace is lovely as well."

She blushed and fiddled with the buckle on Petal's reins, her head down.

He enjoyed the color in her cheeks. There wasn't a drop of guile in her. What in the realm was she doing with him? "Time to ride or we'll lose the light and have traveled nowhere."

❧

They fell into their usual pace, Dragon slightly ahead. Jessalyne caressed the gems at her throat. Perhaps she was no longer just business to him after all. Goose flesh rose on her arms when she thought about his fingers on her neck.

As they traveled into the foothills, the landscape changed from gently forested plains into stony ground. Jagged clusters of grey shale rose from the ground and towered above them. The purple gloam of lastlight colored the sky and a filmy rain drizzled over them. Night came fast. She shivered.

Ertemis heeled Dragon. "We'll have to sleep aground tonight, but I think I can find shelter." He nodded toward a break of evergreens. "Take cover there. I'll be back soon." He took off toward a slag ridge.

Petal found a spot to her liking beneath the pines and grazed on some succulents growing through the hard ground. Jessalyne's backside ached but there'd be no hot bath tonight. She hoped he found a dry place for them. She didn't relish the idea of sleeping in the rain. Or the dark.

Just as she thought she might head out to find him, Ertemis returned. He stared hard into the darkness behind her.

"What is it?"

"Nothing. Follow me."

He led her to a wide fissure in the side of the ridge. "We camp here." He alighted Dragon and took the reins in his hands.

"Where?" She hoped he didn't mean there on the ground. They would be soaked by morning.

"In here." He motioned behind him with a tip of his head and began leading Dragon through.

Jessalyne's eyes went wide. "You don't mean...but it's dark in there and probably full of...creatures!" She couldn't see past the jagged opening.

"There's nothing in there. I've been inside already. Trust me, my eyes see what yours cannot. The ground inside is soft sand, and there are breaks enough to let out smoke from a fire." Thunder growled and the sky opened, soaking them.

Jessalyne yelped and jumped off Petal. "Fine, fine, before I'm washed away."

She pulled Petal through the twisted gap and found herself in complete darkness. Soaked to the skin and shivering, she pressed against Petal's side. "I can't see anything."

"I'm trying to start a fire. I gathered brush and branches earlier but my flint is wet and won't spark." His repeated attempts failed. "We'll have to do without."

She faced the direction of his voice. "No! It's too dark. Please, come here. Quickly."

She felt him next to her. "Point my hand toward the kindling."

He did as she asked.

"Leave hold of me and step away." When she no longer felt his presence, she summoned her magic.

The distinct crack of fire splintered the stillness and flames shot up from the stacked tinder.

Dragon reared and Ertemis grabbed his bridle. "You spook like a colt, Dragon. Be still."

A yellow glow filled the hollow and Jessalyne caught the amazement on Ertemis's face. "Well done," he said.

Water dripped from several openings in the cavern ceiling but the sandy floor was mostly dry. Plenty of open space remained between the boulders scattered across the ground. It would do for shelter.

Ertemis removed his leather breastplate and hooked it over his saddle horn. He yanked his shirt off and stood bare-chested in the firelight. "You cannot stay in those wet clothes, no matter how nicely they cling to you."

Jessalyne hugged her arms over her breasts. "I'm fine."

"You're shivering. Take those wet rags off. Or do you wish help?" He raised a brow, his mouth curving seductively.

"No." She moved to the other side of the cavern, away from him. The firelight set his skin aglow, defining every muscle. He looked like living stone. How would it feel to be held in those strong arms?

Ertemis picked up a branch the thickness of a man's arm and snapped it like a twig before tossing the pieces onto the fire. With some of the longer branches, he built a tripod at the edge of the fire. He draped his cloak and shirt there then began unbuttoning his trousers.

"What are you doing?" Jessalyne yelled.

"I'm not sleeping in wet clothes. And as you still haven't taken a stitch off, I'll be over to help you when I'm through."

"You will not!" She turned around and stared at the rugged cavern walls. Beast. Must he carry on this way? Nice one moment, barbarian the next. Obviously, he enjoyed torturing her. She would never be able to sleep in the same room, or cave, with a naked man. Even thinking the words made her cheeks warm. Especially since she knew exactly what that naked man looked like.

Something pulled her off balance. She gasped. He was unlacing her bodice.

He whispered into her ear. "I wouldn't turn around unless you wish to see for yourself how impressive I am in my all-together. Again."

His hot breath sent a shudder down her spine. "You're shameless and wicked."

"Aye." He tugged once more and the bodice came loose. "That I am."

Once the bodice was off, his hands went around her waist. He held her for a moment, the warmth of his skin sinking through the damp fabric. Then his fingers spread over her hips possessively. She inhaled hard. A thick, liquid heat gathered in her belly. He pulled her close, removing any space between them. The contact was so sweet it hurt, but the pain was worth the pleasure. Rational thought disappeared. Every inch of him was hard, hot muscle. No wonder few women ever refused him.

ᛞ

He brushed his lips against the curve of her neck and she mewed. The woman filled him with uncommon urges. He wanted to hold her and kiss her and protect her and yet, he longed to give her good reason to cry out his name.

"Jessalyne," he murmured, his lips still on her skin. She shivered and he pulled away.

Her hands covered her face. He tried to turn her around but she resisted. "You have no trousers on."

He sighed. "I have trousers on."

She peered over her shoulder through her fingers. "You said you didn't." She turned and thumped his bare chest with her fist. Tears glistened in her eyes. "Why must you bedevil me?"

"I bedevil you? Is that why you're crying?"

She shook her head. He brushed a tear from her cheek with his knuckle.

"Why then?" He asked.

"No reason." She dug at the sand with her toe. "We should—"

"I would believe pointless weeping from most women, but not you." He cupped her chin and tipped her face toward him but she kept her gaze lowered. "Jessalyne, look at me."

Through a veil of lashes, she met his eyes.

"Explain your tears."

"I don't know what to say." She paused, her voice almost a whisper. "You…make me...ache."

He closed his eyes. Maybe if he didn't look at her, the desire would fade away. It didn't, so he opened them. If he must suffer, he was at least going to enjoy the view. "I'm the cause of your weeping?"

She nodded.

"You make me ache as well." Again, he found himself confessing feelings he had no intent to share.

Her eyes rounded. "I do?"

"Aye...like no woman I have ever known." He caressed her bottom lip with his thumb. Her very soft, full, kissable bottom lip. She was so warm, how could she not be feeling what he was?

Tortured by her nearness, he bent his head and captured her lush lips with his, kissing her as gently as he could manage. He sucked her bottom lip between his own. She was so soft, so warm. His hands swept down to her waist and he pulled her hard against him. Her breasts pressed against his bare chest, scorching his skin through the damp fabric of her dress.

She let his lips lead, holding tight to his forearms. His mouth moved tenderly against hers, teasing and taking. Tentatively, she kissed him back.

Rivulets of sweat trickled down his spine as he slid one hand to the small of her back, bringing her feverish body closer. Hungrily, he devoured her hot mouth, wondering if every inch of her tasted this sweet.

The heat of her mouth was almost more than he could take. She moaned against his lips. The vibrations rippled across his skin and into his center, shaking him. He craved her so badly, her touch burned him like fire. She put her hands on his chest and broke the kiss with a sob. Reluctantly, he released her.

"I didn't mean to make you weep again, but I'm not sorry for kissing you." He exhaled as he braced one hand against the stone behind her. For the first time in his life, he was losing a battle and didn't care.

"Ertemis?" she whispered weakly.

"Aye, lelaya?" He used the elven endearment without thinking.

"Does the ache ever go away?"

He smiled. "I don't know. I've never felt such an ache before." More confessions. He was well and truly gone.

"Truly?" Flames from the fire danced in her eyes.

"Truly."

She pressed her fingertips to her mouth. "So that's kissing."

Ertemis cocked his head to the side. "What did you say?"

"I've never been kissed before."

"Never?" He raised his eyebrows. No other man had touched her? Hot, possessive desire thickened his blood.

"Not by a…a man." She lowered her eyes. "It was agreeable."

"Agreeable? My kisses have been called many things. I don't recall agreeable being among them," he teased. "I promise a better attempt next time."

She gave him a curious look.

"Aye." He nodded. "There will be a next time."

Dragon whinnied. She looked over Ertemis's shoulder. "What's the matter, Dragon?"

"He's hungry. And Petal as well, no doubt. I'll feed and untack them if you'll lay out our supper."

"I will." She walked with him toward the beasts.

"One more thing."

"Yes?" She looked up from the saddlebags.

"Those wet clothes."

She glared at him.

"Change into your long tunic. On my honor as a gentleman, my eyes will be averted."

She raised her eyebrows. "Your honor as a gentleman?"

He shrugged, grinning. "It was worth a try."

⁊ʊ

She pulled her old clothes out of her pack and untied Chara's knot. While Ertemis tended Dragon and Petal, she snuck off behind an outcropping of rock to undress.

He'd held her and kissed her. She licked her lips to see if the taste of him remained. When she closed her eyes, it was like he was kissing her again. Heat burned her mouth. Her knees weakened and she leaned against the rocks.

Her only shame was her tears, but how could she not weep at the sensations he'd spun through her? His kiss was a magic all its own. And to be held in those arms…amazing. He hadn't been afraid to touch her, of course, he hadn't known better, but she'd stopped the kiss anyway. If she'd burned him...she shook her head. Don't think of it.

Her skin was wrinkling with the damp. She pulled her tunic over her head, knocking the clips from her hair. It tumbled free and she ran her hands through the damp strands, happy to have it down again. Her scalp ached from the weight of it piled atop her head. She gathered the combs and went back to the fire.

The warmth beckoned and her stomach begged for food. She hung her clothes as Ertemis had on the tripod of branches. The hair combs went into one side of her saddlebag and she dug food out of the other. She took out hard cheese, a sour rye roll and an apple for each of them.

Ertemis nodded when he saw her. "You look like you again."

"I knew you didn't like my new clothes."

"I meant your hair. I like it down."

"Oh." She handed him his dinner. What else did he like about her?

They ate by the fire, neither saying much. Ertemis fed the apple cores to Dragon and Petal. He returned with their bedrolls. "Have you ever slept outside before?"

"No. This is truly an adventure."

He laughed. "Aye, an adventure." He spread out their bedrolls on either side of the fire, first the canvas on the sand, then the blanket on top for a covering.

"Be warned, these damp trousers are coming off. Before you protest, I'll get beneath my blanket as soon as they're hung so you needn't see anything that might drive you to temptation." He paused, wickedness glinting in his eyes. "Of course, if you want to look, I'll gladly leave the blanket off until you've had your fill."

"Beast." She turned abruptly, but now she faced the drying rack. Ertemis would have to walk directly in front of her to get to it. She buried her face in her hands instead.

In a few moments, he called out, "The cave is safe for fair maids once again."

He lay on his side, head propped on one hand. The coarse blanket bunched around his waist, leaving his broad muscled chest exposed. Indecent behavior obviously pleased him. With the firelight gleaming off his dark skin, she couldn't help but think he looked very much like the silky chocolate cakes Valduuk had served them as a dinner sweet. Her mouth watered.

She situated herself into the bed he'd made for her. Not greatly comfortable, but it would suffice. She wiggled a bit, trying to shift the sand beneath her into a more agreeable sleeping surface.

"So? What do you think?" he asked, gesturing with one hand.

She turned to face him, blushing as she spoke. "I don't know why you need to ask such things but yes, your chest is very nice to look at."

Ertemis snorted. "I meant about your bed."

Mortified, she ducked her head under the blanket. He laughed louder.

"Come out before you suffocate yourself."

She uncovered her head. "It was getting stuffy." She rolled to her side and propped herself on her elbow, mimicking him. "Why are your ears and back marked with those runes?"

"Where did you get your magic?"

"First asked, first answered."

"Are you always so bold?" He shook his head. "No one has ever asked me such questions. At least not and lived."

She shivered.

"I would never hurt you." He sat up, keeping the blanket about his waist. He poked a stick into the fire. "It's a long story."

She rolled all the way over onto her stomach and crossed her arms into a pillow, turning her head so she could see him. "So tell me. I'm not going anywhere."

His gaze seemed caught on something in the flames. "As you know, I'm a dark elf, an outcast. I know the names I'm called. Dark elves are rare, because by tradition, they're not allowed to live beyond birth. When my mother knew she carried me, she fled the city of..." he paused.

"She fled the isle of Elysium, the elven homeland. A band of Travelers gave her shelter. When I was born, they tolerated us but every bad thing that happened was my fault. They wanted to use me in their carnival but my mother wouldn't let them. Eventually, they turned us out."

The reflection of the flames in his dark eyes mimicked the storm raging across his face. A vein pulsed in his neck. "Before she left, she begged their tashathna..."

"The what?"

"Tashathna is an elven word for something like an elder wizard and chieftain. Anyway, her magic was long gone so she begged him for a charm of protection. She knew there were those who wouldn't hesitate to rid the realm of me."

His eyes grew liquid. "He tattooed the spells onto my flesh with molten silver."

"Oh my. I cannot imagine the pain of that." Jessalyne winced.

"I was three. I have little memory of it. My mother always told me I took it bravely."

"Do you truly not miss her?"

He shrugged. "Without her magic, she couldn't protect me. And I know she missed her home and her family. She conscripted me into the Legion for my own safety. I choose not to miss her because there's no point. She lives in a place I'm forbidden to go. I'll never see her again."

"I miss my mother every day." Jessalyne sat up, pulling her knees up under her chin. "Do you remember your mother well? What she looked like? What she sounded like? I have the hardest time keeping those memories sharp."

"My mother is a high born light elf. As beautiful as anything you've ever seen. Her hair is the color of the egret's feather, as pure white as you can imagine. I remember her as having a constant glow about her, like she was bathed in moonlight. Except for the color of your eyes, you favor her considerably." A bitter smile grooved his mouth.

Jessalyne bowed her head, hiding the heat in her cheeks. She picked at the blanket. "What's her name?"

"Her name is Elana-naya. But before I was born she was known as Shaylana."

"Shaylana is so beautiful. Why did she change it?"

"She didn't. It was punishment for her indiscretion. Elana-naya means 'daughter of none' just as my surname, Elta-naya, means 'son of none'."

"That isn't fair."

"Fair has nothing to do with the rule of the Tashathna, the Elders."

"What about your father? Did the Elders punish him?"

"My father is human. That's why I am who I am. Only a human male and an elf female can produce a dark elf."

"Maybe he didn't know about you?"

"He knew enough to destroy her life."

"Who is he?"

"I don't know. My mother refused to tell me. I only know he deserves..." He ground his fist into the sand.

"Why didn't your mother just take you to Elysium with her? You're half elf."

He laughed, a sharp, harsh bark. "The Elders would never allow that. My human half offends them."

Jessalyne pulled the blanket a little tighter. "Why?"

"Elysium is the heart of elven magic. On the isle, the elves' magic is strong and pure. On mortal soil, their magic weakens and distorts until it ceases altogether. I don't have that problem. Nothing I've encountered yet has hindered my magic. They fear me because they have no hold on me."

"You still haven't told me about your gifts."

He changed the subject. "How old were you when your mother died?"

"Not quite seven. My father left the day he put her in the ground. After that, I saw him once every few years. Mostly, he just left sacks of coins on my doorstep."

Ertemis grunted. "He shouldn't have left you, a female child alone in such an isolated spot. You did well raising yourself."

She looked up at him. "So did you."

"The Legion raised me."

"That's where you met Valduuk."

"Aye. He saved my life. My skin made me the favorite target of some of the older conscripts. He overheard them plotting to rid the camp of me once and for all. He changed their minds with a broken jaw, a few cracked ribs, and a dislocated shoulder. They never bothered me again."

"What was your job in the legions?"

He shifted uncomfortably. "I was a messenger of sorts."

She swallowed. "Have you killed many men?"

"Do you really want an answer to that?"

She nodded.

"I've killed...my share."

"Is that why Valduuk called you the Black Death?"

He groaned at the name. "Aye. I earned that name because of my ability to come and go unseen."

"So, what other abilities do you possess?"

He laughed.

Indignation tensed her jaw. "Why are you laughing at me?"

"I'm not laughing at you. I'm just not used to the way you treat me." He shook his head. "You speak to me without fear. You look at me without shrinking back. I'm not used to that. Don't I frighten you?"

She smiled. "You look a little frightening but you haven't really given me a reason to fear you. Now, answer the question."

"Such temerity in one so young. What abilities do you possess?"

"Fire."

"I'm aware of that one."

"I can heal."

"I don't think knowledge of herbs counts."

She shook her head. "More than just with herbs. Lord Tyber's son Orit fell and shattered the bone in his rear flank. I healed him with my magic."

"I haven't seen you practice."

"Practice my magic?"

"If I didn't practice with my sword, I might lose my skills. At the very least, I wouldn't get any better. If you don't practice, how will you learn the scope of your power?"

"The thought never occurred to me. Where would I begin?"

"You have fire. Start there. Call fire into your hand," he suggested.

"A flame? It would burn me!"

"Nay, I don't think it will."

She held her palm out and closed her eyes. She imagined a cool flame.

"Well done!" Ertemis said.

She opened her eyes to see a weak blue flame flickering in her hand. She gasped and the flame went out. "Well, that didn't work."

"You doubted yourself. Try again, with your eyes open."

She held her palm out and the flame reappeared. She willed it larger and it grew. "Did you see that? I just did that. I imagined it bigger and then it was." She closed her hand and the flame disappeared. "I cannot believe I never thought of practicing. I've wasted so many years."

"You may be the king's magewoman yet. I've never met a human with a quarter of your abilities." He lay down and pulled the blanket up to his chest. "Best get some sleep."

"Very well. Good dreams." She settled under the covers. Firelight flickered on the rock ceiling.

"Good dreams."

"Ertemis?"

"Aye."

"Who is Lelaya?"

"It's not a name, it's an elven word. Now go to sleep."

His half answer was puzzling but sleep called. "I'm glad nothing happened with Dalayna." She yawned.

She dreamed of her mother. They walked hand in hand through the forests of Fairleigh Grove, as they had when Jessalyne was a little girl. The woods grew dark and she was alone. Her mother's voice called to her. "Jessa...Jessa..."

She ran through a thicket of brush toward the voice. When she cleared the thicket, her mother lay still and pale in the coils of a white, two-headed serpent. The beast laughed with one mouth and frowned with the other.

A huge falcon swept down and caught the serpent in its claws, tearing the scaled flesh into red shreds. Jessalyne raised her hands to strike the serpent with magic and it laughed at her from both mouths. Try as she could, no fire came. She dropped her hands to her sides, powerless to help.

In a flash of white, the serpent struck the falcon and it fell to the ground, its breast bright with blood.

Jessalyne bolted awake, gulping air. "It was just a dream," she whispered. The cave was completely dark. The coals of the fire had ashed over and shed no light. She shivered and held out her palm, calling up the small blue flame. The little light it gave off cast odd shadows on the uneven walls.

The shadows flickered and she jumped. She couldn't hold the flame all night but if she restarted the fire, she would wake Ertemis. She stretched her little light toward him. He slept soundly, his back to the fire. She touched the pendant at her throat.

With the flame to light her way, she pulled the blanket around her shoulders and tiptoed to his side. The sand muffled her movements. She sat on his canvas, turning so they were back to back. Please don't wake up. She balled her fist to extinguish the light and shimmied down a little before curling up next to him. Slumber washed over her and she drifted, vaguely aware of him shifting.

࿇

Ertemis turned and tucked his arm around her waist, drawing her close. She roused at his touch so he held still, hoping she'd think he moved in his sleep. He breathed her in, enjoying her nearness.

"What kindness brings you to my bed, Jess?" His lips brushed her ear as he spoke and she shivered.

"I had a nightscare and it's dark and you were sleeping," she mumbled.

He pulled her a little closer. "Shhh...go to back to sleep. You're safe now, lelaya."

Chapter Seven

Firstlight flushed pink the thin slice of sky visible through the cavern's entrance. Ertemis squinted. Jessalyne slept curled around him, entwined in the blankets. Her head rested on his shoulder, her breath heating his skin. There were worse things than being her pillow. Her hair trailed across his chest like a ribbons of captured moonlight.

He smoothed a strand with his fingers, reluctant to wake her. He could hear Dragon snuffling, waiting to be fed. He could wait a few more moments.

"Mmmm..." Jessalyne murmured and slipped her arm around his neck. Was she dreaming of him?

The feel of her tucked against him was pleasurable beyond words. He listened to her heart beating. Impetuously, he felt the urge to imprint its rhythm. At least when they parted, he'd have that piece of her.

He opened his senses and let the steady thump pulse into him until it ran through his blood as his own. The only other heart he'd ever imprinted was his mother's.

Jessalyne nuzzled her head against his shoulder and he reached for her, pulling her on top of him. "Good morning, sweeting. Sleep better on this side of the fire?"

Jessalyne's eyes opened sleepily. She yawned and blinked a few times. Suddenly, her eyes widened and she stiffened. "Are you still naked?"

He motioned toward the makeshift clothes rack where his clothes hung. "I haven't left this bed since you joined me."

She rolled off him, inadvertently taking all the blankets with her, yelping when she hit the ground.

In the few seconds she'd been gone, he already craved her warmth again. "If you wanted a good look, you only need ask."

She scrunched her eyes shut. "Put your clothes on!"

"Nay, not yet." He scooped her up, blankets and all, and cradled her in his lap. "You shared my bed and kept your innocence, didn't you?"

She nodded, eyeing him warily.

"But I'm a mercenary, not a knight." He embraced her, one arm beneath her back. "I promised I would have another kiss."

ᛒ

His lips were gentle, restrained, teasing her mouth. She yielded, wanting more. His kiss turned ravenous.

Jessalyne lost herself in the crush of his mouth. A new heat forged in her and she reached for him, twining her fingers into his silky black locks. The desire to obey her mother's letter warred with her hunger to be held and touched. *It's just a kiss. Just the most delicious kiss from the most delicious man.*

His tongue caressed hers and sparks shot through her. She balled her fists in his hair, arching against him. She quivered at the unexpected touch, her spine tingling with fire as he tasted her.

He released her, closing his eyes and breathing deeply.

She lay quietly in his arms for a moment. "I liked that very much."

"As did I." He smiled at her and glanced down as he lifted her slightly. "Overmuch, perhaps."

"What do you mean?"

"Nothing." He kissed her forehead. "Are you hungry?"

She shook her head. "I don't want food yet. I want a bath."

"A bath? The stream we passed last night doesn't look deep enough for that. Perhaps it pools somewhere. When I take the animals out, I'll have a look."

"Thank you." If she didn't get some relief for her aching muscles, today's ride would be torture.

He stood up with her still in his arms. "I'm going to set you down so you best keep your eyes toward the wall."

Although she did as he suggested, she saw movement out of the corner of her eye. She turned her head slightly and glimpsed his exquisite backside as he pulled his trousers up. With heat creeping into her cheeks, she decided naked suited him well. She spun back toward the wall before he turned.

He walked past on his way to the animals, grinning wickedly. "Did you enjoy peeking at me?"

Her jaw dropped. "I did not..."

He tapped a finger to one ear. "These never lie to me, you saucy wench. Your heartbeat and your breathing quickened. Besides, the flush on your face betrays you." He kept walking, shaking his head as he went. "The impertinence…"

She stuck her tongue out at his back.

"I heard that too," he called out.

As soon as he left with Dragon and Petal, she dug out the salve from her pack. She was glad to be alone. The agony of two days' ride was hard to hide from Ertemis but the pleasure of his kiss had dampened the pain considerably. Now it throbbed to life as she rubbed the last of the salve into her bruised thighs and backside, each stroke freshening the pain. She didn't want him thinking her unable to manage the journey.

With the salve used up, she worked on securing the bedrolls. She wound them twice before they looked right. Rain had kept the night air damp and her skirt was still damp. She stoked the fire, adding some of the remaining brush and twigs to the coals. It sparked to life and she moved the tripod of branches a little closer.

Ertemis walked back inside. "I found a place where the stream pools enough for bathing, but the water is frigid."

"It will be hot before I bath in it." She took a shard of soap from her pack, the remnant of her bath at Valduuk's.

They walked past Dragon and Petal grazing on a small mound of oats. Ertemis grabbed her hand, bringing them to a stop. He scanned the horizon, a finger to his lips.

She looked at him, questions in her eyes.

He shook his head. "I thought I heard something." They walked a little further and he pointed to a spot where the stream curved into a quiet pool.

"Wonderful." Jessalyne started toward the water, but Ertemis held her hand.

"There's room enough for two."

Just like Valduuk's tub. She shivered at the memory.

He gently tugged her close and filled his hands with her hair. "I'll be on my best behavior. Or not. You may decide." He winked and added, "On my honor as a gentleman."

"Since when are mercenaries gentlemen?" His hands in her hair dissolved the urge to pull away.

He clutched at his heart. "I'm wounded you think so lowly of me."

"Ertemis..." She hesitated. If she told him about her mother's letter, he might stop kissing her. If she told him what she'd done to her father, he would undoubtedly never touch her again.

"I didn't mean to distress you. Take your bath and when you come back, I'll have breakfast ready."

"Thank you." She looked into his starry sky eyes and saw he spoke the truth.

She picked her way across the rocky bank, moving as well as her legs would allow. Kept thinking how lovely the hot water would feel.

When she got to the pool, she set her soap on a rock and crouched close to the water's surface. She dipped her fingers in. Icy cold. The stream must be snow fed from the mountains. Cupping her hand, she drank her fill.

Raising her hands over the pool, she started to close her eyes. No, she must practice. Eyes open this time; she beckoned heat into the water. Power surged up her spine and into her hands.

Wisps of steam rose off the surface. She trailed her fingers through the water, delighting in the warmth it now held. She stood and looked back toward the fissure in the ridge. She saw Dragon and Petal but nothing of Ertemis.

She lifted her tunic over her head and let it drop to the bank before easing into the water. The warmth soothed her and when she reached the full depth of the pool, she sunk beneath the surface. When she came up, she grabbed her soap and started scrubbing.

She dipped under to rinse her hair, then stayed submerged up to her neck. The water's heat relaxed her muscles. She closed her eyes and leaned her head against one of the larger rocks edging the bank, letting the warmth sink into her.

Her legs kept floating up, so she stopped fighting the buoyancy and let them rise. Something wriggled over her toes. Her eyes went wide. A red and black striped water serpent curved across the rippling surface. The same kind of serpent that had killed one of the cervidae.

Heart pounding, she froze. Her dagger was in her saddlebag. Now she wished Ertemis were bathing with her.

Panic rose in her but she held her tongue. Screaming had not helped the cervidae. She would not risk drawing the serpent any faster by sending sound vibrations through the water.

Ertemis, where are you when I need you? She called out to him in her head, wishing him to her side. This wasn't the way she wanted to die.

From behind her, a voice. "I'm here."

"Ertemis," she whispered. How had he known?

"I see the serpent. Stay still."

She heard him moving but kept her eyes on the creature slithering toward her. It passed the middle of the pool, almost close enough to touch. A moan caught in her throat.

The brief glimmer of sun-struck steel flashed before her. Swirls of red bloomed from the two wriggling halves of the serpent as it sunk.

His hands slipped beneath her arms and lifted her out of the blood-clouded water.

Water ran off her naked body in rivulets, but that didn't stop him from holding her tight. She tucked her face against his hard chest and inhaled his comforting fragrance. A man like this was good to have around.

"You're safe now." He kissed the top of her head.

"Thank you." She reveled in the press of his hands on her bare back.

"You're shivering. I'll fetch your gown."

Ertemis jumped down and grabbed her tunic off the bank. He held it up, keeping his eyes averted. She raised her brows at his refusal to take advantage of the situation. The gown clung as she tugged it over her wet body. "I'm dressed. How did you know to come?"

−

He looked up and the breath left him. Sunshine filtered through her gown, outlining her in light. The fabric hugged her damp skin, sheer where it was soaked through.

Desire welled in him. The fabric cupped her breasts the way his hands ached to. Sweeping over the curve of her stomach, his gaze went lower before he could stop himself. Painful need course through him. He was lost and he knew it.

Turning away, he struggled to keep the desire from his voice. "I was saddling Dragon when a feeling of panic came over me. I opened my senses and I heard you calling. I came as fast as I could."

"You heard me? But I only spoke to you in my head. I was afraid to call out for fear I'd draw the serpent faster." She shivered as a breeze swept past.

"The elves call it mindsight. But no one's ever called me as clearly as you did." He stepped up onto the rock next to her. "You need to be by the fire."

Jessalyne faltered on a wobbly rock and Ertemis grabbed her arm before she fell. "You're handy to have around. If that serpent had bitten me..." She shuddered.

He squeezed her hand and turned the conversation to something lighter. "So I'm an agreeable kisser and handy to have around. I'm beginning to bore myself."

She cuffed him lightly on the shoulder. "That's not what I meant."

He slipped his arm beneath her legs and picked her up. "Since I'm so handy, I'll just carry you back. You've used up all your rescuing for the day and I can't risk you breaking something on your way to breakfast."

She wrapped her arms around his neck and rested her head on his shoulder. Her fingers played in his hair, but the ripples of pleasure affect his entire body. "Very well. I'm too hungry to be contrary." She paused. "And I do want to get my money's worth."

He slanted his eyes at her. "Saucy wench," he muttered, unable to repress a grin.

He didn't set her down until he reached the fire. "I'll finish saddling Petal while you change. Then we'll eat and be on our way."

As soon as he left, she dressed in the pale green skirt and blouse, cinching the leather bodice tightly around her waist. She finger-combed her hair by the fire to dry it. Her hands went to his beautiful gift about her neck. She smiled. Black Death, indeed. The name really didn't suit him.

"Jessalyne!" Ertemis called. "I am nigh to death with hunger, woman! Are you dressed yet?"

"Yes, come in." Hands on hips, she stared at him. "I thought you were getting breakfast for me?"

"Patience, mistress. Your handy hireling is overloaded with so many chores." He held up a linen square full of food. "Saddle the mounts, save you from serpents, carry you, serve your breakfast..." He opened the linen cloth across one of the larger boulders and set out their meal, sighing with the great effort.

She laughed at his teasing, snatching a pear off the cloth. "Do you think we'll make a town by this evening?"

Finishing a bite of cheese and bread, he answered. "Sleeping aground not to your liking?"

"I prefer the comforts of an inn."

"The closer we get to Shaldar City, the more towns there will be." He finished the last of his breakfast, tucking an apple into his pouch.

She gathered up her tunic, still drying by the fire, and stuffed it into her pack while he covered the coals over with sand. The combination of the salve and the hot water had lessened the ache in her legs but the thought of more riding bothered her. She was out of salve and by nightfall, she might not be able to walk at all.

The land grew more mountainous the farther they traveled. Bruised clouds drifted across the midday sun.

"Ertemis, can we stop? It's chilly. I want to get my cloak out of my pack."

"Aye." He turned Dragon around, reaching to get her cloak for her. He fished it out and tossed it around her shoulders, brushing her cheek with his hand.

She fastened the clasp and opened her mouth to thank him but he put a finger to his lips. He scanned the landscape, his face stern.

After a moment, he spoke in a low voice. "We're being watched. I sense it. Stay close." Wheeling Dragon back around, he scanned their surroundings as they traveled. Ahead of them, the passage narrowed between sheered rock walls.

A stone fell in the distance and they turned. Four figures on horseback stood on a ridge behind them. Ertemis reached over and grabbed Petal's reins. "Hold on," he yelled, urging Dragon and Petal faster.

Jessalyne looked over her shoulder. The men charged down the ridge after them. Fear shot through her. "Who are they?" she yelled.

He ignored her question. "We need to get through the pass."

Wind whistled in her ears as she looked again. Their pursuers were gaining, the two nearest now brandished blades, bloodlust in their eyes. She glanced ahead. The pass was so far away.

Jessalyne gulped air. The ground passed rapidly beneath them. She clung to Petal, her heart pounding in her chest. Tyber was right. All the realm was not Fairleigh Grove.

She saw Ertemis tug on Dragon's reins, slowing the warhorse down to stay beside her. Petal's nostrils flared and foam speckled her mouth. Jessalyne's stomach sank. They weren't going to make it.

"Stay behind me," Ertemis commanded, wheeling around to face the four horsemen, dust billowing.

"We're going to fight them?" Jessalyne pulled Petal around.

"Nay, I'm going to fight them. Stay on Petal. Be prepared to run for the pass."

Petal sidled up next to Dragon and Jessalyne tried to pull the jenny back. This was not staying behind.

The men were almost upon them. All four had weapons ready. They slowed as they approached, fanning out into a semicircle. One of them shot her a wicked smile that gave her a feeling only a long, hot bath would rid her of.

The men were so filthy it was hard to make out their features. The stench coming off them wrinkled her nose. She swallowed and glanced at Ertemis.

His cloak was thrown back over his broad shoulders, revealing the measured rise and fall of his leather-clad chest. One hand caressed the hilt of his sword, the other rested on his thigh, holding the reins. How could he be so calm?

His hood shrouded his face from the men but she could see it. A predatory sneer twisted his mouth and his eyes—his eyes chilled her blood.

From the shadows beneath his hood, his eyes glittered preternaturally bright with a raw, savage sheen. It was an unearthly, feral glow as frightening as anything she'd ever seen. Everything the name Black Death implied seemed right at that moment and yet, not enough. A reflexive shudder ran through her.

"Get behind me, Jessalyne." He spoke without looking at her, his voice low and menacing.

She tugged at Petal's reins, trying to pull the jenny back.

The first highwayman spoke. "We'd like to thank ya for bringing the wench along. That's an extra bit a fun we didn't count on. Maybe we'll let ya watch, if yer still alive. Course the Legion don't care how we bring ya back." Spittle flew from the man's lips. He dragged the back of his hand across his mouth, smearing his already filthy face.

"I never had an elf wench before," another chimed in.

"She ain't elf. She ain't got the ears."

The leader spoke again. "Don't matter to me what kind of ears she got, so long as her other parts is the same."

The four broke into laughter. The leader nudged his horse a little closer. "Ain't you gonna fight us, muddled blood? Ain't you gonna protect your woman?"

Jessalyne wanted to know the same thing.

Ertemis raised his head. The man flinched and the laughter ceased.

"I'm not going to fight you." Ertemis's voice rumbled like thunder. "I'm going to kill you."

One of the four started to laugh again but his partners didn't join him.

The shush of metal against leather sang out as Ertemis unsheathed his sword. His Feyre gleamed in his other hand. He dug his heels into Dragon's side and the horse charged between the men. He struck with both blades, unhorsing one man and opening a gash in the leader's cheek. Dragon pivoted and Ertemis was on the next two men before they could turn, a symphony of horse and rider.

With an angry howl, the leader came after Jessalyne, his cheek bleeding rivulets through the dirt on his face. She yanked at Petal's reins, kicking the jenny into a run. The clatter of hooves on stone drowned the rush of blood in her ears. The man was right behind her, cursing at her to stop.

She fumbled for her dagger, trying to free it without dropping it. He was so close, so close and gaining. A sharp pain snapped her head back and jerked her off Petal. Jagged rocks bit into her as she smacked the ground. She yelped in pain. Stones tore through her skirt and scored her skin. The man on horseback hauled her across the ground by her braid.

He reined his horse and jumped down, winding her plait around his fist. He yanked her up and looped his arm around her neck, pressing his bloody face against her. "Now we'll see how much yer halfling wants to fight."

Jessalyne gagged. His breath stunk almost as much as the muck-crusted fabric of his tunic. She yanked her arm up to elbow him but the deadly sparkle of his dagger stopped her.

"Don't think I won't use it," he snarled, pressing it into her ribs. She staved off the warm tendrils of fear curling over her skin. If she burned the man, he would kill her for sure.

"Let. Her. Go." Ertemis stood over the bodies of two of the men, Dragon behind him. The third man was simply gone, horse and all. Ertemis's eyes glowed like moonlight.

The man shook his head. "Drop yer blades and get on yer knees. Yer life or hers, you decide."

Ertemis met Jessalyne's gaze. He mouthed the word fire then slanted his eyes away.

He wanted her to use her magic? He was the Black Death, couldn't he do something? She shook her head.

"Don't move," the man seethed in her ear.

The blades slipped from Ertemis's grasp, falling to the ground with a dull clang. The sound tore at Jessalyne's heart. He was giving up. He dropped to his knees, head down. She couldn't use her powers to hurt after what she'd done to her father. She just couldn't. She'd vowed not to.

The man yanked her along as he walked toward Ertemis. His arm tightened around her neck. She coughed and his blade dug into her side. "Quiet."

The man tugged her head back and lifted his blade to her throat while he spoke to Ertemis. "Did ya think ya could kill my men and I'd let yer wench live? Shame to snuff such a fair piece."

He nuzzled his crooked nose into Jessalyne's hair, inhaling. The blood from his cheek matted the loose strands to her face. "Course with all the coin yer hide'll bring me, I'll be able to buy the finest wenches in town."

He pushed the blade into her skin. Something warm trickled down her neck. The man spat on the ground in front of Ertemis. "Look at me when I'm talking to ya. I want ya to watch me slice her pretty throat."

Ertemis raised his head. His eyes blazed with lethal fire.

The man recoiled. Ertemis sprung. He grabbed the man's hand and forced it up with a sickening snap, whipping the man around and spinning Jessalyne out of his grasp. She landed on her hands and knees, gulping deep draughts of air.

Like a great black sea, Ertemis's cloak swelled around him. There was a soft crunching sound and the man dropped to the stones by Ertemis's boots. She crumpled onto her side, exhausted, panting. She closed her eyes. It was too much.

"Jessalyne," his voice was fraught with concern. He was at her side, brushing her hair back, cradling her. "Open your eyes. Speak to me, lelaya."

He'd killed those men as easily and thoughtlessly as swatting gnats. "I want to go back to the grove," she whimpered. Her throat hurt, her backside and legs were bruised from riding and scraped from being dragged, the back of her dress was shredded, her head ached from having her hair pulled, and the man she had hired to protect her was being hunted by men who wanted to kill him – men he had no issue killing in return. Time to go home.

"Open your eyes. Please."

She did. His eyes were silver-speckled black again. No lethal glow, no deep threatening glitter. She rubbed her throat. There was blood on her fingers.

"I know, sweeting, he nicked you." He hesitated, as though it hurt to speak. "You don't want to go home," he whispered. "You want to see Shaldar City."

She breathed a deep shuddering breath. "Why were those men after you?"

His mouth creased, but he didn't answer. Instead, he lifted her gently and carried her to Dragon's side. If he noticed her flinch at his touch, he didn't show it. He set her down, unhooked his waterskin and offered it to her. "Drink."

She managed a little water, then asked again. "Why were those men chasing us? That man was going to kill me."

"No danger of that now."

"Answer me." She fisted her hands to stop the shaking. It didn't work.

He went to brush a strand of hair off her cheek and she pushed his hand away. His jaw twitched. "There's a bounty on my head."

A bounty? She limped to a large boulder and sat, wincing when her bruised backside came in contact with the stone. He'd dispatched the highwaymen so fast he'd been hard to follow. She shuddered, remembering how the leader had slumped at his feet in a boneless heap. Her imagination took over. Thief. Murderer. Rapist. She spoke in a very small voice. "Why is there a bounty on you?"

"I left the Legion without paying my conscription price."

That didn't sound so awful. "Why didn't you just pay it? Isn't that what Valduuk did?"

"I tried. Every time I had enough, the amount increased. They didn't plan on letting me leave. Ever."

"Why leave, then? You made it seem like it wasn't such a bad life."

"It wasn't the life, it was the work they made me do."

"Why? You said you were a messenger."

He scanned the area. "Leave it at that."

"No, I won't. I paid you to protect me. I deserve to know." You kissed me, she wanted to say, you kissed me and that gives me some right, doesn't it?

"You ask too many blasted questions." His eyes swept the horizon.

"Ertemis."

"What?"

"Tell me," she demanded.

He looked at her then, his jaw set, his eyes dark and liquid. "I was the Legion's most proficient assassin. That's why I'm called the Black Death." His mouth twisted. "I couldn't do it anymore." The sky rumbled, threatening rain.

She sat quietly staring at the stones by her feet. An assassin. Who'd saved her. Held her. Kissed her. A man whose values went against everything she believed in. "Why not? Killing those men didn't seem to bother you."

He shifted his weight to his other foot. "Those men would have killed you. Or worse."

"Wouldn't make for good business, would it? Dead employers give poor references."

"Jessalyne, that's not—"

"Please, I've had enough." She twisted away from him, the pain in her legs now seeming like fair payment for aligning herself with such a creature.

"Do you think I enjoy the blood of others on my hands? Do you? Do you know that my senses let me hear each dying heart beat? Let me feel the waves of fear and pain and pleading desperation? With every death I've dealt, I've died a little myself. I had to leave before there was nothing left of me."

"You were right to leave, then." She picked bits of debris off her skirt. "Perhaps you should have left sooner."

"I tried."

"Really? That implies failure. I don't see you as a man who fails to get what he wants."

"I wouldn't expect a healer to understand."

"Good, because I don't."

"Would you rather I let those men take you?"

She met his eyes then. "No."

"Then let that be your first lesson in understanding, healer." He exhaled a long, ragged breath. "That nick on your throat needs cleaning." Wetting a corner of his cloak from his water skin, he knelt beside her and gently wiped off the crusted blood. "Why didn't you call fire when I asked you?"

His soothing touch couldn't keep her chin from lifting. "You had no right to ask me to use my power to hurt someone. I'm not...." She wanted to say like you, but didn't. "I just won't is all."

"All I wanted was a distraction, something to get his attention away from you. I wasn't sure I could get to him before he hurt you."

"A distraction?" She twisted her hands together.

∞

Ertemis felt shame and guilt swirl off her, sad replacements for the fear he'd felt from her earlier. It gutted him that she now held him in such low regard, but why should she be any different from anyone else. "What aren't you telling me?"

"Nothing. I'm ready to go."

He put his hands on hers to keep her seated. "I told you the truth, Jessalyne, and regardless of how poorly you liked it, you will do the same for me."

Her anger washed over him then. "Fine, you want to know? I'll tell you. I'm the reason my father left. I am. I couldn't control my power and I burned him so badly he couldn't stand to be near me. That's why I wouldn't help you. After he left, I vowed never to use my powers to hurt anyone. Ever. Do you understand?"

Haemus's scars were from her. Ertemis nodded. "But you didn't burn him on purpose, did you?"

"Of course not. He was my father." She rested her forehead against her palms. "My mother had just died, I was upset, he grabbed me...it just happened. I didn't even know I was capable of such awfulness."

"You can't blame yourself." He tipped her chin up so he could look into her eyes. "It wasn't your fault."

"Yes, it was. If I were normal, it never would have happened. You don't know what it's like..." The words spilled out of her, anguish burnishing her eyes.

"I know very much what it's like to be despised for something you can't help."

"You do know, don't you?" She looked at him with new understanding. Perhaps she would forgive him yet. "Does it make you afraid of me?"

The tremor in her voice pierced him. "Nay, sweeting, it doesn't make me afraid of you."

"But I could burn you."

He cupped her face in his hands. "But you won't. Just as I would never hurt you. I know you fear me, at least a little. I don't blame you. I would fear me too."

She bit the inside of her cheek. Her gaze imprisoned him more tightly than the Legion ever had. "No one ever wanted to touch me—"

"I want to touch you. Will you let me?"

She nodded.

He kissed her firmly, trying to tell her with his mouth that she had already branded him with the sweetness of her mouth, already set him aflame with her silky skin, already kindled a fire in him that wouldn't be put out. She was everything good that he was not. If ever he'd had a reason to leave his past behind, she was it, and he wished for the thousandth time since meeting her that he was a better man. A man worthy of her.

A blasted clap of thunder broke them apart. He searched the sky. "Rain won't hold off much longer. We should go."

"I don't feel like traveling but I don't want to camp here." She rubbed her throat, but her fingers strayed to her lips, still swollen from his kiss.

"We'll go only as far as the next town. There should be one on the other side of the passage." He brushed a strand of hair back behind her ear. "You're so beautiful."

She shook her head. "No, I'm not."

"Aye, you are." He took her hand and pressed it to his chest. "I swear it."

Her eyes sparkled. "No one's ever told me that but my mother." She took her hand back, brushed it over her hair, and tugged the leather thong from the end of her braid. "My hair is a mess."

"Here, let me." He moved behind her and worked his fingers through her hair, unweaving the silky braid. She moaned softly and leaned into his hands. He picked out the debris, brushed it smooth with his fingers and plaited the top section the way he'd once done his mother's. He tied it off with the leather thong. "There."

She reached back, feeling the braid with her fingers. She pulled it over her shoulder. "I've never seen a braid like that. It's lovely. Thank you."

"It's an elven plait." He offered her a hand. "Let's get out of here."

She started to rise but her legs buckled. She dropped back onto the boulder and winced.

"What's wrong?"

"I'm fine, just a little sore." She groaned as she tried to get up again.

"It's my fault." He frowned. "I should know well enough you aren't used to this riding."

"I'm fine," she muttered through gritted teeth. She stood, grimacing.

"Enough. You'll ride with me." He lifted her onto his saddle and threaded Petal's leads through Dragon's tack.

Easing up behind her, he put her across his lap, supporting her with one arm around her back. She nestled against him without argument. She soon drifted off, her hand on his chest.

He held Dragon to a brisk pace until they were through the pass. For Jessalyne's sake, he hoped they reached a town soon. She deserved a hot bath and a soft bed.

She shifted just as a town appeared on the horizon.

"Are you awake?"

"Mmhmm."

"There's a town ahead. Do you see it?"

"No, but I believe you. How much longer before we arrive?"

Ertemis checked the sun's position. "Probably before lastlight. You'll have your hot meal and long soak soon enough."

"How did you know I wanted those things?"

"You said you wanted a hot meal, a bath and to sleep on a feather mattress."

"I wished for those things but I didn't say them out loud."

"You didn't speak them?" He raised an eyebrow.

"No." She shook her head.

He muttered under his breath.

She tipped her head. "What did you say?"

"I said you infect my brain. Mindsight has never been one of my stronger gifts."

She went quiet. "I don't want you listening to my thoughts."

"Do tell. Are they full of impurities concerning me?" He teased. Just tell me what they are and I'll make them come true.

She gave him a wicked look.

"I know," he sighed. "I'm a beast. Perhaps you should have considered that before you hired me, sweeting." He winked at her. "Are you feeling better?"

"A little. I'll be fine tomorrow."

He patted Dragon's neck. "We will all be better tomorrow."

Chapter Eight

They passed through the town's gate and Jessalyne's curiosity at the sights and sounds took over. The women wore delicate bell-sleeved gowns, the skirts split down the front to reveal another decorative skirt beneath. She would gladly replace her tattered outfit for one of those beautiful dresses.

She realized the townspeople's odd looks were not just for Ertemis but for her as well. "Why are they looking at us so?"

"Elysium is somewhere close to Shaldar City, which we steadily approach. These people must see light elves on occasion. With your hair covering the tips of your ears, you pass for one. They stare because an elfess without a large guard of male elves is rare. Not to mention you're sharing my saddle. They'll leave us alone. We're only gossip fodder to them. They wouldn't dream of bothering us." He winked. "Little do they know how dangerous you are."

"It's still impolite," she said. "They judge what they don't understand."

"You judge them by life in the grove. That's a high measure to live up to."

"You're right." She stared back at a few, making them turn their heads. "So we're gossip fodder, are we?"

"Aye," he sighed.

"Sir!" She called out to a well-dressed gentleman crossing the street.

"Jessalyne," Ertemis hissed.

The man looked over his shoulder as if searching for someone else. He removed a hat of crumpled brown felt, brushed his hand across his hair and swallowed. Tugging down the points of his vest, he came toward them. "Yes, mistress elf?"

"Where is your best guesthouse located?" Fortunately, the front of her clothes was in better shape than the back.

"Down two streets at the end of the market quarter. The Gilded Rose, my lady." The man's gaze darted from Jessalyne to Ertemis to the ground.

She nodded and gave him her best highborn smile. "Thank you, sir." She turned to Ertemis. "Shall we?"

He grinned and shook his head. "Impetuous wench."

On the way to the inn, Jessalyne noted several clothiers in the market quarter. The gowns in one of the shop windows deserved a second look before they left in the morning. She'd have to have something new after being dragged.

Ertemis helped her dismount. Jessalyne smiled as they walked into The Gilded Rose. The décor reminded her of Valduuk's private quarters; lush fabrics, delicately carved woods, thick rugs. She tugged at Ertemis's sleeve. "Very nice."

"And very expensive, no doubt." There was no one at the desk, so he rang a little crystal bell dangling from an ornate brass stand. Jessalyne laughed when he rolled his eyes at the frippery.

A thin man with spectacles came through a door behind the desk. His eyebrows rose when he saw the pair waiting for him. "Welcome to the Gilded Rose. What might I do for you?"

Ertemis spoke. "We need one night and stable space for two animals."

"Yes, sir, let me see..." He paged through a leather bound book. "Ah, yes, I have a fine room for you and your..." His brows rose again, punctuating his unspoken question.

"Wife." Jessalyne grinned. Now that was gossip fodder.

Ertemis narrowed his eyes at her.

"Will you require anything else?" The innkeeper asked.

"Have a hot bath sent up immediately." Ertemis answered. "Afterwards, we'll have dinner in our room. Send ale for me and honeyed wine for the lady." He looked at Jessalyne. "Does that suit you?"

"Do you have any of those little chocolate cakes?" She asked the man behind the desk.

"We do, my lady."

"Fine. A plate of those and some cinnamon tea," she added.

"Send breakfast at firstlight," Ertemis finished.

"Very good, sir." The proprietor handed them a key and rang for a groom to collect the animals.

Ertemis gave Jessalyne the key and went to get their bags.

The innkeeper busied himself behind the desk, glancing up at her occasionally. "Lovely inn you have," she commented.

"Thank you, my lady. Have you traveled through our town before?"

"No." She pursed her lips, giddy with the charade of being an elf. "My lord husband rarely lets me out. He has such a jealous temper. So quick to draw his blade." The man's eyes went big and she bit her cheek to quell a giggle.

Ertemis came in, bags slung over one shoulder. "I thought you would have gone up to the room."

"Not yet." She gestured toward the innkeeper. "We've been chatting."

Ertemis looked at the man, who blinked furiously. The proprietor nodded, muttered something about his wife calling and scurried back through the door.

"What have you been up to?"

She walked toward the stairs leading to the rooms. "Nothing. Nothing at all," she called over her shoulder, unable to suppress her laughter this time.

The room met Jessalyne's expectations, but the bed exceeded them. Never had she seen such a bed. Carved of some pale wood, the bed stood high off the ground, with matching stairs on either side. At each corner, tall posts supported a gossamer silk canopy and silk curtains to close the sides of the bed for privacy.

"Oh," she sighed. "I've never seen anything so lovely." She ran her hand over the pierced work coverlet. "This bedding is silk." A delicate pattern of roses and vines edged the linens. "It's beautiful."

"It should be considering the coin this room cost." He threw his cloak across a nearby chair and unbuckled his sword belt. "We could have a week's lodging at any tavern for the same amount."

"If the townspeople are going to talk, we might as well give them something worthwhile to talk about."

He gave her a curious look. "Is that why you told the innkeeper you were my wife?"

She nodded. "I didn't want him thinking I was some pink skirt."

He raised his hands. "Jessalyne, you look nothing like a courtesan. With your coloring, they think you're high born, trust me. And never in all my days have I seen an elfess fallen to that profession."

A knock sounded at the door.

"I believe your bath has arrived." Ertemis moved to open the door and two valets came in, carrying a large copper tub between them. A maid followed with the first of two steaming buckets of water.

The parade continued until the tub was full. The maid put a basket of toiletries and towels next to the tub and left.

Ertemis sat on the edge of the bed and removed his breastplate, grinning. "This will be very entertaining."

"You're not staying while I bathe."

"Don't I get a bath too?"

"You may bath when you return."

"You would prefer your husband dally with the wenches at the local tavern while you stay here? You do want the townspeople to talk."

"You are not my husband." She scowled at him. Why must he be so difficult at times?

"You told the innkeeper I was. Now, you either shame yourself or deal with the consequences of your falsehood."

He pulled his boots off and settled back on the bed, arms folded behind his head.

Jessalyne clenched her fists. "Very well. I'm tired and sore and I don't have the energy for this. You may stay but you will not watch!"

"How do you intend to stop me?"

She looked around the room. There had to be something...she went to her pack and dug though it.

"The water's getting cold," he called to her.

"Aha!" She pulled a linen square from her bag.

"I fail to see how that will help."

"Failing to see is exactly the point. I am going to blindfold you. Then you may stay."

Shaking his head, he sat up as she came toward him. "I can't believe I'm letting you to do this to me." He spread his knees and she moved between them.

"Very kind of you," she said sarcastically. Brushing his hair back over his shoulders, she wondered if he could sense her body's response to being so close to him. Best get the blindfold on him quickly.

"You know, everything you're trying to hide I saw quite clearly when I pulled you from the pool by the cave."

"Hush!"

He put his hands around her slender waist and listened as her heart beat a little faster. Like sun-warmed seedberries, the delicate scent of desire drifted into his senses. She fought it, but she wanted him. His hands slid up her ribcage, settling beneath the curve of her breasts. Her soft warmth seeped into his skin, tightening the muscles in his thighs.

She finished tying the sash and stepped out of his embrace. "Can you see?"

"I can see exactly what you looked like as the sun sparkled through the water, your hair swirling around your shoulders, the fullness of your—"

"Enough! Can you see through the blindfold?" She clamped her hand over his mouth and he kissed it, causing her to pull it away.

"Nay. Most unfortunate, considering you're about to bathe in front of me." He did his best to sound dejected, and stretched back on the bed, allowing his senses to take over.

She waved a hand in front of his face.

Never in his life had suppressing his tongue been so difficult. He wanted to tell her the blindfold couldn't stop him from sensing the movement of her hand and wouldn't stop him from imagining her in the tub.

He settled onto the bed, listening to Jessalyne turn. The muffled drop of fabric told him she'd undressed. Heat traveled down his spine at the thought. The basket of toiletries scraped across the floor. Dulcet tones of moving water reached his ears as she stepped into the tub.

Her soft gasp revealed he'd been right. The water had cooled. Air moved as she waved her hand. The room warmed slightly. She'd used her magic to reheat the water. Water sloshed. "Ohhh...this feels so good."

"I'm sure it does." She went still. He could feel her staring at him. "Did you forget about me?"

"No."

He listened to the soft splashes and imagined her bare, wet body only steps away. The aching need to touch her resurfaced, lancing through him like sharpened steel. He moaned softly, mad with distraction.

"Did you say something?"

"Nay." Did she have any idea the torture she put him through? He should have left.

Water splattered and something skittered across the floor. The soap. Ertemis heard it spin to a stop on the other side of the bed. "Lose something?"

"Yes. My soap."

"Tell me where it is and I'll fetch it for you."

"No, I'll get it." Water sloshed as she started to get out.

"Jessalyne, I'm blindfolded and you're in the bath. Don't be silly, you'll get everything wet. I told you I can't see."

"All right. It's on the other side of the bed."

Ertemis got up and made a show of feeling for his surroundings, arms out, feet shuffling. "Here?"

"No, further toward the wall, over the other way...there, yes, that's it."

He snatched the soap and walked directly to the tub.

"What are you doing?"

He knelt behind her. "So many questions. If I must be sightless, perhaps you should be soundless, lelaya." He pulled his shirt off and threw it back toward the bed. "Lean forward."

A gentle sloshing said she complied. He dipped the soap into the water and lathered her back.

She flinched at his touch then relaxed as his fingers massaged in slow sudsy circles. "Ohhh...," she sighed.

He smiled, moving her hair over her shoulder. The warm velvet of her skin set his body aflame. Pressing along the bow of her spine, he ran his thumbs below the water line, stopping above the lush rounding of her backside.

"Maybe you shouldn't—"

"Don't like the way it feels?"

"It feels wonderful, but—"

"Shhh...it's been a long day, sweeting. Let me take care of you."

She bent farther forward, giving him access to more of her back. His calloused fingers drew gasps of pleasure from her, filling him with satisfaction.

Her pulse quickened, and her scent filled his nose. Images flooded his head; waking up to her sleepy form curled around him, the tilt of her head when she asked him a question. What was she doing to him? It occurred to him that without the blindfold, the sight of her wet body would probably finish him.

Releasing the soap, he cupped water in his hands and rinsed her back. His lips grazed the side of her neck and she bent her head to his kisses. Whispering her name against her skin, he felt her shudder.

Keeping one hand on her shoulder, he slipped the other below the water's surface, splaying his fingers over her the curve of her belly. What she would look like ripe with his child? Stunned, he shook the image from his head and pulled her tight against the back of the tub. Water sloshed onto his trousers.

Inhaling sharply, she grabbed his wrist. "I can't..."

"I just want to touch you. You're as soft as rose petals. I promise, my hand will go no lower, sweeting."

Feathering kisses on her neck, he moved higher, nipping her earlobe between his teeth. She moaned and reached for him, weaving her fingers into his hair to draw his lips harder against her flesh.

"Ohhh, Ertemis..."

Encouraged by her whispering his name, he slid his hand higher, grazing the underside of her breast. She was softer than rose petals, softer than any woman he'd touched before; deliciously, decadently, velvety soft. And she wanted him. The thought was almost his undoing.

She tipped her head back. "I shouldn't do this..."

"Don't you like my kisses, lelaya?"

"I think I like them too much."

He found her trembling lips and was reminded of her innocence but she met his kiss with a hunger that begged to be sated. He kissed her hard, and she moaned.

His hand swept up to cup her breast, the fullness spilling over his fingers. She arched, pressing further into his hands. Desire overwhelmed him. He felt powerless to control himself.

The pad of his thumb brushed a tender bud and she recoiled, a tremor running through her. She pulled out of his embrace. Water spilled over the tub sides. "I can't," she whispered. "I can't do this".

Ertemis knelt at the end of the tub. His empty hands ached to feel her silk again. "Please, I need you." He dropped his head, stunned by the raw urgency coursing through him. Never had a woman made him beg.

He heard her rapid breathing, the staccato rhythm of her heart. He was too filled with his own desire to read her feelings but her silence sounded like refusal. Maybe she didn't want him after all.

"You can't cast your spell over me, then leave me unsated. I am not a toy to be played with."

Wet footstep squeaked across the floor. "I wasn't toying with you. And I certainly didn't mean to upset you. I just can't do this. I'm sorry."

He stood and ripped the blindfold off. "If you deny you want me, you're lying." She had wrapped herself in a towel.

"I'm sorry." She gripped the towel so hard her knuckles were white.

"Sorry?" Rejection overwhelmed his aching need. Furious for pushing her, he stood, clenching his fists at his sides. He should have taken things slower. He growled a curse, unable to temper the pain of her refusal. He was such a fool.

Her gaze fixed on the bulge in his trousers. Her eyes widened. "Does that hurt?"

He stared at her in disbelief. "Your ignorance does not amuse me." Jaw set, he grabbed his shirt and pulled it over his head before tugging his boots on. He sensed her fear. He needed to leave before he frightened her further.

"Ertemis, please..."

He grabbed his sword belt. "I know I'm low born, but this is the first time you've truly made me feel it. You needn't worry about me touching you again."

Her eyes glittered angrily. She clutched the bath sheet around her.

"Don't look at me like that," he snapped. "This is who I am. The cold hearted assassin. You've made it clear you think me a beast, don't be surprised when I act like one."

He finished buckling the belt and gave her one last look. "Would it have been the worst thing in the realm to give yourself to me? To be with a man who truly..." He leashed his tongue, unwilling to finish. What black magic did she possess to fill his head with such thoughts? He cared for no one.

"My mother's letter said I must remain chaste or lose my powers."

"If you believe that, you're a foolish child. I know one thing. The men of Shaldar's court will make short work of your precious chastity. Magewoman? Try mistress." He yanked the door open.

"Go ahead, leave. I'm used to being left. Why should you be any different?" Jessalyne said.

Snarling, he slammed the door behind him.

Jessalyne melted to the floor, unsure if crying or screaming would make her feel better. How dare he say those things to her? A deep, shuddering sob racked her body. What if he spoke the truth about the king's court? She shook her head. It couldn't be.

Her hand went to the pendant around her neck. There was such heartache in his eyes. She realized suddenly what he had been about to say and her throat constricted. No. She would not cry over that wretched creature another time.

Instead, she dressed in her tunic. A knock rang out and her first thought was of Ertemis. She answered, expecting an apology, but instead found the valets come to remove the tub and serve dinner.

It took them a few trips to carry away the bathwater and Jessalyne sat looking out the window while she waited. She kept hearing his voice in her head. The more she thought about what he'd said, the more her blood rose.

"My lady?" The steward called to her.

Jessalyne turned. "Yes?"

"Shall I serve dinner now or will you be waiting for your husband?"

"You may serve me now." Ignoring the raised eyebrows, she sat at the small table with her head high. The time had come for more than just a change of clothes. Her future lay in Shaldar City, not with some temperamental ex-assassin. Her mother would cringe that she'd felt affection for such a man.

Making a concerted effort not to think about him, she ate her meal with great concentration, every bite studied and tasted thoroughly. She nibbled one of the chocolate cakes but her appetite for such things had disappeared.

After dinner, she practiced her magic and discovered she could make both hot and cold spheres of flame. Still, no Ertemis.

Exhausted from the day's events and the knockdown with him, she got into bed. She was almost asleep when a raucous thumping on the door startled her. She opened it to find Ertemis, eyes glazed. He smelled like a tavern, ale and smoke and horses.

"Miss me, princess?" He stumbled into the room, pulling at his shirt.

She wrinkled her nose, backing away. "You're sotted!"

"Sotted with the softness of your skin..." He reached for her, just as he saw the remainders of dinner on the table. "Food! Fine idea. What have we?" He rummaged through the leftovers.

"I'm going to bed." She turned down the coverlet, hoping he would take the hint and leave.

He whirled around, almost tripping himself. "That's a wonderful idea." He yawned, tugging at his shirt again but it caught in his belt and held tight. After some struggling, he realized the problem and unbuckled his belt, letting both sword and belt clatter to the floor.

"What's a wonderful idea?"

He winked at her. "That innocent country act is very charming, lelaya." He dropped into one of the dining chairs, causing it to scrape across the floor. Yanking his boots off, he set one in the middle of the table.

"What are you rambling about? And why won't you tell me what that word means?" She climbed under the covers, keeping an eye on him.

Standing, he mumbled something she could not understand.

"What did you say?"

"Lelaya means heart of my heart."

Heart of my heart. The words echoed in her head. Even in his current state, she couldn't take her eyes off him. His hair spilled over his bare chest as he fumbled with the fastening on his trousers. Soused or not, he was a stunning sight.

"What are you doing?" She watched him teeter backwards.

In his attempt to undress, he fell back into the chair, nearly splintering it. At last, he drew his trousers off and stood up.

Jessalyne's eyes went wide. "Put your trousers back on, you sotted beast!"

"Pet names for me already?" He flashed her a grin, clearly pleased with his own wickedness. "Better than Black Death, I s'pose."

"Put your clothes on right now!"

"Stop looking." At that, he laughed so hard he almost fell over.

Jessalyne turned away, clamping her hand over her eyes.

"Aye, small glimpses are best at first. I am told 'tis quite overwhelming to see all of me at once."

The bed sank as he sprawled next to her.

"Let's have a kiss before bed, hmmm?" He slurred. "So beautiful..." His fingers skimmed her arm.

She stiffened at the touch that had so recently filled her with pleasure. How could he be so tender one moment and so wretched the next? She couldn't take it any longer. Turning to face him, she snapped. "Stop this behavior or...or...I will set you on fire."

He blinked, reeling back at her words. Blank faced, he stared at her for a moment then erupted in laughter. "Saucy wench! Games, is it?" He swept her into his arms and made to kiss her.

She cried out to him in her mind, begging him to stop.

As if struck, he pulled back. "No need to yell, sweeting."

"Ertemis, please, this isn't you. It's the ale and your hurt feelings." She held his face in her hands. "I'm sorry."

"Hurt feelings? Assassins don't have feelings, silly girl." He went an odd shade of greenish grey. For a moment, she thought he might retch. "I would never hurt you, lelaya. Never." Grabbing one of the bedposts, he hoisted himself up, lurched to the other side of the bed and collapsed face first onto the coverlet.

She stared at the naked, besotted elf snoring beside her. In all her dreams of the future, never had she imagined this.

Chapter Nine

A bird twittered on the windowsill, waking Jessalyne. Yawning, she stretched and propped herself up on her elbows. Ertemis hadn't moved from where he'd fallen.

In the golden glow of firstlight, she studied him. Despite all that had passed between them the night before, she still found him fascinating. His luminous soot-dark skin and muscled curves mesmerized her and for once, she looked as much as she wanted. She was as bad as Corah. Pity, he was such a barbarian. She sighed. Did it matter if he was a barbarian? If not for her mother's letter, she'd be curled around him, as naked as the day she was born. Wouldn't she?

Blushing at her bold thoughts, she slipped out of bed before she did something foolish. It wouldn't do to have him wake up and find her hands tracing the runes along his spine, trailing down to cup his... Enough. She forced the thought out of her head.

Breakfast would be here soon, and the room was a mess. She righted the chair he'd tipped over and snatched his tunic off a bedpost. His trousers were crumpled beneath the table. She laid his clothes over a chair on his side of the bed.

One of his boots sat squarely in the tureen. She pulled it out and wiped off the traces of soup. Just as she put the pair by the door and leaned his sword against the wall, there were two sharp taps on the door. Breakfast had arrived.

On her way to let the valet in, she yanked the bed curtains shut. No need for the man to see Ertemis lying there naked. Besides, she would never manage breakfast with the elf's bare rump in plain sight. Her gaze lingered on the offending body parts. No, it simply would not do.

Another sharp knock. She hurried to the door. "Quietly please," she whispered. "He still sleeps."

The steward nodded and quickly removed the dinner dishes and laid the morning's repast on the table. He gave her a short bow and left, shutting the door softly behind him.

She poured a mug of tea. Her stomach grumbled. She lifted the platter covers to reveal honeycakes, slices of smoked eel, and baked eggs. How Ertemis slept through the aroma, she had no idea.

Fixing a plate, she planned to bolt her breakfast, change out of her nightrobe then walk across the street to the clothiers she'd seen yesterday. Ertemis would undoubtedly snore the morning away. He showed no signs of rousing.

She rummaged through her saddlebags for a pouch of coins, setting each of the heavy sacks on the table. The smallest she left on the table, hefting the others in her hands. Her gaze drifted to Ertemis again. There was one more thing to take care of before she left.

ꙮ

The clothier's shop made mistress Chara's seem pitiful. Jessalyne felt the country girl through and through. Trimmed with embroidery and lace, ribbons and velvet, the gowns kindled a longing in her for a life never known. She imagined the ladies in King Maelthorn's court wore gowns just like these. She ran her hands over the beautiful fabrics, dreaming of days to come.

"May I assist you?" A red-haired woman with a boy's build approached her. Haughtiness dripped from her words like grease off a rasher of bacon.

"Yes, thank you. I would like a dress."

I see." The woman's gaze swept over Jessalyne, stopping at her neckline. A thin smile crossed the woman's lips. "That's a lovely pendant you're wearing. Let me select a few of our finer dresses for you to try, my lady."

She clapped her hands and a young girl scurried out from the back room. "Fetch the new gowns from Romman." She turned back to Jessalyne. "Right this way, my lady."

The young clerk brought dresses out one by one for Jessalyne's approval. Each one was more beautiful than the next, but the last dress surpassed them all.

"Ohh, that is most lovely," Jessalyne said. "I will try that one, please."

In a flurry of fabric, the sales women undressed her and fit her into the gown. They led her to a tall mirror on the rear wall.

Made of luminous sea-green silk, the dress cut low and straight across Jessalyne's bosom. Belled sleeves revealed snug undersleeves of indigo. Matching vines and leaves of gold crept around the hem and up the front edges of the over skirt, split down the middle to show the underskirt of indigo silk. Ribbons of indigo crisscrossed her narrow waist.

"Of course, the look is not complete without the matching slippers and waist belt." The red haired woman tallied the goods on her fingers, smiling. "I'm sure a lady of your bearing will want every piece necessary."

Still focused on the image in the mirror, Jessalyne nodded. "Yes, of course."

The woman sent the young clerk to fetch the items and fussed about, smoothing the skirt and chattering on about the fabric quality until the girl returned.

"Ah, here we are." After buckling the belt around Jessalyne's waist, she slid Jessalyne's feet into the deep green leather slippers. "Lovely. Just lovely. You'll be wearing it, I assume? Pity to put your other...outfit back on," she sniffed.

"Yes, yes of course." Jessalyne couldn't look away from the mirror. She barely recognized herself. Because she was looking at the king's magewoman in training.

"Now, about your hair. We have some combs—"

"No. I wear it down." Let that foul halfling be reminded of what he'd no longer have.

"As you wish." The woman barked at the young clerk to wrap Jessalyne's things. "Then there just remains the rather tiresome matter of the bill."

Jessalyne opened her money pouch, accidentally spilling two gold coins onto the shop floor.

The young clerk's eyes widened. The woman snatched up the coins, smiling. "That will settle your bill nicely."

The innkeeper nodded to Jessalyne when she returned. "My compliments on your purchase, mistress elf. You are as lovely as the isle of Elysium is purported to be. Most sheyneya," he said.

She gave him a curious look.

"I apologize, my grasp of your mother tongue is weak at best. I thought sheyneya elven for 'beautiful'."

"We accent the end not the middle," she bluffed. "Very kind of you." She hurried back to the room before he got a better look at her ears. Pretending was tricky business.

Fitting the key in the lock, she opened the door. Dressed in trousers only, Ertemis stood at the window. The runes along his spine shone softly. His breakfast sat uneaten on the table. She shut the door. He said nothing.

She set her bundled outfit on the bed and gathered up her other things, packing them into her saddlebags. She struggled for something to say to him, desperate to ease the tension. "What does sheyneya mean?"

He answered without turning. "It's pronounced shey'naya. It means radiantly beautiful."

Well, he was speaking to her. "Thank you." She packed the last saddlebag and stood by the bed, wondering what to do next. The silence didn't bother her so much as the reason for it. At the very least, he owed her an apology.

"I'm ready to go." Perhaps that would rouse him out of his foul mood. Nothing. "I'm ready to go," she raised her voice.

"I heard you the first time." He rubbed his brow. "Must you shout?"

"I wasn't shouting." This was going to be a fun day.

৪৩

Ertemis had watched her crossing the street below, sure he was prepared for the sight of her. He wasn't. Even his aching head didn't diminish her beauty. Shey'neya, indeed.

Saladan's trousers, he was such a fool. She should hate him for how he'd treated her. He groaned at the ache in his head and the anguish in his heart. She belonged at court, not his side.

Mortified by how he'd acted, he still thought it best not to apologize. Let her hate him. Leaving her in Shaldar City would sting less if she wanted nothing to do with him. It tore at him not to gather her into his arms and beg her forgiveness, but he was done making a fool of himself.

"Well?" She stared at him.

"Aye, the gown suits you," he groused. Her shapeless tunic and overvest had a new appeal.

"I asked if you were ready to go. I would like to leave sometime today." Jessalyne's eyes sparkled with irritation.

Good. The more she despised him, the less this would hurt. He hoped. Scowling at her without answering, he went to get his tunic. She backed up as he came toward her, skirting around the table to pour a cup of tea. Her hand shook as she lifted the teapot.

So that was it. She was finally afraid of him. "Don't worry." The fabric muffled his voice as he pulled his tunic on. "I've learned my place." He continued dressing, his back to her. "I said I would not touch you again and I meant it." He turned and looked at her directly. "Even if you beg."

"I'm not afraid of you and I wouldn't beg you for water if I were burning in Hael," she snapped.

He threw both their packs over his shoulder. "I'll be sure to remember that when I see you there." Grinding the heel of his boot into the floor, he moved toward the door without waiting for her.

She charged after him, muttering under her breath. When he stopped at the desk, she stormed past and went outside to wait. He paid the innkeeper, watching through the window as a groomsman brought Dragon and Petal round. Jessalyne mounted, ready to be on her way.

Ertemis dawdled inside until her frustration became evident. From the hard crease of her mouth to the tapping of her fingers on the saddle, she looked sufficiently tired of waiting.

He walked outside. "Get down."

"What?"

"Did I stutter? I have to put the saddlebags on." He didn't need her to get down to attach the bags but she wouldn't know that. Besides, getting her off the saddle kept distance between them.

She dismounted, sighing loudly. Standing with her arms crossed, she watched him work.

"Done." Ertemis lit up onto his saddle. "Let's go. I'm tired of waiting for you."

Her mouth dropped, a low growl rumbling out of her as she climbed back onto Petal. "Beast."

"Princess."

"Oaf."

"Brat."

"Brat? You…you…"

The urge to kiss her nearly unhorsed him. The angry sparks in her eyes made her more beautiful than ever. "Come now, surely you can think of better names for such a wretched creature as myself. Killer of babes, perhaps? Nay, too wordy. Dunderhead? Perhaps not, as I am, after all, quite clever. Boor? Aye, that would work nicely. Go ahead, give it a try."

She glared daggers. "Incorrigible reprobate."

He grinned. "Now, then, I knew you could do better."

She ignored him until they left the confines of town, where she drew her dagger to check what direction it indicated. "Stay on this road."

"We'll reach Shaldar City today." Ertemis said.

"Good." She kneed Petal, leaving him behind.

His stomach churned like a boy on his first battle line. He would never see her again after today and she would loathe him for the rest of her life. It was for the best. What life could he offer her? Why did she have to smell so good? He tried to think of anything but her.

The man who disgraced his mother had once lived in Shaldar City. Concentrating on how he would punish the blackguard once he found him, Ertemis lost himself in thoughts of revenge.

ଔ

Jessalyne's joy at reaching Shaldar City faded as she realized Ertemis would be leaving her there. She would never see him again. Not that he cared. Sorrow welled up at the thought. She glanced back at the angry set of his jaw. Did he have to make it so obvious how much he despised her? He would be rid of her soon enough. Maybe that would make him happy. She know it would make her happy to be rid of him. Happy to be rid of him. She repeated the phrase over and over. It wasn't very convincing.

"What did you say?" Ertemis pulled along side.

"Nothing." She nudged Petal and moved away from him. Had he heard her thoughts again? She distracted herself by thinking about how much Sryka would teach her. At last, someone would show her what to do with her gifts. Wasn't that what she always wanted?

"Jessalyne."

Ertemis's voice pulled her back to the present. "Yes?" Maybe he was finally going to apologize.

He gestured up the road, past fields of blonde wheat and green-gold hops. "There's a village ahead. We'll stop to eat there."

"I'm not hungry."

"I am."

"It's not my fault you didn't eat breakfast."

"Actually, it is, but you don't want to have that discussion with me."

"Fine."

A group of children playing on the road ahead stopped to watch the pair approached. They stared at Ertemis, little mouths agape. One boy whispered something to the lad next to him before calling out. "Sir, why are you that color?"

Ertemis grinned at the huddled group. "Because I sassed my mother and failed to do my chores."

The children looked at one another and took off running toward the village.

Jessalyne slanted her eyes at him. "Does that amuse you?"

"Trust me, their mothers will think them angels for the next few days."

They dismounted before entering the village, walking the animals in. Ertemis pulled his hood up.

An old woman, her face weathered and rough, sat outside a thatched cottage, shelling peas. Ertemis approached her. "Old mother, might someone here sell us a meal?"

She gazed up through clouded blue eyes. "Coin will get you just about anything. I've a pot of stew on for me own supper but I'll sell it to you for a handful of coppers or a piece of silver."

"Have you bread?"

"Aye, and so will you for a few more coppers."

Ertemis filled her palm with a mix of silver and copper coins.

She smiled a toothless grin. "Come in then." She sniffed the air. "You have beasts?"

"Aye."

"Brynden!" She yelled.

A young man, well tanned by fieldwork, came round the back. "Aye, Grams?"

"Feed and water the animals, lad."

He nodded. "Aye, Grams." He bowed his head in Jessalyne's direction. "My lady, you're the fairest of the lot what's passed through here in many seasons."

"How sweet of you. Brynden, is it?" She smiled at the young man's compliment.

"Aye." He nodded shyly. "You'll win the prince's hand for sure."

She furrowed her brows. "What do you mean?"

"Haven't you come to vie for the prince? To be Shaldar's next queen?"

Ertemis stepped forward. "Nay, sapling. That's not why she's come." Brynden stepped back.

"Brynden! Chatter don't get the animals tended."

"Aye, Grams." He snuck another glance at Jessalyne as he took Dragon and Petal to the village trough.

Ertemis and Jessalyne followed the woman into her cottage. The savory smell of hot stew greeted them. She motioned for them to sit at a small table near the fireplace.

"What's your name, old mother?" Ertemis asked.

"Magda." She felt along the counter for bowls.

"Mother Magda, you don't see clearly, do you?" Jessalyne's heart went out to her. How hard her life must be.

"Aye, the years have taken most of my sight. There is some light, bit of color if it's bright. Not much else. Brynden is my eyes." She ladled the stew out carefully.

Jessalyne stood. "Mother Magda, please come sit for a moment. I think I can help you."

"There's naught that can be done for an old woman."

"Please, let me try." She took the woman's arm and led her to the chair.

Magda's filmy blue eyes stared blankly across the room.

"Close your eyes, now. I'm going to touch you for a moment." When Magda shut her eyes, Jessalyne gently rested her palms on the woman's lids and called magic to her hands.

She drew the woman's blindness into herself. A veil of darkness fell over her eyes. Magda's blindness was now hers. Jessalyne imagined the film burning away and saw Magda's eyes clear and blue as a young child's. A sudden piercing pain racked her head. Her lungs ached with the effort to breath. Then, a long warm pulse of power ran through her body and it was done. Her hands dropped to her sides. "Open your eyes."

The old woman blinked several times. A smile lit her face. "My lady, I don't know what you done, but I can see. I can see clear as day!" She stood up and hugged Jessalyne. "Thank you, my lady." Her smile disappeared. "I've nothing to pay you with."

"I don't want payment." Jessalyne staggered back, reaching out to steady herself on the table. If only the room would stop spinning. Her gut twisted, but fortunately, she'd not yet eaten and had nothing to vomit. She blew out a breath and the nausea with it.

Ertemis jumped up. "Are you all right?"

"I'm fine. Just winded is all."

Magda stood and held Jessalyne's face between her calloused hands. "Child, you are most beautiful. Surely, you could win the prince if you wanted." She hesitated. "Tis a pity one such as you would end up with the likes of him, though."

"She's going to the city to study, not wed some blasted prince."

Magda glanced over at Ertemis and stiffened.

Ertemis's hood had fallen back and his ears were visible. He raised a hand, "Not to worry, old mother. I mean you no harm."

"I've heard tales of your kind..." She stopped as if she shouldn't have said anything.

"I'm the lady's hired shield, nothing more." A slight smile softened his face. "We only want a meal and then we'll be off."

"Aye, your meal." She relaxed a little as she hurried two bowls of stew and half loaf of brown bread onto the table. "My pardon, Master elf. If you travel with the lady...I meant no disrespect."

"None taken. All is well, you have my word."

Magda left, glancing back over her shoulder.

"That was a great kindness you did," Ertemis said.

"Look around you. Her life is hard enough already," Jessalyne shrugged. "It seemed right."

They walked back outside after finishing their meal and Magda rose to greet them, still smiling, "A thousand thanks for giving my eyes back, my lady."

Brynden stood holding Dragon and Petal's reins. "Aye, 'tis a great gift you've given my Grams."

Magda held a handful of coins out to Ertemis. "You gave me too much for the meal, master elf."

He shook his head. "You undercharged us. Keep it."

"Be well, both of you." Jessalyne wished her gifts could transform the thatched hut into something better.

Ertemis took the reins from the boy and mounted up, holding Petal's reins until Jessalyne mounted as well. She looked toward Shaldar City and then back at him. He tugged his hood down just as their eyes met.

Jessalyne turned back toward the city. It was definitely time to move on.

ဆ

Ertemis finally broke the silence. "Near the horizon. Can you see them?"

Jessalyne squinted. "I'm not sure what I am looking for."

"The spires of King Maelthorn's keep. Castle Ryght is known for its tall north and south towers. I can see the pennants streaming in the wind."

She stared off into the distance, her face a mask.

Wondering what kept her so silent, Ertemis opened his senses. She was a confusing mix of happy and sad. Wasn't she excited to be reaching Shaldar City?

The countryside changed the closer they traveled to the city. Fields of crops and cattle dotted the landscape. Small hamlets gave way to villages. At last, Jessalyne answered, "I see the towers now."

"Aye, we are close." Close to her forgetting him.

Before long, the city came into full view. Granite walls encompassed a colorful scene. Bright pennants flew along the wall walk and the dark shapes of guards patrolling passed beneath them. Castle Ryght rose from the city center, a majestic stronghold built of blue stone, glowing in the late afternoon sun.

"It's so much more beautiful than I expected." Jessalyne stared, eyes sparkling.

Ertemis wrinkled his nose. Cities stunk, regardless of their size. Knowing his mother's disgracer had lived within those walls made the stench of Shaldar City even harder to bear. He pulled his hood down as far as it would go. Despite the danger, he would go to the castle gates with her. Leaving Jessalyne to navigate the city alone didn't sit well.

The massive wood and iron gates of the main entrance were swung wide for daily traffic. Ertemis and Jessalyne passed through with a multitude of others; merchants and farmers with carts full of goods, carriages bearing wealthy nobles to and from the city, travelers on foot and horseback.

Ertemis read the crowd around them for greed or ambition, anything that might indicate someone was thinking of collecting on the Legion's offer. There was some apprehension, but it was mostly an undertone to the steady wave of curiosity. He scanned the crowd. Strictly human. He channeled his magic to blur his image in their minds, the best he could do in bright sun.

Jessalyne stared at each new sight drifting by in the sea of swirling activity. Her head swiveled in every direction.

Ertemis touched her arm lightly. "Mind your staring. You mark yourself as a green traveler. Thieves look for such signs."

"Thank you, I will be more careful." She glanced around, her eyes darting from woman to woman. A subtle smile lit her face. Smoothing her skirts, she announced, "I believe I will fit in well here."

He grunted. "Don't lose yourself in this melee, Jessalyne. Things are very different here. This is not Fairleigh Grove, not by any stretch of the imagination."

She pursed her lips. "I realize that. I am not a simpleton. I know life here will be different."

"I was not implying...never mind." He didn't have it in him to argue with her. Leaving things unsaid between them knotted his insides. The last time his gut had twisted this way, his mother was kissing him goodbye while a Legion commander backhanded him to stop crying. To the commander's credit, he'd never shed another tear since.

Jessalyne's voiced snuffed the memory. "I need to check my dagger."

"The king's magewoman will be in the castle."

"I just want to be sure." Sneaking the dagger out, she held it in her lap while she grasped the hilt. She turned it until the lunestone leapt to life. The line of the blade arrowed straight at Castle Ryght. She glanced at Ertemis to see if he had noticed.

"Where else did you expect her to be?" His gut twisted a little more. "Let's get this over with."

Her eyes were fixed on the stone monstrosity. "I'm going to live in the castle." It came out as a breath but Ertemis heard.

"Beware, Jessalyne. The men in the king's court are treacherous."

"I didn't think you cared."

He started to reply but shook his head. He was done bickering.

Two pairs of the king's men, resplendent in black and gold, guarded the castle gates. Their eyes locked onto Ertemis, hands tightening on their sword hilts and stances widening. He redoubled his efforts to disappear in their minds. After a moment, they relaxed.

Ertemis halted Dragon and dismounted. He motioned for her to do the same as he approached the nearest guard. "The lady has business with the king's magewoman, Sryka. She seeks entrance alone."

The guard nodded and called his superior over. They exchanged a few words and the senior guard waved his hand. The gates opened and the guard called out, "Entrance granted for the woman alone."

Jessalyne turned to face him, her lavender eyes bright with anticipation. The air was too thick. He couldn't breathe. Someone had thrown a blanket of hot, wet wool over him. She was leaving.

"I guess this is where we part." A gentle smile curved her mouth as she studied his face. She raised her hand toward him but stopped halfway, brushing an invisible strand of hair from her eyes.

"Aye." Words left him and he stood quietly, unable to say much else and feeling the fool. He burned to touch her matchless skin, to take her in his arms and kiss her honeyed lips until she forgave him of every thickheaded, dimwitted thing he'd ever said or done. With her at his side, he could be a better man, he knew it. Now he would never get that chance. He tried to read her but his roiling emotions overburdened his power. Kiss her, you dumb ox.

She bit the inside of her cheek, her smile fading. "Well, goodbye." She turned to go, and he caught her hand.

"Jessalyne..." The heat of her skin made the breath catch in his throat. Ask her to stay. Beg her.

"Yes?" The sun sparkled in her eyes, setting her face aglow.

"Be well," he mumbled, unable to get anything else out.

Her jaw went taut and the glitter in her eyes turned anger. "I'll do my best." She spun, Petal's reins in hand, and stalked through the castle gates.

Dragon whinnied softly and Petal nickered back.

He watched her go, listening to the familiar rhythm of her heartbeat, inhaling the last bit of her perfume. An undergroom came and led the jenny off. Even from the back she was the most beautiful woman he had ever seen. And he was the biggest fool to ever draw breath. A complete and utter fool.

When she disappeared from view, he trudged away from the gate, Dragon beside him. A familiar pain sprang up in him, sharper than the edge of his Feyre. He was alone. Again.

ᏇᎢ

Jessalyne hardly noticed the whirl of activity inside the castle gates. All she could think was Ertemis. Three words! That's all he'd said. Two, really. Saying her name didn't count. He must hate her. She ached for him, and he hated her. Or perhaps his cold assassin's heart didn't feel anything. She balled the fabric of her skirt in her fists. Maybe setting something on fire would make her feel better.

She was almost to the main hall when she stopped and ran back to the gate. She knew she must look like a child but she didn't care. One last glimpse, just one last look. He would see her and smile and everything would be better. When she got to the gate, he was gone. The edges of her vision blurred.

She rested her head against the iron scrolls. Why should she expect him to still be there? No one stayed in her life for long. By now, she should be used to being alone.

ൽ

Ertemis hitched Dragon outside the first tavern he found. He sat in a dark corner without touching the mug of ale in front of him. He pitched his elbows on the table and sank his head into his hands. The rhythm of her imprinted heartbeat drummed in his ears, mocking him.

The ache inside focused his thinking, and two things became clear. He needed to know his good for nothing father's name, and how to win the heart of a woman above his birth. Only one person could provide both answers. His lady mother.

He dug his fingers into his scalp. Not only did he have no idea how to get there, even if he could find it, the Elders would never let him in.

Then he recalled something his mother had once told him about finding Elysium. "You must close your eyes and open your heart," she'd said. Poor directions at best, he thought, shaking his head. Open his heart? How in Saladan's name was he supposed to do that? He pushed the ale away. Blast it! Why must women complicate everything?

Chapter Ten

Jessalyne stood in the great hall of Castle Ryght feeling invisible. Five of her cottages would not the fill the massive space.

Mosaics covered the floor and ceiling of the great hall, depicting scenes and people that meant nothing to her. The walls and support pillars were of the same blueschist granite as the exterior walls. Ornate banners hung from the rafters, displaying the king's crest as they swayed in the breeze wafting through the windows around the hall's balcony.

So many people. Which one to talk to? Someone must know how to find Sryka, but they all rushed by so quickly.

"Pardon me, miss?" She approached a young girl cleaning ashes out of one of the massive fireplaces.

"Yes, milady?" The girl wiped at her face but only succeeded in smearing another streak of soot across her cheek.

"Do you know where I might find the king's magewoman?"

"Ya doan want her."

"But I do."

The girl's eyebrows rose. "Ain't ya afraid of her, milady?"

"Afraid of her?" She smiled at the poor girl. Those who didn't understand magic were often frightened by it. "No, I'm not afraid of her."

The girl pointed one black finger across the hall. "Ask the blue thing listenin' to the troubadour. She does Mistress Sryka's biddin'." The girl curtsied and went back to shoveling ashes.

Jessalyne smiled. No one had ever curtsied to her before. She started across the hall toward the troubadour in search of a "blue thing". What the girl meant, she couldn't imagine.

The words of his song became clearer as she approached. He sang about how handsomely the prince of Castle Ryght dressed. Odd. Weren't those sorts of songs usually about sword skills or some heroic battle won?

She stood just outside the small crowd of lords and ladies gathered to listen. The tune was pleasant enough, but the nobles responded with such relish she thought city tastes were certainly different from country ones.

On the other side of the group, a tiny blue-skinned girl huddled against the wall. Jessalyne walked over and extended her hand to her. The girl ducked and Jessalyne pulled her hand back.

"Did I frighten you? I'm sorry. I only meant to introduce myself." She smiled. "I'm Jessalyne Brandborne of Fairleigh Grove." She extended her hand again.

The creature raised her head. "You don't mean to hit me?"

"Hit you!" Jessalyne started. "Why would you think that?"

"Never mind, milady." She held her hand out as Jessalyne had done. "I'm Fynna."

Jessalyne shook Fynna's hand. "Nice to meet you Fynna. You're the first person I've met with blue skin. It's a lovely color."

"Really? You think it's lovely?" Fynna smiled. "I'm a pixie. You look fey but you aren't. Your ears are round. They should be pointed, like this." She tapped the tip of her ear.

"You're right, I'm not fey. You're also the first pixie I've ever met." Jessalyne squinted at Fynna. "I thought pixies had wings?"

Fynna's mouth tightened to a hard line. "We do. Usually. That's another story. What can I do for you, milady?"

"I'm looking for Mistress Sryka."

Fynna's big eyes got even bigger. "Are you sure?"

"Yes, I've come to be her apprentice."

"Does she know you're coming?"

"Yes, but I think she expected me many years ago."

Fynna nodded. "I'll take word to her. Wait here 'til I come back and let you know what she says."

"Very well. Thank you." The pixie dashed off to a far set of steps.

౭౦

Fynna took the steps more quickly than usual. She couldn't wait to pass this tidbit on the old crone. An apprentice, indeed. Sryka would take one look at that beautiful young face and turn the lady into a toad. Or something worse.

She bounded up the last few steps. "Mistress Sryka," she called out.

The old woman came in off the wall walk. "Must you shriek, Fynna? I swear you are more bother than you're worth."

"Pardons, mistress. I have news."

"Well? Spit it out!" Sryka stared at her.

"There is a girl in the hall who says you might be expecting her. Something about being your apprentice." Fynna could not help but add, "She is quite beautiful. And young."

Sryka's mouth opened slightly, her gaze distant. "The child is here. She's here." Her eyes refocused on Fynna. "Bring her here. Now!"

"Yes, mistress." Fynna started back down the stairs. She could not recall the last time Sryka had looked so pleased.

୫

Ertemis rode without really knowing where he was going. Frustrated and disheartened by the whole day, he stopped and dismounted near a stream. Searching through his packs for an apple, his finger's brushed against something unfamiliar. He pulled the bag off Dragon's back and dumped it out. Four heavy suede pouches tumbled to the ground. Guilt lanced through him at the sight of Jessalyne's gift. Why would she do that?

She knew he needed the money to buy his freedom but he didn't understand. After everything he'd said to her and the way he'd behaved, she'd done this.

Dragon munched grass while Ertemis sat on the bank, staring at the swirling water, feeling more unworthy than he ever had in his life. He needed to talk to his mother and soon.

"Open your heart. What is that supposed to mean?" He looked at Dragon. "Do you know what that's supposed to mean?" Nose deep in a patch of young clover, Dragon ignored him.

Ertemis groaned. He leaned back against a nearby tree and closed his eyes. All he could think of was Jessalyne. He should've apologized. He should've kissed her one last time. His fingers curled, remembering the delicate silk of her skin. Her heartbeat thrummed through him. The aching melody tortured his soul. "Open my heart for what? More pain? First my mother, now Jessalyne..."

Suddenly, his mother's words became clear. He knew how to find Elysium. Besides Jessalyne, the only other heartbeat he'd imprinted was his mother's.

He threw the saddlebags back over Dragon and leapt into the saddle. "Dragon! Quit filling your belly."

Straining his senses, a sound spun through him on a tremulous thread of hope. His mother's heartbeat called to him.

Hours passed and forest gradually gave way to moor. The air softened into mist, parting to reveal a trail winding through the marsh. He knew from his mother's stories what waited on the other side.

His heart hammered when the inland sea of Lythe came into view. A long pier ran from the end of the trail out into the water. The Ferryman lingered at the pier's end, waiting. Although Ertemis saw nothing but swirling brume, he knew the isle of Elysium was there, somewhere beyond even fey sight.

The Ferryman beckoned. Ertemis dismounted, leading Dragon. There was no sound as they walked down the pier, no hooves against wood, no jangling tack, not even birdsong. It unnerved Ertemis but he remained calm. He knew the Ferryman served as the final line of defense for the isle.

Dragon walked onto the ferry first, surprising Ertemis with his willingness. With both of them aboard, the Ferryman pushed off soundlessly and they evanesced into the rising, rolling fog.

ꝏ

Fynna grabbed Jessalyne's hand. "Come, she wants to see you immediately, milady."

"Wait! My bags!" She scooped them off the floor, trailing after the pixie. "Fynna, slow down! And please call me Jessalyne."

"Very well, she wants to see you immediately, milady Jessalyne."

"Just Jessalyne."

Fynna kept tugging her toward the stairs. "You look like the others but you aren't."

"What does that mean?" Jessalyne asked, trying to keep up as they mounted the stairs.

"The other ladies are all here to win the prince." Fynna wrinkled her nose. "They tease me. Are you going to tease me because I don't want to waste time liking you if you are."

"I give my word, I will not tease you." She wondered if the steps actually ended somewhere or if this was some of Sryka's magic. They passed a small landing with a single door but still kept climbing.

At last, Fynna led her into a large room at the tower's top. Old books, pottery jugs and little glass jars crammed the shelves covering every available wall. What looked like a stuffed gryphon's foot sat next to twin crocks labeled simply, Big and Small. A fire raged in the fireplace, boiling the smelly contents of a caldron and warming the room considerably.

One door, bolted shut, stood across from another one. That door was wide open and led to the outside, to some sort of wall walk.

"Mistress! I've got her!" Fynna yelled.

Sryka walked through the open door, wind whipping her untamed grey hair around and billowing up under her robes making her look larger than she was.

Jessalyne tensed as the woman's eyes studied her. She looked down, unsure what to do.

"Shy, are we?" The old woman's voice rasped across Jessalyne's skin and she met the woman's gaze again.

Sryka smiled and Fynna hiccupped. "You are far lovelier than I expected, child. You will do nicely." She quickly added, "As my apprentice."

"Thank you, Mistress Sryka." Jessalyne relaxed slightly. "I'm pleased to be here."

"You will room with Fynna, who will now leave and straighten up her chamber so that it is suitable for human occupation." Sryka glared at the pixie, who scuttled out the door and down the steps.

The old woman eased herself into a well-stuffed chair near the fire. "Ah...the heat feels good on old bones. Come, sit, child." She pointed a gnarled finger at a footstool next to the chair. "Tell me your name."

Jessalyne crouched on the low stool. "My name is Jessalyne."

"I expected you sooner, Jessalyne. I requested your mother send you when you reached your tenth year."

"My mother passed when I was very young. She did leave your instructions with my father but he was...remiss in getting them to me. I apologize."

"I must ask you a very important question." Sryka positioned her scratchy fingers beneath Jessalyne's chin.

"Yes, mistress?" The woman's skin was ice.

"Are you still pure?"

"Mistress?"

Sryka sighed. "Your virtue, is it intact?"

Jessalyne cast her gaze away. "Yes, Mistress Sryka. My virtue is secure. I've known no man." Although she longed for one.

One with dark skin and star-sparked eyes and lips warm as…she swallowed and need flooded her belly.

"Are you all right, child? You look unwell."

"Just tired, mistress. The traveling has worn me out."

Sryka nodded. "You will rest today, then. Tomorrow your training begins."

"Thank you, a rest would do me good."

"Through the door on the lower landing you'll find your chambers. Don't worry about Fynna. If you cannot bear the wretched creature, I'll find another place for her."

"I'm sure she will be fine. Tomorrow, then?"

Sryka nodded and waved her off.

She headed down to the first landing. She was relieved her late arrival had not cost her the apprenticeship. She pushed the door open. "Fynna?"

The pixie swept the bare stone floor with a worn broom. "Jessalyne!" The broom clattered to the floor, and she clapped her hands. "It will be nice to have company." She looked around. "The room isn't the best, but it's serviceable."

The room was almost as large as Sryka's above but without any other doors. Unlike Sryka's, this room was nearly empty. Two straw-stuffed mattresses lay on the bare stone floor. Between the mattresses sat a trunk covered with melted candle stubs. A worn, double door wardrobe stood against the far wall, across from the fireplace.

"Is this all there is?" Jessalyne hands went to her hips.

Fynna frowned. "I'm afraid so. My comfort isn't really Sryka's concern."

"How long has it been this way?"

"Since I been here." Fynna plopped onto one of the mattress. "Five years."

Jessalyne thought of the comfort of Valduuk's and the luxury of the Gilded Rose. She threw her bags onto one of the mattresses and shook her head. "This will not do."

Fynna jumped up. "Please, don't say anything to Sryka. She'll get cross. I made that mistake when I first got here. The house stewardess won't help either. She won't even talk to me. Wretched old biddy. Mistress Wenda deserves to be bent over with rheumatism."

"Rheumatism?" Jessalyne thought for a moment. "Take me to her. Let me see what I can do."

Fynna shrugged. "Fine. Follow me. You'll see for yourself, I guess."

⅋

The ferry skimmed the water, barely disturbing the surface. The intense fog made it impossible to see anything beyond the edge of the skiff. Ertemis imagined the fog was what sucked up every bit of sound as well.

A single shaft of sunlight broke through, splitting the mist cleanly. The fog pulled back like curtains being drawn. The brilliant, sudden daylight caused him to squint. Elysium rose out of Lythe, sparkling like a jewel in the distance.

Elysium was more magnificent than any story his mother had ever told him. Built of washed limestone and polished marble, soft curves dictated the architecture of the city. Not a single hard line or sharp angle broke the seamless flow of one building into another. Carved into the pale cliffs, a wide serpentine staircase led down from the city to twin piers sweeping out into the water like welcoming arms.

The ferry eased to a stop at the end of one pier. Ertemis led Dragon off the ferry. He wondered if he should thank the Ferryman. He turned, but the skiff already disappeared into the fog.

Chanting and music floated in the air. Drawn by the sounds, he stepped off the curving pier and onto elven soil. Like a swarm of wasps, magic buzzed over his skin so strong his teeth clenched and the muscles in his back tightened. He rolled his shoulders, breathing deeply as the buzz lessened to a whisper. Elysium's allure was instantly recognizable. A sense of well being washed over him and in that moment, his human half retreated, bested by the vibrating power of the elven homeland. No wonder his mother had been unable to stay away.

Ertemis ascended the stairs toward the city and came to a landing. There an elder in pale robes stood behind a rostrum. Three thick plaits pulled his white hair back from his face, revealing his slanted ears. He closed the book he leafed through and nodded at Ertemis. "You seek someone." It was not a question.

"Aye, my lady mother." Distrust knotted Ertemis's gut. He wasn't welcome here but, so far, no one had stopped him.

"Her name?"

"Shaylana Elana-naya" Ertemis thought it best to give both names. He didn't know what she went by after so many years.

The elder paged through the book, looking for what, Ertemis couldn't guess. He tried to read the elder.

His head snapped up, eyes flaring with light. "Your magic will not be tolerated here. Do you understand?"

"Aye." Ertemis rested his hand on his sword's hilt.

The elder went back to his book. He read something, then looked up again.

"Ertemis Elta-naya." Another statement. "You will wait here until I return." The elder moved with a quickness Ertemis did not expect.

A carved marble bench offered the only seat on the landing. After a short span of time, chimes rang out. Curiosity took over. He tried to read his surroundings. A sudden heaviness clamped down on him. It was like the fog he'd felt in Jessalyne's cottage but thicker, more visceral. They'd shut him out.

He sat on the bench for what seemed like a day. What was time to a race of near-immortals? Or perhaps they made him wait because they could.

At last, the elder returned. A smaller cloaked figure followed behind. Ertemis sighed. He had the feeling they were about to tell him to leave.

The elder moved aside to let the second elf pass. They exchanged a brief nod and the elder backed away.

The smaller elf walked up to Ertemis. Slender hands slipped the hood back. Luminous beryl eyes stared up at him, edged with tears.

"Mother," he whispered.

"Mi elta. Oh, I've missed you." The words tumbled out of her in one short ragged breath. Tears spilled as she embraced him.

At the feel of her arms around him, Ertemis froze. Memories flooded him. He was eight and she was telling him to be brave and kissing his forehead and his cheeks and her tears fell hot against his face.

He wrapped his arms around her and hugged her back.

She glanced up, a wisp of a smile replacing the tears. "The tashathna has granted us some time together here. They will not allow you into the city."

He scowled. "Why grant me entrance at all if they're so afraid?"

She pressed her hand against his cheek. "They wanted to see you for themselves." She took his hand. "Please, sit."

He did as she asked. His mother was more beautiful than he remembered. "What are you called now?"

She sat beside him, her gaze sweeping him hungrily. "Just Elana, to most."

Daughter. Just daughter.

"It pleases me to see my son as a man." She smiled a little broader. "You want something, I sense it."

"True. I do want something." He returned her smile. "How is your life?"

"My life is…good. My needs are met." She twisted her hands. "Every day I regret what I did to you. You deserved better. I was weak and young. I'm so sorry."

He took both her hands in one of his. "Don't be sorry. You did what you thought best. The Legion gave me a place in the world and a way to earn my keep."

"You are kind, even if you're not truthful." Tears still twinkled in her eyes as she reached up to cup his face between her hands. "You've grown into a handsome man. Have you a wife? Sons of your own?"

He looked away, turning his face out of her hands. "Mother, you know what I am. Women seek me for other things, but not to wed."

She tipped her head. "But there is love in your heart. I feel it. Love and sorrow." She put her hand to her mouth. "She's why you're here, isn't she?"

"I am not…in love." He spat the word out. "That is a weak human emotion. Weakness has no place in my life."

"Love knows no race. You can't deny what your heart feels. You miss her." She put her hand on his arm. "You doubt her feelings for you."

He pulled away and stood, facing Lythe. "She's an innocent and very gifted, a firemage in training. Fair beyond words..." He shook his head. "She deserves better than what I can give."

"And you're the one to decide this? You sound defeated from the start. If you went to battle that way, how long would you survive? Tell her how you feel."

Ertemis turned to face her. "This isn't a battle. If it were, I would know what needs doing." Anger crept into his voice. "The Legion raised me and you expect me to know how to speak sweet words to a beautiful woman above my station?" He threw his hands up. "I am lost."

She reached up and took his hands, pulling him back down beside her. "If you love her, isn't it worth finding out if she loves you in return? And you do love her, so don't tell me differently."

He dropped his head into his hands. "Aye, I love her." His answer was muffled through his fingers. "I'm sick with it."

"I think those words would be enough. Speak your heart to her, dash the consequences. Find her and do it at once. If she's as beautiful as you say, some man will win her heart soon enough."

Ertemis looked into her eyes. "She's not the only reason I'm here." His voice went gravely serious. "I want the name of my father. I've waited long enough."

The color drained from her face. "I can't give you that." She looked away. "Leave him be, son. He isn't the wicked man you think he is. You don't know what passed between us. Both sides paid.

"Why won't you tell me? Why protect him? I'm your son. Don't I deserve to know?"

She stared at the ground. "He's an old man by now, if he even still lives. Please, let him be."

"Why? Why do you hold this from me?" He pounded his fist on the bench between them.

She turned to look at him, her jaw set. "I loved him and he loved me and we talked about making a life together, when...when things became different. Then I realized you grew in my belly and I panicked, fearing it would ruin everything and so, I fled."

"I don't understand what you're talking about."

"I was in Shaldar City as part of the Council sent to broker an alliance between Elysium and Shaldar. When I disappeared, the elves blamed King Maelthorn for the misdeeds of his court. In return, he blamed the elves for fouling the proceedings apurpose. Any hope for an alliance crumbled under the accusations.

"Shaldar lost the wisdom and strength of the elves and we..." Her voice lowered. "We are more isolated than ever. Our bloodlines are so weak, many chose not to bear children instead of losing them in birth."

"I didn't realize the elves suffered but that's not my concern. I already knew my father was in Shaldar City. What I want is a name." Ertemis's hand sought the hilt of his sword. He would find his father somehow. Then he would pay.

"The desire for vengeance seeps out of you like water from a cracked bowl. I cannot allow you to harm the man I love. Try to understand."

Chimes rang out again and she stood. "Our time is gone. I won't say goodbye, only tu'layan fa naltha."

"You really think we'll meet again? I doubt the elders will admit me twice."

"I see you haven't lost the language." She smiled. "I expect an invitation when you wed your firemage."

He pursed his lips. "Elysium truly is a dream world."

"Only to those who don't live in it, my son." She slipped her fingers beneath the opening of her cloak, drawing out a thin gold chain. A finely woven band of gold dangled from it, sparkling in the sun. She pulled the chain over her head and held it out.

He stared at the glittering ring.

"It was a gift from your father, a symbol of his unending love for me. Give it to your beloved." She reached up, sliding the chain over his head. "Go to her and speak your heart."

The chain was so fine, he couldn't feel it on his skin. He picked the ring up from where it lay against his leather breastplate. Woven of thin gold strands and set with tiny diamonds, it reminded him of something he'd seen before. "It's beautiful. Are you sure you won't miss it?"

She shook her head. "I'm not allowed to wear it here. It would please me greatly to give you this one thing."

"Then I will take it. Thank you."

She reached up to kiss his cheek. "Be well, Ertemis."

"Be well, mother." He returned her kiss and fresh tears sprang to her eyes.

As she walked away, images of Jessalyne spun through his head. He rolled the band of gold between his fingers. His mother was right. A woman as beautiful as Jessalyne would not remain a maid forever.

Chapter Eleven

Jessalyne followed Fynna into the kitchen. The scullery was busier than she'd imagined. Staff bustled about making breads, plucking chickens, scaling fish and bundling herbs to dry.

At the end of a long table sat a dour-faced woman, her hair scraped back into a tight knot. She pored over an open ledger. Gnarled fingers gripped a quill as she scratched figures into the book.

Fynna nodded toward the woman, stepping back against the wall, out of the way of two boys hefting a huge pickle barrel.

Jessalyne smoothed her skirts, and approached. "Pardon me, Mistress Wenda?"

Wenda's head stayed down, her eyes fixed on her work. "Aye." Her tone was stern.

"I'm sorry to bother you, mistress. I've just come to the castle and I have a request."

She looked up, eyeing Jessalyne's dress and necklace. "You have any idea how much work it takes to keep this place in order? If I listened to every request from every skirt come to chase the prince, nothing would get done. Now out!"

Jessalyne's head snapped back. "I'm not here to 'chase the prince'. I'm here to study under the tutelage of Mistress Sryka. And I don't expect you to grant me anything without my giving you something in return."

The woman's eyes narrowed. "What do you mean?"

"Is there somewhere else we might discuss this?"

"Nay."

Jessalyne sighed. She didn't want the entire kitchen witnessing her gifts. Leaning over, she whispered into the woman's ear.

Wenda rubbed her chin with the knuckle of one swollen hand. "If this is some trick, some foolery, I will make your life here as unpleasant as is within my means. Do you understand?"

"Yes, mistress."

"Fine. Come with me."

The girls followed Wenda to her chambers. The room of the house steward lacked nothing.

"What do you want in return for this healing?" Wenda asked.

"Fynna and I share the room beneath Sryka's quarters. There is barely any furniture to speak of, no lanterns...it's unfit to live in."

Wenda forced a smile. "Take this misery from my body and I will embarrass you with goods."

Jessalyne nodded. "Thank you. Please sit. Fynna, stand at the door. I want no interruptions."

Wenda sat in high back tapestry chair near her fireplace, resting her gnarled hands on the arms. "Will this hurt? Not that it matters...what is one pain over another?"

"No, I don't think so. At least it won't hurt you."

Fynna watched Jessalyne with intense curiosity, barely blinking.

Pulling the chair's mate in front of Wenda, Jessalyne sat. She rested her hands over the woman's, feeling the swollen joints of her twisted fingers.

She gave herself over to the growing power inside, willing the woman's pain into her own flesh. She inhaled as her joints began to throb. Crumpling forward, she waited for her powers to dissolve the deep ache. The welcome flush of heat passed through her. The swelling subsided. The twisted fingers straightened. A soft inhale of breath told her the heat had passed into Wenda.

The heat drained out of Jessalyne, and she relaxed back against the chair, tired but not spent. Each time she called her power, she grew stronger. Ertemis was right about practicing.

Fynna's mouth hung open.

Wenda extended her hands, wiggling and flexing her fingers. She stood and stretched, pleasure lighting her face. "I feel like a girl again. This is most wonderful, most wonderful." She jumped lightly. "There's no pain. None!"

Jessalyne smiled as Wenda hugged her. "I'm glad to have helped."

"Helped? This is more than help, child. You're gifted. I've been here almost as long as Sryka and she's never even attempted such a thing! You should school her, child."

Panic niggled at Jessalyne and she looked at Fynna, nodding furiously by the door. "You must promise me, both of you, not to breathe a word of this to anyone. Fynna, promise me on your wings and Mistress Wenda, please..."

"Hush, girl. If any ask where my rheumatism has gone, I'll tell them I bought a potion off the Travelers at the shade market." She smiled. "Come, now. I've my end of the deal to uphold."

Wenda led them back to the kitchen, where she directed a maid to clean the girls' room. Lantern in hand, she bade the two pickle barrel boys to follow her. Through a series of stairs and long passages, she at last stopped at the end of a dreary hall, lit only by high narrow windows. Handing the lantern to one of the boys, she selected a key from a large ring dangling off her belt and unlocked the door.

With a wink to the two girls, she snatched the lantern back, pushed the door wide, and sauntered through. The circle of light revealed a vast storehouse.

Mistress Wenda's meticulous organization was evident in the neat rows and precise placement of each object. Pieces of furniture were draped with muslin. Rugs were rolled and bound with twine.

"Now," she said. "What does the room need?"

Fynna's blue hands caressed the edge of a nearby rug. "Can we have a carpet?" she asked timidly. Even Jessalyne was unsure of when Wenda's new generosity might evaporate.

"Boys." Wenda's now limber fingers snapped. "Mark that rug to go. What else?"

Jessalyne thought quickly. She rattled off a list of goods. "Two lanterns, with stands. Two chairs, padded if possible, and a table to go between. Bed boxes to get the mattresses off the floor. If it can be spared, a tapestry for the north wall. A fire screen, a footstool, coverlets for the beds, and a wash basin."

She peeked at Mistress Wenda, aware of how much she had asked for, but Wenda was busy pointing the boys in the direction of each item.

Fynna jumped up and down in a way that Jessalyne imagined would have sent the pixie flying if her wings were still attached.

Wenda spoke softly. "Thank you, child. Thank you so much."

"Your generosity is thanks enough," Jessalyne said.

"Now, off you both go. Everything will be delivered today."

Both girls nodded their thanks again and Jessalyne did her best to keep pace with the pixie so as not to get lost in the maze of halls and stairs.

When they got back, they stared. The room had been scrubbed clean. Jessalyne dug through her bag for some dried lavender and sprinkled it over the floor before the carpet went down.

"This room will be livable after all."

Fynna did some more jumping, and before long the boys came knocking with the carpet.

Woven of blues and greens, the rug covered nearly the entire room when unrolled. Jessalyne and Fynna moved the mattresses upright against the wall to await the bed boxes.

Fynna spread out on the rug like a child making snow faeries. "It's as soft as kitten fur!"

Jessalyne smiled and leaned on one of the mattresses propped against the wall. She rubbed the bed linens between her fingers. "How well do you know your way around the city?"

Big blue eyes blinked up at her. "Pretty good. Why?" Fynna rolled over onto her knees.

"There are still a few things this room needs. Like decent linens."

"But that takes coin. And I'm not allowed out without Sryka's permission." Fynna's stuck her tongue out, her gaze returning to the carpet. She petted it like a cat.

"Coin isn't a problem. I'll beg Mistress Sryka to let you go. If you take me, I'll buy you some sweets. Put on your good tunic."

Fynna looked at her tunic, plucking it away from her body with two fingers. Her mouth bent into a frown. "It's the only one I got."

"I apologize, I didn't mean to upset you." Jessalyne wondered why the pixie hadn't been given a new tunic. Surely the cost of a few new clothes would not empty the king's coffers. "I didn't realize it was your only one. Why haven't you been given another?"

"I get a new one every year but Mistress Sryka always takes it away as punishment for some dumb reason or another." She shrugged. "It doesn't matter. Pixies aren't worth noticing in this kingdom."

Seeing the hurt in Fynna's eyes, Jessalyne knelt down beside her. "Why?"

Fynna traced the carpet's woven pattern with her fingertip. "The prince can't stand any creature not human. Pixies, sprites, the weer, trolls, goblins, any being not human...especially elves. Ever since King Maelthorn attempted an alliance with the elves a long time ago. Some say he wants the prince to try again, but the prince refuses. That might be why the king hasn't blessed a bride for him."

"Why does that matter?"

"Tradition says that for the prince to get the throne, he has to marry a woman the king approves. Without the king's blessing, the prince can't marry and until he does, he can't be king. If the king dies before the prince marries..." She paused, a shudder running through her. "Shaldar will be a kingdom without a king."

"I take it that's a bad thing."

Fynna's eyes widened. "Shaldar will be overrun by every lord who sees himself as the next king. Eventually, there won't be anything left to rule."

"The king must realize this. Seems silly not to bless a bride for the prince and keep Shaldar safe."

Fynna glanced around. Jessalyne wondered who could possibly be listening when they were alone in the room.

Lowering her voice a bit, Fynna answered. "Lots of people think the king has no intention of letting Prince Erebus rule. With Erebus on the throne, the realm would suffer anyway. He's a cruel man who only cares about his own pleasure. He taxes the people wickedly to pay for his fancy clothes and big feasts. But worst of all, he hates his father."

"Truly?" Jessalyne whispered back, caught up in the moment.

Fynna nodded. "And the women that come here to win the prince's hand..." The pixie rolled her eyes. "Mean-spirited, foolish wenches that only see the promise of the queen's crown on their head and jewels on their fingers. I don't blame the king one bit."

"Poor King Maelthorn. He must be so disappointed in his son."

Fynna hopped in place. "I've got it! You can heal the king like you did Mistress Wenda! You can save his life and then all this will be over."

"What ailment does the king suffering from?"

Fynna stopped hopping. "Old age, I think."

Jessalyne shook her head. "I doubt I can cure that. Growing old isn't a disease."

Fynna's face fell.

Jessalyne patted the girl's hand. "Shopping will cheer you up. I'll go talk to Mistress Sryka."

Jessalyne bounded up the steps and knocked at Sryka's door. The old woman took her time answering. "What do you need, child?"

"I wish to go into the city to purchase a few things. I would like to take Fynna with me."

"Fine. You shouldn't have to carry your own packages. If she gives you any problem, let me know. I will deal with her."

"Yes, mistress."

"And Jessalyne, mind yourself. If any man tries to talk to you, ignore him. Remember who you are at all times."

"Yes, mistress." What would Sryka think of the dark elf whose kisses still burned her lips? She turned her head to hide the heat rising in her cheeks.

Sryka closed the door and Jessalyne went to fetch her coin pouch and her new friend.

The memory of Ertemis's mouth pressed against hers was bittersweet, but it was just a memory. He was gone. Her fingers sought the gems at her neck. Small comfort knowing part of him had once cared enough to give her such a gift.

She pushed open the door to her shared quarters. "All right, off we go."

Clapping her hands, Fynna spun on one foot. Jessalyne smiled half-heartedly as she attached her coin purse to her sash. Fynna cocked her head to one side. "Is something wrong?"

Jessalyne shook her head, not trusting her voice.

Squinting, the pixie pursed her blue lips. "You're a bad liar."

A weak smile tweaked Jessalyne's mouth. "Just memories, nothing else." She jangled the coins in the pouch at her side. "Shall we?"

Fynna bounced several times on her little blue toes before the pair headed down the long winding stairs. They exited into the great hall, still bustling with activity.

"There's so much going on here all the time," Jessalyne said. "I never imagined city life would be so busy."

"This is nothing. Wait until nobles visit for holidays or feasting. Then you'll see what busy really is."

They walked out into the sunny courtyard Jessalyne had first entered. A group of heavily painted, over-dressed young women sat to one side, under the shade of two large oak trees. They drank cold tea from crystal goblets while they watched some of the prince's guard practicing swords.

Fynna grabbed Jessalyne's hand and pulled her in the opposite direction.

"The gate is that way." Jessalyne pointed to the way she'd come in.

"I know a better way." Fynna kept tugging.

One of the girls from the group under the tree nudged the one next to her, and pointed at Fynna. "Seems the blueberry is pestering someone new."

The girl stood, tossing blond ringlets over her shoulder. She set her glass down and smoothed the skirts of her lemon-colored gown. "You there," she called out.

Jessalyne turned in the girl's direction. "Me?"

"Yes. Is that little blue bug bothering you?"

Fynna crouched behind Jessalyne's skirts.

"She's not bothering me. And she's a pixie, not a bug."

The girl smiled thinly, staring at Jessalyne with limpid blue eyes. "Whatever it is, it isn't fit to keep company with. You know the prince won't tolerate her kind in the castle once he's crowned."

"That's right, Salena, you tell her." Another of the girls spoke, her freckled nose twitching.

"He has to be crowned first," Jessalyne shot back.

Holding an embroidered linen square to her nose as if damping out some awful smell, Salena raised her eyebrows. "Not interested in the prince? Probably for the best. I doubt he would find your looks the least bit appealing."

The gaggle behind Salena twittered. Jessalyne wished Ertemis were here. He would scare the wits out of them.

Fynna tugged at her skirt. "Please, let's go."

Nodding, Jessalyne felt the tingle of anger heating her spine. She spun on her heel. Behind her, Selena cried out. "Ow! Who poured hot tea in my glass?"

ॐ

The shops in Shaldar City's market quarter shamed every other shop Jessalyne had seen during her journey. The selection of goods overwhelmed her. She wanted one of everything.

Fynna's new tunic was first. But after trying several clothiers, Jessalyne soon found none of them carried anything to fit Fynna's petite figure.

"It can't be helped. None of these shops specialize in pixie." Fynna sighed.

"I don't give up that easily." Jessalyne stood beneath the awning of the shop they had just left. She smiled when she looked across the street. "I have an idea."

The pixie followed her line of sight. "You cannot be serious."

"It won't hurt just to look."

"I am not wearing anything with ruffles or daisies or kittens. Well, maybe kittens." Fynna crossed the street with Jessalyne and entered the children's shop.

When they left, Fynna was wearing a new tunic, simply cut from tea-colored linen, and tied about the waist with a matching embroidered sash. She carried a bundle beneath her arm with two more tunics, one of lightweight grey wool and one of earthy green brushed cotton.

She smiled. "Thank you. But I really only needed one."

"Nonsense. I can't have my quartermate wearing the same thing everyday. It would bore me to tears." She winked.

They wandered in and out of the shops. Jessalyne bought sticks of shortbread dipped in chocolate from a bakery.

"I can't believe how yummy this is," Fynna mumbled through a mouthful of crumbs. "Chocolate is the most best thing I have ever tasted."

"I agree," Jessalyne said. "I only just tried it for the first time on my journey here." She held up a brown paper sack full of chocolate biscuits. "Hopefully, these will last more than a day."

She bought soft cotton sheets for their mattresses, several colors of hair ribbons, lavender-scented candles, and two bars of good, fragrant soap.

She bought dinner from a street vendor. They found an empty bench, and unwrapped the rough paper holding their meals.

"I never knew shopping could make you so starved." Fynna took a bite of crunchy fried trout.

"Truthfully, I've never shopped so much in my life, but I like it," Jessalyne said.

They finished and Jessalyne wondered if they should turn back, but Fynna seemed to be having such a good time so they continued on. As they were passing a shop window, a handsome linen shirt caught her eye. She stopped to take it in. Bleached pure white, it had trailing vines embroidered around the neck in silver.

Ertemis would look so handsome in a shirt like that. She imagined him in it. Then out of it.

"That's a man tunic," Fynna stated.

"I know. I want to buy it anyway."

Fynna furrowed her brow. "For who?"

"No one." Before she changed her mind, she grabbed Fynna's hand and pulled her into the shop. The shirt was paid for, wrapped up and added to the other bundles without Jessalyne trying to figure out the point of buying clothing for a man she'd never see again. It was too painful to think that way. Better to imagine him as away for a while than gone for good.

On the long walk back to the castle, Jessalyne stayed quiet, content to let Fynna talk. It was not until they opened the door to their quarters that Jessalyne spoke.

"Oh, look at it all!"

The boys had finished delivering and setting up all the furniture and household goods promised by Mistress Wenda. Transformed from bare to beautiful, the room looked nothing like it had when they left.

Atop the lush carpet, the canopied bed boxes were placed against opposite walls. Folded coverlets lay on each mattress, next to a feather pillow. A rich tapestry hung on the wall between the beds with a carved wood table holding candlesticks beneath it. Two lovely upholstered chairs sat paired with a small game table off to one side.

Jessalyne dropped all her packages except for the sheets. She unwrapped them and threw Fynna's onto her bed. "Here, make your bed and then we'll put the rest away."

When that task was completed, the pair laid out the rest of their purchases. Fynna put her new tunics in the wardrobe and then lit the lanterns on their stands.

Jessalyne unwrapped the shirt she'd purchased for Ertemis and sat on the bed holding it in her lap, stroking her fingers across the soft fabric.

Fynna watched her. "Why won't you tell me who you bought that for?"

Sighing, Jessalyne shrugged. "He isn't in my life anymore."

"But you bought him a shirt." Fynna looked confused.

"I know...I didn't say it made sense." Jessalyne rolled the black pearl between her fingers, staring at the shirt again.

"Love never does."

"What did you say?" Jessalyne's head snapped up.

"I said love never does make sense."

"I'm not in love with him." Jessalyne shook her head.

"You bought a shirt for a man who isn't in your life no more but you aren't in love with him? I guess he isn't in love with you, either."

"He's definitely not in love with me."

"Where'd you get that?" Fynna pointed at Jessalyne's neck.

"What?"

"The pendant you can't quit touching. Did you buy that for yourself?"

"He gave it to me." Jessalyne bite her lip, remembering the day he'd put the necklace on her. If she closed her eyes, she could feel his fingers brush her skin.

"So, he doesn't love you but he gave you a necklace worth a whole heap." Fynna put her hands on her hips. "Makes perfect sense to me. Humans."

"What do you mean a whole heap?"

Fynna sat next to her on the bed. "The amethyst alone is something, but the pearl..." She raised her eyebrows. "That's a black Thrassian pearl, biggest I've ever seen. Rare and real expensive."

Jessalyne looked sideways at her. "How do you know all that?"

Fynna shrugged. "I've lived in the castle long enough and seen enough nobles showing off to know a bit about this and that." She smiled broadly. "Plus I eavesdrop a lot on Salena and her chickens when they don't know it."

Jessalyne laughed. "Really? What else do you know?"

"I know he probably does love you and if he's like most men, he'll come back for a woman he loves."

Closing her eyes, Jessalyne sighed deeply and shook her head. "I don't think so, Fynna. He barely said a word to me when we parted."

"Maybe he's not the talkative type."

"We quarreled the day before." A single tear burned down her cheek, her voice cracking. She covered her face with her hands. "I can't love him. I loved my mother and she died when I was little. I wanted my father to love me but I scared him away. If I love Ertemis, he'll never come back either."

Fynna put her arm around Jessalyne. "Don't judge him by your past. That belongs to you, not him."

Jessalyne wiped her eyes. "You really think he loves me?"

Fynna nodded. "Men give cheap jewels to the women they want to bed and expensive ones to the women they intend to keep."

Jessalyne smiled. "You certainly are a wealth of information." She laughed. "No jest intended."

Fynna lit one of Jessalyne's new lavender candles. She started a small fire in the fireplace and hung a kettle to boil for tea. Jessalyne folded the shirt and tucked it away on her side of the wardrobe. She splayed her hand across the fabric before shutting the armoire doors, her mind elsewhere.

They spent the rest of the evening playing Fryst on their new game table, eating chocolate biscuits and drinking tea. They kept the conversation to castle gossip and the day's shopping. Finally giving in to sleep, they crawled between their new cotton sheets as the moon crossed the midnight line.

Jessalyne dreamed of Ertemis.

His arms wrapped around her, fingers splayed over her ribs and belly. Pulling her close, he snuggled her against the warm muscled length of his body, nuzzling soft kisses onto her neck.

"Lelaya," he whispered. "I've missed you so much. Missed touching your warm silky skin, missed kissing your sweet mouth."

He turned her onto her back, his dark eyes wild with want. Smiling, he dipped his head and ran his tongue across her collarbone. His raven-black locks fell over his shoulders and dusted the swell of her breasts.

She moaned as goose flesh covered her skin. Her hands traveled up his arms to caress his bare chest.

"I love the color of your skin," she whispered. Fingertips grazing his chest, she smiled at the feel of him. He growled in response.

Midnight eyes stormy with need, he kissed her hard, resting his elbows on other side of her. His hands tangled in her hair. He kissed her until tremors ran through her, shaking her...

Jessalyne woke with a start. Fynna was poised to jostle her one more time. "Get up! Mistress Sryka will be expecting you!"

She opened her eyes and yawned. "I was dreaming."

"That explains the moaning."

"What?" She swallowed her embarrassment.

Fynna held her hands up. "Hurry up and dress. If you're late, Sryka will blame me, and I don't want to be punished because you lolled in bed dreaming of a man you're not even in love with."

Chapter Twelve

Jessalyne knocked at Sryka's door. A voice called out, "Come in."

She entered, knowing how sheepish she must look. "My apologies for my lateness, mistress. I fear the traveling wore me out more than I realized."

Mistress Sryka sat at the long table that took up a great portion of the room. Thick tomes spread out around her. She hastily shut one she'd been reading as Jessalyne came closer.

"No harm done. Sit." Sryka gestured to the chair across from her.

Jessalyne did as she was bid.

"Have you come into your powers?" Sryka's eyes narrowed.

"I...I have some gifts but I don't know their full extent." Not a lie.

Sryka nodded. "We'll begin your training today. In a week's time, if you show yourself to be as gifted as I think you are, I will introduce you to the prince. After all, you'll be serving him when I am gone. Eventually, I will perform a binding spell to bind your powers to you. Until then, I must restate that you are to remain chaste."

"Yes, mistress." Jessalyne couldn't stop thinking about her dream.

"Are you listening to me, child? You'll be meeting the prince of Shaldar, the heir to the throne. Does that mean nothing to you?" The look on Sryka's face told Jessalyne it had better mean something.

"Yes, of course, it will be a great honor." She feigned a smile.

The answer seemed to appease Sryka. "You'll meet the king as well, if he lives long enough. The position of magewoman is thankless, but we serve the greater good."

Another knock at the door and Fynna slipped in.

"Late as usual." Sryka scowled. "Get to your chores."

As soon as Sryka turned back toward Jessalyne, Fynna did her best silent imitation of Sryka, complete with wagging finger.

Jessalyne pinched herself to keep from laughing. Sryka was already on the next topic, gazing out the open door that led to the wall walk and talking about seasons and something else Jessalyne had not caught.

She did her best to look interested even though her attention truly belonged to an onyx-eyed, smoky-skinned elf.

The day passed quickly as she learned the difference between spells and charms, incantations and glamours, how to levitate small objects and the basics of scrying.

"There is so much to learn." Jessalyne's eyes swam from reading the cramped text in Sryka's books.

"That's enough for today. Put the books away before you go."

"Thank you, mistress." Jessalyne started shelving the multitude of volumes on the table.

"Have Fynna bring your dinner up to you. I would prefer you not take your meals in the hall just yet. For your own safety. I don't want the men in the castle chasing after you like rutting dogs. Understood?"

"Yes, mistress."

"Very well. Tomorrow morning then."

Jessalyne nodded and finished shelving the last few books, glad to be done. She couldn't concentrate any longer. A walk in the gardens might be just the thing to clear her head, but she didn't want to leave Fynna behind. "Mistress Sryka, may Fynna go too? I have some things that need mending."

Fynna shot Jessalyne an odd look.

"Very well." Sryka didn't look up from the herbs she was sorting.

Jessalyne winked at Fynna, and the two made their way down to their quarters.

"For a moment, I thought Sryka was rubbing off on you," Fynna said.

"I didn't want you to get stuck up there for the rest of the night. Besides, I want to walk in the gardens, and I hoped you would come with me."

"I would love that! We should stop by the kitchens. I bet cook will give us a basket dinner so we can eat outside."

"That's a wonderful idea. Especially since Sryka doesn't want me dining in the great hall." Jessalyne rolled her eyes. "She seems to think the castle's male population will find me irresistible."

As they headed to the kitchen, Fynna nodded. "The old witch might actually have something there."

Blooming with fragrant flowers, the gardens delighted Jessalyne. She named all the flowers and herbs she knew for Fynna. They walked the maze of rosemary hedges, inhaling the spicy woodsy scent. Near one of the large ponds they found a shaded spot. They sat and spread out their meal.

Jessalyne smoothed a linen napkin over her lap. "This is really lovely. I'm glad you came along."

"I'm glad you got me away from Sryka. I hardly ever get to come out here. These gardens are the only good thing Prince Erebus has done, even if they are just to impress the women that cluster around him."

"I'm supposed to meet him in a week's time." Jessalyne took a bite of cheese.

Fynna looked aghast. "What? Why?"

"Sryka thinks the future king should meet his future mage."

"And she's worried about the rest of the castle's men? Hah! The prince is the one she should be worried about. They don't call him the Prince of Hands for nothing."

Jessalyne's appetite waned. "The Prince of Hands?"

"I'm sure he won't bother you," Fynna reassured her. "His tastes run to a very different sort of woman, more like Salena and those twits."

Jessalyne wanted to believe her but the seed of apprehension sprouted.

Fynna changed the subject. "Look!" She pointed to the pond. "The swans are out."

A pair of elegant gray birds sailed across the still water, rippling the pond's surface with swirling eddies.

"I've never seen swans before. They're so beautiful." An unnamed yearning wrapped around Jessalyne's heart.

"Swans mate for life," Fynna said.

Jessalyne followed the feathered beauties as they glided side by side. A thought occurred to her, and she turned to Fynna. Her voice was hushed when she spoke. "What do you know about elves?"

"Being pixie, probably more than most. What do you want to know?"

Jessalyne chose her words carefully. "I'm curious why the prince thinks they are such a threat. I saw some elves at home once. They came to the naming ceremony of a noble's son. They were intimidating but not in a threatening way. They just seemed so very perfect and regal."

"I don't really know the whole story of what caused the rift between King Maelthorn and the elves. As for Prince Erebus, he just thinks any creature not human is below him."

Fynna continued, "I'm sure the elves think the same of him, since they consider themselves a noble class and rightly so, I guess, considering they hold so much of Shaldar's old magic. It's said only the faerie have more."

"The elves live on an island called Elysium. It's impossible to find except for them. It's supposed to be paradise and the source of their power. Sometimes they leave Elysium, the males, mostly, to visit other towns, but you won't ever see them in Shaldar City, not since the alliance went bad all those years ago."

Jessalyne nodded with interest. "That's the only kind of elves?"

Fynna shook her head. "Well, there is sort of another, but most folk don't like to talk about them. The dark elves. Born of mixing blood. The midwives that birth them are supposed to snuff them." She shivered. "I've never actually seen one but people say there's a few in the realm. They tell tales about one."

She lowered her voice and narrowed her eyes. "They call him the Black Death, the fiercest, most bloodthirstest assassin the Legion's ever had.

"Skin black as night and eyes like fire. They say he'll kill a man for breathing wrong and that he can turn himself into a crow at midnight. And on the night of the new winter moon, he devours a newborn babe to renew his powers."

"That is absolutely not true," Jessalyne snapped. "He does no such things! My word, that is the most ridiculous bunch of piffling I've ever heard."

Pulling back, Fynna wrinkled her brow. "Well, you asked! How do you know what he does and doesn't do?"

Jessalyne took a deep breath and tried to calm herself. "It just sounds like foolishness. Like an old mother's tale. Eating babes. Really now," she huffed.

Were these atrocious lies what people actually thought of Ertemis? Her heart sank as she imagined a life plagued with such prejudice. The sudden urge to wrap her arms around him and kiss the hurt away filled her. She closed her eyes, wondering if she'd ever touch him again.

Leaning back against a tree trunk, Fynna bit into a juicy slice of melon. "Just telling you what I've heard. Dark elves are very dangerous creatures. Unless you're a woman. They're supposed to be quite knowledgeable in other areas, if you know what I mean."

"No, I don't know what you mean. Why are you grinning like that?"

"You know, in other areas..." Fynna made a rude gesture with her hands.

"Fynna!" Jessalyne's eyes widened. "Oh my, that was uncalled for."

The pixie fell over laughing. "You asked!"

They finished their meal, and watched the sunset unfurl in ribbons of lilac and coral before heading back to their quarters.

"Tomorrow is bath day." Fynna flopped onto her bed.

"Wonderful! What time will the tub be brought up?" Jessalyne asked.

Fynna shot her an odd look. "We bath in the scullery."

"You cannot be serious. In front of everyone?"

"Behind a screen, silly. I've got the feeling you'll get to go first, if Sryka has anything to say about it. And she does."

"I don't want to interrupt the normal routine. I'll bathe in whatever order works best."

"Trust me, you do not want to bathe after the houseboys. Especially during the summer months." She wrinkled her nose.

Jessalyne stared, unsure she fully understood. "Do you mean we share the same bath water?"

"Of course! What did you think I meant?"

"That is disgusting! I cannot bathe in someone else's dirty water."

Fynna shrugged. "Unless you suddenly become nobility, you better get used to it."

"I would prefer not to bathe, then."

"So would the houseboys but Mistress Wenda makes them. I'd think anyone who spends as much as you on fancy soap would want to put it to good use."

"Not like that." Jessalyne changed into her nightrobe. Out of habit, she lit the bedside lantern with a nod.

Fynna clapped her hands. "Do that again!"

"I didn't mean...you must keep this between us, like the healing."

"But that's what you're here for, isn't it?"

"Yes, but..." Jessalyne wasn't sure how to put into words the reluctance she felt to let Sryka know the extent of her gifts. Silliness, that's all it was.

"You don't want her to know, do you?" A wise grin played on Fynna's lips.

Jessalyne shook her head, feeling shamed at the admission.

"I understand, trust me. If I know anything about the old bat it's that if she can't benefit, she won't bother." Fynna winked. "This pixie's lips are sealed."

At firstlight, Jessalyne went to the scullery and begged two pails of water off cook. She carried them back upstairs, and after a wave of her hand, she and Fynna washed with the hot water and orange blossom soap.

"I prefer to soak in a tub but clean is clean." Jessalyne wrung out the linen square she had used to scrub herself with.

"This soap is so much better than cook's lye and ashes concoction."

"Lye and ashes? No wonder the houseboys hate to bathe. I'll give cook a better recipe."

Fynna pitched the dirty water out the window before Jessalyne could stop her. "Fynna!"

"Everyone does it. Well, everyone who hopes Salena is down below." She giggled.

Jessalyne rolled her eyes as she finished dressing. "Sryka's waiting. Try to be on time today, I want to eat dinner in the garden again."

"Me, too." She pulled her tunic over her head and tied the sash. Wisps of blue hair stuck out in every direction. "Ready!"

The days passed quickly and Jessalyne fell into a routine of mornings and afternoons with Sryka learning as much magical knowledge as she could, sunset dinners in the garden by the swan pond, and nights filled with dreams of Ertemis.

On the eve of Jessalyne's meeting the prince, they dined on bread bowls brimming with barley stew and honey-glazed apricot turnovers. In trade for Jessalyne's soap recipe, the meals cook fixed for them achieved new heights of deliciousness. Fynna sucked the stickiness off her fingers while Jessalyne rinsed hers in the pond.

"Are you nervous about meeting Prince Gropes-a-lot?"

"Calling him that doesn't help, Fynna." Jessalyne sat next to her friend, both of them watching the play of colors in the sky as the sun descended.

"Sryka sure has done a good job of keeping you from crossing his path this week. Between eating up your hours with all that study to no dinners in the hall..." Fynna shifted. "I wonder why she doesn't want you to see him."

"Maybe she doesn't want him to see me."

Fynna looked sideways at her. "Could be. You do look a little—"

"Elven—I know. You commented on that when we met. Besides, I've heard it before."

"From who?" Fynna sucked a bit of parsley out of her teeth.

"You ask a lot of questions." Jessalyne leaned forward, resting her chin on her bent knees.

"I would ask less if you would answer more. I can't help it. Pixies are very curious by nature. So tell me, what are you hiding?"

Jessalyne whipped her head around. "What does that mean?"

"You keep secrets." Fynna shrugged. "But they're yours to keep."

"What makes you say that?"

"You moan in your sleep. You daydream constantly, rolling that pricey pearl between your fingers. Please, before it kills me, tell me about the man you bought the shirt for?"

"I can't." Jessalyne shook her head.

"I am very good at keeping secrets."

Jessalyne sighed. "You must swear to keep it."

"I swear on my wings, I won't tell a soul."

"He's not the monster people think he is. Well, he was, but he isn't anymore. I don't know if he can turn into a crow, I never saw that, but I swear he would never eat a newborn babe. Although he does like to eat." Eyes on the sunset, Jessalyne took solace in correcting Fynna's misconceptions about the dark elf. Smiling, she added, "And he's a wonderful kisser."

Silence greeted her. She turned to look at Fynna. The pixie stared back, mouth open, wide blue eyes topped by raised eyebrows.

"You wanted to know."

"Are you talking about who I think you're talking about?" She whispered. "The Black Death?"

"Please don't call him that. His name is Ertemis."

"Oh my oh my..."

"You're babbling, Fynna."

"Did you see him kill anyone? How did you meet? Is the rhyme true? Well, no, you probably wouldn't know that. Or maybe you would. What does he look like? Is he handsome? Does he have sharp teeth?"

"I saw him kill...a water serpent." She refused to further color Fynna's idea of Ertemis with the tale of how he'd dispatched the bandits. "How we met is a long story for another time. As for what he looks like, he is very handsome, well-muscled, and tall. His skin is the color of soot, but with a sheen like this pearl. His eyes are black ringed with silver and I could stare into them endlessly. And his lips...they're very soft."

"You definitely kissed him?"

"More than once."

The pixie hopped up and down. "What was that like?"

"It was a magic all its own." Jessalyne let out a delighted sigh and laid back on the ground, arms crossed beneath her head for a pillow. Through the leaves of the rowan trees, a few bright stars twinkled in the early evening sky.

"A magic all its own and you still don't think you're in love with him? Just admit it, already!"

"What good will it do me to be in love with a man I won't ever see again?"

Fynna plopped down. "Why do you think that? You don't know for sure. If he is who you say he is, he's used to getting what he wants. If he wants you, he'll be back. And from that bauble, I'm guessing he wants you very much."

"I cannot think about that now." Jessalyne hugged her knees tighter. "I meet the prince tomorrow and I'm dreading it."

Fynna slid closer and wrapped her little arm around Jessalyne. "It will be over before you know it. Let's head back and have some tea and finish the rest of those chocolate biscuits. Then you can go to sleep and dream about your lover."

Jessalyne gave Fynna a good-natured shove. "Don't call him that. Are all pixies so bothersome?"

Fynna nodded. "I thought I mentioned that."

Jessalyne stood. "I think I will eat all the chocolate biscuits myself."

Jumping up, Fynna put her hands together. "You wouldn't really do that, would you?"

Hitching up her skirts in both hands, Jessalyne grinned wickedly. "If I get to them first, I will." She took off running, Fynna close at her heels.

Panting as she ran into the room, Fynna crashed onto her bed. "If I had my wings, you would still be in the garden."

"If I had used my magic, I could have just blinked myself up here."

Fynna sat up. "Really?"

Jessalyne grinned. "No. But it sounded good, don't you think?" She dodged a pillow as it flew past her head.

"I think I will beat you in a game of Fryst as soon as the tea is ready." Fynna hopped up to fill the kettle and hang it over the glowering coals.

"Well, you can try." Jessalyne was glad for the distraction and friendship Fynna provided. The pixie deserved more than a few new tunics and some soft sheets for her bed. She deserved her wings back.

Chapter Thirteen

Prince Erebus posed before his full-length looking glass while Sryka waited. He adjusted his white silk tunic. A flurry of valets brushed imaginary lint from his embroidered velvet cape and polished the sapphire-crusted buckles on his goblin-skin boots. He twisted the waxed point of his dark beard one more time before waving his staff away with one heavily jeweled hand. "Out! All of you."

Finally, the prat turned to face Sryka. "You're sure you can get my father to bless her?"

"I'll find a way." Sryka wished the prince paid as much attention to the politics of state as he did to his appearance.

"I still favor you casting a spell to get him to bless Salena." Erebus licked his lips. "She's a very willing wench and much to my taste."

"We have been over this, your highness. The Oath of Amity between the king and I makes that impossible. The oath serves its purpose. It has always been that way between king and mage. Besides, I have searched every grimoire and tome I possess trying to find a way to break the oath. It cannot be done." Idiot. Sryka shifted her bones on the hard wooden seat.

"Why don't you bind the girl's powers now so I may bed her this evening?"

Sryka closed her eyes, willing herself to stay calm. "She is not ready to have her powers bound. Once you are wed, you may do as you wish with her. All in due time, Erebus."

ဢ

Jessalyne and Fynna stood outside the carved wooden doors of the prince's chambers. Jessalyne took several deep breaths, unready to walk through them yet.

"Remember, he needs you more than you need him." Fynna squeezed her friend's hand.

Smiling weakly, Jessalyne nodded. "Thank you."

"Now go or we'll both get into trouble. Dinner by the pond?"

Knocking loudly on the heavy doors, she whispered, "Dinner by the pond will be just what I need."

Fynna slipped away as Sryka's voice bid Jessalyne enter. Pushing the door wide, she did her best to look calm and confident as she entered the Prince's private chambers. Sryka sat in a wide carved chair looking highly uncomfortable. The prince stood opposite. Jessalyne dropped into a curtsy as Sryka had instructed. "Your Highness. Mistress Sryka."

With difficulty, Sryka eased herself out of the chair. "Lord Prince Erebus of Shaldar may I present my apprentice, Jessalyne Brandborne of Fairleigh Grove."

Clasping her hands in front of her, Jessalyne kept her eyes focused down. She knew not to make eye contact until spoken to.

"Jessalyne." The prince spoke her name like he was tasting a new food, testing it to see if it suited him. "Welcome to my home. Are you enjoying your stay in my fair kingdom?"

Jessalyne raised her head and looked at the man speaking to her. He was almost the same height and his dark, sparkling eyes reminded her of the water serpent. She imagined he must fancy himself a great man to wear so many jewels at once. "Yes, your lordship. Castle Ryght is a marvelous place."

Slowly, the prince circled her. She felt like the last sweetcake on a platter set before a starving man.

"Quite lovely." His palm grazed her backside as he walked behind her.

She gasped and almost started forward but quickly steadied herself. Heat sparked in her belly. She forced a civil response. "Thank you, your highness."

"You look a touch fey. Have you any impure blood in your line?" He came around to face her, making no effort to hide his attempt to peer down her dress.

"No, your highness, I do not." It took great control to keep the rising anger out of her voice. "I believe that would make me dark as night, not pale as day."

He raised one well-groomed eyebrow. "So it would. But then, of course, you'd not have been suffered to live."

Leaning closer, black lust flickered in his eyes as he scanned her figure, "And you are very much alive, aren't you?"

His words crawled over her skin, making her want to retch. To her great relief, he turned his attention to Sryka. "She will do."

Jessalyne knew she should be happy with the prince's approval. It secured her position as mage-apprentice. But the prince looked at her in a way that made her feel worthless and ashamed to be a woman. For all his wicked ways, Ertemis had never made her feel that way.

Sryka leaned to the side to see around the prince. "You're dismissed for the day, Jessalyne. You will dine tonight in the great hall at the prince's table. Tomorrow your lessons start anew. That is all."

Jessalyne curtsied again and ran to find Fynna. The pixie had been right about how quickly it would be over and how salacious the prince was. Did the women competing for his hand actually think his behavior acceptable? Or worse, appealing?

ॐ

Fynna sat in the scullery, picking stones out of the lentils. She glanced up as Jessalyne stormed in. "Well? How was it?"

Jessalyne put a finger to her lips and shook her head. "Cook, is there anything Fynna and I might have for a picnic lunch?"

Kneading dough on the long table, the rotund woman who ran the kitchen used her elbow to point across the kitchen. "In the cold larder, there's lots of pickles, all kinds of breads and cheeses, vegetable cakes, honey braids...help yerself, love. Fynna's done a fair share of work in here today. Sneak yerself a few of them chocolate cakes if ya want. They're for the prince's tea but his royalness don't really deserve them."

"Thank you." Jessalyne took a basket from a shelf and lined with a linen square before loading it with goodies.

Fynna set the bowls of lentils down and hung up her borrowed apron. "Thanks, cook."

As soon as they were outside and out of earshot, Fynna asked again. "Well, what happened?"

"The man disgusts me. He looked at me like some kind of sweet to be eaten." Jessalyne's gait increased the angrier she got.

Fynna jogged to keep up. "Really? I didn't think he would like you that much."

Jessalyne shot Fynna a look.

"You're plenty likeable! Just not what he usually goes after. For the love of Queen Menna, slow down."

Jessalyne halted, crunching gravel under her slippers. "He ran his hand across my backside!"

Just as Fynna stopped, Jessalyne spun on her heel and started off again.

"What did Sryka say?" Fynna panted.

"Nothing. She seems to have forgotten how concerned she is with my chastity."

"Well, he is the prince."

"But she works for the king!" Jessalyne set the basket down in the shade of the rowans but stayed standing, her hands on her hips.

"Stupid old hag." Fynna sat cross-legged on the ground and began setting out their lunch.

"He asked me if I had any fey blood."

She looked up. "He did?"

"Right before he tried to look down my gown. Ugh. The man is a slug." Jessalyne shuddered.

Fynna patted the ground next to her. "Sit. It's over. Tell me more about your dark elf while we eat."

"I know you're trying to change the subject."

"Can you blame me? You're talking about my two least favorite people."

"Is that also why you're eating the chocolate cakes first?" Jessalyne laughed.

"I didn't think you noticed that." Fynna tried to hide half a cake in her small blue hand.

Jessalyne shook her head. "You're too much, Fynna...you make me laugh. Thank you."

"If you want to thank me, tell me about the kissing again."

Still smiling, Jessalyne rolled her eyes. "Can we just eat in silence and enjoy our lovely surroundings?"

"So you aren't going to be thinking about the kissing then?" Fynna ate the rest of the cake, then licked the chocolate off her fingers.

"Have you ever been kissed?" Immediately after Jessalyne asked the question, Fynna's face went purple. "Fynna, what's wrong? Are you choking?"

"Haven't you ever seen a pixie blush before? Yes, I've been kissed but not in a long while. This is hardly the spot for me to find love." She fished a plum cake out of the basket. "So now can I hear about the kissing?"

Leaning back against one of the tree trunks, Jessalyne obliged her. They sat talking for quite a few hours.

The evening meal chimes rung. Jessalyne jumped up. "I'm supposed to eat dinner at the prince's table. It slipped my mind!"

Scooping the remnants of their lunch into the basket, Fynna waved Jessalyne on. "Go! You still have time before the final chime ring."

Jessalyne burst into the scullery, barely noticed by the bustling staff. She took a moment to blot the beads of perspiration off her lip and brow with a nearby apron.

She must smell awful. Maybe it wasn't such a bad thing, since she had to sit at the prince's table. She grabbed a stem of rosemary from the cook's herb jar anyway and crushed in her hands, then rubbed her hands over her neck and hair. Straightening her skirts, she felt ready for whatever came next. Mostly.

Everything about the great hall at dinner overwhelmed her. So many people going in every direction, so much clatter. Each platter carried past by the kitchen staff wafted new smells.

Three long tables sat on a dais at one end of hall. From the finely carved chairs to the crystal goblets, it was obvious the tables were reserved for royalty and their noble guests. The center table, although decked in the king's colors, had no one at it. The left table held only a few elder noblemen. The right table was full of people, most of who seemed to be busy looking important. Jessalyne thought a preening bunch like that could only be seated at the prince's table.

Of the few seats left, she had no idea which one she should take. Deciding the one furthest away would be most to her liking, Jessalyne sat in the very last one, next to a young boy in noble dress.

"Greetings." Jessalyne did a small curtsy to cover her general bewilderment of the whole situation.

Busily rummaging in his left nostril with one finger, he stared at her. "Who are you?"

Not quite the response she expected. "I'm Jessalyne, mage apprentice to Mistress Sryka."

The boy inspected his fingertip before shoving the digit up his other nostril. "I'm Fert."

As she sat next to the little monster, she took comfort that his poor manners had kept him from offering a hand in greeting. "Are you related to the prince?"

With a great sigh, Fert stopped foraging and explained. "My mother, Lady Fenlyck, is the daughter of the king's sister."

"Is that your mother there?" Jessalyne pointed a few seats away toward a broad-faced woman with elaborately coiffed red hair. Her plunging neckline dripped with faceted carnelian beads.

"You don't know very much, do you?" Fert gave her a cold look.

Deciding she'd had enough conversation with the sanctimonious child, Jessalyne turned her attention to the scene before her. Of the low tables that ran out from the dais end to end, the center rows were filled with other lesser nobles, judging by their accoutrements. Salena and her ever-present cluster of gnats took up almost an entire table. If they noticed Jessalyne, she couldn't tell.

The next row out held the castle guard, many accompanied by painted women who looked happy just to be in the great hall. Beyond that, an assortment of travelers and merchants filled the tables.

The last chimes rang for the evening meal and colorfully dressed jugglers strolled between the tables. Following them came a troupe of lithe tumblers. In the gallery, minstrels played a lively tune. When the tumblers reached the end of the hall, trumpeters appeared on the balcony above the dais. They announced the prince with three short bursts. He strode into the room and as if on cue, the seated guests erupted in hoorahs, stomping their feet and banging their pewter mugs.

"Is it like this at every dinner?" She asked Fert.

In the middle of wiping something onto the bottom of the table, he looked at her as if she smelled of the stables.

"Never mind," she growled.

Waving as he made his way to the dais, Prince Erebus nodded and smiled, sucking up the adoration. Two valets scurried to pull out the prince's chair. He stood before the cheering crowd, hands raised against the swell of the throng. At the softening of the din, he clapped his hands and announced, "Dinner is served!"

Another cheer rose as the kitchen staff came forth with platters for the head table. Wine was poured for each guest, starting with the prince.

The prince's taster sipped the wine then sampled each dish before it was placed before Erebus. With a yea or nay, his plate was filled with the selections he chose. He looked down both sides of his table. When he saw Jessalyne, he leaned back and whispered to one of his stewards.

The steward came and bent to Jessalyne's ear. "The prince requests you dine at his side."

Even Fert looked interested by that bit of news.

Without waiting for Jessalyne's assent, the steward pulled out her chair, forcing her to stand. She moved to the side as everyone shifted down a chair. The steward set Jessalyne's goblet of wine at the now vacant spot beside the prince.

"Your highness." She tried to smile as she sat next to Prince Erebus. As a dinner companion, Fert was infinitely more desirable.

"Jessica, how does the evening find you?" He leaned closer than necessary.

"It's Jessalyne, your highness. I'm well. And you?" If politeness did not dictate she ask after him in return, she would not have uttered another word.

He was about to answer when a steward came forward with some pressing business and took the prince's attention off her. She sipped her wine, looked out over the feasting and locked eyes with Salena.

Jessalyne could not believe this girl actually wanted the prince. Rage danced across Salena's face. Jessalyne was in no mood to deal with the prince's unwanted advances and some simpering skirt's ill will. The girl needed something else to focus on.

Concentrating on the candelabra in the middle of Salena's table, Jessalyne called her magic. The flames shot into the air. The girl next to Salena jumped, toppling a carafe of wine onto Salena's gown.

The prince's hand found her knee, distracting Jessalyne from the ensuing melee at Salena's table. She turned to find him still in conversation with his steward. The prince's fingers moved higher, massaging her thigh. Jessalyne cringed at his touch. Ertemis, where are you?

Maybe Ertemis was right about her virtue being required as proof of her fealty. It crushed her to think what this pretentious fop might expect of her. She would turn her back on Shaldar City before she gave Prince Erebus one shred of herself.

Chapter Fourteen

Once finished with his conversation, Prince Erebus turned to Jessalyne. This close it was easy to see he groomed himself to appear younger. Over the spicy musk he doused himself in, the scent of henna wafted from his hair.

He smiled, reminding her of a dog snarling. One of his bottom teeth was an odd yellow shade. It took her a moment to realize it was carved ivory and not a real tooth at all.

"You look lovely this evening, Jessalyne."

An empty compliment, considering she had not changed. "This is the same gown I wore when I met you this morning, your highness."

"Is it? Perhaps I'll have my clothier provide you with a selection of gowns. I take great pains to ensure those around me are well taken care of."

Since when? She'd had to buy Fynna a new tunic. "If that pleases you, your highness."

He patted her arm and she was relived to have his hand off her thigh. "Very well, it shall be done. I will send one of my stewards into the city to take care of the matter."

"Very kind of you, Prince Erebus." Jessalyne saw a chance to get away. "Tomorrow will be a very full day, and I am already so tired. If your highness would be so kind, I would very much like to retire to my chambers."

The prince's gaze found Salena as she reentered the hall, freshly changed into a deep red gown. The neckline left no question as to what Salena considered her best assets. She met his gaze and drew her tongue slowly across her lips.

Without turning back Jessalyne, he dismissed her. "I believe I shall retire myself. I have matters to attend to in my chambers. Good evening." He motioned for one of his stewards and pointed toward Salena while whispering something.

Unnoticed, Jessalyne slipped away and hurried up the steps to her chambers. She wanted nothing more than to scrub herself free of every trace of his touch and climb into bed. At least she could find solace in her dreams, even if the man she dreamed of was just a memory.

Morning came pale and early. Jessalyne sipped her tea while she dressed and wondered if the day would bring another skin crawling encounter with the prince.

Fynna broke Jessalyne's reverie by poking her in the stomach.

Jessalyne swallowed quickly and set her cup down. "What was that for?"

"Are you ready to go? I've asked you twice and you haven't answered me."

"Oh. Sorry." Jessalyne gulped the rest of her tea. "Ready."

They walked into Sryka's chambers as they had every day for the past week, expecting lessons and chores.

"Fynna, it's about time. I want this entire floor scrubbed with lye and then the carpets taken out and beaten. The ashes need to be shoveled out as well. If you finish that before we get back, you are to dust these shelves, but mind you do not break anything or I will take it out of your hide. Am I understood?"

Fynna cringed. "Yes, mistress."

Sryka turned to Jessalyne. "Today you meet the king. I must attend to more pressing matters, but I will take you to his chambers first."

Jessalyne wondered what could be more pressing than visiting the king.

"You will stay there until I return for you, understood?"

"Yes, of course." Jessalyne tired of Sryka's patronizing attitude. A hint of frustration crept into her voice. Sryka's eyes narrowed but she made no comment.

They passed the guards posted outside the king's chambers without notice. The guards seemed to want little to do with the old sorceress.

In the king's foyer, Jessalyne admired the royal crest, inlaid in marble into the floor's center. The room had eight sides, with six sets of double doors. The only solid walls were on either side of the main entrance and low carved benches sat against them.

A young squire came out from one of the side doors to greet them. Sryka cut him off before he could speak. "Where's Laythan?"

"In the king's bedchambers, mistress." The boy pointed toward the doors across from the entrance.

The first of the king's inner rooms felt like it belonged in the warm, comfortable home of a wealthy scholar rather than a castle. The showiness that saturated Prince Erebus' personal rooms didn't exist here. King Maelthorn's library was lined not just with books but also with objects that looked rare and expensive. The walls were covered with detailed maps of Shaldar and the neighboring realms.

Sryka trudged through the room as if she wanted to spend as little time there as possible.

When they reached an arched door at the far end of the room, Sryka stopped and rang a small crystal bell hanging from a tapestry pull.

The door opened and a simply dressed white-haired man greeted them. Jessalyne at first thought he was the king but remembered Fynna telling her the king's ill health kept him abed.

"Here's the king's tonic." Sryka handed him a stoppered earthenware jug. "The prince wishes the girl be introduced." Sryka barked the words in such a way Jessalyne felt like she was somehow to blame for bothering the man.

The old man took the jug and adjusted the spectacles on the end of his nose. Peering through them, he nodded. "Very well. Be seated. I will fetch you when his majesty is ready for visitors."

He gave Sryka a sideways look before closing the door. Jessalyne sensed there were few in the castle who found Sryka's presence enjoyable.

"Who was that?" Jessalyne whispered.

"That dried bit of flesh is Sir Laythan." Sryka almost shouted. She narrowed her eyes at the closed door and muttered something under her breath. "He's the king's man."

"You mean like his steward?"

"Yes. Now sit and wait. When your time with the king is over, sit here again and I will collect you when I am finished."

"Yes, mistress." Jessalyne sat on the wide leather bench trimmed with age-darkened nail heads. Sryka leaned heavy on her staff as she exited the king's antechambers.

Alone in the room, Jessalyne itched to examine the books and the maps and the curiosities filling every available space in the room. She listened for footsteps. Hearing none, she got up and tiptoed over to the nearest bookshelf.

The first book was on Ulvian mourning rituals, the second was a book of plays by an unknown author. The spine of the third was in a language she didn't recognize. Sitting next to the volumes on that shelf was a small, hinged box made from a raven's egg. She picked it up and, unable to contain her curiosity, opened it.

"Perhaps you shouldn't touch what doesn't belong to you." Sir Laythan stared at her disapprovingly.

Jessalyne nearly dropped the egg box. She hadn't heard Sir Laythan open the door. "I'm truly sorry, sir. I meant no harm." She gingerly placed the object back on the shelf.

"Follow me." His tone was clipped.

"Yes, Sir Laythan."

Heavy drapes shuttered the bright sun from the king's bedroom. It took a moment before Jessalyne's eyes adjusted. Stale air swamped the room, both sweet and foul at the same time. Only the measured rasps of breath coming from the high curtained bed broke the quiet. Through the sheer inner curtains, Jessalyne glimpsed the propped up form of a man.

Sir Laythan stood by the bedside. "Lord King Raythus Maelthorn, Ruler of Shaldar, Right Royal Heir to its throne and Benevolent Monarch to its people, the prince wishes I present to you..." Sir Laythan looked at her, eyebrows raised as if he expected something.

Jessalyne looked at him blankly.

"Your name, child. What's your name?" Sir Laythan sighed heavily.

"Jessalyne Brandborne of Fairleigh Grove."

"Jessalyne Brandborne of Fairleigh Grove, your highness." Sir Laythan pulled the inner curtains back a bit, bowed, and backed away from the bed until he reached the door and left.

The king motioned her closer with a withered hand. Jessalyne curtsied, then approached a few steps. The king looked older than Sryka but beneath the mask of age, there were signs he had once been a handsome man. The sparkle of intelligence still danced in his eyes. "Come closer. Don't be frightened by the ravages of time."

"I'm not afraid of you, Sire, just unsure of myself. I'm unused to courtly ways. I don't wish to make a dunce of myself."

He smiled softly. "Fairleigh Grove is most beautiful. Deep in the southern valleys of the Wyvers, is it not?"

Amazed the king knew of her home, Jessalyne took a step closer. "Yes, your highness, it is. Have you been there?"

"I passed through there once as a boy, traveling with my mother. She took me all throughout Shaldar. She thought it important I know the land I would someday rule."

"A wise woman."

"Yes, she was. Taken from me too soon. She died birthing my twin sisters."

Jessalyne felt a twinge of familiar pain. "How old were you, Sire?"

"Not yet twelve years of age." The pall of longing clouded the king's face.

"I lost my mother when I was a child also. The pain never really leaves."

King Maelthorn nodded, still lost in memory.

"I should leave you, your highness. I don't wish to wile away your day with casual chatter."

"Casual chatter is something I've not had the pleasure of in many ages, child." He smiled. "I was beginning to fear my son's taste in women ran only to the gossipy skirts he's paraded past me these last few years now. You're a welcome change."

Jessalyne furrowed her brow. "Your highness, it's not my place to correct you, but I'm not here to win your blessing as a bride for your son. I'm here as mage-apprentice to Mistress Sryka."

The king's face fell. "Unfortunate news. Nonetheless, you are the first bright spot in my day for quite some time."

"You might have more bright spots if you let some sun into this room." Jessalyne slapped her hand over her mouth too late to stop the brash comment. "Forgive me, your highness."

The king chuckled. "Despite what my physicians say, I think you're right. I doubt the sun could speed the inevitable any more than fate allows." He tugged the bell pull hanging next to the bed. Sir Laythan appeared through the door.

"Laythan, open those drapes and windows and bring a chair for my guest."

Arching one eyebrow, Laythan hesitated. "But your physicians, your highness—"

"Blast the physicians. I want sunlight and fresh air."

"Yes, Sire." Laythan did as the king requested and the room took on the golden hue of the sun filtering in. Jessalyne inspected the space as the warm light revealed what the gloom had kept hidden.

Bookshelves and curiosities lined the walls just as in the outer chambers. The jug Sryka brought sat on a table near the king's bed, a small mug next to it.

Laythan brought the chair from the king's desk and set it next to the bed. Jessalyne nodded her thanks. "Have you read all these books, King Maelthorn?"

"Tell me your name again, child. My mind is not what it once was."

"Jessalyne, Sire."

"Lovely name. Yes, Jessalyne, I have read all these books. Some many times over." He clasped his hands together. "Age does terrible things to the memory. I can remember things that happen in my youth as though they occurred yesterday and yet things just discussed slip from my mind like water over a fall." He reached for the mug on his side table, took a sip and grimaced

"You don't care for Mistress Sryka's tonic?"

"It's an awful, vile tasting concoction. She assures me it's the only thing giving me strength. My physicians agree but in truth, they would rather face Saladan himself than argue with Sryka."

"If it tastes as bad as it smells, you have my sympathy." Even as the opened windows brought in fresh air, the stench lingered.

She sat and talked with the king until he began to grow tired. Laythan insisted the king rest and he agreed, bidding Jessalyne farewell but not before insisting she return the next day to talk with him some more.

Laythan escorted her to the bench outside the bedchamber. "I must apologize for my behavior earlier. I incorrectly assumed you were another one of the prince's women. It was good to see the king happy and I have you to thank, so, my apologies."

"I have met some of the prince's women." She grinned. "Don't apologize, I would feel the same way."

Laythan smiled. "I shall look forward to seeing you tomorrow then. There is one thing you should know, however."

"Yes?"

"The king sometimes...loses his place in time as it were. He slips back into the days of his youth, thinking the past is really the present. If it happens, don't be alarmed. It usually passes quickly. He's a good man and with him goes the end of an age, I fear." Sorrow lit Laythan's eyes as he gazed back toward the bedroom.

"I can tell he's a good man. As are you for keeping his interests at heart." She sat on the bench. "I will wait here for Mistress Sryka and not touch anything."

"Until tomorrow then." With a chuckle, he added, "Touch anything you want."

"Thank you. Until tomorrow."

Laythan closed the door. Jessalyne leaned her head against the wall, closing her eyes and wondering what it would be like to be the king's age. The thump of Sryka's staff woke Jessalyne from the nap she'd slipped into.

"Well?" Sryka looked at her expectantly.

"The king invited me back tomorrow."

The old woman's face softened and her eyes brightened. "Did he? Excellent. You may take your dinner in the garden tonight if you wish."

"I'd like that very much." Anything to avoid the hands of the prince. "May Fynna join me? I do hate to carry the food basket," she added, appealing to Sryka's need to keep Fynna subservient.

"Fine. I will send her down when I return to my chambers but she better have done her work and done it well."

As soon as Sryka turned her back, Jessalyne rolled her eyes. Poor Fynna.

༒

Instead of going directly back to her quarters, Sryka sought out the prince. She found him in his chambers, having high tea with the usual group of insignificant females.

"Out, all of you. I must speak with the prince alone." She glared at the pouting lot of them, daring a retort to pass their rouged lips.

The girls filled out quickly and the prince looked none too pleased. "This better be of great importance, old woman."

"The king met the girl today," Sryka said.

"So?" The prince sat with one leg thrown over the arm of his carved chair.

Sryka held her temper, eager for the coming days when she would ensorcell this unbearable twit and bend him to her will. "And the king has asked her back tomorrow. It bodes well, don't you think?"

The prince studied his nails. "How soon before he blesses the union so that I may be crowned?"

"You've waited this long. A little while longer will do you no harm." You will wait until I'm ready, you simpering fool.

"Just see that it happens. I'm tired of waiting. I want to be king now." The prince jumped to his feet, causing the crystal on the table to clink.

"As do we all, your highness. As do we all. I shall return when I have more to tell you."

"You're dismissed then. Stewards! Send the women back in!" He yelled loud enough to be heard beyond the double doors of his chamber.

The flood of women that rushed in nearly knocked Sryka down. She held tightly to her staff until they passed, placating herself with the thought that very soon she would turn the whole lot of them into salamanders.

Calmer, she left the prince to his giggling women and walked back to her quarters. It was good the child had done so well with the king. She desperately needed the renewal.

Soon, she would no longer have to suffer in this weak, aged body. She would have youth and beauty and power. Prince Erebus would be her puppet and she would be the true ruler of Shaldar.

She made a list of the few remaining things she still required for the incantation. The hardest to come by would be the nails pulled from a babe's coffin, but the undertaker would certainly supply her with them in exchange for the love spell he desired. The most vital ingredient of the spell was already in the castle.

Under the blackest sky of the next new moon, she would gather all the necessary components, speak the ancient words and cast the spell that would begin the next phase of her life as queen of Shaldar. She couldn't help but snicker aloud. Poor simple little Jessalyne, who could barely grasp the levitation spell, had no idea what an important role she was about to play.

Chapter Fifteen

Jessalyne waited in the scullery for Fynna to come down. She busied herself by teaching cook a cervidae recipe for seeded brown bread. When Fynna finally stumbled in, Jessalyne wanted to cry.

"Fynna! You look awful!" Jessalyne rushed to her friend's side.

"That miserable old hag worked me to the bone. Look at my hands!" Fynna held up her palms as Jessalyne helped her to the bench. The skin was cracked and bleeding, the nails torn and ragged.

Wrath blossomed in Jessalyne's heart against Sryka. "She cannot treat you this way. Something must be done."

"There is nothing that can be done." Fynna slumped her head on her folded arms. "I'm so hungry I could eat bugs but I'm too tired to chew. I don't think I can walk to the swan pond."

Jessalyne petted Fynna's tousled mop of indigo curls. "You just rest, let me take care of you." Fortunately, the scullery was nearly empty. Bread and pies had already been baked and most of the staff was out tending the spits of meat roasting over the fires in the great hall.

"Cook, may I use a few items from your store?"

"Whatever ya need, love." Cook shook her head and clucked her tongue while she looked at Fynna. "Take care of the wee one."

"Thank you. Will you fetch Fynna a mug of water? I need a few things from my own supplies in my chambers."

"Aye, I'll fetch it myself from the well so it's good and cold. You go, I'll keep an eye on the child."

Nodding, Jessalyne hurried out of the room and up the length of stairs. When she returned, the mug of water was drained but Fynna was in the same spot, head down, her arms crossed in such a way that her ravaged palms faced up.

In one of cook's pestle and mortars, Jessalyne muddled a selection of fresh and dried herbs into a dollop of tallow to make a salve for Fynna's hands.

"Fynna? Are you sleeping?"

The pixie shook her head silently and sat up.

"I want to spread this on your hands. It will sting a bit at first but then it will numb them slightly and take the pain away while they heal, all right?"

Fynna nodded and stretched her arms out.

Jessalyne spread the mix onto Fynna's palms with as little pressure as possible. Fynna gasped as the salve covered the first bit of cracked skin. "It's all right, keep going." She winced as she spoke.

Once Jessalyne finished, she began making a restorative tea to give her friend some energy back. "You'll feel better soon."

"The pain in my hands is gone and the bleeding has stopped." Fynna wiggled her fingers slightly.

Cook set a plate of cheese and dark bread with raisin butter in front of Fynna as she looked at Fynna's hands again. "I must be daft! So sorry, love, ya can't eat that with your hands such a sight, can ya? Leave that for Jessalyne. I've something better than that for ya." She disappeared into the cold larder and came back with a large bowl of creamy egg custard.

She scooped the pale cream into a smaller bowl and added a healthy dollop of raspberry preserves on top. "Now, that should be manageable." She set the bowl and a spoon in front of Fynna and gave the pixie a wink.

"Thank you, cook." Fynna held the spoon in her fingertips and took a large bite. Closing her eyes, she swallowed the custard. "Mmmm. Almost as good as chocolate biscuits."

Jessalyne finished brewing the tea and set a mug next to the bowl of custard. "Drink this. It'll give you some energy."

"Thank you, both of you. I feel better already. It's nice to be taken care of for a change." Fynna sipped the tea and made a face. "I might take that back. What is this stuff?"

"Just drink it. It'll help, I promise." Jessalyne smiled but inside she was seething. Something had to change in the wretched way Sryka treated the pixie.

Fynna gulped the tea down with a grimace. "Ugh. That is truly awful."

"But good for you. Why don't we go back up to the room and you can lie down?"

"I thought you wanted to go out into the garden?"

"Don't be silly. You need rest."

"A nap sounds like a great idea."

They took the stairs at a slower pace than usual. When they entered the room, Jessalyne's bed was mounded high with fancy dresses. A slip of parchment lay atop the pile of gowns.

"What's all this?" Fynna asked as she eased onto her bed.

Jessalyne groaned. "The prince mentioned something about sending out to his clothier for a selection of gowns for me."

She snatched the parchment from the top of the heap and read it aloud. "Please accept these as a gift from your future Lord King. I am sure you will do me the honor of wearing one at dinner. Prince Erebus"

"Wonderful. Sryka told me I could have dinner in the garden. I suppose the prince's request tops that." Sighing, she held up the first dress, a ruffled confection in peach and green. Jessalyne wrinkled her nose. "This is..."

"Hideous? Abominable? Very Salena?" Fynna laughed so hard tears seeped from the corners of her eyes.

"You obviously feel better."

"Yes, I do. Let's see the next selection."

Jessalyne held up the second gown. Done in orange velvet and lace, strands of pearls dripped from the bodice. "Oh my...this is worse than the first one."

"I really think you should try them on."

"Shouldn't you be sleeping?"

"There has to be one gown in that pile worth wearing. What is that bit of blue I see?"

From underneath several gowns, Jessalyne pulled out the dress Fynna pointed at. She held the dusty blue brocade gown with pale ivory satin trim in front of her. "What do you think?"

"Quite lovely, actually. I wonder how that found it's way into that pile."

"Purely accidental, I'm sure."

"You should get ready soon."

Jessalyne laid the dress down. "There's time. I need to heal your hands."

"But you put the salve on them."

"Sryka's not about to release you from your duties long enough for you to heal properly. Stretch them out so I can see them."

Fynna sat up and held her hands out in front of her.

Jessalyne held her own hands overtop Fynna's small blue ones and let the magic rush through her. A quick sharp flash of pain washed over her hands and was gone.

"Amazing." Fynna flexed her fingers. "The pain is gone." She threw her arms around Jessalyne's neck. "I've never seen such power in Sryka. You mustn't ever show her your true abilities. Her jealousy would not be a good thing."

"You needn't worry about that. When I'm under her teaching, I let her think I'm a complete novice."

"Good. You must protect yourself. Now, you'd better dress. The dinner chimes will ring before you know it."

While Jessalyne changed, she told Fynna of her day with the king. "How long has Sryka been providing the king with that awful smelling tonic?"

"Quite some time now. I've never seen her make it and I never have to wash the pots when she is done. She must keep it locked in her room. I never have to deliver it either. Usually one of the king's stewards comes for it early. I used to pass them on the stairs as I was going up for the day. Now that you're here, they must come very early because I never see them at all any more."

"She delivered it herself yesterday. I don't know how the king can drink the stuff. Maybe she's poisoning him. Do you think?" Jessalyne looked at Fynna.

"No. She can't do him harm. The Oath of Amity prevents it. She took it when she became the king's magewoman and you'll take it when you become magewoman to the prince."

"The Oath of Amity?"

"It's a barrier spell to prevent the king's mage from using magic against him or doing him harm."

Jessalyne finished tying herself into the prince's gift. "I guess it's just some awful tonic, then. How do I look?"

"Lovely. I have a feeling the prince's hands will be lively tonight."

Jessalyne rolled her eyes. "I'm not looking forward to this evening."

Fynna lay back down. "You could always set him on fire."

"Ah yes, that should do it. Thank you so much for your help." Jessalyne stuck her tongue out before heading to the great hall.

The days continued and Jessalyne's stayed the same. Mornings spent learning insignificant charms and spells from Sryka, afternoons chatting with the king, and dinners finding new ways to divert the prince's attentions.

At night, much to Fynna's delight, she practiced her magic in the confines of their quarters. The ache in her heart increased. She missed Ertemis more every day.

One morning she woke as the weak glow of firstlight barely edged the horizon, another dream of her dark elf filling her sleep with visions. She slipped out of bed quietly so as not to wake Fynna and stood by the window. The dream had been so real, more so than any before it. The remembered feel of his arms around her made her weak and the most awful thought crept into her head. What if he never came back? What if she never saw him again?

She pressed the necklace he'd given her to her lips and her eyes burned with unshed tears. Tipping her head back to keep them from falling, a sob escaped her throat.

"What's wrong?" Sleep thickened Fynna's voice.

Jessalyne shook her head. Her voice would crack if she tried to speak.

Fynna padded across the floor and slipped her arm around Jessalyne's waist. Are you crying? Did you have a nightscare?"

Jessalyne pressed the heels of her hands against her eyes. Tears solved nothing.

Fynna rested her head against Jessalyne's side. "You dreamed of him again, didn't you? You must miss him so."

"He isn't coming back, is he?"

"Don't say that. He'll return, I know it."

Sniffing deeply, Jessalyne shook her head. "No, he won't. It's been too long." She gazed out the window at the brightening sky. "I've been here for more than a month, Fynna. He told me he could hear my voice in his head."

"Mindsight?"

Jessalyne nodded. "I've called out to him every day and still he doesn't come. It's time I give up my foolish fantasies and just forget him or I'll live the rest of my life longing for a man who doesn't even remember me."

༄

Ertemis turned as his mother walked away. The Ferryman waited for him at the end of the curving pier. He led Dragon down the steps and back onto the skiff.

The fog rolled in when the Ferryman pushed off, blocking all sight of Elysium. Ertemis took one last look at the ring his mother had given him and tucked it beneath his breastplate and tunic. He was so wrapped in thought, he barely noticed they reached the far shore in half the time it took to get to Elysium.

Dragon followed him off onto the small pier and although Ertemis knew the Ferryman would already been gone, he looked back anyway. Nothing but swirling mist and gray water remained.

The sun set as he made his way through the bog, lighting the sky with fire. He stayed on the high path as lastlight descended. He urged Dragon on, unwilling to spend the night in the marshland that served as a buffer between the mortal world and Elysium.

He approached the forest line, his elven sight picking out subtle differences. Everything was somehow different. The leaves were larger, the greens slightly darker. Blooms replaced buds. The boom of bullfrogs greeted him instead of the trill of tadpoles.

Panic twisted his gut. The day spent on Elysium had been much more than a day in Shaldar. He studied the constellations. Spring was well over and summer was in full sway. He cursed the time lost.

He opened his mind and comforted himself with the cadence of Jessalyne's heartbeat. Digging his heels into Dragon's side, he took off for Shaldar City, forming a plan as he rode. By now, any number of men could have wooed Jessalyne. She must think him gone for good. If she still thought of him at all.

The overwhelming need for sleep grew the farther he traveled. The effects of time spent on Elysium were catching up to him. He would have to sleep, even if just for an hour or two.

He jerked back and realized he had drifted for a moment. Even Dragon plodded along in a fog. Ahead sat a small cluster of thatched cottages. Magda and Brynden. He could make it at least that far.

Focusing on a small square of candlelit window, he kept on until he and Dragon were at last in front of the cottage. He slid off Dragon and dropped to the ground with a thud.

The light inside the cottage went out.

Ertemis knocked softly on the door. Nothing. He knocked again and waited. The door opened a crack and he could see Brynden peering out.

"I was here with Lady Jessalyne, she healed your—"

"Master elf?" He spoke to someone inside the cottage. "Grams, relight the candle, it's all right." He turned to Ertemis. "What brings you back to our home?"

"I need a place to sleep and Dragon needs tending. I also have a matter to discuss with you in the morning."

Magda pulled the door open and chided her grandson. "Let the man in, Brynden. Where's yer manners, child?"

"Sorry, Grams." He slipped past and took Dragon's reins. "I'll take care of your horse."

"Thank you, Brynden. Mistress Magda, pardon my intrusion at such a late hour. I seek shelter for the night and of course, I will compensate you for your trouble."

She looked past him. "The lady ain't with you?"

"No." Not yet.

"Come inside. You were more than generous during yer last visit. You can have the boy's bed."

The soft glow of embers in the stove cast the cottage in a warm light. Half a loaf of seeded bread sat on the table. His stomach growled.

"Hungry, are ya?"

"Aye."

She unwrapped a hunk of cheese from some waxed linen and set it next to the bread. After rummaging in a cabinet, she added a pot of honey. "Eat then. I'll have fresh eggs in the morning and porridge. Nothing fancy but it'll fill ya."

He tore into the bread, smearing it liberally with honey before stuffing it into his mouth. He swallowed, then spoke. "If you can spare him, I want to hire Brynden as my squire for a short time."

She nodded, mulling it over. "I'll give ya my answer in the morning." She started behind a curtain doorway, then paused and pointed to a bed tucked into an alcove in the wall. "That's yers for the night. Snore all ya want. My hearing ain't that good."

He devoured the last of the meager fare and collapsed fully dressed onto Brynden's bed, asleep more quickly than he could whip his sword from its sheath.

The smell of breakfast and his growling stomach pulled him from his dreams of Jessalyne. Someone had closed the curtain across the alcove. He opened it and squinted at the bright daylight. Why couldn't it be overcast more?

Magda stood at the fire, stirring a pot of porridge. "Good morning, master elf. Sleep well?"

"I don't remember." He stretched and threw his legs over the side of the narrow bed. "Have you decided about the boy?"

"Don't mince words, do ya?" She ladled porridge into bowls. "I've thought it over and if Brynden agrees to it, it's all right by me."

He sat at the small table and dug into the hot porridge. "Where is he?"

"Tending your horse. He'll be in shortly. You'll keep him from danger, won't ya? He's all I have since my son passed."

"You have my word he won't be in harm's way."

The cottage door opened. "Good morning, master elf. Grams, there were only two eggs." Brynden set them on the counter and sat next to Ertemis. "Dragon's fed and watered. He ate three portions of oats."

"That horse bears the soul of a fat man." Ertemis emptied his bowl. "Brynden, I want to hire you as my squire. Temporarily."

The boy's eyes lit up. "Really?" He glanced at Magda and quickly hid his excitement. "I can't. I have duties here. I'm sorry."

Magda patted Brynden's shoulder. "It's all right. Yer chores'll wait."

"Thanks, Gram." He smiled. "When do we leave?"

Ertemis leaned back. "After you bathe."

Brynden frowned. "Truly?"

"Aye! Being next to you is like standing downwind of a sty. Mistress Magda, has the boy any other clothes?"

"We ain't city folk. We wear what we got." She furrowed her brow. "Wait." She went behind the curtain, then reemerged with clothing draped over her arm.

"These were Brynden's father's. I imagine they should fit him now." On the bed where Ertemis had slept she laid a slightly worn cloak of navy wool and a simple cotton shirt and trousers in pale grey. "Will those do?"

Ertemis nodded. "Very well. Very well indeed."

With Brynden mounted on Dragon beside him, Ertemis entered Shaldar City for the second time. Even with Brynden playing decoy, Ertemis took great care to keep himself covered with his cloak and used his magic to make himself insignificant to any eyes that found his face.

He glanced up. The boy had certainly taken to his role as knight-in-training. Ertemis's sword hung at his side. Brynden had yet to take his hand from the hilt.

Holding tight to Dragon's reins, Ertemis opened his mind, listening for the familiar sounds of a tavern. Following them, he led them away from the bustle of the main streets and into a less crowded quarter.

"Ertemis." Brynden whispered out of the corner of his mouth.

"Aye?"

"This doesn't seem to be the best part of town."

"Exactly what we want."

"It is?"

"Aye. I want to be noticed as little as possible. Blending in is out of the question, but in the lesser parts of town, people have their own worries and aren't as inclined to notice strangers."

Brynden nodded and stayed quiet.

They found a tavern inn and Ertemis felt at home immediately. The Boot and Buckle was just the sort of place a dark elf could disappear in. He made arrangements for a room with two beds and stable space for Dragon.

Ertemis took his pack and Brynden's while the boy followed the innkeeper's directions to the stable with Dragon in tow.

The room was sufficient. Two pallets, a washstand and a fireplace were all any man truly needed. He pulled the shabby curtains back and studied the lay of the land visible beyond the window. The room was on the third floor, overlooking a back alley. The window opened easily. He would be able to come and go without notice.

Brynden came up a few moments later, his excitement at everything going on barely contained. "Dragon's settled in. What now?"

ᴥ

Jessalyne barely heard a word of Sryka's lesson. She tried but there was little in the casting of runes for better crop growth that could pull her thoughts from Ertemis.

Where was he? A brief image of him, wrapped in the arms of some tavern doxy flashed in her head. She shoved it away. Even if it were the truth, she didn't want to see it.

"Are you listening to me?" Sryka rapped the table sharply with her staff.

"Yes, mistress. Forgive me, I didn't sleep well last night."

"Did that pixie keep you up?" Sryka glared at Fynna, busy in the corner polishing the sorceress's crystals.

"No. It had nothing to do with Fynna." Jessalyne knew the tone of her voice was less than respectful but she didn't care.

"Very well. You are dismissed to visit the king."

Without another word, Jessalyne got up, happy to go but wishing Fynna could come with her.

"Before you go, take the king's tonic to him. His steward must be ill, he hasn't been by to pick it up yet." Sryka pulled the jug from a pouch deep inside her robes, her back to Fynna.

"Yes, mistress." Jessalyne took the small, stoppered jug from Sryka's hands and turned to leave. At least her visit with the king would be a pleasant distraction. Lately she had been reading to him from a book of poems. She shot Fynna a parting glance and took her leave.

On her walk through the castle, she again found herself thinking of Ertemis. If he didn't come back, maybe there was a way she could send him a message. Perhaps Valduuk could help her.

She didn't see Sir Laythan until it was too late. He swerved to miss her, she went the same way, and they collided. Sir Laythan stumbled but stayed upright. Jessalyne fell backwards, knocking the stopper loose from the jug. The vile liquid splashed over her, staining her gown with the liver-colored tonic.

"Ugh!" She tilted her face away from the stench rising off her dress.

"My dear, are you all right?" Sir Laythan offered his hand even as he wrinkled his nose.

"I'm fine, but my dress may never be the same." She took his assistance and stood. The stain spread further.

"I was just on my way to fetch that nasty draft myself. Jeremy's mother had her third child last night and I granted him the day off to help her."

"Sryka dismissed me early and asked me to bring it." She suppressed a gag at the sickening smell. "I must change, I cannot bear this stench any longer. I'll return shortly."

She ran back to her room, ignoring the wrinkled noses and puckered faces of the people she passed. Once inside, she stripped off the gown and left it in a heap, making sure none of the stain touched anything else in the room. At least it was one of the prince's gowns. She could care less if it was ruined.

She selected another dress of lavender brocade trimmed in deep red and hurriedly threw it on, cinching the waist and buttoning the bodice. Gagging, she opened the window wide. Already the smell of Sryka's tonic doused the room.

She tucked a lavender sachet into her waist sash and crushed it to release the fragrance of the small dried flowers. She closed the door and made her way back to the king's chambers. The guards on duty outside his doors gave her entrance without question.

Sir Laythan was shelving a selection of books as she walked in. "Greetings again. I must say, you smell much better."

"Wouldn't take much after being drenched with that awful stuff, would it?"

"It would not."

"I think the king might be happy to have a day free of Sryka's elixir."

"Actually, there was some left from yesterday. I already gave it to him."

"Oh." Jessalyne wished his majesty never need taste the vile stuff again.

"He's not well today. I thought it might help. He's lost in remembrances of the past, but I'm sure he'll listen if you read to him. Your voice seems to soothe him."

She rested her hand on Sir Laythan's arm, the pain in his eyes evidence of his love for his king. "You're a kind man. I cannot imagine anyone serving the king better."

"Thank you." He smiled and slid the last book into place. "I'm brewing a pot of tea. I'll bring it in to you."

"That sounds wonderful." She squeezed his arm before entering the king's bedroom.

Laythan had already placed a chair next to the bed and pulled the bed curtains back. The king was propped up with pillows but he made no sign to indicate he noticed her enter. He stared blankly out the windows, mumbling quietly to himself.

Laythan came in with the pot of tea and a mug on a tray. He set it on the table near the bed, glanced at the king and shook his head sadly before leaving the room.

Jessalyne poured tea into the mug and sipped at it, but the king kept staring out the window. Not knowing what else to do, she starting reading. At the sound of her voice, the king's mumbling ceased and a slight smile softened his face. He whispered something she couldn't hear.

She paused to take another sip of tea. When she looked up, the king's eyes were fixed on her.

"Good afternoon, your highness. How are you feeling today?"

His dark eyes glimmered with tears, and he whispered the same word again.

Unable to hear, she nodded and smiled.

With trembling lips, he said it again more clearly.

She hadn't heard him correctly. That had to be it. She set the book down and moved to his bedside, sitting on the edge.

"Again, your highness. Please."

He uttered the word once more. Disbelief filled her. It couldn't be. How could he know that name? She took his hand in hers. He smiled again and words spilled out of him.

"Shaylana...I knew you would come back." He gripped her hand with surprising strength. "I've missed you so much. Please tell me you've brought our child. I think of you everyday, my love."

"Shaylana? You think...I'm Shaylana?" Realization swept through her with a shudder. It was too impossible to believe. She needed more confirmation.

With the king still begging to see his child, she cried out for Sir Laythan.

He burst through the door. "What's wrong? Should I call the king's physicians?"

"Were you in the king's employ when he attempted to form the alliance with the elves?"

Taken back, Laythan hesitated. "Yes. Why do you ask?"

"Was there an elfess in the council by the name of Shaylana? An elfess the king was especially fond of?"

"How do you know this?" Laythan's eyes narrowed." What sorcery have you worked on him?"

"He got a child on her, didn't he? And when she fled, the alliance fell apart, spoiling the blood between both kingdoms."

Laythan tore her hands away from the king. "How do you know this? I demand you tell me or I will call the guards and have you put out of the city."

"I mean his highness no harm, I swear it. He called me by her name. Shaylana. You see the pendant around my neck?"

He nodded.

"Her son gave it to me. Her only son. The king's son."

"It cannot be," he whispered, staring at the necklace then the king. He slumped into a chair. "Lady Shaylana sent a missive after she disappeared telling the king the halfling child had been dealt with according to custom. He cursed the elves for their intolerance."

"His son is very much alive."

"Do you know what this means?" He straightened. "This child is King Maelthorn's firstborn son. Prince Erebus is no longer in line for the throne. There is hope yet for the kingdom. What kind of man is the king's son? He is half-elf, of course..."

Laythan paused as his own words sunk in. "A dark elf on the throne of Shaldar or Prince Erebus? I daresay one could be worse than the other."

"Ertemis is a good man, nothing like what people think. He shielded me here, kept me safe and sheltered. He knows nothing of his father. Nothing."

"She never told him, just as she told us the child was killed."

"She conscripted him to the Legions when he was a boy."

Laythan face blanched. "The Legions? I've heard tales of a creature—"

"I don't think most of them are true."

"Are you telling me the king's firstborn is the assassin known as the Black Death?"

She nodded. "And I love him."

He stared unblinking at the floor. "In truth, I always thought the tales more fiction than fact, stories told for frights and amusements...and now you tell me this creature is not only real but the king's own flesh and blood."

The king grasped Jessalyne's hand. "A son or daughter, Shaylana, please tell me..."

"A son, named Ertemis. You would be proud of him, I think. His life has not been an easy one, but he's made his own way."

The king stared out the window again, and she wondered if he'd really heard anything she said.

Laythan looked up. "Where is this dark elf?"

She shook her head. "Unfortunately, I don't know."

"But you love him?"

"Yes, I've tried not to but I cannot help it. We quarreled and when he left he barely spoke to me. I'm sure he's forgotten me by now."

"Forgotten a woman who bears such a lovely resemblance to his lady mother? I doubt that. More likely he berates himself for not finding a way to smooth things between you before he left." Laythan stood and patted Jessalyne's knee. "Not to worry. The Black Death is a man for hire and a man for hire cannot be too hard to find or he will never get work."

She brightened a bit. "I had not thought of that."

"This will be our secret, Jessalyne. Do you understand?"

"But I must tell Fynna."

"The pixie in Sryka's service?"

"Yes. She's my friend and she already knows about him."

"Very well, but no one else. I don't want Sryka or Erebus learning of this."

She nodded. "I agree. There's just one thing I don't understand."

"What is that, child?"

"In order to be king of Shaldar, a prince must marry a woman blessed by his father, correct?"

"Yes, that's right."

"Does that mean Shaylana was the king's mistress? I doubt Ertemis will find that happy news."

Laythan shook his head. "Nay, she was not his mistress. His highness was married at his coronation, as all kings of Shaldar are, but she died in childbirth, along with the babe, about a year after they wed. The king fell into such a state of sorrow that I thought he wouldn't recover.

"Lady Shaylana brought laughter and joy back into his life. He truly loved her and his hope was that a successful alliance would polish the way for them to be wed. He intended she be his queen.

"Some years after the failed alliance, he realized he must have an heir and so he wed again and Erebus was born. But it was a union born of duty, not love. She passed two summers ago."

Jessalyne kissed Sir Laythan's cheek as she slipped off the bed. "Thank you. Take care of his highness. I fear this has been a bit of a shock for him. I'll see you tomorrow, Sir Laythan."

Ertemis was King Maelthorn's firstborn son. Heir to the throne of Shaldar. It was almost more than she could take in. She was rounding the last few steps to the landing when she saw Fynna coming down from Sryka's quarters.

"You're certainly alight with something." Fynna hopped onto the landing.

"I have news." Jessalyne held a finger to her lips and whispered, "I'll tell you inside."

She pushed open the door and the reek of her stained dress greeted them. "Ugh. I must throw that dress out."

Fynna stood in the doorway, quivering. "What...what is that?" She pointed to the stain clearly visible on the crumpled gown heaped upon the floor.

"I bumped into Sir Laythan and spilled that foul tonic Sryka makes for the king all over my dress. Have you ever smelled anything like it?"

Sinking to her knees beside the dress, Fynna nodded. "Yes. I have." She picked up the gown and lifted it to her nose, inhaling where the stain was.

"Fynna! How can you stand to—"

"She's poisoning him. With the dust off my wings." Fynna shook, despair twisting her mouth.

"What do you mean?"

"Pixie wings are covered with a fine powder like butterfly wings. That's where pixie dust comes from. Made into an elixir, it smells like the corpse flower."

She held up the dress. "I would know that smell anywhere. No wonder Sryka has taken such pains to hide the tonic from me."

"But you said she cannot harm him because of the Oath."

"She has found a way around it. In small doses, pixie dust is a powerful restorative. In large doses, it's deadly. By giving him the elixir every day, she's slowly poisoning him." Fynna sobbed. "And destroying my wings in the process."

"Not for much longer. I have news that will change everything. Everything."

Chapter Sixteen

Ertemis relaxed on one of the pallets, arms folded behind his head. "We wait." He closed his eyes, ready for a nap.

"We wait? We just got here!" Brynden muttered, his dissatisfied with Ertemis's decision evident in his voice.

"Just until lastlight. You'll need to be alert later. Once I leave, I want you to keep an eye on Dragon."

The boy sighed as he lay on the other pallet. "Fine."

"Brynden?"

"Aye?"

"Take my sword off, please. You're liable to slice yourself in two while you sleep. "

"It's still sheathed!"

"Take it off. Now." Ertemis suppressed a grin. The boy's enthusiasm was undaunted.

With another great sigh, Brynden reluctantly took off the sword and lay quietly.

As the boy's breath slowly evened out with sleep, Ertemis grinned. No doubt the excitement of the day had taken its toll. Sleep would do them both good. His eyes closed, Ertemis opened his mind and found Jessalyne's heartbeat, drawing it into his body until his heart beat in time with hers. Knowing she was so close and not being able to go to her was excruciating. He ached to hold her and kiss her. He would never leave her again. If she would have him.

He pulled free the chain his mother had given him and studied the delicate band of gold and diamonds. It confounded him to think of himself, the infamous Black Death, actually in love. And with such a woman as Jessalyne. He moaned softly at the thought of her smooth skin.

She would say yes. She had to. He would find them a place to live, near Valduuk perhaps. Jessalyne could work as a healer or maybe just stay home and fill their home with babes and every night he would hold her tight and inhale her intoxicating scent and remind himself that she was his. He would make sure she wanted for nothing.

His head full of the promise of the future, he fell asleep clutching the ring, his hand over his heart.

ಬ

Fynna kept her eyes fixed on the blotch staining the gown.

Jessalyne took her friend by the shoulders and turned her, forcing her to look up. "Listen to me. When I was with the king today, he was lost in remembrances of the past. Sir Laythan told me to expect that at times, but today is the first I saw of it. He was mumbling and staring out the windows and making little sense. I started reading to him and when I paused, he was staring at me.

"I thought he was himself again, then he called me by someone else's name. I went to his bedside to hear him better and he said the name again, as clear as a summer day."

Jessalyne hesitated, looking into Fynna's weepy eyes. "Fynna, he called me Shaylana. Shaylana."

Fynna shook her head slowly. "I don't understand."

"He called me Shaylana and asked me if I had finally brought our child to him."

Still, the pixie looked confused.

"Of all the stories you've made me tell you about Ertemis, does that name not mean anything to you?"

The fog in Fynna's blue eyes cleared. Her mouth dropped open. "Do you mean..." She covered her mouth with her hand. "He is...His mother was... is it true? Can it be?"

"Sir Laythan confirmed it. I told him everything about Ertemis and me. Well, not everything, but the important bits."

"Your dark elf is heir to the throne of Shaldar." Fynna whispered the words as if saying them too loud might make them untrue.

Jessalyne nodded and whispered back, "Fynna, we must keep this between us and Sir Laythan. Sryka and the prince must not find this out."

"A secret of the utmost importance. Keeping it will be my first duty to his highness, King Ertemis."

King Ertemis Elta-naya. Except the Elta-naya no longer fit, Jessalyne thought. The firstborn son of Shaldar's king could hardly be called the son of none.

"Fynna, I must take this dress down to the scullery and throw it into the fire. I cannot bear the stench any longer. You must also keep secret what Sryka is about with your wings. I can only imagine how terrible it is for you to know she's doing this, but I promise it won't be for much longer."

"The knowledge that Prince Erebus's day is coming will help, rest assured."

Jessalyne bundled the dress so that the stain was in the middle. "Is there anyway to get Sryka out of her chambers?"

"Why?"

"I want to try my hand at scrying for Ertemis. I must find him and I don't know how else to do it. I need her crystal."

Fynna smiled. "You leave that to me. Now get that foul dress out of here and ask cook for some chocolate biscuits while you're down there."

Jessalyne laughed. "I'll see what I can do."

ജ

Sryka was in no mood for the prince's behavior. After searching inside the castle for him, she had finally found him in the front courtyard, playing childish games. "Your highness, we must go see the king. Immediately."

"I'm busy, old woman." Prince Erebus kept his eyes on Salena as she took her turn at Fox and Geese.

She moved closer and whispered in his ear. "You no longer wish to be king, then?"

His eyes sparked with interest. "Why didn't you call me sooner?" He spun on his heel and Sryka hobbled after him, leaving Salena pouting in the sun.

Sir Laythan greeted them warily. Never had both Prince Erebus and Sryka come to see the king at once. "His highness is not well today. Perhaps tomorrow would be a better time."

Erebus pushed Laythan out of the way. "How dare you tell me what I can and cannot do? Out of my way."

Sneering at Laythan as she passed, Sryka had the prince secure the bedroom door to keep the old man out until they needed him. How odd. Fresh air wafted in through open windows and the king stared out at the blue sky.

"He looks well enough to me," Erebus grumbled.

She moved toward the bed. "Your highness?"

The king twisted, revealing a faraway look in his eyes. Even better. She smirked. "Let Laythan in to witness. The king will give the blessing."

Prince Erebus stepped away from the door and Laythan burst in. "You should not be in here. The king needs his rest."

"Be quiet, old man. You knew this day would come." The prince stroked the hilt of his sword in a poorly veiled threat.

Sryka focused her attention on the king. "Your highness, we are here to receive your blessing on the child Jessalyne. Your son wishes to wed her and take his rightful place on the throne."

"My son?" The king's words were feeble.

"Aye, your son wishes you to bless Jessalyne as his bride so that he may marry her."

"Jessalyne?"

Sryka ground down her exasperation. Just a little while longer and she'd be free. "The pale-haired girl who has been visiting with you?"

"Beautiful hair." A faint smile crossed his face.

"Aye, lovely hair. Do you give her your blessing to wed your son?"

"Hair like moonlight..." The king seemed to be searching his memory. "My son is here?"

"Aye, Sire, your son is here."

His face lit in a way Sryka had not seen in a long time. "I give my blessing."

છ

Jessalyne returned with a bundle of the requested biscuits tied in linen.

"Oh good." Fynna smiled. "I brewed a pot of tea. I knew you'd come back with them. Cook loves you. Did she say anything about that dress?"

Jessalyne handed the biscuits to Fynna. "She sent me down to the laundry, to pitch it in one of the furnaces so it wouldn't stink up the scullery. I promised her a recipe for pepperberry preserves."

"Do you have to go to the great hall for dinner?" Crumbs spilled out of Fynna's mouth.

"Regrettably, yes. I am running out of ways to distract Prince Erebus. I swear, if he does not stop petting me like a kitten, I may show him my claws."

Fynna spit more crumbs out as she laughed. "I would like to see that!"

"Mark my words, as soon as I become his mage, I will waste no time making sure he understands his hands are not welcome anywhere near me."

"When you become the new mage..." Fynna hesitated, twisting her toes in the carpet.

"Yes?"

"I would like to be your apprentice. If you think I could do it, that is."

"Of course you could do it, but wouldn't you rather return home?"

"For everything Sryka puts me through, I like castle life. At least I like it since you've gotten here."

Jessalyne was touched by Fynna's words. "When I am mage, you will always have a place here. But you will come and go as you please. None of this asking permission rubbish."

Fynna stuffed another biscuit in her mouth.

"You keep eating those biscuits like that and you'll be too fat to fly." Jessalyne opened the wardrobe to select a gown for dinner. "How awful is this one?" Jessalyne pulled out a spinach green sateen gown with mustard ribbons lacing up the sleeves and banding the waist.

"Must I answer?"

"You just did. Do you think the prince's clothier is blind?"

Fynna laughed and set the biscuits down long enough to lace Jessalyne into the gown. She smoothed her hair into a simple braid. "All right, I best go. I'll see you after dinner. Maybe we'll play some Fryst when I get back, if you feel like it."

"I'll walk with you. I think cook is making liver dumplings."

Jessalyne raised an eyebrow. "And you're going to eat those after eating chocolate biscuits? Not only do I not know where you store all that food, I don't know how you keep it down."

At the bottom of the stairs, Fynna veered the back hall toward the scullery and Jessalyne reluctantly took her seat at the prince's table.

Prince Erebus entered with his usual pomposity. He wore a purple velvet cloak, trimmed in peacock feathers and gold braid. A bit much, even for him.

Somewhat distracted by the extravagant cloak, she at last noticed two familiar faces in the procession with Prince Erebus. Sryka and Sir Laythan were walking behind the prince. Sir Laythan's mouth was crumpled in an unhappy frown, but Sryka was oddly buoyant even as she leaned on her staff.Jessalyne tried to catch Sir Laythan's eye as the party made its way onto the dais but he didn't look in her direction.

At the trumpeters' final flourish, Prince Erebus raised his hands to silence the crowd. "Citizens of Shaldar, visiting nobles and distinguished guests! As always, your love and affection for me is overwhelming."

Jessalyne thought she might retch. Laythan but he still would not look at her. Sryka's eyes were fixed on the prince as he continued his address.

"As you all know, I have been searching for a bride. A woman who must not only serve me as wife and companion but who must also serve you, the people of Shaldar, as your queen. A woman who will bear the heirs to Shaldar's throne. A woman who most importantly must receive the blessing of King Maelthorn."

Finally. The king had blessed Salena and the prince would leave her alone at last. Great relief swept through her knowing this would be the last dinner spent fending off the prince's advances. Salena preened in the audience, staring at the prince with a haughty expectance.

Jessalyne felt a hand on her shoulder and looked up to see the prince. He still spoke to the crowd. "It is my great honor to introduce you to the woman who will be my mage." He gazed at Jessalyne, his smile wide enough to show his molars. "And in one week's time, my queen. I give you Jessalyne Brandborne of Fairleigh Grove!"

Chapter Seventeen

The visceral howl erupting from Salena barely registered in Jessalyne's mind. The room spun as she gasped for breath. His queen. All sound faded. Lights dimmed. She clutched for the table, for anything that would keep her upright. Her knees failed. She grabbed a handful of fabric as she slipped from her chair.

In her grasp, the prince's sumptuous cloak tore loose from its jeweled fastenings at his shoulders and fell over her. Strangely detached, she stared at the ceiling. The prince stood above her, his hands on his hips.

He addressed the crowd. "Seems once again I am too much man for one woman."

The crowd erupted with cheers and hoorahs and the prince motioned for his stewards. "Take this girl to her chambers," he snapped. "I am about to make her queen and this is how she reacts? Foolish chit."

Sryka hobbled up beside Erebus. "Well done, your highness."

"Sit." He ordered. "I will not have an empty chair at my table."

ଚ୍ଚ

The loud rapping startled Fynna. She opened the door to find Jessalyne draped across the arms of one of the prince's stewards.

"What happened?"

The man barged in and dumped Jessalyne onto the closest bed.

"She passed out, what does it look like?" He stomped out without bothering to shut the door.

Fynna secured the door, then went to Jessalyne's side and lifted her head to slip a pillow beneath it. She felt Jessalyne's forehead. Not hot. Not cold either. What was wrong with her?

"Jessalyne, can you hear me?" Fynna took Jessalyne's hands between her own. "Your hands are like ice! What happened?"

A quiet moan answered Fynna's pleading. Jessalyne took a deep breath as she struggled to sit up. "I didn't pass out but I wish I had."

"I don't think you should be up yet." Fynna gently pushed her back.

Jessalyne moaned again, covering her face with her hands. "Oh Fynna, it's just so awful. I cannot marry him. I will not marry him, I refuse."

"Marry who? What's awful? What happened?"

Jessalyne grasped Fynna's small hands and stared into her eyes. "The prince somehow got the king to bless me as his bride. In one week we're to be wed and he will be king."

"Oh no." Fynna shook her head. "I wondered what the noise in the great hall was. This cannot be. We must find Ertemis now."

Sitting up, Jessalyne sighed. "I need Sryka's crystal."

Smiling, Fynna reached into the pouch dangling from her waist sash. "When I was in the scullery, I heard the servers commenting on how odd it was to see Sryka at dinner. I made a little visit her chambers." She pulled out a long black cord with a single onyx crystal swinging from the end.

"You got it!" Jessalyne hugged Fynna. "Thank you so much."

"How do we make this thing work?"

"I need a bowl of water sprinkled with ashes."

Fynna jumped off the bed and grabbed the washbasin. "Will this work?"

"It will have to." Jessalyne cleared the game table and fetched the water jug while Fynna set the bowl on the table and scooped some ashes from the fireplace.

Jessalyne filled the bowl then nodded for Fynna. She sprinkled a small handful of ashes over the water's surface. "Enough?"

"It looks right, from what I remember."

Fynna clapped the dust from her hands. "Now what?"

"Now I scry." Jessalyne dangled the crystal over the water and uttered the words Sryka taught her. "With powers of fire and water bound, what is lost shall now be found."

They waited. Nothing happened.

"Maybe I added too much ash." Fynna stared into the sooty water.

"Maybe I said it wrong." Jessalyne cleared her throat and tried it again.

"I think it moved that time." Fynna said.

"That was a breeze from the window." Jessalyne shook her head. "I have a feeling we could try this all night with the same results. It isn't going to work. It probably only responds to Sryka." She handed the crystal back to Fynna.

Fynna hid her disappointment. Jessalyne had enough troubles. "It was worth a try. I'll put it back in the morning, she'll never know it was gone."

Jessalyne sunk onto her bed. "What am I going to do? I cannot marry Erebus. He repulses me. To think of him touching me..." She shuddered.

Fynna patted her hand. "Wait until dinner is over, then go speak with Sir Laythan about the poison tonic. The prince will probably spend the evening with that tramp Salena. The guest quarters are far from the king's, and after the prince's announcement this evening, he'll have to go to her, because she won't be coming to him."

"I should try to cleanse the poison out of the king's system. He's a good man, Fynna. He doesn't deserve to suffer," Jessalyne said.

"The good in this kingdom rarely get what they deserve." Fynna tucked her knees up and wrapped her arms around her legs.

"It doesn't make sense, though. Why would Sryka poison the king? When Erebus becomes king, I will become the mage in power. She stands to lose everything."

Fynna shook her head. "Trust me, Sryka does nothing that doesn't serve her own goals. How she'll benefit from Erebus on the throne, I don't know but it cannot be good."

Jessalyne squeezed Fynna's hand. "Oh, Ertemis. Where are you when I need you most?" She whispered his name over and over while clinging to the pendant around her neck.

౸

Jessalyne's voice ripped through Ertemis's mind. He sprung from the pallet, instinctively reaching for his sword before realizing what had happened. He opened his mind to her. Desperate unhappiness overwhelmed his senses and he pulled back, astounded by how much she filled him. It was time. He tucked the ring beneath his breastplate before waking Brynden. "Get up. I must leave. I need you in the stables watching Dragon."

In truth, Dragon didn't need watching. Anyone foolish enough to try stealing that animal would be soundly dissuaded by a well-placed hoof or sharp bite. But it couldn't hurt to make the boy feel useful.

"I'm up. I'm up." Brynden did little to hide his disappointment when he saw Ertemis buckling the sword onto his belt. "I guess you're taking that with you?"

Ertemis shot him a glance.

"Well, what if someone tries to steal Dragon? I have no weapon!"

"You have Dragon. That's enough, trust me."

He grumped, but threw his cloak around his shoulders as Ertemis did the same. Ertemis flipped him a silver. "Take your dinner to the stables. Whatever you don't spend, you may keep."

"Thank you!" Brynden's eyes rounded, the matter of weaponry forgotten.

"If anyone asks, I've off drinking. If I'm not back by firstlight, tend Dragon, then come back to the room. Stay here in case I need you."

"Aye. Good luck to ya."

"Men like us make our own luck, Brynden."

The boy smiled. "I'll remember that, master elf."

As soon as Brynden left, Ertemis went to the window overlooking the alley and opened it, taking in the night. Thick clouds allowed only brief glimpses of the waning moon, darkening the night almost completely.

Celebratory sounds drifted in with the night air. Focusing, he heard snippets about the prince's engagement. Unconcerned with such petty matters, he shifted his thoughts to finding Jessalyne. He slipped out the window and with elven agility dropped silently to the ground below, his cloak billowing out around him. Both directions down the alley were clear. He tugged his hood up and wrapped the night around him. With each step, he disappeared a little more into the shadows until he walked onto the street, completely veiled in the night's embrace.

ॐ

Fynna returned from her spying mission. "The hall's clear. Just a few drunken revelers passed out by the fires."

Jessalyne didn't want to leave the room but she needed to tell Sir Laythan about the tonic and find out how she had suddenly become Prince Erebus' betrothed. "All right, I'm going. Don't wait up, I have no idea how long I'll be gone."

Fynna nodded and whispered, "Be careful."

Jessalyne tip-toed into the great hall. Fynna's assessment was accurate, but she still kept to the back wall as she crossed to the other side. The castle was so quiet. Perhaps everyone had drunk themselves to sleep.

The guards outside the king's chambers gave her a curious look. The tall one spoke. "The hour is very late. His highness is asleep, miss."

"Please, I must speak with Sir Laythan. It's urgent."

They glanced at each other.

"I'll be quick and quiet, I promise."

The shorter guard smiled. "Miss Jessalyne, you have yet to be noisy." He gave her entrance.

Once inside, she knocked lightly on Sir Laythan's door. "Sir Laythan? It's Jessalyne. Are you awake?"

When he opened the door it was obvious he had not yet retired for the evening. "My dear, I am so sorry. There was nothing I could do."

"May I come in?"

"Yes, of course." He stepped aside then closed the door behind her. He motioned toward the chair by the fire, bringing another chair from the desk.

As soon as he was seated, she began. "The tonic is poison. Sryka is making it from the dust on Fynna's wings."

His eyes went wide.

"You must stop giving it to the king. Don't tell Sryka, just send the steward to fetch it every morning like you usually do. We cannot tip our hand yet until we have some sort of plan."

"A plan? What can we do? I am an old man and you're a mage apprentice."

She smiled softly. "There's much I've kept hidden. Will you take me to the king? I believe I can strip the poison from his body."

"Do you really think there's anything you can do?"

"I can only try."

He nodded. "Come with me."

༄

Ertemis approached the castle gates with caution. The guards would not be able to see him, but his warrior instincts stayed wary for anything that might go wrong. Two guards on either side of the barbican and two guards on either side of the inner gate. Even for him, climbing the large iron gates without making noise would be difficult. He couldn't chance it.

He crept along on the far side of the main street in front of the castle entrance. The guards gave no sign they sensed his presence. Further down, guards were stationed at regular intervals along the parapet. He kept moving, studying the walls. He ran his hand over the polished granite. It was as slick as it looked.

There was no way he could scale those walls without alerting the guards. He would have to use a little magic and an ample portion of cunning.

Of the two guards on the outside, one was a might stouter than the other. Ertemis slipped between the guards, careful not to touch against the gates, lest the hinges groan. Leaning toward the portly guard, Ertemis whispered into his ear. "Had enough at supper, didn't you, lard bottom?"

The guard jerked his head around at stared at the man across from him. "What did you say?"

The other guard gave him an odd glance. "I didn't say a word."

"I heard you!"

"I didn't say anything."

The stout guard turned back to his post, tugging his tunic down.

Ertemis leaned in again. "I'll wager your shadow weighs more than I do."

Again, the fat guard whipped around. "I guess you didn't say that either!"

"Said what?" The thin guard made a face. "Maybe your ears are failing."

"Or they're stuffed with butter." Ertemis added softly in Turl's ear.

"That's enough, you weedy varlet. I won't stand for another word, Pieter." Turl punctuated his sentences by jabbing the air with his spiked lance.

"Weedy varlet? Is that the best you can do, you suety barrel of pig innards?" Pieter narrowed his eyes and planted his feet wide.

"Pig innards?" Turl's face bloomed bright red.

Turl dropped his lance and lunged at Pieter. Ertemis stepped out of the way. As the two tussled, the guards inside yelled for them to cease. It did no good. With much swearing and name-calling, the two guards rolled around in front of the gate, beating each other senseless.

Inside, the other two guards opened the main gate to come to the aid of their fellows. Stepping around the scuffle, Ertemis walked straight into the bailey.

℘

Jessalyne followed Sir Laythan into the king's bedchambers. He drew back the heavy bed curtains first and then the sheer inner ones.

"Should I wake him?" Sir Laythan asked softly.

"No. Let him sleep. Just give me a little room." Jessalyne kept her voice low as well.

Laythan backed away. "Do you need more light?"

She shook her head. "The candle is sufficient." The king looked ill even as he slept. His skin was almost grey and Jessalyne suspected a few more days of the tonic might finish him. Turning back, she gave Laythan a reassuring smile.

She rested one hand lightly on the king's forehead and another over his heart, slowly shutting out everything around her. She tried to sense the poison, tried to feel for it with her mind before she drew it into herself.

Eyes closed, she envisioned the king's body as whole. In her mind, she saw dark oily patches rise to the surface of his skin. Her whole body tingled. She snatched the first of the dark stains away. It burned her skin like acid. She called more fire for strength. Over and over, she plucked the caustic stains and fed them to the fire inside her, wincing as they gnawed into her flesh.

Laythan gasped. She opened her eyes. Blue fire washed her hands and arms.

When the stains were gone, she searched for anything else ailing him but found nothing. She directed the healing heat into the king before taking her hands away.

Her head spun and dark spots clouded her vision. The poison's magic had taken its toll. She slumped into a chair near the bed, exhausted and panting.

Laythan went to the king's side, staring in astonishment. He shook his head. "How...I...thank you." Concern bent his mouth. "Are you all right?"

She nodded. "I'll be fine after some rest. How is his highness?"

"He looks utterly restored. He's still sleeping, but I imagine he'll be much improved come morning." Tears glimmered in his eyes. "I doubted you. I'm sorry. I won't make that mistake twice. You have my word."

"I've hidden this power from Sryka and I would like to keep it that way."

"What's one more secret?"

At that they both smiled. Laythan offered her his arm and helped her out. He shut the door quietly behind them. "We have more to discuss."

"We do, but I'm shattered. Can it wait until tomorrow?"

He nodded. "Tomorrow is time enough. Thank you again."

ಬಿ

Ertemis hugged the walls as he slunk into the great hall. The fires had burned down to glowing ember beds. People snored beside the hearths. He inhaled the scent of strong drink. Good. A man in his cups slept well.

One of wolfhounds dozing by the fireplaces raised its head. The dog looked directly at Ertemis. Its great black nose worked the air. He held his breath. At last, the animal lay its head back down.

He honed in on Jessalyne's heart rhythm, moving toward the stairs on the far side of the hall. Back flat to the wall to avoid anyone coming or going, he made his way up.

ಬಿ

Jessalyne bid the king's guards goodnight and set off through the maze of passages. She hadn't had dinner, and as tired as she was, her grumbling stomach wasn't going to let her sleep until she ate something. She changed course and took the back hall to the servant's entrance into the scullery.

Lost in a swirl of thoughts, she walked blindly. What would happen when Sryka learned the king had been healed? And when the king learned what his son and his mage were up to? A strand of hair dangled before her eyes and as she tucked it behind her ear, she collided with a dark figure.

A small platter of chocolate biscuits and gingerbread clattered to the floor. She bent to retrieve them. "Pardon me, I wasn't looking where I was—"

"Let them be. The future queen of Shaldar should not scuttle around the floor like a maid."

She held her breath. The biscuits were scattered around a pair of goblin skin boots with jeweled buckles. No, not now. She had neither the strength nor the desire to deal with the prince. Straightening, she met his gaze. "And yet you fetch them from the pantry yourself, your highness?"

"I am not coming from the pantry, although where I am coming from is none of your business." He moved toward her. She stepped back.

She could smell perfume on him and judging by how poorly he had redressed himself, she knew Fynna's guess had been correct. Fresh anger over the night's events welled up. "So kind of Salena to give you her leftovers."

Amusement warmed the prince's cold stare. "Jealousy becomes you. I'm pleased to know you have some spirit after all."

He took another step toward her and she backed into a wall.

"I hope to see that spark when I bed you." He put a hand on either side of her, pining her to the stone. "I'm so used to Salena's fiery disposition, a cold fish would bore me to tears."

"Then keep her in your bed." Jessalyne ducked under his arm but he shoved her back.

"I plan to, but I can have Salena anytime I choose. Innocent flesh is much rarer." He leaned in, lips puckering.

Jessalyne pressed her hands against his chest and twisted her face away. Erebus's tongue slicked the side of her neck. She gagged. Anger and disgust boiled up insider her, desperate for a way out.

ଛ

Ertemis rounded the corner and found Jessalyne in the arms of another man. Wounded, he stumbled back. He was too late. And if that was the way her tastes ran now, she definitely wouldn't want him.

With a scowl of disgust, she pushed the man away. Not her lover after all. The man lunged at her and Ertemis's relief faded. Jessalyne's assailant laughed at her attempt to stop him and roughly pawed her breast. She yelped.

Rage overtook Ertemis. No one hurt Jessalyne. Still cloaked in magic, he grabbed the man's collar and yanked him back at the same time she shoved.

Jessalyne looked at her hands in surprise as if she hadn't known she possessed such strength.

The assailant slumped against the wall, rubbing the back of his head where he'd smacked the stone. "Pasty wench. How dare you deny me? How dare you lay hands on me? I swear, you will not survive this kingdom long when your usefulness is up." Who was this weasel?

She flung her palms toward him, fingers curled up around blistering balls of flame. The man flinched. Good. She stared him directly in the eyes and spoke in a slow, deliberate voice. "If you ever touch me again, I will show you my true fiery disposition."

Ertemis grinned. She'd been practicing. Her refusal to back down made him proud. How could he not love a woman this fierce?

The man swore and backed away. "Witchspawn," he whispered, his gaze lingering on the flames she held. He whimpered and took off down the passage. She doused the fireballs as soon as he was out of sight.

"Well done," Ertemis whispered.

She spun around, hands up. "Who's there?"

Ertemis pushed the hood of his cloak back and dropped his enchantment. "You called and I came."

Her hands fell to her sides as her mouth dropped. "Are you real?"

He could wait no longer to touch her. He gathered her into his arms. Her soft curves and warm skin against him felt like coming home. "You tell me, lelaya." He pressed her closer and inhaled her scent. "Do I feel real?"

She nodded. "Oh yes...very real." Her eyes blazed as she pulled away and jerked her hand back, her open palm flying toward his face.

He caught her wrist inches before she struck his cheek. "What the devil is that for? You called me!"

She wrenched her hand out of his grasp. "I've been calling you for a month. You just show up now and expect me to thank you? Why don't you just go back to whatever alehouse you crawled out of?"

Heat radiated off her in waves, warming the passage uncomfortably.

"Jessalyne, I can explain..."

She grabbed his tunic and pulled him close, sniffing him. "You don't have to. I can smell her." She glared at him and swallowed hard. "Get away from me. I don't ever want to see you again."

Chapter Eighteen

He inhaled. The chain holding his mother's ring was steeped with her perfume and the warmth of the passage was releasing the scent. "You have no idea what you're talking about, Jessalyne. The woman you smell is my lady mother."

The air cooled as Jessalyne's disposition calmed. She narrowed her eyes, unsure. "You went to see your mother?"

"Aye. In Elysium." He watched her face softened and realized that he desired her just as much when she was angry as when she was not.

"You visited with her for a month?"

"Nay, I was in Elysium for less than a day. When I stepped foot on mortal soil again, a month had passed. Time on Elysium is as meaningless as money in Fairleigh Grove." He took a step closer. "Believe me, I came as soon as I heard your call."

Her gaze dropped to the floor. He reached for her again, desperate to hold her. "Don't be angry with me, sweeting."

She looked up, not quite meeting his eyes. "I'm sorry for what I said about the alehouse."

"I'm sorry I gave you reason to think that of me, and I'm sorry for many other things." He bent his head to whisper in her ear. "If I don't kiss you this moment, I will die."

Closing her eyes, she tipped her head and offered her mouth to him. He captured her lips and devoured the sweetness he had missed for too long. She melted against him, wrapping her arms around his waist. Her lips traveled down to the curve of his neck, and she kissed him there as he had once done to her. He rewarded her efforts with a low moan. By Saladan's bollocks, he wanted her. Perhaps too much at the moment. He pulled back and brushed a strand of hair from her eyes. "If he touches you again, I will kill him."

Catching his hand in hers, she kissed his palm. "I'm fine."

"Aye." he smiled. "That you are."

She traced his jaw with her fingertip. "You pulled him off me, didn't you?"

"Aye. Does that disappoint you? You seemed so pleased with yourself."

"It doesn't disappointment me in the least." She rested her head against his chest and he embraced her again. "I missed you."

Words left him. He struggled against the rush of emotion. "I missed you, too, lelaya. And as much as I would like to keep you in my arms, I cannot risk being seen. I need to hide myself again then we should get out of this hall."

"We can go back to my quarters."

He cloaked himself, knowing the instant she could no longer see him by the change in her face. She turned down the passage. "Stay close to me."

Chuckling, he replied, "You needn't worry about that."

Her stomach grumbled again. She paused, unsure of where to look. "I was on my way to the kitchens. Do you want anything?"

What he wanted wasn't food. "I haven't eaten since breakfast."

"I'll get enough for both of us."

Only the bakers occupied the kitchen at such an hour. They paid little attention to her as she filled a basket with bread, cheese, pickles, cold sausages and honey cakes. He wished she would hurry. He ached to be hidden away with her.

Finally, she started up a new set of steps. He whispered, "Will anyone see us here?"

"Highly unlikely."

He took the basket from her. "Let me help, then."

At a landing, she paused in front of the door. "Wait here. I share these quarters."

His heart sunk. "Why bring me here then? I don't want anyone to see me." And he wanted to be alone with her.

"Fynna knows all about you. I just don't want you to scare the blue out of her."

"The blue?"

"Don't move." She took the basket back from him and slipped inside. "Fynna," she whispered.

The pixie was curled on top of her coverlet, still dressed in her tunic. Obviously, she had tried to wait up. She yawned. "I smell food."

"Are you awake enough for a surprise?" Jessalyne set the basket on the table.

Fynna opened her eyes a little more, a sleepy smile on her face. "Chocolate biscuits?"

"Not that kind of surprise, silly goose."

Fynna stretched. "What is it?"

Jessalyne smiled. "Better than chocolate." She opened their chamber door. "You can come in now."

"Who are you talking to?"

Ertemis emerged out of thin air. Fynna fell off her bed and onto the floor with a soft thump. She peeked over the edge. "Is that..." She pointed then snatched her finger back. "Are you him? The Bla—I mean, Ertemis?"

"At your service." He bowed slightly. "And you are?"

"Fynna." She popped her head up a little more. "I'm a pixie."

"I'm a dark elf."

She climbed back onto her bed. "I know."

Ertemis winked at Jessalyne. "Talking about me behind my back, are you?"

Jessalyne unpacked the food basket while Ertemis unclasped his cloak and threw it across her bed. He reached into the basket to help. Their hands touched. His fingers briefly interlaced hers. Smiles drifted across both their faces.

"No liver dumplings?" Fynna grinned at her friend. "I think I'll go to the scullery and see if there are any in the cold larder."

She left, only to pop her head right back in. "I'll knock before I come back in. You know, just in case—"

"Fynna!"

The pixie giggled as she shut the door.

"I see subtlety is not one of her virtues." Ertemis sat at the game table.

Jessalyne took the chair across from him, trying to find a place to start. "I have so many questions and so much to tell you. So much has happened."

"There's something I need to say first."

He tore a hunk of bread into pieces, keeping his eyes down. "I owe you an apology. Before we parted, I treated you no better than that beast in the hall. You deserve better. Much better. Please...please forgive me."

Her eyebrows rose.

He glanced up. "Does my apology surprise you?"

"Yes."

"I'm sorry for that also. They don't come easy to me."

"Why did you say so little to be when we parted?"

"Another chance to practice my apologies." He rubbed his chin. "I thought it best if you just forgot about me. I was a fool."

He leaned back in his chair. "I'm sorry for that as well. The sight of you walking away, disappearing into this castle...it was not easy."

She slid her hand over his. "What made you go see your mother?"

Leaning forward, he looked into her eyes. "I needed some advice."

"You?" She couldn't imagine him needing advice from anyone. "I didn't think you were coming back. I was sure of it."

"I knew time on Elysium meant nothing but it never occurred to me what that would mean when I returned. Lelaya, I'm most sorry for that." He came around the table and picked her up in his arms, kissing her forehead. "Do you forgive me?"

She'd ached for him. Cried over him. "Do you promise not to do it again?"

Still holding her, he sunk into the chair she'd been sitting in. "You want me to stay?"

"Yes," she whispered as she kissed his mouth. "What was it like to see your mother after so long?"

He broke the kiss reluctantly. "Bittersweet. She's happy enough. She still refuses to tell me the name of my father, though."

Jessalyne stiffened. "I need to talk to you about that. That and so much more." She slipped off his lap and walked toward the fireplace.

"What is it?"

Before facing him, she took a deep breath. "I know who your father is."

His dark eyes fixed on her. "You do?"

"Yes. But you must promise to hear me out and that you won't hurt him."

"I'll listen but I won't promise more than that."

"I don't know how else to say it so I'll just come out with it. You're the firstborn son of King Maelthorn. The man you yanked off me in the passageway is your half-brother, Prince Erebus."

His jaw tightened and the muscles in his neck corded. He sat silently, unmoving, staring past her into the dying embers of the fire.

"Ertemis? Are you all right?"

After a long moment, he spoke. "I'm the son of a king?"

"Yes, but it's more than that. You're first in line for the throne."

He shook his head. "That cannot be right."

She knelt in front of him and took his hands. "It is right, and I would very much like to take you to meet your father in morning, if you are willing. But there is one more thing you must know."

"There is more?"

She sighed. "Yes. In less than a week's time, I'm to marry Prince Erebus. Somehow he persuaded the king to bless me as his bride."

"What?" Ertemis sprang to his feet.

She groaned at the thought of all that had expired. "I'm betrothed to him. I had little choice in the matter."

"You will not wed that slavering animal. I'll kill him before that happens."

She twisted her hands. She'd expected his anger. "It's not up to me. As soon as we wed, he will become the new king of Shaldar. That's all he wants me for."

"I'll meet the king tomorrow morning and see for myself what can be done about this." His shoulders straightened. "If he has any desire to right the wrong he did to my mother, he will end this betrothal."

"Your father still loves your mother."

He ran a hand through his hair and dropped back into the chair. "She still loves him."

"I know how she feels." Jessalyne walked over to him, trembling at how easily the words slipped out. If only he would say them back.

His jaw unhinged. "What did you say?"

"I love you," she whispered before reseating herself on his lap and burying her face against his neck.

ಬ

Ertemis closed his eyes and inhaled deeply as the stone wall around his heart crashed down. She loved him. The thought rippled through him, tingling down his spine and quickening his breath. Before he lost his nerve, he fished his mother's ring from beneath his breastplate. Shifting Jessalyne off his lap and onto the chair by herself, he knelt before her.

Her face was buried in her hands.

"Jessalyne, look at me."

"No." She swiveled away from him.

"What's wrong, sweeting?"

"I never should have said it. You didn't say it back."

"Jessalyne." He paused to take a breath, willing himself to speak the words of his heart. "I love you desperately and if you would look at me, you would see I am trying to ask for your hand."

"You are?" She peeked through her fingers. "Even though I'm betrothed to your brother?"

"Half brother, and if you will have me, I will rectify that matter. One way or another."

With tears in her eyes, she nodded. "I will. I will. Of course, I will!"

Emotion thickened his voice. "My mother gave me this ring to give to you. My...father," the word was hard to say without grimacing, "gave it to her many years ago." He slipped the ring from its chain and onto her finger before pulling her into a tight embrace. "I promise never to leave you again, lelaya."

She pulled away. "Then tell me again."

He paused, losing himself in her pale violet eyes. "I love you, Jessalyne."

Smiling, she kissed him softly. Rapping at the door turned both their heads and they stood. Jessalyne smoothed her dress. "Come in, Fynna."

Fynna peeked around the door. "I couldn't eat anymore."

Ertemis laughed. "We haven't even started our dinner."

"Well, that explains why it's safe for me to come in." The pixie shut the door behind her.

"Fynna!"

"It will be firstlight soon." Fynna crawled into her bed.

Ertemis looked out the window. "Aye, that it will."

Jessalyne smiled. "Then I shall be better able to inspect my new ring."

Ertemis rolled his eyes. "Is there going to be a great deal of noise now?"

"What ring?" Fynna popped up.

Holding out her hand, Jessalyne wiggled her fingers. "Ertemis asked me to marry him."

Fynna squealed, then shook her head. "The Prince of Hands isn't going to like that."

"The Prince of Hands?" Ertemis growled. "Your betrothal to him ends tomorrow."

Fynna shrieked and started jumping on the bed.

Ertemis folded his cloak into a pillow. "Jessalyne, could ask your friend to contain herself long enough for us to sleep a few hours?" He settled onto the carpet, stuffing his cloak beneath his head.

"Fynna, he's right. We need some sleep." She stared at Ertemis with curiosity as he stretched out on the carpet.

Fynna stopped jumping. "Yes, your highness." She erupted into a fit of giggles.

Ertemis shot her a look. "Pixie, please."

She tucked herself back under the covers. "Sorry, master elf. But it is very happy news."

He smiled. "That it is."

Jessalyne looked at him. "You're going to sleep on the floor?"

"Aye. And you are going to sleep in your bed."

"Are you ill?"

Just lovesick. "As tempting as you are, that bed could barely hold me, never mind another." He wouldn't torture himself by having her so near, but so unavailable. He winked at the tempting pout of her lips. "Your days of sleeping alone are about to end."

Jessalyne shivered. Did she fear their joining? But then she smiled. "Good night, my love." She hung over the side of the bed, watching him.

"Sweeting, go to sleep or I will take the ring back."

She lay back and pulled the covers up. "Try it and I'll toast your fingers, elfling."

"That's a fine way to speak to your betrothed. I can see this marriage will be a labor of love." He shifted toward the door so she would not see the grin on his face.

"Hmmph." Jessalyne wriggled deeper under the covers.

"That's what I thought," Ertemis whispered as he drifted off to sleep.

৪০

It seemed to Jessalyne that she had only just shut her eyes when the gossamer wings of firstlight flew in the window. As she stretched, the events of the past few hours came flooding back. She felt for the ring on her hand. It was still there. She propped herself up on her elbows and glanced down. So was Ertemis.

She smiled helplessly at his lanky form sprawled on the carpet. Strands of glistening black hair spilled over the folded cloak beneath his head. One hand gripped the hilt of his sword.

Slipping out of bed, she knelt beside him and studied his handsome face. She traced the angled line of his right ear, running her fingertip delicately over the silver-inked runes.

His hand snaked up and grabbed her wrist as his eyes came open. "I promise very soon to show you just how much your touch on that particular part of my body affects me, but for now it would be best if you did not do that."

She bit her lip. "Sorry."

He smiled and winked at her. "I can think of worse ways to be woken." He nodded toward Fynna. "If we were alone, I would not have stopped you."

She bent to kiss him and he kissed her back, rolling her on top of him. Her squeals of delight woke Fynna. She stared down at them sleepily.

"You're ruining my appetite for breakfast." She stuck her little blue tongue out.

"My apologies for Jessalyne's indecent behavior this morning." Ertemis laughed as Jessalyne's eyes went wide.

She sat up and thumped his chest with her fist. "You're still a barbarian."

"Too late, you've already said yes. No taking it back now." He tugged her back down and kissed her soundly.

Fynna yawned. "Will you two be rolling around on the carpet all morning?"

Jessalyne wrestled out of Ertemis's embrace. "We do have quite a day ahead of us, don't we?" She turned to him. "Are you ready to meet your father?"

He stood and shook out his cloak out. "Perhaps you should be asking if he is ready to meet me. I'm not the son most men dream of."

"He will be very proud of you." She hoped. "And you needn't worry, King Maelthorn is a good man."

"What about Sryka? She'll expect you this morning," Fynna said.

Jessalyne clenched her jaw. "I have no desire to spend another moment of time with that woman, but she cannot find out about Ertemis. I won't have her ruin our chances at displacing Erebus."

"Whatever your normal routine is, stick to it." Ertemis tossed his cloak around his shoulders. "I'll wait here until you return."

"You'll stay here?"

"I have little choice. My cloaking enchantment doesn't work well in bright sun. I need shadows at the least."

"I'll be back as soon as I can."

"Patience. I have waited this long to meet him, a few more hours is nothing."

Fynna shrugged. "Don't worry. If she does anything to make Sryka suspicious I'll break something and distract the old hag."

As the girls prepared to go, Ertemis settled onto Jessalyne's bed. It creaked but held. He closed his eyes. Was he thinking of how the meeting with his father might go? Trying to comprehend that he was the son of the king? She put her hand on his shoulder and he opened his eyes. "We're going now."

He pressed a kiss to the back of her hand. "Take the ring off."

She shook her head in objection. Fynna responded. "He's right. Sryka will notice it immediately."

"Very well." Jessalyne slipped it off her finger and tucked it into the pouch on her waist sash.

"Keep an eye on her, Fynna." Ertemis followed them to the door.

"Yes, your majesty." Fynna giggled and did a sloppy curtsy.

Ertemis rolled his eyes. "I'd do better asking a hungry man to mind a sweet shop. I'm going to bolt the door so give three rapid knocks when you return and I'll know it's you."

"Three quick knocks it is." Jessalyne squeezed his hand, then she and Fynna slipped out and up the stairs to face Sryka for what she hoped was the last time.

∞

Three raps in quick succession woke Ertemis and his hand instinctively sought the hilt of his sword. He shook himself awake. He could not remember falling asleep but Jessalyne's small bed was more comfortable than he'd imagined. If only she'd been in it, too. Three taps on the door. He slid the bolt back and let Jessalyne in.

"Where's Fynna?"

"She always stays later. Sryka invents a myriad of unnecessary chores for her to do. It makes me mad but there's little I can do about it."

"Sryka didn't suspect anything?"

"No. I'm sure of it." Jessalyne fished in the little pouch hanging at her waist.

"Good." Happiness filled him as she slipped the ring back onto her finger.

"Are you ready to meet the king?"

Ertemis shrugged and held his hands out. "I'm not sure battle leathers are the most appropriate outfit but it's all I have."

"I'm glad you mentioned that. I had completely forgotten." She went to the wardrobe and took something out.

Ertemis narrowed his eyes at the sight of a man's shirt in her hands. "Who does that belong to?"

"Do you like it?" She shook the shirt out for him to see.

"Do I like the fact that you have an expensive man's tunic in your wardrobe? No, I don't. It looks like it belongs to the prince."

"It belongs to a prince. You. I bought it for you as a present but with all the excitement last night, I forgot I had it."

His jaw hung slack as he sat on the bed. "You bought that for me?"

Nodding, she grinned hopefully. "Do you like it?"

Save his mother's bestowal of his Feyre, no one had ever given him a gift. "When...when did you buy it?"

"My first day here. Fynna took me into the city so I could buy a few things. I saw this in a window and thought of you. It was foolish, I guess. I didn't know if I would ever see you again, but..." Her voice trailed off and she twisted the toe of her slipper into the carpet.

"Come here."

She walked over clutching the shirt in front of her.

He pulled her near, his hands cradling her forearms. "I was wretched to you. I barely acknowledged our parting, and yet you bought this for me that same day?" He bent his head, ashamed by the memory of his actions. He didn't deserve her.

She tossed the shirt on the bed and wrapped her arms around him. His forehead pressed against her ribcage.

"You're too good for me." Their closeness muffled his words, but not the pain in his soul. How would he ever be the man she was worthy of?

"Hush now. We were both cross with one another." She kissed the top of his head and petted his hair. "You still haven't told me if you like it."

He looked up then. "It's the finest thing anyone has ever given me. I will put it on right now." He pulled her onto his lap. "Well, maybe not right now."

She gasped as his warm mouth nibbled the tender spot beneath her ear and closing her eyes, arched into his embrace. He trailed hot kisses trailed lower, down her neck and across her collarbone until he reached the soft rise of her breasts. He paused to take her in. She opened her eyes.

"You're the most beautiful woman I've ever known." He took her hand in his and kissed the delicate skin on the inside of her wrist. "The only woman I ever want next to me." He worked his way down to her arm, nibbling her skin.

Jessalyne wove the fingers of her free hand into his hair. "You think I'm beautiful?"

"You know I do." He traced a finger down the path his lips had taken, starting at her jaw line. "But I'll tell you more often."

Her eyes shuttered and goose flesh rose on her arm where his fingers played. She shivered. "Perhaps you should undress."

His eyes widened. "I'll tell you you're beautiful every day if that's what it gets me."

She playfully pushed him away. "I meant so you could put your new shirt on. You do still want to meet your father, don't you?"

"Aye." He tugged off his leather breastplate and made a show of being disappointed. "I thought my attentions were finally getting to you."

She sat up and fanned herself. "I enjoy your attentions very much. Too much, perhaps. My thoughts have gotten quite wicked."

He laughed as he removed his worn tunic. "Now that's my saucy wench."

Her eyes fixed on his bared chest and a sigh escaped her.

"You like what you see?" He raised his eyebrows.

She nodded slightly and her cheeks went scarlet. The sight made him lightheaded with pride and wanting. He took her hand and placed it against his bare skin. "Can you feel my heart thumping? You do that to me."

Slowly, she splayed her fingers out, her hand soft and warm and smooth. "Your skin reminds me of silk tumbled with sand. I didn't know a man could be so soft and so hard at the same time."

He bit back the words he really wanted to say, how he'd like to show her just how hard he could be. Instead, he groaned as her hand moved across his skin.

She started to speak, then faltered.

"What is it?"

"I don't know the right words."

"Just speak your mind."

"I think…I think you are beautiful, too."

He smiled and captured her hand in his, kissing her fingertips. He would do anything for her. Anything. His smile faded as he considered what that meant. "If this meeting does not go well, I may have to leave quickly."

"You won't go alone."

"You would give up this life for what little I can offer you?"

"Without looking back. In truth, I might have left soon anyway. I find little purpose in being trained by a woman who seeks to destroy the king she serves. And Erebus makes my skin crawl." She shuddered.

Ertemis stood and dressed in the white linen shirt. He ran his fingers over the embroidery. "I have never owned anything white. Not the most practical color for a man of my profession." He planted his hands on his hips. "How do I look?"

"Like a prince." Her eyes focused on the vee of bare chest visible where the neck of the tunic lay open. His ears picked up her quickening pulse. "I cannot imagine a more handsome man. Pity you have to hide yourself until we get to the king's chambers. I could stand to look at you a bit more."

"Be careful what you wish for." He winked at her before cloaking himself. "Lead the way."

"That is most disconcerting." She frowned at the disembodied voice, squinting as if it might help her see him. "Stay close when we go through the chamber doors. The guards won't know to hold the doors open long enough for two."

He pressed himself against her from behind, wrapping his arms around her waist and pulling her snug against him. "Is this close enough?"

"Oh! You are so poorly behaved. It is entirely unfair to use your enchantment that way." For all her words, she stayed tucked against him.

"Poorly behaved? Unfair? And yet you don't struggle to get away." He nuzzled her neck with his lips, finding the spot that made her sigh.

She giggled and he pulled away. "That's not the response I expected."

"I just thought how odd I must look, being ravished by some invisible lover."

"I have not yet begun to ravish you." He bent his head to whisper in her ear. "Although, I am entirely ready to fulfill my position as lover, invisible or otherwise."

She wobbled, as though her knees had given way. "We should go now, before we do not go at all.

Chapter Nineteen

Jessalyne held her breath the first few times they passed someone in the hall, but she soon relaxed. As long as he stayed in the shadows, Ertemis was truly invisible to the eyes of those around them. He stayed behind her and moved so quietly, that if not for his hand against the small of her back or occasionally lower, she wouldn't have known he was there.

The king's guard greeted her as she approached. "Fair lady, how does the day find you?"

"Well, Reginald, and you?"

"Fine, fine." He opened the door and swung it back for her.

She hesitated, feeling Ertemis's hand leave her back. She paused to give him time. "How is your lady wife? Did she find the salve I sent her useful on that burn?"

"It healed without a scar. We're both much obliged to you."

Patting his arm, she smiled. "Tell her I asked for her."

"I will, miss."

With that, she went inside. Reginald shut the door behind her.

"Ertemis!" she whispered.

"Here." His hand returned to thee small of her back and she reached behind, covering his hand with hers for a moment.

Laythan opened the sitting room doors. "Jessalyne! I thought I heard the doors. Oh, child..." He reached to embrace her. Ertemis's hand left her back.

"I have not seen the king in such fine form in many years. You did a wonderful thing. He's waiting for you in the library."

Laythan reached for the second set of latches, and she caught his arm. "Sir Laythan, wait. I need to talk to you first."

"What is it?"

"What have you told the king about his son?"

"Nothing. I thought it best if it came from you."

"Ertemis is here."

Laythan's eyes widened. "He's in Shaldar City?"

"Yes, and he's here."

"In the castle?"

"In the room."

His eyes narrowed as he glanced around the foyer. "I'm not a young man but my eyesight is still sharp. I believe if the Black Death were here, I would know."

Jessalyne wondered if Laythan could hear the low growl Ertemis gave in response. "Trust me, he's here and he doesn't care for that name. Would you like to meet him?"

Laythan crossed his arms. "Indeed."

Jessalyne looked behind her. "Ertemis?"

The light in the room seemed to shift and the air shimmered as Ertemis emerged from the shadows against one wall.

Laythan clutched his chest. The color drained from his face. "Saints and sinners! I meant no disrespect."

Ertemis nodded. "So long as I don't hear that name again, it's forgotten."

"Ertemis, this is Sir Laythan. He's your father's man and a good friend to me as well."

"Anything you have done for Jessalyne is greatly appreciated."

Still wary, Laythan smiled weakly. "She's been a welcome addition to life here at Castle Ryght." He hesitated and then spoke again, not quite making eye contact with the dark elf before him. "I knew your mother."

His face softening a bit, Ertemis stared at Laythan. "You knew her?"

"Aye. Shaylana was the light of the king's life."

"Hmmph."

Laythan pursed his lips. "You may not believe that but it's true. He loved her very much. I believe he still does."

"If he loved her so much why did he do so little for her when she found out about me?"

"Perhaps this is a conversation better had with your father."

Ertemis crossed his arms. "Very well."

Jessalyne moved between the two men, facing Ertemis. "Let me speak to the king with Sir Laythan first. I fear seeing you without being properly prepared might shock him."

"Whatever you think best. I'll wait here."

"Thank you." She reached up to kiss his cheek and whisper in his ear. "I love you."

His lips curved up in a smile that she knew was for her alone.

"I won't be long."

Nodding, he stepped back into the shadows and vanished.

She turned to face Laythan. "Shall we?"

He opened the library doors and stepped aside to let her pass, then shut them with a wary glance into the foyer. "The king is in the map room."

As Laythan led her through the library, Jessalyne realized the king's chambers comprised almost an entire wing of the castle.

The king closed the book he was reading as they entered the room. Laythan bowed before him and Jessalyne followed with a deep curtsy. "Your highness, Jessalyne is here."

"So I see." He rose to greet her, a wide smile on his face. "Greetings, child."

He looked like a different man. His cheeks were flush with color and his eyes had a new sparkle. "You look well, your highness."

"Because of you." He clasped her hands in his. "I owe you my life, Jessalyne. I'm in your debt. Whatever you need, whatever you desire, you shall have it."

She smiled softly. "Then perhaps today will be easier than expected."

He looked at her quizzically.

"May we sit?"

"Of course, of course." He pulled another chair close to his and waited until she sat before joining her.

"I don't quite know where to start so I'm just going to begin and hope for the best." She ran her hand along the chair's leather arm. "When you were ill, you called me Shaylana."

Emotion flickered across his face. "She was a very special woman."

Jessalyne smiled. "I know who she is."

"You know her?"

"I don't know her, but I know her son and that's what I want to talk to you about. Shaylana's child, your son, is very much alive."

"The child is alive? A son? It cannot be." He sat back. "Shaylana sent a message not long after she disappeared that the child had been dealt with. I knew enough of elven customs to know what that meant."

She laid her hand on his arm. "I promise you, he's alive."

His eyes locked onto the ring glinting from her finger. "Where did you get that?" Emotion edged his words.

"From your son. His mother wanted him to give to me."

King Maelthorn stared at the gold band. "I gave that to her on the night of the Hunter's Moon. She was so beautiful in the warm golden light. I thought my heart would break from the sight of her. I promised as soon as the treaty was signed, we would wed. She was gone a month later."

He looked up, eyes liquid. "Where is he? Where is my son?"

"He's here." She stood, happiness filling her. "I'll get him."

The king jumped up, almost knocking his chair over. "Yes, please, immediately."

She ran back to the foyer and burst through the door. "Ertemis, come now, your father wants to meet you."

He reappeared and she grabbed his hand, pulling him into the library.

Ertemis dug in his heels. "Jessalyne, I'm a grown man. I prefer to walk like one, not be dragged in like a child."

"I'm sorry, it's just that your father wants to see you so badly."

Ertemis straightened the hem of his new tunic. "Lead on."

She could barely contain herself as she walked back into the map room. When Ertemis entered behind her, she was torn between watching his face or the king's.

Neither one said a word. Ertemis's face was unreadable. He might as well have been carved of granite for all the emotion he showed. The king's chest heaved at the sight of his son. His mouth came open as if to speak but nothing came out.

Jessalyne felt the need to break the strained silence. "King Maelthorn, meet your son, Ertemis Elta-naya."

King Maelthorn's face froze. "No one calls my son a bastard."

Ertemis narrowed his eyes. "You understand elven?"

"Well enough to know what elta-naya means." The king faced Ertemis without fear.

"Then my name should come as no surprise to you." Ertemis's voice ground down to a low growl. "It's what I am.

Bastard born halfling, mixed breed, muddled blood. The product of an unwed mother."

Jessalyne cringed. She had hoped for a more peaceful meeting. "Stop it!" she hissed.

Ertemis glared at her, his face full of uncertainty. "He needs to know what my life has been because of what he denied my mother."

"He can imagine, I'm sure. But he didn't even know you existed."

Ertemis's face steeled. All trace of emotion disappeared again.

"What Jessalyne says is true. I never denied your mother," King Maelthorn countered. "The last I heard from Shaylana was a brief message sent by a courier who had no recollection who'd given him the message or where he'd come from., but he'd been paid in elven gold. Your mother erased herself from his memory." He sank into his chair. "At times I wished she'd done the same to me."

He shook his head at the memories. "The message came around the time she would have delivered. It was all of six words but I understood perfectly. 'The child has been dealt with.'"

"She told you—" Ertemis paused. "You thought I had been killed at birth?"

King Maelthorn nodded, his eyes focused on the distance past. Sir Laythan stepped forward and put his hand on the king's shoulder. "Your father suffered greatly. I'm sure it cannot compare to the life you've led, but you must understand, he too has suffered."

"Before your mother came here, he had already lost a wife and child. Shaylana seemed liked a new beginning. The alliance with the elves was eminent. It was an unparalleled time in the history of Shaldar."

Ertemis spoke softly, "I didn't know. She never told me that part of it."

The king looked up. "Perhaps we might start over. I am an old man and very aware of what little time I may have left. I am not willing to waste that time. You must have questions. I know I do." The corners of his mouth turned up in a slight smile. "I want to get to know my son."

Ertemis swallowed hard. He moved slowly across the room and sat in the chair next to King Maelthorn. "I do have questions."

Jessalyne covered her smile with her hands. The sight of Ertemis and King Maelthorn sitting side by side pleased her to no end. She caught Sir Laythan's gaze and he motioned toward the door. Nodding, she slipped out of the room behind him.

"We should give them time alone. I'm sure there's much they would like to discuss in private."

"I agree." She couldn't stop smiling. "It's wonderful, isn't it? I'm so happy for both of them."

"Aye. I never would have thought to see such a day. The king is like a man reborn. His health restored and now this…" His face darkened. "He still doesn't know about Sryka. Just that someone was poisoning him. She must be dealt with."

Her smile turned into a scowl. "Indeed. I would prefer not to have to see her again. I had to spend this morning with her as usual, pretending I knew nothing of what she'd done to his majesty."

Laythan nodded. "Once the king finds out what she's been about, he will deal with her. He may seem a kind old soul but he has a fierce temper, especially when it comes to disloyalty."

"So that's where Ertemis gets it." Jessalyne twisted a bit of hair around her finger.

"Why don't we sit in the parlor for a bit and I'll send one of the squires to fetch some lunch?"

They entered the parlor and Laythan tugged the bell pull. Jessalyne sat near the window overlooking the gardens and the swan pond. She smoothed out the folds in her skirt. Laythan took a chair near her and tried to make conversation, but she couldn't focus. Her mind kept wandering to what Ertemis and his father were discussing. The sun slipped lower and still they talked. She stared out the window, watching the swans glide across the purple-glazed surface of the pond.

The doors into the parlor swung open to the sounds of animated conversation. Jessalyne and Laythan turned in unison to see Ertemis and King Maelthorn enter, engaged in passionate discourse.

"I agree you have nothing to worry about from Myssia. It's the Akuza that pose the most threat."

King Maelthorn clapped Ertemis on the back. "We have nothing to worry about, you mean."

Ertemis shook his head. "That will take some getting used to."

He turned to face Jessalyne and she greeted him with a smile. He winked back, obviously in good spirits.

The king beamed. He kept his hand on Ertemis's shoulder as he spoke. "Jessalyne, I promised you a boon earlier and I mean to honor that. However, when I tell you my plans I believe you'll have little left to ask for."

He glanced at Ertemis, a determined cast settling over his face as he continued. "Laythan, call my scribe. I have a proclamation to write and Ertemis needs a message sent to his squire. Also, send a royal emissary to the Legion to establish a reasonable price for my son's bond. He is now a free man."

Ertemis lifted his chin proudly, but kept his eyes on his father.

"Tonight before I sit down to dinner in the great hall, I will proclaim Ertemis as my heir and crown prince to the throne of Shaldar."

The king nodded toward Jessalyne. "In two weeks time, a coronation and royal wedding will take place. As you are still the Blessed Bride, my dear, it falls to you marry my first born." He smiled broadly. "I hope that will not be too much to ask?"

Jessalyne flew off the window seat. "Of course, I will marry him, your highness." She laughed out loud. "In truth, I was going to marry him regardless of what happened today." Her smile faded. "What about Prince Erebus?"

"Please, call me Raythus. We are family now." Raythus looked exceptionally calm for a ruler about to create chaos in his kingdom. "Prince Erebus may be a foppish peacock of a man but he understands protocol. I am ashamed to admit it, but I have known since he was very young he would never be fit to rule. Why do you think I put off blessing a bride for so long? Soon enough he will have all the time he wants for visits to his tailor and chasing skirts."

Ertemis spoke, perhaps seeing Jessalyne's disbelief on her face. "Raythus, I doubt Erebus will give up the throne so easily. Or Jessalyne, for that matter."

Raythus punched his fist against his palm. "I'm his father and his king. He has no choice but to abide by my ruling. I need a man with a spine of steel and the heart of a warrior to take my place. Too many of Shaldar's neighbors eye us like some plump stonefruit, ripe for the picking."

Laythan stood, clearing his throat. "Your highness, there is something more you need to know."

"Yes?"

"Jessalyne and I have knowledge that Sryka was the one poisoning you."

"What?" The volume of Raythus's voice threatened to shatter the parlor windows. "How dare she break her oath. But how can it be? Her magic should be useless against me."

"It should be, but she found a way around the oath. The tonic she sent you was laced with pixie dust, an ingredient that could save your life in small doses or kill you in large ones."

Jessalyne stepped in. "She's harvesting the dust from the stolen wings of my friend, Fynna. She used a separation spell to take her wings away as a punishment."

"Call my guards." Raythus clenched his hands in anger. "Then send for Erebus and my scribe," he growled. "I have work to do."

Jessalyne and Ertemis waited in the parlor for Raythus to call them back into the library. Her fingers dawdled with the pendant around her neck.

"I was surprised to see you still wearing that." He smiled at her in a way she was not yet used to.

"I thought many times about taking it off but I couldn't." She rolled the pearl back and forth between her fingers. "I've been told this is a very costly piece. What made you buy such a thing for me when we barely knew each other?"

His mouth was partially hidden by his hand on his chin, but she still saw the corners of his smile. He motioned for her from his overstuffed chair. "Come here."

"I'm right next to you."

"Come here or I'll come get you."

Jessalyne stuck her tongue out. "Hah."

He raised one eyebrow as he uncoiled from the chair and swept her up off the window seat, reseating himself with her on his lap before she could scarcely blink. He nuzzled her neck, making her forget what she'd been saying. Reluctantly, she pushed him away. "You haven't answered my question."

"A beautiful woman should be adorned with beautiful things." His lips against her ear. "I shall shower you with fine things for the rest of your life."

At the sound of footsteps, they both looked up. Laythan cleared his throat, his eyes on Ertemis. "Your father would like you to join him. Lady Jessalyne, you may come with us if you like."

Ertemis kissed Jessalyne's temple as he stood, setting her feet on the ground. "If you don't want to face Erebus, you don't have to come in."

"I'm not afraid of him."

"After last night, it's more likely the other way around." Ertemis nodded to Laythan. "Lead the way."

༚

They entered as Erebus slammed his fist onto the table. "You cannot do this!"

Raythus stayed calm. "But I am. It's time you meet your brother." He gestured toward Ertemis.

Erebus spun around, his face clouded with rage. The crimson flush darkened like the underbelly of a thundercloud as he realized what other bloodline ran in Ertemis's veins. Ertemis nodded, taking pleasure in seeing the man suffer who'd hurt his beloved. "Hello, brother."

Erebus slammed his fist down again. "You expect me to accept this baseborn spawn as my brother? Never! I will not pay for your dalliance with some elven w-whore." He sputtered with fury.

Jessalyne's hand clamped onto Ertemis's arm as he started forward, but he shook it off. He tightened his grip on his sword hilt. "Refer to my lady mother with such disrespect again and I will slice your tongue from your mouth."

"Erebus, enough!" Raythus moved to stand between them. "Ertemis is my first born. He will marry the Blessed Bride and be crowned king. That is the end of this matter."

"You would break my betrothal? Is there no end to your duplicity?" Erebus's mouth curled into a sneer.

"I gave my blessing for her to marry my first born son. There is no duplicity." He stared down Erebus's fierce gaze. "The proclamation is written. It will be read in the great hall tonight when I introduce Prince Ertemis to the people of Shaldar."

"So it is done, and I am cast aside." Erebus was rigid with rage. He smoothed his velvet tunic, obviously trying to compose himself. "In truth, I'm happy to be free of the witchling bride."

Ertemis growled and Erebus laughed bitterly. "You've been well matched, brother. A marriage made in Hael, to be sure."

Raythus stepped back. "It doesn't need to be like this, Erebus."

"Yes. It does. I will not be made the fool in my own kingdom."

"Where will you go? Do you want me to arrange for a delegation to travel with you? You could sail to Myssia as my emissary."

"Your concern overwhelms me." Sarcasm poured from Erebus' words. He sneered at Raythus as he brushed past, keeping wide of Ertemis and Jessalyne.

He paused at the door. Straightening to his full height, he schooled his face to indifference. "The people will never accept this creature in place of me. I will always be the rightful king of Shaldar in their minds." He pointed at Raythus, the slightest tremble betraying his attempt at apathy. "You will rue this moment, old man. Mark my words."

Chapter Twenty

Blaring trumpets announced the processional as the king waited to make his way into the great hall. Almost three years had passed since he had dined amongst his people. How would they receive him? How would they receive the news of his newly discovered son?

He glanced back at Ertemis. Shrouded in a voluminous black cloak with the hood pulled low over his face, his son loomed like a shadow. In truth, he had some fear of the man, but also a great deal of sadness over what his life had been.

His gaze shifted to the beautiful woman beside his son. Like a beam of moonlight, Jessalyne radiated with an ethereal glow. Her hand rested on Ertemis's arm as she offered him a slight smile. How perfect a pair.

The music changed. Raythus took a deep breath. The doors into the great hall were pulled open by a pair of valets wearing his colors. He went forward with head held high, smiling and nodding to greet his people. The crowd in the hall sat briefly stunned at the sight of him, but before he passed the first table, they stood as a whole and erupted with adulation.

Chants of "Hail the King" rang throughout the hall and eased his mind as he headed for the dais. Today was the start of new promise for Shaldar.

ॐ

Through the parted doors, Jessalyne's gaze swept the assembled mass. How they would react to the king's news? What would the sight of Ertemis do to them? She turned her attention back to Raythus as he began to speak.

"Noble people of Shaldar, gentle folk of this great kingdom, I am so pleased that my return to good health allows me to join you in our great hall."

Again, applause filled the room, echoing against the high mosaic ceiling.

Raythus raised his hand, stilling the crowd. "It is with even greater pleasure that I announce the most wonderful news. Many years ago you will recall I attempted to forge a union between Shaldar and Elysium. The elves sent a council here for many months as we worked on building this alliance. That much you know. What is not widely known is that one of the women in that council captured my heart. I promise you that she shared my feelings."

The hall went deathly quiet, then a hum rose like a swarm of bees coming closer. The buzzing stopped when the king continued.

"With respect for this elfess, the most I will reveal is that a child was born of that love. Not just any child but my first born. A son I've just been reunited with."

He looked back at Ertemis, still veiled in his cloak. Voice fraught with emotion, Raythus gestured toward the man beside her. "Fine citizens of Shaldar, nothing would please me more than to introduce you to my first born son and rightful heir to my throne, Prince Ertemis."

Ertemis stepped forward, slipping his hood back as he did.

A collective gasp broke the silence as the crowd realized what Ertemis was. Whispers of "dark elf" and "halfling" murmured through the hall.

Raythus raised both hands to regain their attention. "Gentle folk! Please!"

When they had quieted enough, he spoke. "The wedding planned for just a few days from now is not being canceled, merely pushed back a week. The Blessed Bride has been promised to my first born son and in a fortnight's time, my first born will indeed marry the lovely Lady Jessalyne. Tonight we feast in celebration of their troth!"

The cacophony of cheers and hoorahs erupted filling the great hall with happy noise once again. Jessalyne smiled as she and Ertemis made their way to the dais and their seats at the king's side. The promise of a wedding feast and the king's assurance seemed all the people needed to overlook Ertemis's notorious reputation. Or perhaps it was Erebus's displacement they cheered for.

Raythus quieted the assembly one last time. "Before the feasting begins, I must bring a serious matter to your attention. The matter of treason."

Again, whispers hissed through the great hall.

"Through her vigilant observations, Lady Jessalyne discovered the affliction ailing me was due not to age or illness but a deadly poison. The traitor behind this poison was none other than my mage, Mistress Sryka. She now enjoys the full benefits of Castle Ryght's dungeons."

He turned toward Jessalyne. "For your fealty and courage, I bestow upon you the Star of Shaldar."

Laythan came forward, a velvet pillow in his hands. Hung on white silk ribbon and embossed with the king's crest, the Star rested on top of the pillow.

The king draped the medal around Jessalyne's neck, kissing her on each cheek when he was through. "You're like the daughter I never had, child. Thank you for all you've done for me," he whispered.

"Thank you, Sire." She curtsied, not sure what the proper response was to being honored in such a way. She looked from the medal around her neck to Ertemis. The pride in his eyes overwhelmed her with bittersweet emotion. In a day's time she had become betrothed to the man her heart desired and awarded the kingdom's highest honor. If only her mother were alive to see her.

The next few days passed in a blur. After Jessalyne approved the invitations, royal scribes worked through the night to finish them. Messengers were dispatched to the furthest parts of the kingdom. She made sure their first stops were Fairleigh Grove and Warren on the Wick.

Dressmakers demanded Jessalyne's time for fitting her wedding gown, cook sought her input on the menu for the feast, and when she wasn't consumed with a myriad of other details, she poured over Sryka's books, looking for a way to reverse the separation spell that had stripped Fynna of her wings.

"Found anything yet?" Fynna peered over the pile of cleaning supplies in her arms as she pushed open the door to Sryka's old quarters with her elbow.

Jessalyne placed a leather ribbon between the pages and shut the book. "No reversal spell but I did find this." She held up a key worn shiny with use.

Fynna's eyes widened. "Is that the key to the armoire?"

"It has to be. We've tried every other key possible. I wanted to wait until you got here to try it." Jessalyne stood and pushed open the door into Sryka's bedchamber where the armoire stood. "Ready?"

With a deep breath, Fynna nodded.

The key fit perfectly into the lock and turned with ease. Fynna gasped as Jessalyne swung the doors wide. Like faded panes of stained glass, Fynna's wings rested on the large middle shelf. Sryka had nearly stripped them clean. Only small patches of iridescent color remained.

A great wrenching sound erupted from Fynna. "No, no, no..." she moaned, covering her face with her hands. She sank to her knees, unable to look at her desecrated wings. Sobs racked her small body.

With a lump in her throat, Jessalyne kneeled beside her friend. "I promise we'll make this right. We will." She wanted to believe that. She glanced at the wings again. The underside of the middle shelf held a small latched door. She stuck her nail in the groove and pushed it open. A book fell out. Weird runes scarred the blood red leather covering.

"Fynna, I think I've found what I was looking for."

"Jessalyne? Are you in here?" Ertemis's voice rang out from the other room.

"Yes, in the other room."

He leaned through the door, his broad shoulders tensing as his hands gripped the opening. "What's wrong? Is Fynna hurt?"

"No...yes. Her wings." Jessalyne nodded toward the shelf.

He winced at what was left of Fynna's once beautiful wings. "Can you—"

Jessalyne cut him off with a shrug.

Fynna exhaled one last sob and stood, knuckling the tears off her face. Without taking her eyes off her wings, she spoke softly. "I'm going to the gardens. I need to be alone for a while."

"Of course." Jessalyne rose and brushed her skirt off. "I'll start studying this book immediately."

Fynna wandered past Ertemis, her footsteps fading as she trudged down the stairs.

"Poor Fynna. I've got to find a way to help her. This might do it." She heldup the book. "It was tucked away in a hidden compartment. I don't recognize any of these symbols, do you?"

He glanced at it. "Nay. Can you heal her?"

"It's not a matter of healing. The wings need to be reattached. Without the right spell, there's nothing I can do." She shook the book in her hands. "This has to be it. I've read almost every other book in these chambers and found nothing."

He reached for her hand. "Come with me out onto the wall walk."

She set the book on the worktable as they passed it. "Why are we going out here?" Maybe for more kissing.

"To talk." He released her hand only to pull her close with an arm around her waist. His fingers stroked her cheek. "I must leave for a few days."

She clamped a hand over his. "What? Why? Where?"

"My lady mother insisted I beg your hand in marriage. She also insisted she be invited to the nuptials."

Jessalyne's eyes widened. "Elysium? You're going to Elysium? You told me yourself time has no meaning there. You may never return." She crossed her arms and pursed her lips. "No. I forbid it."

He grinned. "You forbid it? I don't think anyone has ever forbid me to do anything before."

"Well, I am, so get used to it, you big oaf." She slipped away and moved further down the wall. How could he do this? What if he missed the wedding? Or never came back? She needed him right now.

"Jessalyne? Your dress—"

"I'm not talking to you right now." A curl of smoke drifted past. She glanced down. The smoke came from her dress. She breathed deeply to dispel the heat of her anger.

Ertemis chuckled softly. "Before you set me on fire, lelaya, I am only delivering a message. I promise I will not set foot on Elysium."

She kept her back to him. "Then why not send a messenger?"

He braced a hand against the wall on either side of her. "Because no else can find Elysium but me. I will return well before the ceremony. I still have one more blasted fitting for my coronation attire." He kissed her shoulder, his lips burning against her skin. "Nothing will keep me away from you. Nothing."

"I don't know." She bit her lip to keep from smiling. There was perverse power in having such a powerful man bend to her will.

"Jess, sweeting, I give you my word." He brushed the hair from the nape of her neck and feathered kisses across the exposed skin.

She settled her hands over his. "Will your lady mother come? I would very much like to meet her."

"I'm sure she would, if only I could deliver the invitation."

She twisted to face him. "Rotten beast. Fine. Go. I have plenty to do anyway." She frowned, thinking of Fynna.

"You'll find a way to help her."

"Did you read my mind now?" She tried to read his. Nothing.

"Nay. Just the turn of your mouth and the look in your eyes." He kissed her forehead. "The view is breathtaking, isn't it?"

She snuggled against him and gazed over the city. "It is. Even more so when you think you're to be king of it all."

He sighed at her words, his face somber, and his eyes thoughtful. "King. It brings such responsibility." Turning his gaze toward her, his expression softened. "At least you will be at my side as queen."

"The thought frightens me so much I don't even want to think it." She shook her head, pale strands coming loose around her face.

"We'll find our way together." He gave her a quick squeeze. "I must go. Brynden will think I've changed my mind. Which reminds me, I want to lend him Petal. He has no horse of his own and it's a long walk."

"Why not give him a horse from the royal stables?"

"Character is not built through gifts, my love."

She held him tightly. "Stay a moment longer. Please."

He nodded and she pressed against him, resting her head on his thickly muscled chest. He smelled of leather and the spiced soap she'd made for him.

"I love you, Jessalyne." He kissed her soundly, his hands slipping down to cup her backside

She gasped. "I love you, too, your wickedness."

"Saucy wench." They walked back inside and he kissed her once more before he headed off to find Brynden and Dragon.

The sun felt good on his skin as he exited into the courtyard and walked toward the stables. Castle Ryght was the most magnificent castle he'd ever been in. That it should become his home staggered him.

Servants nodded as he passed, greeting him with a respectful curiosity. Gathered beneath some shade trees, a throng of girls watched the castle guards at sword play. They fell silent as he approached.

"Good afternoon, ladies," he greeted them as he passed, trying on the role of lord of the manor.

Whispers filled his ears but before he could listen closer, he detected footsteps behind him. He whirled, his cloak billowing out around him.

She yelped, then giggled. "Oh my, you startled me. You're unusually quick." Eyes the blue of an early spring sky lit a face framed by corn silk curls. A coquettish smile turned up the corners of the girl's berry colored lips. She looked at him from beneath a fringe of kohl-darkened lashes.

"Not in all things, I assure you."

Her smile widened and the pink tip of her tongue played across her teeth. She held out a dainty hand. "We have not been properly introduced, your highness. I am Salena LaPierre, daughter of Baron LaPierre."

He hesitated, unsure of what to do. Finally, he took her hand and brushed his lips across it the way he'd seen noblemen do when introduced to a woman of their class.

"Such a light touch for a man of your size. I will assume you are Prince Ertemis, the new heir to Shaldar's throne?"

Dropping her hand, he realized he should have offered his name in return. He bristled at his lack of aristocratic skills, an unnecessary reminder of how unfit he felt to be king. "Aye. And I am leaving unless you have some further need of me."

By the gleam in her eye, he saw she read more into his words than was there.

"Perhaps it is I who should ask if you have any needs. As a citizen of Shaldar, it is my duty to serve you, my lord prince." She toyed with the neckline of her gown, her fingertips brushing the fullness of her breasts.

Ertemis growled. The scent of Erebus clung to her, poorly masked from his sensitive nose by her oversweet perfume.

She mistook his displeasure for lust and moved toward him. "It's regrettable that you'll be forced to marry that ghostly shrew. I would be more than willing to offer you a bit of solace, your highness." She stepped closer, her voice a little softer. "You will find me quite capable of sating your most wanton appetites. Compared to Lady Jessalyne, I am a very different woman."

Her boldness was startling, but her belittling of Jessalyne stirred a cold rage in him. Struggling to compose himself before his temper bested him, he closed his eyes, only to feel her hand slide down his arm. He wrenched her wrist away.

She gasped. "A bit rough for my taste but I will adapt."

Jessalyne's voice suddenly filled his head. Travel safely, my love. I'll be waiting for you. Her words hushed the thrum of anger rushing through him. He glanced toward the north tower and a quiet sense of joy unlike anything he'd ever known flowed into his being. She loved him. He threw his head back and laughed.

Tearing her hand away, Salena rubbed her wrist, her eyes filled with hurt. "Are you laughing at me?"

"Compared to Lady Jessalyne, you are a very different woman indeed. As different as dung is from a rose. Did you really think to seduce me with the scent of my half-brother still clinging to you?" He shook his head, slitting his eyes at her as he dismissed her.

"Disrespect your future queen again and you will be sent home to your baron father with instructions that your family is no longer welcome in the king's court. Do you understand?"

"Yes, your highness," she hissed before rushing back to the stunned girls behind her.

Ertemis strode toward the stables, wishing Jessalyne walked beside him. He very much wanted to feel her hand in his, to inhale her perfume and hear her voice. Away for such a short period of time and already he longed to return to her.

Brynden ended his flirtation with a young scullery maid as Ertemis approached. Dragon snuffled, nudging Brynden with his nose. Brynden bowed awkwardly. "Your highness, Dragon is ready."

"Brynden, the bowing and such…" Ertemis shook his head. The boy was so eager to please. "Less is more. Now, saddle Lady Jessalyne's donkey for yourself."

"Aye, your high—er, master elf."

Ertemis rubbed Dragon's nose while he waited for Brynden to finish. He stared at the polished walls of Castle Ryght. Not only did he now have a place to call home, but he also had a woman to come home to.

ॐ

Jessalyne picked up the book she'd found and settled onto a padded bench near the window, eager to determine if it held the spell she needed. There was no organization to the information it held. The first spell was for turning mice into locust, something Jessalyne couldn't imagine a use for. The next spell was for intensifying a thunderstorm. She clapped the book shut when the third involved a mix of swan's blood and children's tears.

"What kind of book is this?" She starred at the cover again, trying to decipher the runes.

"It's a grimoire." Fynna walked back into the room, her face and voice bereft of emotion.

"What is it?"

"A book of the dark arts. Not something to be taken lightly." She slumped onto a bench at the worktable.

"Fynna, are you okay?"

"No. But I will be."

Jessalyne hoped so. She'd never seen Fynna so brokenhearted. "I guess I need to finish reading this wretched book."

"I saw Ertemis and Brynden preparing to leave out in the courtyard."

Happy to change the subject, Jessalyne smiled. "I thought Ertemis a message. I wonder if his mindsight heard me."

"I think Salena was trying to send him a message, too."

"What do you mean?"

"She was talking to him. Flirting. She put her hand on his arm but judging by his reaction, she won't do that again soon."

A bead of sweat trickled down the back of Jessalyne's neck as her temperature rose. "She'd best not or I'll deal with her."

Fynna fanned herself with her hand. "I shouldn't have said anything. You're toasting me! Calm down. Ertemis is capable of taking care of himself." She picked up a broom and began to sweep.

"I know. You're right." She sighed and opened the book again. "There's too much to do to worry about Salena."

ঙ

"For the fifth time, you will not even glimpse Elysium." Ertemis shook his head at Brynden's questions.

"Not even just a little bit?"

"No!"

"Will I see any elves?"

Ertemis pivoted in his saddle. "What am I? Or don't I count because I'm only half-blooded?"

"I'm sorry, I didn't mean...nay, your lordship, of course you count." Brynden's cheeks went red.

Ertemis turned back around. "If you want to see full blooded high born elves, you will have to wait until my lady mother's arrives for the ceremony."

"Aye, sir."

"I've asked you not to call me that. Lordship and highness are bad enough. No sir."

"As you wish."

"Quiet now. I need to listen for the way." He regulated the beat of his heart to match his mother's, the rhythm strengthening as the landscape changed. Familiar scenery gave way to the bog path.

He spoke to Brynden again. "Stay on the path and keep me in sight at all times. Do not deviate, do not hesitate, and you will be fine. This is enchanted ground we tread, between the worlds of fey and mortal. There are creatures here you cannot begin to imagine."

A birdlike cry pierced the silence and Brynden jumped, fresh fear rounding his eyes. "Aye."

Ertemis was beginning to see the affect of his human companion on the trip to the Ferryman's pier. The sky was darker than his first visit. The bog seemed closer to the path. Muddy ooze sucked at the higher ground as if trying to drag the path under.

He kept his pace slow so there was no chance Brynden would fall behind. When they reached the pier, the sky was a murky soup of thunderclouds. Fingers of wind tore at their clothes. The Ferryman waited at the end of the jetty, his skiff level although the inland sea of Lythe foamed around it.

The Ferryman shook his head at Brynden.

Ertemis called out above the wind. "I'm not seeking passage for the boy or myself. I only wish a message be delivered to my lady mother."

The winds eased as he pulled the sealed scroll from his pack and held it so the Ferryman could see it. The Ferryman beckoned for the scroll. Ertemis dismounted, motioning for Brynden to stay put. He walked down the pier, mindful of the churning sea.

Turning the scroll over to the Ferryman, Ertemis wondered if he should await a response. The Ferryman pointed back toward Brynden and the animals, then pointed to the ground. Ertemis guessed that meant he should.

The Ferryman disappeared into the fog before Ertemis stepped off the pier.

"What now?" Brynden looked anxious to leave.

"We wait."

∛

"Fynna! I found the separation spell. I think the spell on the next page is what we're looking for. It has to be." Jessalyne spread

245

the book across the worktable. Fynna dropped her dusting rag and came to look for herself.

"A joining spell." She shook her head slowly. "I don't know, this is dark magic. Are you sure?"

"How can it be dark magic when we're using it for good?"

"But this spell is for things like attaching an enemy to a tree or for giving someone donkey ears."

"So why shouldn't it work for wings? I think the spell is only in this book as an accompaniment to the separation spell."

"Well, I'm willing." A slight smile brightened Fynna's face. "Then let's do it."

Fynna nodded. "I agree. We can use the worktable."

"Will you fetch a quilt from our room to lay over it? I want to read the spell again and gather the ingredients." Fynna skipped out of the room. Jessalyne sat down with the book. She checked the spell for any nuance that might cause it to go wrong. Anything belonging to Sryka was suspect in her mind. No reason for Fynna to pay a greater price than she already had.

Seeing nothing overtly dangerous, she ransacked Sryka's stores for the ingredients. A few of them, like shaved horse hoof and dried stitcher beetles, made her grimace, but most of the others, like sap from a speckled elm, seemed perfectly normal. She added them to the caldron and heated them as directed.

Fynna came back in and spread a quilt over the worktable. "Are you ready?"

Jessalyne ladled some of the mixture into a dish. "I guess so. You?"

"Definitely." The pixie hopped up on the table and lay face down.

"Slip your tunic down in the back so I can see the scars."

Fynna adjusted herself on the table, fixing her tunic as Jessalyne had asked, then rested her forehead on her arms and waited. "I trust you."

"Thank you, Fynna. That means a lot to me. I'm going to get your wings now." And hope she lived up to that trust. Jessalyne swung the unlocked armoire doors open and gently lifted the wings. Almost weightless and brittle as autumn leaves, they rested in her hands like shadows. She moved slowly back toward the table so the air didn't lift them out of her hands.

Just below the small of Fynna's neck, two indigo crescents marked the points where her wings had once been. Jessalyne smeared a bit of the potion on each crescent, then laid each wing as close to the spots as possible.

"I don't know if this will hurt or not."

"It can't hurt any worse than it already does." The quilt muffled Fynna's voice. "I'm ready."

Jessalyne picked up the grimoire and with a calming breath, began to read. "Whether lost or newly found, these two objects shall be bound, and when the two have been combined, leave no seam for eyes to find. Joined together as flesh to bone, joined together as if grown, bind them now for evermore with this spell do I implore."

A quick, sharp sucking sound rent the air. Fynna cried out and arched her back. The wings began to spread. With a painful mewling, she collapsed onto the quilt. "It hurts so bad...they're too damaged...I cannot bear it." She fell silent, her clenched fists going limp.

Without hesitation, Jessalyne dropped the book and raised her hands over her fallen friend. She called her magic, focusing on Fynna's desecrated wings. She imagined them as best she could, whole and beautiful and healthy.

Pain tore through her as she absorbed the damage. Heat built in her, burning the pain away. The room wavered and she closed her eyes, tipping her head back slightly. Awash in fiery magic, her awareness began to melt. She saw Fynna's wings. Brilliant blues and greens flashing like jewels. Gossamer beauty alive and fluttering. Heat darkened her vision and the wings were gone.

She stumbled away from the table and fell to her knees. The cold stone floor felt so good. She pressed her cheek against it, letting it leach the heat from her body and drifted off as darkness claimed her.

"Lady Jessalyne, are you all right?" Sir Laythan shook her. "What happened? How did Fynna get her wings back?" He helped her sit.

"Where's Fynna? My head hurts and I'm starving."

"Fynna's asleep on the table. It's no wonder you're starving, you missed lunch and dinner. That's why I came looking for you. Are you all right? What happened?"

"I found the joining spell to fix Fynna's wings but then I had to heal her because they were so damaged. It took more out of me than I expected. Did you try to wake Fynna? I'm sure she's hungry too."

"When is Fynna not hungry?" Laythan helped her stand.

"Oh...look at her wings. They're so beautiful. No wonder she missed them so much."

Curled around Fynna's sleeping form, her wings created a beautiful crystalline blanket of swirling blues and greens. They were very much like butterfly wings, as Fynna had described them, and now, they pulsed with life.

"Wake up sleepy head. We missed dinner."

"Mmm...dinner." Fynna stretched and yawned. "Why didn't somebody wake me sooner? I'm nearly dead with hunger."

Jessalyne laughed. "Is that all you're concerned with?"

Fynna sat up, her wings fluttering out behind her. Recognition lit up her face. "I have my wings back! Thank you!" She launched herself off the table and hugged Jessalyne.

"You're welcome. It was my pleasure to give them back to you."

Fynna clapped. "Let's eat!"

ॐ

After a restless evening, Ertemis woke to a clear pink firstlight. Even the fog had dissipated to little more than mist. He stretched, glancing over at Brynden. The boy sat wrapped in a blanket, huddled in front of Dragon and Petal. By the dark circles under his eyes, he hadn't slept.

"Did you sleep at all?"

"I wasn't tired."

Ertemis stifled a laugh. "We will be here until the Ferryman returns, so try to sleep a little."

"If you insist." He laid down right where he was.

Soft snoring serenaded Ertemis as he rummaged in his pack for breakfast. He ate staring into the mist, hoping the Ferryman would come soon so he might return to Jessalyne. Once Dragon and Petal had been fed, he sat on the pier, waiting and watching.

The mist split like a curtain and the Ferryman's skiff floated into view. He was not alone. A pale grey horse stood beside the Ferryman. Another figure held the horse's reins. Ertemis squinted. The figure's hood dropped back to reveal his mother.

He hadn't expected her to return with the Ferryman, only to send her response. He swallowed. Besides the day and time, the only information contained in the message was that he was getting married and if she wanted to attend, a guide would meet her outside Shaldar City's gates to take her the rest of the way. He had planned on being that guide so he could tell her he knew who his father was during the trip. There was no chance he could hide anything from her on the ride back. One 'your highness' from Brynden and the bird would be out of the cage.

"Mother. I didn't expect to see you." He reached for her hand and helped her onto the pier, taking her horse's reins. It spoke volumes that the tashathna had let her come unescorted. Either they considered her expendable, or assumed he would be guide enough. Both were probably true.

"You sound unhappy I came." She raised an eyebrow.

"Nay, it's my great pleasure to be your escort. Jessalyne looks forward to meeting you."

"As I do her. That's why I decided to come so quickly, so that I might get to know this woman who's captured your heart." She smiled broadly and kissed his cheek. "I'm so happy for you, my son." He returned her smile, still trying to determine the best way to tell her where they were going and who she would be seeing. The Ferryman faded back into the mist. Ertemis helped her mount.

"Who is that sleeping boy?" She nodded toward Brynden.

"My squire."

She tipped her head at him. "You have a squire?"

And so it began. "I will explain as we ride. Brynden, get up."

Brynden opened his eyes. He looked directly at Ertemis's mother. The morning sun rose behind her, illuminating her with a soft glow. "Am I dreaming?"

"Nay. My lady mother has decided to return with us. Mount up so we might leave. You may lead."

Brynden hopped up and bowed low. "Nice to meet you, mistress elf."

"You may call me mistress Elana. And there is no need for bowing."

"I keep telling him that," Ertemis said.

Brynden nodded and scrambled up onto Petal, stealing glances at her every chance he got. They stayed single file on the path until they left the bog behind. Then Brynden held the front, while Elana dropped back next to her son.

Keeping her eyes straight ahead, she spoke. "Your mind is swirling with thought. I can almost hear it."

"There is much that still needs to be said. I don't know where to start."

"Start with what burdens you the most."

"You must promise me you will not turn back."

"A promise given blindly is a fool's demise."

"Please don't quote Aramaeis to me. The Tashathna Precepts lost their meaning when I entered the Legions."

She bowed her head, obviously discomforted by his words. "I am sorry. They come as quickly to my lips as song to a bird."

"I didn't mean to upset you. Between you and Jessalyne, I shall be apologizing for many years to come, I fear."

She smiled. "I will not leave, but I will not promise."

"I cannot ask for more than that." He cleared his throat. "I know who my father is."

She stayed silent, eyes never leaving the way ahead.

"Jessalyne saved his life and brought us together."

When she finally spoke, her voice was husky with emotion. "So you know then. Your father is a great man."

"He is a great man and not just because he's king. He recognized me as his son, his first-born heir. The ceremony is more than just a wedding. It's also a coronation. My coronation." No matter how many times he said it or thought it, the idea remained foreign to him.

She turned to him, her eyes wide and sparkling. "You're to be king?"

"Aye."

"My son is to be king." She paused, letting the words sink in. "I never thought I would see the day when the king of Shaldar would have elven blood running through his veins." She nodded. "This is remarkable news."

They talked more and day wore away. Lastlight drew in around them. Crickets sang and the first evening stars glimmered in the sky

Ertemis pointed. "Are you tired, mother? There's a clearing ahead. We could camp there for the night."

"I might be too excited to sleep, but I could eat a little supper."

Ertemis dismounted when they reached the spot and helped his mother down. "Brynden, see to the horses while I start a fire. Mother, I don't see a bedroll among your things."

"I didn't bring one."

"You can use mine." He unpacked his and tossed it to the ground before handing Dragon's reins to Brynden.

"Ertemis!"

Jessalyne's frightened cry pierced his mind. He felt her anger in his bones. The bitter taste of her fear filled his mouth. Snatching Dragon's reins back from Brynden, he leapt into the saddle. "Brynden, see my mother safely back to Shaldar in the morning. I must leave now. Something's wrong. Jessalyne needs me." And with that, he was gone.

Ertemis arrived at the castle gates well before firstlight, his mind racing with possibilities. He hadn't heard Jessalyne's voice again, no matter how many times he called out to her. He could still hear her heartbeat but it had grown progressively fainter. Nothing had ever filled him with such fear.

Judging from the lights still burning in the great hall and the amount of people milling about, something significant had happened. He handed Dragon off to a stable boy and strode inside. He headed for the king's quarters, nearly colliding with Laythan on the stairs.

"Prince Ertemis, we thought you were gone." He rubbed his brow.

"What happened to Jessalyne?" Ertemis clenched his fists at his side.

"How did you—"

"What. Happened. To. Jessalyne."

Laythan's face blanched. "She's gone."

Chapter Twenty-one

Three grown men hovered over a small blue female.

"Oww!" Fynna squirmed.

"Fynna, please hold still. Your head needs to be bandaged." Laythan tried again to clean the cut near her temple.

Raythus patted her knee. "Be brave, little one."

"Here, squeeze my hand when it hurts." Ertemis went down on one knee beside the chaise and offered his hand. She grabbed his first two fingers, gripping them as Laythan continued his ministrations.

"Almost done." He spread salve over her wound and then wrapped a swath of linen around her head and tied it off. "There. You can stop cutting off the prince's circulation."

"She's barely touching me." He slid onto the chaise next to Fynna. "Do you feel up to telling me what happened?"

"Mm-hmm." A sob hiccupped through her and she worried the hem of her tunic as she spoke.

"Jessalyne had already gone to bed when I decided to go to the kitchen for a snack. When I came back, our door was open a little and I heard noises, like a scuffle. I shoved the door open and someone was standing over Jessalyne, holding her down on the bed with a cloth over her face. I ran in, and they hit me and knocked me down. Before I could get up, they held the cloth over my face and I must have passed out."

"Did you get a look at their face at all?"

"No. They had a dark cloak on and a scarf wrapped around their face." She started to weep. "I'm sorry. I should have yelled for help."

"It's okay, Fynna. You tried to help. Do you remember anything else?"

"No, I'm sorry. Maybe I will when my head stops hurting."

He turned to look at Laythan and Raythus. "Has the substance on the cloth been identified?"

Laythan nodded. "Fynna knew it immediately."

Ertemis looked at her, trying to maintain his patience. He should be out searching for Jessalyne. "What was it?"

"Bitterlace. I'd recognize it anywhere. Sryka used it to stun all manner of insects and rodents."

"Did you touch the intruder at all?"

"I grabbed a good handful of their cloak before they hit me."

"Which hand?"

"My left."

Ertemis lifted her hand to his face and inhaled. The scent hit him hard and he growled, low and throaty. Fynna snatched her hand away.

He looked up at his father, his face contorted with rage. "Erebus."

Raythus turned to the guard awaiting orders near the parlor entrance. "Take another guard with you to the dungeons and bring Sryka back to me. We will see what she knows." He scowled. "If Erebus is indeed responsible for this…"

Ertemis stood, his hand on his sword. "If he has harmed Jessalyne, blood or not, I will kill him."

Raythus nodded. "It doesn't make me happy but I understand." The parlor doors opened and they all turned.

Two pages entered with breakfast trays, doing their best not to look overcurious about what was going on. They did a quick bow and placed the trays on the table, lifting the silver covers off and stepping back.

"Son, you should eat. You will need your strength."

"I don't much feel like it but I agree. I will also need food to take with me." He went to the table and bolted down a few mouthfuls of meat and cheese.

Raythus spoke to the older page. "Have cook fix a parcel of food for traveling and have it sent to the stables for Dragon's packs. Tell her it's for the crown prince."

The pages bowed and barely avoided being knocked down on their way out by the king's guard rushing in.

"Sryka's gone, your majesty. The night guard's had his throat slit and the door to her cell was unlocked. There's nigh a trace of her."

Ertemis threw down the morsel of meat in his hand. "Blast it! They are in league. Where I find one, I will find both. And there I will find Jessalyne."

Raythus held up his hands in dismay. "But we've no idea where they've gone."

Ertemis turned to Fynna, who'd found her way to the table. Her mouth was full of bread and both hands held more food.

"Do you recall seeing a dagger among Jessalyne's things? She used to wear it on her belt."

Fynna nodded, swallowing before answering. "She stopped wearing it after she arrived here. It's tucked away in her things."

"Do you feel well enough to find it and bring it to me at the stables?"

"Of course!" With a flutter of her wings, she lifted off the floor and hovered for a moment. "I'll be right there." She snagged one last slice of bread before flying out of the room.

Ertemis clasped his father's forearm. "I will explain when I return. Brynden should be arriving with my mother by midday. I must go after Jessalyne."

"My prayers go with you that you both come home safe."

℘

Ertemis had finished saddling Dragon when Fynna flew in, dagger in hand.

"I found it."

Ertemis reached for it but she pulled away, hovering just beyond his reach.

"I have no time for games, pixie."

Fynna floated back, a little less sure. "I want to come with you."

"Nay. This is my business. I will deal with it as I see fit."

"Jessalyne is my best friend. I am coming with you."

"You will slow me down."

"I can fly faster than your horse can run."

"Your head is still bandaged. You need rest."

"Did you sleep last night?"

"Are you always this infuriating?"

"You have no idea."

He cursed. "Fine. Give me the dagger. Now."

She handed it over, her wings a blur of color as she waited for him to finish.

Just as he was about to mount, a voice called out to him. "Has the wedding been cancelled?"

Ertemis looked up. "Valduuk."

"Who else? Or were there other trolls invited?"

"I did not expect you to arrive so soon." He alighted Dragon's back.

Valduuk narrowed his eyes. "What's wrong?"

"Jessalyne's been kidnapped by my half brother and the king's magewoman. I go to hunt them down and bring her back."

Valduuk eyed Fynna. "If that's the best muscle this city has to offer, I think I'll come along."

"Jessalyne is my friend. She needs me," Fynna said.

"My apologies, mistress pixie, I meant only to offer my services to my legion brother, not to slight you."

"Enough! You two can chatter while we move." He nudged Dragon and rode past them toward the castle gates. They quickly caught up.

Fynna gave Valduuk a once over. "I'm Fynna." She held out her hand as she hovered along at his eye level.

Valduuk bowed as he lifted her tiny hand with one finger, brushing his lips across it. "I wish we were meeting under better circumstances, Mistress Fynna. I am Valduuk. I must tell you, I have never seen a more beautiful shade of blue."

Outside the city walls, Ertemis brought them to a stop and extracted the dagger. With the handle firmly in hand, Ertemis called up his love's imprinted heartbeat, meshing it with his until the two harmonized as one. He turned in a slow circle until the lunestone came alive with a lambent glow.

"How did you do that?" Fynna asked.

"I didn't do. Jessalyne did."

Fynna scrunched up her face in confusion. "You aren't making sense."

"Her heartbeat is imprinted into my memory. When I adjust my heart's rhythm to hers this dagger reacts as though Jessalyne's holding it. Somehow it knows the way to Sryka, and where Sryka is, Jessalyne will be. I feel it."

"Can't you just listen for her heartbeat? You've found me that way in battle several times," Valduuk said.

Ertemis's fought to keep his emotion from his words. The clearest head in battle usually won. "I tried. It's too faint. Whatever

Erebus and Sryka have done to her, they will pay." He nudged Dragon forward.

Fynna shuddered. Valduuk looked at her. "What's wrong?"

"Sryka." Fynna spit. "She is a mean, spiteful, evil hag. She stole my wings but Jessalyne got them back for me."

Valduuk raised one bushy brow. "I'll see she gets what's coming to her."

"If she's hurt Jessalyne, all you'll have to deal with is scraps." Ertemis pointed north. "We follow the line of the dagger."

Valduuk grunted. "The land beyond Shaldar's borders is dangerous territory. How far north do you think they went?"

"Since when does danger bother you? Tavern keeper's life making you soft?"

With a fierce growl, Valduuk threw his shoulders back exposing a leather band laden with throwing stars strapped across his chest. He put one hand on his broadsword and the other on his battle-axe. "I live for madness and mayhem."

"Good, I have the feeling you're about to get your fill." Ertemis shot him a curious look. "By the way, Valduuk, since when do you attend a royal wedding wearing every weapon you own?"

Valduuk smiled, revealing rows of razor sharp teeth. "Firstly, this is only half of what I own. And secondly, if a woman can tame you, I'm taking every precaution available."

৪০

Jessalyne woke cold and bruised. Her mouth parched as sand. Utter darkness surrounded her. She shivered. Dampness wicked into her from the hard, gritty ground. Every joint ached. She licked her lips and tasted blood. Something reeked like rotting flesh. Groaning, she remembered the cloaked man in her room. He'd hit her across the face when she'd kicked him in the gut. Right before he'd clamped a rag soaked in bitterlace over her nose and mouth.

She tried to sit only to find her hands chained behind her back. Following the links around with her fingers, she felt where it looped through a ring sunk into the stone floor. Tugging, she tested it. Solid as the stone beneath her.

The clank of her constraints being tried brought footsteps down a set of nearby stairs and a bright light. A door was unlocked. Slices of light danced through the bars, but the figure holding the lantern was indiscernible. Jessalyne squinted as the blazing lantern bobbed closer but still couldn't see who held it. She glanced away and something sparkled, catching her eye. A circle of crystals surrounded her.

"Ah, good. You're finally awake. I'll fetch Mistress Sryka."

Jessalyne shook her head to clear the lingering fog of bitterlace. Whoever it was sounded exactly like Salena.

"Oh and another thing. I'm supposed to tell you not to try your magic while you're in the circle. Mistress Sryka says you'll just burn yourself up and that wouldn't do anyone any good."

"Salena?"

"That's right, you pasty-faced wretch. Don't worry, you'll still get to marry a prince. But not that bastard creature the old man claims is his son. You're going to marry the real prince, Prince Erebus. Of course, when Mistress Sryka is done with you, you won't remember a thing and I'll be the one warming his bed every night." Salena laughed as she left, locking the door behind her.

Jessalyne's hip was numb from lying on the cold stone. She struggled to move, trying to bring some circulation back. As her eyes readjusted to the lack of light, she stretched out her legs, reaching one foot toward the circle of crystals. Too far away to touch.

Although her hands were chained, she managed to conjure a small ball of cold fire. The cell holding her was more like a stone cave with a barred front. In a desperate move, she flung the ball of flames toward the crystals. The fire flattened against an invisible wall and washed back over her. Salena had told the truth.

Jessalyne lay in the dark, searching her brain for a solution. Before she thought of anything, more footsteps and the familiar thump of Sryka's staff announced the old mage. Her lantern shone through the bars. Sryka entered slowly, her discomfort obvious. Holding another lantern, Prince Erebus strode past Sryka to leer at Jessalyne.

"Your magic won't save you now, wench." He circled her, his lecherous grin widening. With a glance back at Sryka, he set his lantern down and stepped into the crystal circle. He yanked Jessalyne to a sitting position and caught her chin in his hand. He rested his free hand on her bare ankle, his fingers caressing her skin. The fear growing in her belly blossomed into anger. He leaned closer, his breath hot on her face. "So soft...so smooth...such a shame to waste such pretty flesh on that half-blood animal." His hand slid further up her leg and he leaned closer still.

Too late, Jessalyne realized he meant to kiss her.

Kneading her thigh, he smashed his fleshy mouth against hers. The anger smoldering in her gut flared and a bolt of white-hot rage shot through her as she twisted her head away. With no reason to hide her powers any longer, every inch of her came aglow as though she'd been doused in flames.

Erebus yowled. The stone chamber amplified the sound. His head snapped back, shock in his eyes. He held his hands in the light of the lantern. Blisters covered him wherever his skin had touched hers. He gingerly ran his fingers over his lips, feeling the blisters there, too.

"Witch! What have you done to me?"

Jessalyne glared at him through pale wisps of hair, defiantly lifting her chin. "Touch me again and I'll fill your boots with ashes."

Erebus backhanded her across the mouth. She pitched, her shoulder slamming into the stone. The coppery tang of blood filled her mouth and she spat it out, keeping her eyes on Erebus.

She lunged forward, hissing at Erebus like a cat. The chains snapped her back, but still he recoiled, tripping over his feet to get back outside the crystal circle.

Chest heaving, he glowered at Sryka. "You told me her powers were useless in the circle."

"To those outside it. You chose to step inside." Sryka smirked at him.

Erebus scowled. "Call me when you are prepared to give her the Oath, then bind her powers. I want this marriage sealed and consummated before sun up."

He snatched his lantern, yelping as the handle bit into his scorched skin. Cursing, he stormed out, kicking the metal door shut. With the clang of metal ringing in her ears, Jessalyne barely heard the laughter coming out of Sryka.

ಬ

Fynna crested the ridge first, followed by Valduuk and Ertemis.

"I've never seen anything like it," she murmured.

"I'd hoped never to see it again." Valduuk shook his head.

Ertemis glanced at the dagger's softly pulsing lunestone. "Aye. One venture into Scythe is one more than a person needs in their lifetime."

Rusted pinnacles of iron ore punctured a glowering sky and billows of yellow steam leaked from fissures in the ground. The occasional waft of vapor brought the stench of sulfur.

"This is Scythe?" Fynna came to rest at Valduuk's feet. She sat, staring out over the hellish landscape before them.

"Aye. Hael on earth and home of the Akuza." Ertemis dismounted. "We must be close. Erebus is too cowardly to travel far beyond Shaldar's borders."

Valduuk shrugged. "Unless he's made an arrangement with the Akuza."

"They would spit him and roast him for dinner before that happened."

"That is a likely possibility."

"Do they eat pixies?" Fynna stared at her male companions.

"They eat just about anything they can get their hands on. The Akuza aren't fussy." Ertemis pulled a linen handkerchief from his pack and tied it around the lower half of his face.

"I don't suppose we're allies with them?"

"The Akuza have no allies."

Shivering, Fynna moved closer to Valduuk. "I can believe Sryka would come to a place like this but Erebus?" She shook her head. "Poor Jessalyne."

"Let's just hope we find her before the Akuza realize they have company."

Picking their way through the jagged rubble and spurts of hot sulfuric steam, the trio hiked deeper into Scythe. The sky roiled with green gray clouds and despite the heat from the fissures, lastlight brought a cold dampness. Even with the linen square as a mask, the fumes rendered his elven sense of smell useless.

Had he been able to see the night sky through the foul mist clinging to the land, Ertemis knew he would have seen the first stars twinkling through. The thought made him sick for Jessalyne. He ached to be back on the wall walk with her, counting stars and naming constellations. He imagined her silky hair filling his hands and the sweet press of her kiss.

With renewed determination, he listened for her heartbeat, praying the silence filling his ears would be met with a gentle thumping if he just listened harder. The faint pulse he had clung to since the castle was completely gone.

ᵔᵝ

Sryka watched Jessalyne for a moment before she spoke. "I am sorry for the pain he caused you. I would not have had you harmed but then I couldn't give him a reason to suspect anything, could I?"

"Since when do you care what happens to anyone but yourself?" Jessalyne eyed the old crone suspiciously.

Leaning heavily on her staff, she moved a bit closer to where Jessalyne lay. "Hah! You think I care for you? You poor deluded child. I simply don't want my new body damaged. I'd hate to spend the first few weeks of my newfound youth healing from some unnecessary injuries."

Jessalyne struggled to sit up, wincing at the pain in her shoulder. "What are you talking about?"

"There's no binding spell, you dimwit. Erebus will witness you taking the Oath of Amity as Jessalyne and then he'll leave, thinking as you do that your powers must be bound so he may safely bed you. In truth, I shall cast a spell of renewal."

She extracted a stoppered vial of ashes from her pocket. She tossed the cork aside and shuffled around the crystal circle, spilling the powder over it. "Ring of ashes all around, now fire within is fire bound."

She smiled. "I was a little surprised when Erebus told me of your encounter in the hallway, but fire is a simpleton's trick. You couldn't master even the novice level skills I tested you with at the castle." She gestured toward the circle of ashes. "Try your fire tricks again and this ring will ignite, burning you alive."

"Soon my spirit will leave this worn out shell and come to reside in your young tender flesh. Of course, it may take a while for your spirit to surrender, but I'm prepared for that. Not only am I a much stronger mage than you but I am much smarter."

The desire to set Sryka aflame pulsed through Jessalyne. "I refuse to take the Oath. I'll tell Erebus what you have planned. I'll fight you with every scrap of power I can muster or I'll die trying."

Sryka shook her head. "No, you won't. You'll be a good girl and do as you're told."

"Give me one good reason why," Jessalyne sneered.

Reaching beneath her robes, Sryka pulled out a glowing lunestone pendant. It swayed in her decrepit hand. "The dark elf approaches. If you don't do as I command, I'll do to him what the midwives should have done ages ago."

৪১

Ertemis sunk down onto the hardscrabble, ignoring the shards of stone pressing into his knees. She was not dead. He would not accept that. She would have to lie cold in his arms for him to believe that.

Gravel crunched under Valduuk's feet as he approached, rubbing Dragon's nose before setting his mammoth hand on his Ertemis's shoulder. Fynna hovered nearby.

"We can rest a moment, if you need."

Ertemis shook his head and stood. His voice threatened to break. "I cannot hear her heart any longer."

Tears welled up in Fynna's eyes. "What does that mean?"

Gruffer than he meant to be, Ertemis snapped, "I don't know."

Fynna swallowed and pointed to his hand. "But..."

Ertemis glanced at Jessalyne's dagger still clenched in his fist. The lunestone shone intensely. He lifted the dagger and turned it in all directions until the stone burst forth lighting up the night around them. His gaze followed the line of the dagger. Sharpening his vision, he recognized what lay ahead.

He pulled the cloth from his face and inhaled deeply. "Time for this to end."

"Aye." Valduuk nodded.

"There's an abandoned Scythian garrison ahead and from the scent of smoke in the air I'd say Erebus couldn't bear a cold dinner." A wicked grin curved his mouth. "Or Jessalyne's set someone on fire."

Ertemis flipped the dagger in his hand and held it up to Fynna. "Here."

She took it, shaking her head. "I can't make it glow."

"You need a weapon. Valduuk and I will try to watch out for you, but you must be able to protect yourself."

She nodded. "Thank you."

He glanced at Valduuk. "You take the old witch. I want Erebus to myself."

"Aye, brother, he's all yours. And may Saladan have mercy on his soul."

Chapter Twenty-two

The glow from the lunestone pendant lit the chamber with a cool, callous light. All Jessalyne's anger, all her purpose, all her desire to protect herself drained away as if she had been punctured. Nothing mattered to her but Ertemis. She would do whatever Sryka bade her to keep him safe.

Another set of footsteps sounded in the chamber, but Jessalyne didn't bother to look. She didn't care. Once she took the oath, this would all be over. Salena's voice echoed in the chamber. She sounded overly pleased to be helping Sryka. Her jubilant tones pricked Jessalyne like needles in her skin.

Shutting Salena out, she searched for some thought to take her away from the dank chamber. With no idea if it was day or night, she wondered if Ertemis was back from Elysium yet. Did he know what had happened to her? By the time he found her, if he found her, she'd be wed to Erebus and possessed by Sryka. A lone tear slanted down her face. No. No crying. That would solve nothing.

She called out to him, not knowing if he heard her but needing to talk to him, to warn him of what lay in wait for him. More than anything, she wanted to see his face and touch his midnight velvet skin. Wrapped in his imagined arms, she felt his illusory kisses on her face, skimming her broken lip and soothing the pain away. She could almost feel his throaty growl resonating against her skin.

A gentle, soothing heat radiated through her. He would come, wouldn't he? She resolved to fight until she saw his face one last time, heard his voice, and told him she loved him.

"Get her up."

"I don't want to touch her," Salena whined. "I saw what she did to Prince Erebus."

"You silly twit. I bound her with acacia ashes. She'll fry herself if she creates fire in that ring now."

With a great martyred sigh, Salena grabbed Jessalyne by the shoulders and hoisted her up. As soon as she was upright, Jessalyne hissed at the girl as she had at Erebus. Salena stumbled back, knocking a few of the crystals askew.

"Clumsy girl," Sryka screeched.

Jessalyne squared her gaze through the opening in the circle and gathered her power to give the girl a good scare. She summoned a bolt of cold fire and sent it in Salena's direction. The blast exploded off the floor in front of Salena and she stumbled, thumping her head against the stone as she fell.

Sryka hurried toward Jessalyne, nudging the crystals back into place with her staff. She ignored Salena, motionless on the floor. "Keeping the best for last, are you?" She smiled. "I have always wanted inborn powers. Fire will do nicely."

Jessalyne's body trembled with the flow of power. She glared at the woman. "I hope you blow yourself to bits."

"Now, now. It will all be over shortly." She glanced at Salena. "I wish you hadn't done that. I hate to climb stairs and now I have to fetch Erebus myself."

When she returned with Erebus, his hands and mouth were smeared with grease. Jessalyne smirked at the thought of how it must aggravate him to look so unfashionable.

"Let's get this over with." He looked highly uncomfortable and kept his distance from Jessalyne.

"Your darling Salena doesn't seem very interested," she teased. Even so, she cringed at the thought of hurting someone with her power.

"Shut up, witchling," he growled. "If you were as replaceable as she, you'd feel the extent of my wrath."

"Wrath? You don't know wrath until you've raised the blood of dark elf." She smiled her sweetest smile. "You do know he's on his way, don't you?"

His eyes widened as Sryka seethed. "She doesn't know what she's talking about."

"Didn't Mistress Sryka inform you? Pity. If I knew a creature called the Black Death was coming for me, I'd want a little time to prepare." She shrugged. "Oh well."

Erebus clenched his fists, only to howl at the fresh pain. "Witch, why didn't you inform me?"

Sryka frowned. "She's lying. He isn't coming. He doesn't know where we are. How would he find us in the wastelands of Scythe?"

"The Oath. Now," Erebus demanded.

Sryka nodded, glaring daggers at Jessalyne as she handed her a sheet of parchment. "Read this aloud."

Jessalyne read the first line to herself. "If I read this I'll be a liar."

Erebus unsheathed his short sword, groaning at the torment it caused. "Read it or so help me, I will sever your fingers one by one until you do."

With a catch in her throat, Jessalyne read the words. "I, Jessalyne Brandborne, take this oath of amity by my own free will. On this day I vow to serve my king blamelessly as his mage, to protect him from harm and be his shield."

"I denounce all powers and magics, swearing never to invoke such against my king, using them only as he commands and only for his good. I promise this with my heart and mind in like accord."

Sryka blew a pinch of white powder at her and she sneezed. The split in her lip bled anew.

"It is done." Sryka turned to Erebus. "Be gone and I shall send her to you when her powers are bound."

"See that you are quick about it. We return to Shaldar immediately."

Sryka waited to speak until he had retreated up the stairs. "So many years I have waited to perform this spell, more years than necessary thanks to your selfish mother. I worried she would keep you longer than agreed, and I was right."

"She didn't try to keep me. She died when I was young and my father hid her instructions."

"I knew she would die when you were still a child, but I thought she would last long enough to see you on your way to me."

"You knew she would die young?" Pain laced Jessalyne's words.

"She wanted too much. She knew such strong magic came with a price."

"What did she want from you?" Even Sryka's bitter memories of her mother seemed sweet.

"The homely creature wanted a husband and a child. I taught her how to cast the glamour for beauty so she could find a man who would marry her. I gave her fertility potions and she drank them down like summer wine. When she told me she had nothing to pay me with, I made her promise her child would serve as my apprentice. She was easily beguiled. She drank the last few potions without even asking what they were." Sryka snickered.

"What were they? What did you do to her?"

"Your concern is touching albeit late. You should thank me for those final draughts. They made you what you are. One to give you gifts from the earth, another to enhance that gift. One to ensure your appearance surpassed that of your mother and father. I can only imagine what he must look like. Another to brighten your mind and the last to make you hale and hearty."

Sryka laughed. "Everything you are, you are because I made you that way. Now, enough of this chatter. It's time for you to fulfill the destiny you were born to."

Numb, Jessalyne nodded. She barely felt Sryka prick her finger with a needle and catch a few drops of blood in vial before unlocking her wrists. Her hands fell to her sides and feeling rushed back into them with a sharp prickle of sensation. The pain freshened her awareness. Sryka began the ritual.

With the same needle, Sryka pricked her own finger, dripping the blood into the vial with Jessalyne's. She corked the vial and set it down before pulling a book and several small pouches from her robes. The black leather grimoire was a twin to the one left behind in the armoire. She opened the book and read aloud in a tongue Jessalyne had never heard. From the first pouch, she took three small nails, drawing runes in the air with them as she spoke.

Jessalyne's vision narrowed, closing down until everything seemed far away. She squinted; trying to watch what Sryka did next. Whatever came out of the next pouch was too small for her to see. Sryka drew in the air with it as well. A low whine filled Jessalyne's ears until she could no longer hear Sryka's voice.

The room tilted. She fell forward and caught herself with her still tingling hands. A feeling of lightness filled her. She tried to grip the stone floor but the sense of floating overwhelmed her. Her mind reeled as images from her life flared and faded away. She cried out. Her spirit was being sucked out of her.

The thought enraged her and she fought back. Struggling to hold on to her memories, she focused on Ertemis. She called to him over and over. Her voice echoed in her head, the sound flattening and washing over her as her fireball had earlier. The circle was holding in her pleas.

Her sight almost gone, she reached forward and found a crystal. Just beyond it, her hand brushed through the line of ashes. Pushing the crystal aside, she scoured the floor and opened a hole in the ring.

Tipping her head back, she gathered breath for one last plea and screamed Ertemis's name.

⁊

"She's here." The relief sweeping through Ertemis was short-lived. "I hear her heart again, but the rhythm is wrong, echoing, almost double." He gestured to Valduuk and Fynna. "You take Erebus. Hold him until I secure Jessalyne."

Ertemis motioned with two fingers up a flight of steps. Valduuk responded with a turn of his fist and disappeared up the stairs, Fynna close behind.

The dark elf honed in on his beloved and entered a narrow hall. The garrison reeked with the stench of death. The Scythians had suffered great losses at the hands of the Akuza invaders. He had seen the atrocities with his own eyes. The bloodscent revived images better forgotten and tightened the muscles in his jaw. He reached for the hilt of his sword. The cold metal comforted him.

From the sounds above him, he surmised Valduuk was upholding his end of the mission. Erebus shrieked like a woman. Farther down, the hall narrowed and turned. He followed it, eager to get to Jessalyne. Ahead, pale light slipped out around the edges of a door. Flakes of rust beneath the heavy iron latch and hinges were evidence the door had been recently used.

He would have to be quick. With so much rust, the hinges would protest and any chance for surprise would be lost. Steeling himself for what he might find, he drew his sword and wrenched the door back, tearing it loose from its top hinge. He flew down a set of stairs, barely touching them as he descended.

In a cell ahead of him, Jessalyne huddled on her hands and knees on the filthy stone floor. Her head hung down, her beautiful moonlight hair, disheveled and dirty. The ground around her was littered with crystals sparkling in the lantern light.

"Jessalyne," he roared as he barreled through the cell door.

She lifted her head.

The sight renewed his rage. Her ring and pendant were gone. A purple bruise marred her pale cheek. Trickles of dried blood trailed from her mouth. Her gown was torn and stained. Recognition flickered in her eyes as she focused on his face. Her face contorted as she struggled to speak.

"Ertemis." A whisper so soft only his ears could have heard it.

"I'm here, lelaya." He knelt beside her, his hands shaking with outrage at what had been done to her. She moaned as he cradled her in his arms. He gently brushed the hair from her face. Her skin was so cold.

She opened her mouth to speak but a spasm tore through her, stiffening her body. Pain veiled her face, changing her expression into that of a stranger.

"So you came after all, elfling?" Her voice was strong but edge with bitterness. Not the Jessalyne he'd ever heard before.

"Of course, sweeting. Did you think I wouldn't?" His brow wrinkled as he studied her. She was Jessalyne, and she wasn't.

She laughed, a dry rasping sound. "Love has made you weak."

Her eyes lost their focus. She went slack in his arms. Another grimace of pain twisted her mouth. She grabbed hold of the edge of his cloak.

"Sryka's in me…"

"I don't understand," he shook his head.

"Listen," she gasped, another spasm shaking her.

Opening his senses, he did as she asked. Pushing everything else aside, he listened to the rush of her blood, the scrape of air through her lungs, the throbbing of her bruises. And then the echoed heartbeats, one gaining in strength, one diminishing. The latter was Jessalyne's. If Sryka had indeed possessed her, the crone was winning.

"Nay…this cannot be."

The intruder in his arms sneered at him. "But it is, halfling."

He shook her, desperate to help but not knowing how. "Jessalyne, fight her. You are stronger than she'll ever be."

A low moan parted her lips and the woman he held was Jessalyne once again. With his cloak, he gently wiped dirt from her face.

"Kiss me," she breathed.

"I don't think—"

"Please." Her grip on his cloak loosened and her hand slipped down his chest.

Pulling her close, he embraced her mouth with his. Her lips were cold and still beneath his press. Tears wet his face as he feathered kisses across her bruised skin, whispering her name as he drew breath, pleading with her to respond.

"Not like this," he moaned. "Fight her, Jessalyne."

Her eyelids fluttered at the sound of her name. "Kiss me," she whispered again, her face a storm of emotion as the battle within her seethed.

He bent closed the distance between them and kissed her again as tenderly as he could. Her lips parted slightly. The delicate response quickened him. She nodded and he imagined the beginnings of a smile.

Abandoning his timid approach, he captured her mouth and savored it like rare fruit, suckling their sweetness. Her hand grasped his arm, her touch assuring him, urging him on. Her lips warmed in answer to his kiss.

She squeezed his arm and cried out as another spasm stiffened her. Her head snapped back and her eyes flew open. A mask of anger altered her gentle expression. Her mouth twisted as she spoke.

"Get away from me, mongrel!"

"You will not win her, hag." He lifted Jessalyne's hand and kissed her fingers. The warmth building in her spurred him on. He pressed her palm against his cheek. "I love you, Jessalyne. You are the bravest woman I've ever met. Come back to me."

The mask dissolved and her dulcet tones answered him. "You found me…" She smiled weakly. "Kiss me again, my love…"

Without hesitation he reclaimed her mouth, passionately meeting her demands. Her building heat seeped through his clothing, mingling with the fire already burning inside him. Her tongue danced against his. She slid her hand up his arm, cupped the back of his neck and pulled him closer with new strength.

They fed from each other, hungry to salve the pain of separation, eager to find comfort in the love that bound them. The desperation of their kiss became satisfaction. Heat curled off Jessalyne in waves. She tried to pull away, but he refused to let go. He would not lose her again. "Don't fight it."

Ertemis lost himself in her trembling mouth. Another rush of heat coursed through her. Holding her meant being burned. A small price to pay for having her whole. He braced himself for the pain, unwilling to release her even as she pushed him away.

"Let me hold you, lelaya," he whispered. "I'm not afraid of the pain, just of letting you go."

She clung to him then, and he imagined he felt her open herself up to the sweltering surge. Flames danced over her skin, biting into his. Sryka's low guttural wail flooded the room as the old woman struggled against Jessalyne's swelling power. Energy exploded out of her, bathing the chamber with incandescent heat and incinerating Sryka's hold.

The pain rocked him to the core, but he clung to her until her head dropped against his shoulder and the flames vanished. The stone floor around them was scorched. Bits of charred cloth floated down. Their clothes were tattered and singed.

Jessalyne's eyes flickered open. She blinked a few times. Her hand came to his cheek and choking back tears, she laughed and kissed his hot skin. "I love you."

"Then why are you laughing at me?" He grinned as she covered him in fiery kisses.

"Because your ears are smoking."

He kissed her nose. "I get the feeling that if I had let you go, I'd be ashes right now."

"I'm sorry for hurting you."

He clasped her against his chest, tucking her head beneath his chin. "I'm sorry I wasn't here to protect you."

"Jessalyne! Are you all right? It smells like smoke in here." Fynna hovered near the cell door, her wings shimmering in the lantern light.

"Aye, she's fine. I'll explain the rest later. Where's Valduuk?"

"Keeping Erebus at bay. You best come." She glanced around the chamber, clicking her tongue. "Salena. I should have known."

Ertemis followed her line of sight. "The girl from the castle."

Fynna nodded. "Sryka finally got her due as well, I see."

Jessalyne wrapped her arms around Ertemis's neck. "More than you know."

He lifted her and started up the stairs.

"I can walk."

"So can I." He winked as he bounded after the pixie. The thin glow of firstlight seeped into the passageway, brightening as they approached the stairs to the main chamber.

Valduuk's battle-ax rested on his shoulder while the tip of his short sword hovered beneath Erebus' chin. "Move again and I'll see for myself what color royal blood is."

Erebus lifted his chin higher. "You don't frighten me, you fetid animal."

"Fetid?" The point of his blade tickled the prince's flesh.

Ertemis shook his head. "Poor choice of words, Erebus. My brother takes his hygiene rather seriously."

Erebus scoffed. "This creature is your brother? Your mother wasn't particular about what she bedded, was she?"

Valduuk whistled low and took a step back, notching his battle-ax back onto his belt. "Not a good idea to insult the elf's lady mother."

Ertemis narrowed his eyes and let his magic brighten them with an eerie gleam. "He's the only brother I've known, Legion or otherwise." He nodded to Valduuk. "Take Jessalyne and Fynna outside." He eased Jessalyne into the troll's arms. Fynna fluttered behind Valduuk as they left.

Erebus brandished his weapon and winced. Blisters covered his hands. "I am not afraid to fight you."

Ertemis shook his head. "I don't plan on fighting you."

"Hah! I knew you were a coward. That muddy skin hides yellow blood."

"I plan on killing you."

Erebus paled and backed up. "You cannot fault me for trying to protect my right to the throne."

Ertemis stepped closer. "The throne means nothing to me compared to Jessalyne."

"You can have her back. All is settled." Erebus edged around the room keeping the wall at his back.

"All is not settled. You hurt her. Now I will hurt you."

"It was all Sryka's idea." Sweat drenched Erebus's brow. He swallowed, raising his sword a little higher. "I never touched her. I swear it."

Suddenly, the blisters made sense. "You put your filthy hands on her." Ertemis stepped closer. Blisters speckled Erebus's mouth as well.

He shook his head. "Nay, I did not…"

The rage in Ertemis colored everything red. "You put your mouth on her."

Erebus shuddered. "Never! I swear—"

"You lie!" Ertemis growled the words through gritted teeth. He leveled his blade at the cowering man. "The blisters on your hands and face betray you."

The desperation in his half-brother's eyes gave way to terror. "You would kill your own flesh and blood over a wench?"

"Now you claim me? Should that soften me? Perhaps instead of killing you, I'll take you back to stand trial before the kingdom."

"Fine. I'll throw my fate upon the mercy of Shaldar's judges."

Ertemis shook his head, moving closer as he spoke. "I am the only judge you will ever see. I sentence you to die."

"No!" A woman screamed and sharp pain erupted in his back. He spun around, his sword singing in the air. The dagger in his shoulder begged to be ripped out.

Salena tottered in the doorway. "How dare you threaten your king, you dark devil." Her eyes shifted behind him.

Ertemis turned as Erebus made his move. Swinging his sword in a wide arc, he came at his brother with a wild cry.

Ertemis crouched and pivoted backwards, leading with his elbow. He caught Erebus in the gut, doubling him over and throwing him to the ground. Salena leapt onto Ertemis, using the dagger in his back for leverage.

As her weight torn the dagger through his flesh Ertemis thrust up and tossed her onto Erebus. Blood drenched his side, spilling into his boot.

Excruciating pain radiated from the wound, but the legion had taught him to ignore pain. He trained his blade on Erebus's chest.

Valduuk ran back in, Jessalyne still in his arms. Fynna buzzed behind. "I heard the yelling, thought you might need help."

Ertemis staggered but kept his eyes on the pair beneath his blade. "Aye."

Jessalyne gasped. Valduuk held her in one arm and drew his blade. "You're hurt."

Ertemis nodded, unable to speak. He listed to one side, losing the grip on his sword. The floor tilted. His blade clattered to the stone. Fresh pain wrenched his body. His knees buckled, slamming him into the hard floor. Haze clouded his vision and the room pitched again, tilting up to meet him as he keeled over.

∞

"Let me go." Jessalyne struggled to get out of Valduuk's arms. Ertemis needed her.

Erebus pushed Salena aside and stood. He looked at Ertemis, lying motionless in the crimson puddle, and a crazed grin lit his face.

Valduuk helped her stand but held her back. He hefted his battle ax over his shoulder. "Stay with Fynna. I'll take care of this."

Erebus lifted his sword over Ertemis's fallen body.

"No," Jessalyne pleaded. Fynna whimpered softly.

Valduuk lunged forward and Erebus plunged the sword halfway down, stopping the troll dead.

"Say goodbye to your precious half-breed, witchling." Erebus laughed. Light glinted off the sword as he raised it again.

He was going to kill Ertemis. Molten anger spilled through Jessalyne. The same incandescent rush as when she'd burned Sryka. And her father. She embraced the viscous heat, welcoming the savage power. She shook her head, tendrils of dirty hair grazing her cheeks. "Not today." She thrust her hands forward and white-hot fire flared from her fingertips, casting everything in bright light and deep shadow. The fire danced over her skin, sparking and spitting like a fighting dog straining to be loosed.

Erebus' eyes widened but the unhinged look stayed. "Too late, too late," he trilled, plunging the sword toward Ertemis's heart.

Jessalyne unleashed the fire.

With a great crackling whoosh, the flames leapt from her hands and struck him, splintering his sword in a shower of sparks and hot metal. The flames shoved him back and pinned him against the garrison wall. Fire danced over him, hissing and snapping while he shrieked, vanishing only as he dropped to the floor, lifeless and smoldering.

She'd killed him. She'd done exactly the thing she'd vowed not to, but what else could she have done? Let him take Ertemis from her? Suddenly she understood how Ertemis had killed the men that had chased them down. Her heart broke at the heavy burden he bore for every soul he'd taken.

Drained, she stumbled to his side. She bent to kiss him and saw sparks of her own. Her head swam. She rested her head against his chest, listening for a heartbeat. Please be alive, please. She clung to consciousness, desperate to know if he lived, but using so much power in such a short time had exhausted her.

Without hearing an answer to her plea, she slipped into darkness.

Chapter Twenty-three

Ertemis moaned when Jessalyne sponged his brow with a cool, damp cloth. He nuzzled his face against the soft skin of her arm. She smiled at the caress. How much she'd missed him, worried over him. He shifted, entwining his fingers with hers and pulling her with him as he turned.

She tumbled onto the bed beside him. She shook his shoulder gently, trying to free her other hand. He was unmovable.

"Stay," he mumbled, circling her with his free arm and nestling her closer.

Kissing his shoulder, she trailed her fingers down the angle of his ear, stirring a throaty moan of a different sort out of him. His eyes opened, heavy with a mix of sleep and desire. They widened at the sight of her bruised face.

He leaned up on one elbow and his fingers traced the edge of her jaw as he studied the evidence of her ordeal. "Are you all right? Where's Erebus? He will pay for what he did to you." He rolled his shoulders and stretched. "How long have I been abed? Whose bed is this?"

"So many questions! I'm sore and stiff but otherwise fine. You've been abed two days in your father's chambers. He insisted. Erebus..." She paused, staring at her hands. "He was buried yesterday." She sighed. "I vowed not to use my gifts to harm anyone ever again. But he gave me no choice." Her words ran together, one long exhale.

"Don't blame yourself, lelaya. Your father was an accident. And Erebus, well, you saved my life. Are you sorry for that?"

"No, never, of course not." She glanced up but quickly shifted her gaze back to the bed linens.

"Look at me." He lifted her chin with his fingers and stared. "Your eyes..."

She pulled away, looking down. She should have known she couldn't hide that from him. "You weren't getting any better. You

lost so much blood. I couldn't bear the thought of losing you again."
She hesitated. "I healed you."

"And?"

She met his gaze and let him see just what the result of that
healing was. Her eyes no longer held just a hint of lavender. They
were as violet as the amethyst pendant she wore around her neck.

He started to speak, then dropped his gaze to her neck.
"You're wearing the necklace I gave you." He glanced at her hand.
"And my mother's ring. I thought they were lost."

"Fynna found them in Salena's waist pouch, who by the
way, your father sent home with an accompaniment of guards. She'll
be under house arrest for the remainder of her life."

"Very well. Now tell me what happened to your eyes."

"It happened when I healed you. But my eyes are only part
of it." She shook her head, searching for words. "Something
changed." It was all so confusing. "The strangest sounds fill my
head, sounds I could never hear before. And I can pick out the color
of a man's tunic when others can only barely see him." She raised
her brows. "Even at night."

He tipped his head. "When you heal someone, what
happens?"

She gave him a curious look. "What do you mean?"

"How does it work?"

"I absorb whatever is wrong with them into me and then my
gifts just sort of burn it away."

"You did that when you healed me?"

"Yes."

"What kind of things can you hear?"

"Sounds I don't understand."

"Listen right now and describe to me what you hear."

She closed her eyes, listening intently. "Birds outside, people
talking…"

"Listen past that. What else?"

She was quiet for a moment. "Soft thumping, like a distant
muffled drum, but not quite."

He pressed her hand to his lips.

She opened her eyes. "Why are you smiling at me like that?"

"I think you absorbed some of my elven senses. Odd. I
didn't think anything like that was possible. I'm certain you just
heard the beat of my heart."

"Truly?"

"Aye."

Pausing, she closed her eyes and listened again. He placed her hand against his chest, over his heart.

"It's amazing," she whispered, opening her eyes again.

He pulled her onto his lap, feathering kisses over her bruised skin. You're amazing.

Her eyes went wide. "Did you say that? I heard your voice in my head!"

Aye, I said that and it's true, you are amazing. I never knew a woman could cast such a spell over me.

Her eyes sparkled. "I've done no such thing. In fact," she rested her elbow on his shoulder, stroking his ear with her fingers, "I think you're the one charming me."

His eyelids closed and a low, throaty moan vibrated out of him. "You have no idea what that does to me, woman."

"Then tell me."

"My ears are very," he swallowed, "sensitive." He spoke while she caressed the edge of his ear, running her nails from the pointed tip to his lobe. A shudder coursed through him.

She slipped out of his lap to kneel beside him on the bed. Brushing his black locks off his broad shoulders, she bent to kiss the first rune marking his skin. A deep, rumbling sigh escaped him. He grasped her about the waist and spread his fingers over her hips, kneading her flesh. He arched his head back. Her tongue grazed his ear and he jolted. She smiled softly, her lips never leaving his skin.

"You like that?" she murmured, knowing full well the effect it was having on him. The sense of power was more delicious than any chocolate biscuit she'd ever eaten.

"Saucy wench," he whispered, his eyes never opening. "I warned you once about teasing me this way..."

She leaned back. "I guess I should stop, then. We do have a wedding to prepare for."

He grinned, a flicker of things to come dancing in his eyes. "I almost forgot. Tomorrow is our wedding day." His gaze darkened. "And our wedding night."

"Actually, I postponed our wedding until you were recovered."

He narrowed his eyes. "You just said we had a wedding to get ready for."

"We do." She smiled. "But it's not ours."

Ertemis rubbed his temples. "Who then?"

"While we were gone, your father asked your mother for her hand and she said yes."

His jaw hung slack. "They're to be wed? Truly?"

She nodded. "Shaylana will be Queen Mother of Shaldar and no one will ever be able to question your right to the throne again."

"I cannot fathom it." He eased back against the headboard, trying to take it all in. "But when will we marry?"

"Whenever you like."

"I like sooner better than later."

"Is the day after tomorrow soon enough?"

"Nay, but it will do." He reached for her, his voice low and liquid. "Let me show you what else your teasing does to me."

℘

After standing beside Ertemis during his parent's simple ceremony, Jessalyne thought she might never again glimpse such pure joy in his eyes as she saw that day. She was wrong. The light in his eyes outshone the sun as she walked the aisle toward him on the day of their nuptials.

Her breath caught at the sight of him. He was magnificent. Silver-tipped plaits hung from his temples while the rest of his shimmering black locks flowed over his shoulders. To match the tunic she had given him, the king's clothiers had sewn him a pair of white linen trousers and tucked into knee-high silver-buckled boots they fit like a second skin. His flowing grey cloak bore the royal crest of Shaldar. His sword glinted at his side. Ertemis was every inch royalty. She swallowed, overwhelmed. This man was about to be her husband. And her husband was about to be king of Shaldar.

Beneath her intricately embroidered overdress of lilac silk with its long bell sleeves grazing the floor, she trembled. Her gaze drifted to the cluster of white roses in her hands, the heady scent almost too much. Her undergown of white silk clung to her steadily warming skin, the air stuck in her lungs. So many eyes watched her.

I'm right here, lelaya. Just a few more steps and you can lean on me. Like a cool caress, Ertemis's words calmed her. She smiled to let him know she heard.

That's right, keep your eyes on me, sweeting. His gaze echoed his words and she relaxed, the steps coming easier now.

I love you. So much it made her ache.

His smile widened slightly. *And I you, with all my heart.*

The gathered crowd of nobles and dignitaries receded from her sight as she laid her hand on top of his. The feel of his skin against hers, the connection of flesh, centered her.

Raythus bound their hands with gold cord symbolic of their commitment to one another and the people of Shaldar. Ertemis's strength flowed through her; his confident smile reminded her she was no longer alone and never would be again.

Endless litanies were recited before the vows were spoken and the cord removed. Ertemis held her hand as they knelt together. Raythus crowned them with circlets of gold, a shimmer of tears in his eyes and Shaylana at his side

He nodded for them to stand and he raised his hands before the assembled crowd. "It is my great pleasure to present to you as husband and wife the new king and queen of Shaldar, Lord and Lady Ertemis Maelthorn." His voice echoed through the cathedral as the congregation erupted in loud hurrahs and shouts of "Hail the King."

Ertemis caught Jessalyne up in an embrace and kissed her soundly, inciting another swell of cheers and well wishes.

"I've never kissed a queen before," he whispered in her ear.

She smiled as she answered him. "Time to practice, don't you think?"

The feast in the great hall was followed by dancing. Jugglers entertained out in the courtyard and stilt walkers amused the crowds gathered to catch a glimpse of the royal couple.

The day wore away and Jessalyne realized hours had passed since she'd spoken to her husband. She'd seen him at his father's side across the great hall talking with some duke or being introduced to yet another noble. As exciting as it was, holding court at the head table wore her out. All the names and faces of the noblewomen presented to her blurred together. With a whisper in Shaylana's ear, she excused herself and escaped into the kitchen to catch her breath.

"What's wrong?" Fynna followed along, a great hunk of wedding cake in each blue fist.

"I cannot bear to meet another person. I'm tired and I just want to see Ertemis alone, away from all this noise." She frowned. "If this is court life, I'm not cut out to be queen."

"Nonsense," cook chimed. "Your ladyship's just worn thin, poor thing. After all you been through, it's a crying shame for you to be thrown into that rabble out there and expected to endure. Sit and have a cup of tea."

"That sounds wonderful. Thank you, cook."

Fynna winked at her. "You'll be alone with him soon enough."

"Fynna, behave yourself." Jessalyne laughed and bit her lip. Being alone with him was, quite frankly, daunting. She'd never been so nervous about anything in her life.

"You'll be fine. Better than fine. You'll see. I need more cake." Fynna flitted back into the horde of revelers.

She had drunk less than half her cup of tea when Fynna returned. Valduuk followed a moment later. Both had icing smudged in the corner of their mouths.

"It's time, it's time!" Fynna twirled in the air.

Valduuk held out his arm. "He asked us to fetch you. He's had enough as well."

Jessalyne slipped her hand over Valduuk's massive forearm and let him walk her into the great hall. The massive candelabras, lit at sunset, suffused the hall with a rapturous glow. The crowd dissolved around them and knowing smiles met her every glance. Her cheeks warmed.

Ertemis stood between his parents, the circlet of gold gleaming against his obsidian brow. He held out his hand and, with a bow, Valduuk backed away. Jessalyne reached for her husband. Their fingers meshed. The subtle pulse of blood beneath skin filled her ears. The sound of her beloved's heart.

He kissed her hand, pressed it to his cheek, his eyes never leaving her face. "I have a surprise for you," he whispered.

She tilted her head, a slight grin belying the fresh surge of nerves she felt. "What have you done?"

"You'll see soon enough." He turned his attention to the waiting crowd. "Ladies and gentlemen of the court, you have honored us with your presence on this most memorable day." Jessalyne's heart swelled as Ertemis spoke. He had become the king before her very eyes.

The cheering drowned him out until he raised a hand. His dark gaze met hers and he held it as he spoke. "As I'm sure you will understand, the events of the past few days have worn us out. Your queen and I will be retiring for the evening." He kissed her hand again. "Please, stay and celebrate as long as you like. Tonight our home," his voice caught at the word, "is yours."

Again the crowd cheered, turning back to the revelry with renewed passion. The musicians struck up a new tune and dancers partnered off. Wine flowed and servers carried silver trays of sweets throughout the hall.

Raythus clapped him on the back. "Well spoken, son."

Shaylana kissed Ertemis on both cheeks, then Jessalyne. "I cannot imagine greater happiness than what I feel today."

"Nor I." Ertemis nodded, a grin spreading across his face. "Don't expect us for meals tomorrow. I've already left orders with cook to send ours up."

"Ertemis!" Jessalyne cuffed his shoulder, the crimson flush in her cheeks undoubtedly visible even in the candlelight.

With a laugh, he scooped her up in his arms and bid his parents good dreams. He took the steps two at time until he reached the first landing. Leaning back against the wall, he set her down only to enfold her in his arms. Without a word, his mouth found hers in a deep, hungry kiss.

She draped her arms around his neck, luxuriating in the press of his body. His hands slipped to the small of her back as he nibbled the side of her neck.

"Mmmm…" she laced her fingers through his hair, loosening the plaits at his temples. "You're very good at that."

Hot breath tickled her ear as he whispered promises of things to come. "My love, tonight you will find I'm good at many things."

His words shot heat through her at and she shivered, her hands slipping from his hair to his shoulders. "I fear I cannot offer you the same guarantee."

"Your virtue is a great gift, not something to be ashamed of." He smiled reassuringly. "My life started anew today. Nothing else that came before matters. I want no other woman but you for the rest of my life."

Footsteps sounded on the stairs behind them. Ertemis drew his cloak around them and hid them in the shadows. "I've had enough idle chatter with well wishing nobles."

"I agree." Jessalyne huddled against him, watching the torch shadows flicker through the spot where her feet should be. The clean leather scent of him delighted her. "We're invisible," she whispered.

"Aye, but not mute." Shifting, he quieted her with a kiss.

The voices of Raythus and Shaylana echoed in the hallway as the pair made their way hand in hand.

"If I had a few less years on me, I'd carry you in my arms as well. I've half a notion to try it anyway."

Shaylana laughed. "You are a silly man. Sweet, but silly."

"Unfortunately I'm also an old man, my darling. I wish—"

She silenced him with a kiss on his cheek. "I have a thought on that subject…" She paused as they passed the landing, staring straight at Ertemis and Jessalyne. "You two haven't made it very far."

Ertemis threw off the enchantment. "I thought you were guests. I've had my fill of small conversations."

Raythus chuckled. "Your mother used to hide from me like that." He tapped the side of his nose. "I had other ways of finding her." He slipped his arm around her waist, holding her close.

Shaylana clasped his hand, her pale green eyes stayed on his face. "We should be off, lelaya."

He kissed her forehead. "Indeed, we should. Good dreams, children." Nodding at Ertemis and Jessalyne, the pair continued off down the hall entwined like young lovers.

Ertemis dipped slightly, catching Jessalyne beneath her knees and lofting her into his arms again. "They set a good example. Besides there is the small matter of the surprise I promised you."

Her fingers laced behind his neck. "I cannot imagine what you've been up to. Is it a new dress? New slippers? A book of spells, perhaps? A kitten? I would so love a kitten."

"Sweeting, close your eyes."

"I don't think I can. I'm too excited to keep them closed."

"Please."

She covered her face with her hands, leaving large gaps between her fingers.

"Close your eyes or I'll pull your skirt up over your head and do it myself."

She clamped her fingers together. "I swear I cannot see. Where are we going?"

"Patience, love."

She listened to his footsteps on the stone floors. They went up another flight of steps. She smelled the oily tang of chain mail and a male voice greeted them as doors opened. Tallow and floral scents filled the space as the same doors shut behind them. Ertemis put her down.

"May I open my eyes now?"

"Aye."

They were in a small foyer. Similar to the king's quarters, it had the crest of Shaldar inlaid on the floor. Tall candelabras, dripping in crystal, stood on either side of two sets of doors. The candlelight lit a path of white rose petals leading from the foyer into the doors on the right.

"Where are we? I don't recognize this place."

"This used to be the queen's quarters but as my mother is not about to leave my father's side, I have had it refurbished for us. Unless you would prefer your own chambers."

"You did this for us? When did you have the time?"

"Actually, it was my idea, but Valduuk took care of the details." He held her hands as he backed through the doors to their right. "There's more."

The trail of petals led into the massive bedchamber. Candlelight muted the mural of blue skies and wispy clouds decorating the high ceilings. Two enormous armoires flanking one of the tall windows dressed in ivory silk.

Jessalyne kicked off her slippers and wriggled her toes into the luxurious wool carpets. "This room is so beautiful. And this bed…" she stared up at the thick carved posters and snowy damask curtains.

"It reminds me of another bed." Her fingers trailed across the silk coverlet as she walked back to Ertemis.

"I know how much you liked that bed, and I thought it would be a good reminder to me."

She slipped her arms about his waist. Crinkling her brow, she tilted her head. "A reminder of what? That was not exactly the most agreeable evening we spent together."

"I resolved that night that any woman who could put up with me at my worst surely deserved my best, although in truth, I had no reason to believe you'd want me at all. When I left Elysium and realized how much time had passed, I was afraid your heart would belong to another."

"Why would you think that?" She shook her head at his admission.

"Beautiful women aren't alone for long, although you're so much more than beautiful. You're strong and brave and you fight for what you believe in."

She leaned into him. "You see all of that in me?"

A wicked grin lit his face. "Aye, beneath that tempting bosom beats a heart of fire and I've been cold too long."

Her hands traveled lower to cup his backside. "You don't feel cold to me."

His brows shot up. "I thought I was marrying an innocent maid." He lifted her, slipping his hands beneath her buttocks and pulling her hard against him. "Seems I have wed the sauciest wench in all of Shaldar."

Wrapping her legs around his waist, she captured his mouth in a restless, hungry kiss. Her tongue danced against his and he moaned.

He walked them to the bed, resting her on the thick mattress to free his hands. Without breaking their kiss, he loosed the ties on her gown and eased the silk up over her thighs. Suddenly, he backed away.

Her brow furrowed nervously. "What's wrong?"

His words came out husky with need. "I want to see you."

Tentatively, she stood and slipped out of her gown. His hungry eyes grazed over her. The white silk undergown hid nothing. He kneeled at her feet and slid his hands up her calves, under the white silk, and along her heated thighs.

"You're as supple as warm honey and twice as sweet."

She closed her eyes, struggling to balance the fire ignited by his touch.

"Look at me. I want to see your eyes, lelaya."

Shaking her head, she whispered, "I'm afraid." Images from the past swirled in her head as she opened her eyes. Would the past always haunt her?

He lifted her onto the bed and lay beside her. "I would never hurt you."

"I know." She wove her fingers through his black locks. "I'm afraid of hurting you. I fear I'll lose control and burn you like I did my father."

"I held you the entire time you fought Sryka and nothing happened."

She pursed her lips. "Your ears were smoking. You consider that nothing?"

He traced a line across her collarbone and down between her breasts. "The risk is worth the reward."

"No, it isn't." She'd almost killed her father. Had killed Erebus.

"I'm not worth it?" He pulled back.

"No. Yes. What I mean to say is that nothing is worth hurting you."

"You can't hurt me. You might singe me a bit, but I'll heal." He winked.

"Stop jesting." Stubborn, handsome, impossible oaf.

He leaned to whisper in her ear, brushing his lips tenderly over her skin. "I'll set the bed on fire myself if you make me sit here any longer without touching you."

She nestled her head on his shoulder. "It doesn't frighten you?"

"The only thing I'm afraid of is that my wedding night will be spent talking."

Heat spilled over her cheeks. "That will not do."

"Nay, it will not." He stood, his hands working the buckle on his belt.

She reached for him, pushing his hands away. "Let me."

Grinning as he dropped his hands, he watched her nimble fingers unbuckle the clasp. "You do that as though you've undressed a man before," he teased.

She smiled to herself. A taste of his own medicine might cure him. She dropped his belt to the floor. "I have."

"What?" He scowled. "Who? When did this happen?"

"It was you, my love, before I even knew your name." She giggled a tugged at his tunic. "Such jealousy! Perhaps the Green Death is a better name for you."

The muscles bunched in his shoulders as he crossed his arms over his chest, thwarting her attempts to remove his shirt. His black eyes gleamed with amusement. "Shall I remind you of a rather buxom tavern girl by the name of Dalayna? As I recall, you flew into quite a fit over something that never even happened."

"That wicked trollop provoked me apurpose and if you mention her name again, I'll do more than make your ears smoke." She threw her hands onto her hips, daring him to repeat the girl's name. The white silk strained across her body, and his needy gaze dropped lower. He swallowed.

"Now I know I have married the right woman." A familiar silver glitter sparkled in his eyes. "I cannot resist you when you're cross. Kiss me, wench."

She climbed onto the bed, kneeling on the coverlet. "No."

"No?" He moved toward her, but she put her hand out to stop him.

It would be good for him to wait. "You will not say her name again?"

"Nay, it shall never cross my lips again." He promised with his hand over his heart. "Now, please, before I succumb—"

"Tell me you love me," she insisted.

"I love you madly."

He leaned in to kiss her. She scooted back and smiled coyly. "Take your shirt off."

Far too eagerly, he stripped off his tunic. His skin shimmered in the candlelight. She wanted to devour him. "Now have I earned a kiss?"

She shook her head and pointed at his trousers, her face burning at her own boldness. She stared brazenly, waiting for his reaction.

Without hesitation, he yanked his boots off and tore at his trousers, disrobing in a blur. She shrieked and hid her face behind her fingers. She hadn't expected so much of him so fast.

"Is this what you desired, your highness? To see me bare before you?" Need thickened his voice to a deep, smoky syrup.

She nodded without looking at him.

"Look at me, lelaya. I'm your husband. It's your right. And if you're bold enough to ask, you should be bold enough to look."

He's right, he's my husband. I have every right to look. She dropped her hands. There was so much more of him than she remembered. So much dark skin and curved muscle and…"Your eyes are glowing."

He grinned wickedly and crooked his finger at her. "Come closer. Sit on the edge of the bed."

"Turn around and I will."

"You've seen me twice in my skin already, haven't you? Why is this any different?" he asked as he turned.

"Because I didn't intend to see you those times." Her gaze traveled up the steely contours of his legs to the rounded curves of his backside. Every inch of him was hers and hers alone. The thought made her giddy. Light-headed. Wanton.

A shuddered sigh escaped her throat. Her fingers itched to caress his velvet skin. She slid off the bed and went to him, softly stroking her fingers up his thighs, flattening her palms over his hips.

He sucked air in through clenched teeth. The thick muscles in his back constricted as she explored the silver trail of runes tattooed on his spine. Blazing kisses followed as her arms wrapped around him. Her fingers splayed over the ridges of muscle leading to his groin.

"Jessalyne, please," he hissed. "You torture me."

Need had long ago overwhelmed any remaining shreds of shyness. With a shush of fabric, her gown pooled around her feet. She tugged his hand and turned him around.

ಬ

In the candlelight, her skin seemed drenched in new cream. Words failed him. The long ago glimpse of her dressed in the dampened sheath by the pool faded, replaced by the unadulterated vision before him. Her gracious curves captivated him, enslaving him to the marrow. Her power flared around her softly, as if moonlight shined through her skin.

She studied him openly, the pale luminescence surrounding her increasing the more she looked. Obviously, she'd overcome her inhibitions.

"Am I to your liking?" He watched her gaze travel his body.

"The fairest man I've ever seen."

"Aren't I the only man you've ever seen?"

She nodded, laughing softly, but her eyes never strayed from him.

He'd known that much, but her admission filled him with prideful possession. She was his and only his. Now. Always. Forever.

She hesitated, her voice a whisper. "Are all men so…" She gestured with her hands, not knowing how to put words to her question.

He laughed. "You never cease to charm me, wife. A more winsome wench I can't imagine." He gathered her into his arms. "Of course, you'll never know the answer to that question because I have no intention of letting another man near you for as long as I live."

Their lips met in agreement, a bond of fidelity sealed with a kiss. He picked her up, cradling her in his arms like the precious treasure she was, and carried her back to the bed.

"Now," he said, "we shall begin your lessons."

Epilogue

Ertemis hid himself in the shadows outside their door, wanting to catch a glimpse of his wife unaware. He hadn't seen her all day. There was much to do before his parents left for Elysium. Because of that, he yearned for more time alone with her before the pace of their lives increased further.

Whether she was teaching Fynna a new spell, practicing her own magic or drowsing beneath him with the flush of passion coloring her cheeks, he loved watching her. The latter thought filled him with new purpose as he entered their bedchamber.

She sat by the fire, her glorious hair unbound and spilling over her shoulders. His latest gift to her stretched in front of the fire, then left his spot on the rug to seek his mistress's attention. Raisin rubbed against her legs, and she reached down to scratch the little black cat on the head before taking up her needles again. The pink tip of her tongue darted over her lips as she worked the yarn in her hands.

He chuckled softly and she looked toward the door. "There you are. How was your day, my love?"

He glanced behind him. "You can see me?"

"Of course. You're standing right in front of me."

"But I'm hidden. You shouldn't be able to see me."

She shrugged. "Well, I can."

"I thought the residual powers you gained healing me disappeared a few months ago."

"They did." She pursed her lips. "Hmmm…perhaps you should listen to my heart."

He knelt beside her. "Are you ill?"

"Perhaps I am."

With his senses fully aware, he did as she asked. When the sound of her heartbeat came to him, he knew immediately something was amiss. Concern twisted his mouth and he listened again. The faint echo was all too familiar.

A chill shot through him. "Sryka," he whispered.

She shook her head. "Once more, my love."

Again, he concentrated, letting the ebb and flow of her beating heart flow through him. Again, he heard the second, subtle rhythm of another heart. He frowned. "I don't understand."

She held her knitting up, trying to suppress a laugh.

He stared at the tiny bootie dangling from her needles. The realization struck him like a thunderbolt. "Are you…are we…is that…" He sat back on his heels, his mouth open.

A laugh of pure delight spilled out of her. "Yes, my love."

He swept her up into his arms. "A babe! I am the most blessed man in all of Shaldar." He shook his head in disbelief. "How long have you known?"

"Not long. I am glad to see you so happy."

"Happy? I am overjoyed beyond words. I cannot describe it." He spun her around in his arms.

She put her hand on his chest to stop him. "I am dizzy enough of late as it is, I do not need your help."

He stopped immediately. "Should I put you down? Did I hurt you?"

"I am not some fragile flower that needs coddling. I just don't need any more spinning than what my stomach does on its own."

He sat gently on the bed, holding her steady. "Does this mean I should find my own quarters to sleep in?"

"I don't think I've ever seen you look so happy and so sad in such a short span of time," she teased. "There is no reason for you to sleep elsewhere. But in time, sleep is all you'll be doing in this bed."

"In time, you say?" A shameless smile bent his mouth. "I'm sure you'll agree we must use what's left as wisely as possible." He nuzzled his lips her neck and her laughter turned into a shriek of pleasure as his hands slid up her gown.

She dropped her knitting off the side of the bed and nibbled his lower lip. "Oh yes, we mustn't waste a moment. I'm sure there are still things you haven't taught me. And then there are all the lessons I've forgotten."

He shook his head. He could not love her more if he tried. "Are you always going to be such a saucy wench?"

Love shone in her eyes like the stars in the sky. "Kiss me, halfling, and see for yourself."

About the author:

When the characters in Kristen Painter's head started to take over, she decided to exorcise them onto paper and share them with the world. She writes paranormal romance for Samhain Publishing and has the first of three books in her gothic fantasy vampire series, Blood Rights, coming from Orbit in fall 2011. She hopes to add a YA series to the mix as well and has also been published in non-fiction, poetry and short stories. The former college English teacher can often be found online at Romance Divas, the award-winning writers' forum she co-founded. She's represented by Elaine Spencer of The Knight Agency.

Connect with Me Online:

My website: www.kristenpainter.com
Twitter: http://twitter.com/Kristen_Painter
Smashwords:
http://www.smashwords.com/profile/view/KristenPainter
My blog: http://www.kristenpainter.blogspot.com
My Facebook Page: http://www.facebook.com/KristenPainterAuthor

7757531R0

Made in the USA
Charleston, SC
07 April 2011